CW01332836

COPPICE

CHRIS MOTTERSHEAD learned something about bees and bee-keeping in his early years as a Rural Science teacher. Since then he has taught in state and idependent schools, at home and abroad. He is presently Principal of Tabeetha School, Jaffa, Isreal.

Mystole Publications,
Mystole Farm,
Mystole,
Canterbury, Kent, CT4 &DB,
United Kingdom

This Book is a Work of Fiction. Names, Characters, Places and Incidents are either products of the author's imagination or are used fictitiously. Any resemblance to actual events or locales or persons, living or dead, is entirely coincidental.

Copyright © Chris Mottershead 2000

The Author has asserted his moral right to be identified as the author of this work.

ISBN 0953746690

Printed and bound in Great Britain by The Basingstoke Press 75 Ltd.

All rights reserved. No part of this publication may be reproduced, stored in a retrieval system, or transmitted in any form or by means, electronic, mechanical, photocopying, recording, or otherwise, without the prior permission of the publishers.

A copy of this book is held at the British Library.

Cover artwork by Dave Trendell – trendy@hotmail.com
The author wishes to thank all those friends and family who helped him
to complete this book.

COPPICE
Chris Mottershead

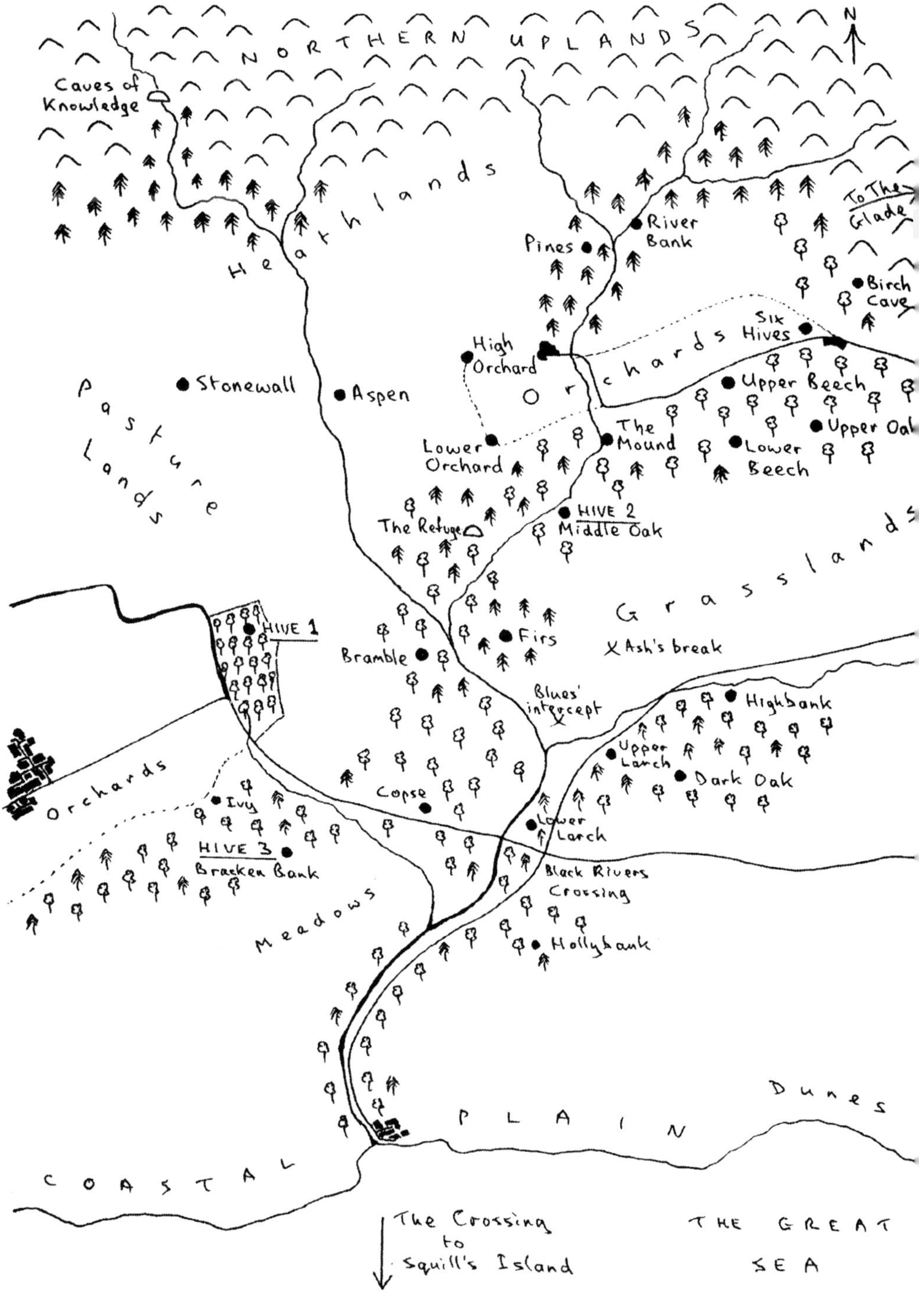
N
NORTHERN UPLANDS
Caves of Knowledge
Heathlands
River Bank
Pines
To The Glade
Birch Cave
Six Hives
High Orchard
Orchards
Upper Beech
Stonewall
Aspen
Pasture Lands
The Mound
Upper Oak
Lower Orchard
Lower Beech
HIVE 2
Middle Oak
The Refuge
Grasslands
HIVE 1
Bramble
Firs
Ash's break
Blues' intercept
Highbank
Orchards
Upper Larch
Dark Oak
Ivy
Copse
Lower Larch
HIVE 3
Bracken Bank
Black Rivers Crossing
Meadows
Hollybank
Dunes
PLAIN
COASTAL
The Crossing to Squill's Island
THE GREAT SEA

HIVE ONE

1. CONSCIOUSNESS

He was gradually becoming aware of his own existence. Slowly he began to sense his immediate surroundings, but even as he did so an alarm was triggered!

'Trapped!' it screamed. 'You're trapped!'

Above him, below him, on all sides – trapped! Any attempt to move failed – he was firmly held in. The alarm persisted, sounding from somewhere deep within. His eyes were useless. He couldn't see a thing. His remaining senses only confirmed that he was entombed. A dark, swirling mist began to thicken around him. The alarm began to fade. Was he running out of time? Was the crisis over? Was he winning or losing? He paused; he thought. Was there nothing to be done? Was there no part of him that could react? He felt an itch on one of his folded antennae and rubbed it with his mandibles.

'Oh!' he exclaimed. 'I can move my mandibles! Maybe I can chew my way out.'

With that inspiration he pushed his mandibles as hard as he could against the cell wall. They quickly cut through and a welcome freshness swamped his head, driving away that ever threatening mist. The alarm had passed; its purpose fulfilled – another drone honeybee was about to emerge from his cell.

He rested for a few seconds only, keen to continue his escape but also needing to recover from the shock of his first experience. Despite using his mandibles in a somewhat haphazard manner, he succeeded in cutting away most of the thin wax capping of his cell. This provided him with an escape route, but there was no way he was just going to walk out! Although he had three pairs of legs, they were all pinned close to his body by his tightly fitting cell. Seeing where he wanted to go, yet apparently unable to move, he tried 'willing' himself out through the opening he had made. Somewhere in his body the muscles responded and, to his surprise, he moved a fraction.

'So that's the answer,' he muttered, and then concentrated on squeezing himself out.

As each pair of legs cleared the rim of the cell, they provided leverage for the rest of his body. Out he popped! Looking back into the cell he had just escaped from, he couldn't believe he had fitted into such a small space.

His legs, all six now working, though a bit wobbly, straddled at least two wax cells. Then something struck one of his rear legs. He clumsily turned round to investigate and let one of his legs slip into a cell. He steadied himself. There were other bees nearby – he could see them and smell them quite easily. Again something hit one of his legs, something sharp. Peering down at the surface of the wax comb, he spotted the cause of his irritation. Mandibles! Another bee was in the process of escaping from his cell.

Curiosity getting the better of him, he kept his close position and observed the prisoner of this particular cell make smart work of his cell capping. This bee had little difficulty squeezing himself out onto the surface of the comb and standing up on all six legs. Here was one strong, confident drone honeybee!

The two drones came face to face. Despite the dimness inside the beehive, they could see each other well enough with their extremely large eyes. The second bee then posed a surprisingly awkward question.

'And who are you?'

There was a short, embarrassing silence, and then...

'*TWENTY-ONE*,' rang out a loud, coarse reply, but not from the other drone bee.

'*TWENTY-TWO*,' boomed the same voice, and both drones cringed. '*TWENTY-THREE*. Oh, if you're lucky! This batch isn't up to standard, is it? Don't see why we have to put up with so many of these useless drones anyway. Good thing supplies are ample this season.'

With that parting comment, the 'loud voice' moved on, reaching twenty-nine before turning to other matters.

'Well,' said the somewhat bemused second bee, 'I guess that answers my question. You must be Twenty-one, having emerged just ahead of me, and I'm Twenty-two. All very orderly, but who's the bee with the voice?'

'And where's "Twenty-three if you're lucky"?' added Twenty-one.

They paused for a few thoughtful moments, then looked around the immediate vicinity. Was there a half-emerged drone nearby – or what?

'There!' said Twenty-two. 'And look, he's only pushed one mandible through his cell capping.'

'But it's not moving,' observed Twenty-one.

'Quickly, help me cut him free!'

They had the capping off in no time, but the bee they revealed showed no signs of movement.

'We're too late,' said Twenty-two.

Twenty-one shouted at the immobile creature. 'Hey, come on! Don't give up.'

'You're free to come out. Please try,' added Twenty-two.

'Squeeze forwards,' urged Twenty-one, bending down closer. One of his antennae touched the ailing bee, who responded with a slight movement.

'He's still alive,' said Twenty-one. 'We'll have to help him some more.'

They tried grasping hold of his front legs and pulling him out. The more they encouraged him and touched antennae, the more response they drew. Eventually, with his front legs pulled out for him, he began to squeeze himself out.

It was a long and painful process, but with continued assistance 'Twenty-three' at last emerged and flopped onto the surface of the comb. Apart from looking completely shattered, he also appeared to be a bit on the small side for a drone. They helped him to his feet and asked what had happened.

'I thought it was all over,' he gasped. 'That dark mist...only managed one cut...so tired...so trapped.'

'Well, you're safe now,' Twenty-one reassured him. 'How do your legs feel?'

'Very wobbly, but never mind – I'm just glad to be alive and I'm most grateful to you two.'

'No problem,' said Twenty-two, 'but we must find something to replace your lost energy. If we place you between the two of us, we can crawl over the comb together and locate some food.'

The trio set off along the comb face, pushing their way through the many bees milling around, getting in each other's way, it seemed. Their antennae began twitching, Twenty-three's in particular. They soon came to an area of honey cells and dived in with great enthusiasm, their long tongues sucking up enough delicious, energy-rich food to satisfy their needs. In fact they completely gorged themselves!

Twenty-three was soon a different bee, able to walk unassisted and showing a great interest in everything around him. He had slender, almost silvery antennae, which twitched constantly when he was on the move. If Twenty-three was small for a drone, Twenty-two was the opposite. He was well built and looked very powerful. His black and yellow banding was smart and crisp – not the sort of drone bee to argue with. As for Twenty-one – well, he was average in size, regular in colouring, normal antennae. In fact there was nothing special about him, not to look at anyway, but he did think a lot.

As the three drones relaxed after their feed and the bees in the hive began to cluster together at 'heatfall', Twenty-one began to think back over the day's events. He wondered just how close he had come to being in Twenty-three's predicament.

He turned his head to address Twenty-two. 'Did you have much trouble working out how to escape from your cell?'

After a few seconds delay, the reply came. 'No, not a lot. I was in a bit of a panic for a short time, I suppose, but once I'd shoved my mandibles through the capping, it was easy.'

'Hmm,' reflected Twenty-one. 'It seemed strange that emerging from your cell could be such a risky business. And who was the bee with the loud voice?'

As he pondered that one, a rather worrying thought came to him. That particular bee must have seen the problems Twenty-three was having, but Shouter – yes, that was a fair description of the creature – had made no effort whatsoever to assist Twenty-three. Why not?

With that disturbing question still lingering, he drifted into a state of semi-consciousness for the night.

2. MEET THE QUEEN

A jolting movement brought Twenty-one to his senses. For a moment he thought the comb was falling apart beneath him.

A voice came out of the confusion. 'Hey, wake up will you?' Twenty-two was prodding him. 'We were beginning to think you weren't going to bother!'

Twenty-one's beautiful big eyes were at last working well enough to remind him where he was, and the events of the previous day began coming back to him.

'Sorry,' he mumbled.

'So you should be, you're just about the last bee on the comb to stir himself,' complained Twenty-two, 'and we're famished!'

Twenty-one felt Twenty-two had done all the stirring, but he kept quiet and followed his friend, who was already making a beeline for the top of the comb. There were still scores of bees milling around but Twenty-two powered his way through. Twenty-one and Twenty-three tagged along directly behind – Twenty-three twitching his antennae in anticipation.

Close to the top of the comb they found some opened honey cells and helped themselves to the rich, thick liquid. What a pleasant feeling it gave them as it poured into their empty stomachs. Nearby they found some pollen cells and sampled them as well. A little further on they came across worker bees cleaning cells with a strange smelling substance. Being curious, Twenty-one wanted to know more about it.

'Erm, excuse me, what's that stuff you're using?'

The worker bee looked up in surprise and stared at him, as if to ask, *are you talking to me?*

'I just wondered what that stuff is – that you're using on these cells?'

The worker bee glanced all around and then whispered, 'All I know is that the foragers bring it in for us. It's a great polish for cleaning out used cells.'

COPPICE

'Foragers?' queried Twenty-one, while his two friends listened in attentively.

'Yes, you know – the worker bees who fly out for food. They sometimes collect this stuff as well.'

'Hmm.' Twenty-one hadn't thought about flying yet. 'Don't you get to fly out then?'

'Oh I do hope so – one day I…'

'That's enough idle chatter! Get on with your cleaning!' yelled a loud voice. Immediately the worker broke off the conversation and resumed work.

'Shouter,' whispered Twenty-one.

'Who?' asked Twenty-three.

'Shouter. That's what I've called the bee with the loud voice who gave us our numbers.'

'Right,' agreed Twenty-three.

'A worker bee as well,' added Twenty-two. 'Not even as big as me.'

'Not many bees around here are as big as you,' pointed out Twenty-one. 'But I'd like to know more about her. I think she's a bit of a bully.'

'Just let her try bullying me!' said Twenty-two. 'Come on then, let's get after her!'

The trio scurried off with Twenty-two leading the way and the other two tucked in neatly behind him. They passed cells with larvae of various sizes, busily tended by nurse bees. Foragers were bringing in the food they had collected and passing it to other workers for storing. Other bees were cleaning cells. It certainly was a hive full of activity. They had crawled over the top of one comb and down to the bottom of the next one when they came to a sudden halt.

'What's up?' asked Twenty-one, as Twenty-three peered round to try and see for himself.

'She's disappeared,' replied Twenty-two.

'What? She can't have – or weren't you close enough?'

'I beg your pardon! I certainly was close enough, but she was there one second and gone the next, just as we reached a mass of bees.'

'What mass of bees?'

'That one – straight ahead of us.'

Twenty-one looked carefully at the worker bees barring their way. Twenty-three came alongside and twitched his silvery antennae in their direction. Twenty-two was just frustrated and thinking about charging right through them, but he wasn't sure if Shouter was beyond them or not.

'There's a different scent around here,' said Twenty-three. But Twenty-one was concentrating on something else.

'Twenty-two,' he said, 'try walking towards them.'

Twenty-two gave him an odd look but was pleased to have a course of action.

'My pleasure.' And he advanced three or four bee-lengths to meet the nearest worker. She cleverly deflected him to the right where he met the next worker, who did the same thing. Twenty-two soon found himself being detoured around the mass of worker bees. He gave up and returned to his accomplices.

Twenty-one, having watched very carefully, was fascinated. 'They must be hiding something,' he declared. 'Whether Shouter's in there or not, I want to know what they're up to.

'But how do we find out?' asked Twenty-three.

'I could try barging my way through,' suggested Twenty-two.

'I don't think that will be necessary,' said Twenty-one. 'I've an idea. They're forming a deliberate barrier, but in deflecting bees around it they move just enough for a bee to push through. So, if you walk up to them again, Twenty-two, I'll tuck in right behind you. When the first barrier bee moves to deflect you, I'll dive through the gap she leaves. It'll help if you're a bit awkward about being deflected!'

'No problem!' agreed Twenty-two. 'Let's do it.'

'What about me?' asked Twenty-three.

'Um, you just stay here. If anything goes wrong, this is where we'll meet up again.'

Twenty-three wasn't very convinced about that but he had little choice. Anyway, he wasn't exactly built for pushing and shoving – he relied on his antennae and his superior sense of smell. He also sensed danger, but he didn't think his friends would take any notice of him, so he kept it to himself. Anyway, was it possible to smell danger?

Twenty-two walked confidently up to the nearest barrier bee with Twenty-one hiding behind him. Sure enough, he was deflected to the right and a small gap opened up. Twenty-one pulled out from behind his partner and – froze! He stood there; staring at the gap as it was closed by the barrier bee returning to her original position. His chance was gone. He had lost his nerve at the critical moment. Twenty-two turned round, grabbed his friend, and pulled him away from the barrier bees.

'What's wrong? Why didn't you go for it? Didn't I do my bit?'

'Sorry, sorry. You were fine. It was my fault. Hang on a while.'

He thought back over what had just happened. What had caused him to freeze?

'Got it! There was something I didn't expect to see. Some sort of structure I think. It just took my attention and...'

'OK, OK, don't worry about it. Now, let's try again.'

'What?'

'You're not giving up after one attempt are you?'

'Um, well, no...I guess not.'

Twenty-two waved his antennae at Twenty-three to indicate they were going to try again and that he should stay where he was. He then nodded at Twenty-one, who obediently slipped in behind him as he set off once more towards the barrier. Feeling a bit of a fool after his failure, Twenty-one was determined to get it right this time.

Twenty-two approached the nearest barrier bee who deflected him to the right. As a small gap opened up, Twenty-one shot out from behind his partner and dived through it! Taken by surprise, the barrier bees failed to close ranks in time and he was past them with just a slight brushing of abdomens. Immediately he saw clearly what had caught his eye briefly the last time. Two seconds later he found himself surrounded by worker bees – and they were not pleased!

'Just what do you think you're doing?' rasped one of them.

'You've a nerve!' said another. 'Now what do we do about this? First time anybee's slipped through our barrier. Do you think we're here for our health?'

The first bee, hitting on a course of action, interrupted. 'Send for the comb controller, she'll know what to do. She's around here somewhere I'm sure. In the meantime, you stay right here!'

Twenty-one, surrounded as he was, had little option of going anywhere, and he was too frightened to say anything. He did wonder though if his two friends were safe.

Somebee must have gone off to fetch the comb controller because she shortly arrived, breaking her way crisply into the ring of bees around the hapless Twenty-one. He thought he recognised her. When she spoke, he knew he recognised her!

'Number?'

Twenty-one could only stare at Shouter.

'*Number!*' she bellowed.

'Um, Twenty-one.'

'From which comb?'

'I, I'm not sure.'

'Try harder!'

'About the centre, I think.'

'Huh, you've not been out for long, have you? How many heatfalls have you experienced?'

'Heatfalls?' repeated Twenty-one.

'When the temperature drops and we cluster together, nice and cosy like – remember?'

'Oh yes, er just the one then.'

'Only one! And you're already sticking your antennae where they don't belong! Very odd!' She paused for a few seconds as if trying to decide what to do about this most unusual behaviour, then arrived at a decision. 'He must go before the Council. The Queen bee must know of this.'

Shouter nodded to the nearest worker, who responded by pushing Twenty-one forward. Three other workers took positions around him, and the group followed comb controller Shouter as she walked slowly along the floor of the hive. This unusual little party passed under one comb before climbing upwards. Somewhere around the centre of the comb they stopped.

'Wait here,' ordered Shouter, and she walked on a few bee-lengths before disappearing from view. It was some time before she reappeared.

'They're ready now; follow me.'

The party moved forwards a fairly short distance before the comb controller stopped them. She then directed Twenty-one to follow her through a cordon of barrier bees. As they broke through they came face to face with a group of bees, one of whom was very different from the rest.

COPPICE

Shouter whispered to Twenty-one – or she tried to. 'Don't speak unless the Queen gives you permission.'

He wasn't likely to; he was still too scared. At the same time, his curiosity – which had landed him in this mess – was not completely subdued. He looked carefully at what he took to be the Queen. She was much longer in the abdomen than both worker and drone bees. Her wings were larger as well. Her colour was the same as other bees in the hive with one striking exception. He could just make out an area of blue on the top of her back – the top of her thorax in fact. This struck him as very odd because it was so different from all other bee colours, which were browns, blacks, oranges and yellows. It certainly made her stand out – as if her size wasn't enough! There was something else he picked up very clearly – the smell. There was a strong, distinctive but not unpleasant odour all around them. It was as if their little meeting was wrapped in it.

In close attendance to the Queen were about half a dozen workers. There was nothing unusual about them as far as he could tell. They all glared at Twenty-one as though they had better things to do and did not care for this intrusion. Having looked him over with her great, piercing eyes, the Queen spoke.

'I have been Queen of this hive for three cycles. I do not recall ever having to tell off a drone for prying into matters that do not concern him. You will listen carefully to my instruction.

'This is an orderly, well-controlled hive. Our rules and regulations are simple and straightforward. Everybee has its own task. Everybee has its part to play. There is plenty to do and no need to interfere with anybee or anything else. I produce and lay all the eggs for the hive. My workers clean cells, feed and care for the larvae, build and repair combs, guard the entrance, maintain the correct atmosphere in the hive and forage for food outside the hive. We have never, ever gone short of food in my time as Queen. As for drones like yourself, you have an easy time. Make the most of it while you can. Such curiosity as you appear to have shown, however, cannot be tolerated – especially in one so recently emerged. There is only one answer to this. You must fly immediately! That will keep you out of mischief for your remaining time.' She turned to her comb controller and ordered, 'Take him down the tube and make him fly!'

3. BEYOND THE HIVE

Everything was happening so quickly that Twenty-one had little time to think. With four worker bees in close attendance, he was ushered smartly back down the comb to the floor of the hive. From there, the escort party moved in a straight line along the hive floor, with Shouter in front. Their rate of progress was such that Twenty-one was sure that other bees in the vicinity must have been jumping out of their way.

Shortly he detected a breeze of cooler air coming from somewhere up ahead of them. At the end of the combs they came to an opening. It was circular in shape and they walked right into it. A rapid increase in light intensity caused Twenty-one's eyes to adjust automatically, but he was getting quite worried. Where were they taking him? What were they going to do to him?

The 'tube' they had just entered was about five bee-lengths wide. He could see lots of bees, mostly workers, walking along the tube's surfaces in both directions and in all positions. It was, at least, reassuring to find that this part of the hive was well used. It was a longish walk to the end of the tube where another big increase in light intensity hit them, so much so that Twenty-one's eyes could not completely compensate for it. As a result he began to see much more than he could inside the hive. He didn't have to wait long to test out his newly extended vision.

Shouter turned to the escort party. 'Right, here we are. Over the edge with him. Soon have him flying and out of mischief!'

And without more ado, two of the workers shoved a terrified Twenty-one off the end of the tube. For an instant he felt himself falling, but then, quite automatically, his wings burst into action – all four of them – and he was no longer falling. In fact, he was hovering in mid-air.

'What a fantastic feeling!' he cried out, as he began to take a more personal

COPPICE I

control of his movements. First he turned to face the tube – the entrance to the hive from which he had just been unceremoniously dumped. He rose up to the level of the tube but didn't hang around because lots of bees were landing and taking off and he was in their beeline. One of them actually buffeted him out of the way. So he moved backwards and upwards, imprinting a picture of the hive entrance and its surroundings into his memory as he did so. The tube came out of a very large wall, part of which looked more solid than the rest. There was also a coloured marking by the side of the entrance. He flew higher still and could see over the wall, taking in the surrounding vegetation – especially the trees of various sizes.

A lot of what he saw was greenish in colour but he also picked out oranges, yellows, violets, and, up above, a vast expanse of blue with a large yellow spot in it. Flying in ever increasing circles, he firmly imprinted in his mind the broader location of the hive. He was so absorbed with his first flight that he barely noticed the other bees flying around until he felt the need to catch his breath. Landing, with some apprehension, on the nearest branch, he was surprised to find it swaying a little. His suction-assisted feet held on well enough though.

From his vantage point, Twenty-one observed the area around the hive entrance. Worker bees were flying in fairly straight lines to and from the entrance. A few other bees, drones as far as he could tell, were flying around in circles before shooting off somewhere. He wondered where they were going. Then he remembered the two drones he had left behind inside the hive. What had happened to Twenty-two and Twenty-three? Were they OK? Had they been 'arrested' as well? He scanned the drones zooming around but didn't think his friends were among them – there were no particularly large or small drones amongst them. Should he go back into the hive and look for them? Maybe, but he didn't fancy risking the tube just yet. Shouter and company might be hanging around to make sure he didn't return too soon, if at all! Then again, his friends might have been evicted and flown off already. Swayed by the sheer enjoyment of flying, he decided to follow another drone as he flew off to wherever the drones were flying off to. He could try re-entering the hive later – preferably much later!

Twenty-one rejoined the circling drones and soon spotted one setting off on a beeline. Flying up behind him, he noticed the buzzing sound for the first time. He wondered if all bees buzzed. Listening carefully to his own wings, he thought he was probably buzzing as well. He drew up alongside the other drone.

'Er, hullo there. Hope you don't mind me tagging along. My first time out, you see.'

The other drone stared at him. Noticing that Twenty-one still had a lot of body hair he commented, 'You're out a bit early, aren't you? How many heatfalls have you had?'

'Er, just the one.'

'Only one? That's most unusual. You shouldn't be flying until after your third or fourth. I hope you know what you're doing.'

'Well, I think so. Anyway, I couldn't help flying early, I was sort of forced into it.'

'Forced into it?'

'Yes.'

'How?'

'By a comb controller's escort party.'

'What? I can't believe that!'

'Well it's true,' insisted Twenty-one. 'They did it on the Queen's orders, she…'

'Enough! Enough! I don't want to hear any more – could get me into trouble. They don't like anybee stepping out of line here, you know. Every bee to its own task – nothing more, nothing less!'

'That sounds familiar.'

'I bet it does. Anyway, as you're out early, I ought to brief you on the five facts of flight.'

'The what?'

'The five facts of flight.'

'Oh.'

'For a start, when you first leave the hive, get a full picture imprint. You do this by hovering in front of…'

'Done that!'

'OK, OK. Secondly; select and memorise landmarks such as tall trees, streams, aberrations…'

'Aber-what?'

'Aberrations. They're sort of unnatural things built by the giant creatures, as I understand it. They're usually very big so they make good landmarks.'

'And the giant creatures are?'

'Best left alone!'

'OK.'

'So, to continue. Where was I? Ah yes, third fact; make use of the light from the sun – that's the brightest point in the sky. I expect you've already noticed it.'

Twenty-one nodded.

'Then there's the force field – not so easily appreciated.'

Twenty-one looked puzzled.

'Yes, well, when you're a bit more experienced. And finally of course, when time and energy are important, fly in a beeline, as straight as possible – like we are now. Got that? I hope so, because here's the drone zone and I must leave you. Enjoy yourself.'

Before Twenty-one could thank him and ask him his number, the drone shot away – helpful, but not particularly friendly. Never mind, he could explore on his own for a while before flying back to the hive. He zoomed around, surveying the various plants and trees, occasionally approaching other drones, but they were not being very sociable for some reason.

He landed for a rest and his attention was drawn to a worker bee on some yellow flowers nearby. She was very busy collecting nectar and pollen. Being curious, Twenty-one popped over to join her.

'Clear off! I was here first!' she snarled, and then realised she was addressing a drone. 'Who do you think you are anyway? Leave the foraging to us workers and mind your own business – or should I say laziness!'

A shaken Twenty-one backed off, hovered a few bee-lengths away, and then landed on another plant. 'She's not very friendly either,' he said to himself. In fact, no bee's very friendly around here.' This made him wish he was back with Twenty-two and Twenty-three. Perhaps he should go back soon and try and find them. While deciding what to do, he watched the worker bee in action.

She stuck her head right into the tubular flowers, one after the other, in order to extract the food – or so he reckoned. When she flew off, he decided to check it out for himself.

He landed on one of the flowers, stuck his head in and unfurled his tongue as far as it could go. No good. Although he did have some pollen dust on his head, he couldn't reach the nectar, which his sense of smell told him was in there somewhere. He tried another of the tubular flowers, then another, before giving up.

When he stopped, he suddenly noticed that the drone zone had gone very quiet. He scanned the area and couldn't spot a single drone. They'd all gone! As he looked and listened he began to feel an eerie presence in the air that chilled him. What was it? What was happening? He was looking all around for an indication of what he felt when two dark shadows shot over his head, just a few bee-lengths away. He cowered and so missed taking a proper look at them, and he wasn't going to hang around in case they came back.

Twenty-one shot up into the air to begin his return journey. He hovered there, trying to decide which way to fly. He thought back to his departure from the hive and found he could quite easily picture its appearance. He recalled that he had taken the beeline with the other drone, out to the drone zone. Since then he had buzzed around a fair bit and lost his sense of direction. Which way was home?

A very worried honeybee landed back on the plant below. What should he do now? He tried to remember the five facts of flight. He was sure of the hive's appearance and he knew he should fly in a beeline. Then there was the sun – yes, still in the sky – and the force field. Not much help. What else was there? Then it hit him – 'landmarks'. He had no landmarks because he had flown out with the other drone. Now that drone, and all the others, had gone; no doubt scared off by those dark shadows or whatever they were.

Fighting down a rising sense of panic, he forced himself to think through his predicament. Which direction? It could be any direction. In that case, which was the best way to fly? He concentrated on that for a while. Flying straight wasn't going to help much. That left flying in circles!

Up zoomed a revitalised drone. He made a circular tour of his present location,

COPPICE I

looking especially to the outer side of his circuit. Nothing doing. He didn't recognise a thing.

'Very well,' he reasoned with himself, 'so now a bigger circle, then a bigger one and so on, working outwards from here until I spot the hive. But first a landmark to work from.'

Encouraged by his own plan of action, Twenty-one selected a very tall tree as his landmark and set off on his circuits. Round and round he zoomed, in ever widening circles. After some time, and feeling rather cross-eyed, he was still out of luck. He rested on a branch of a tallish tree. Why hadn't he succeeded? What was he doing wrong? In fact there was little else he could do, as flying off in a straight line was sheer guesswork…or was it? Was he missing something?

Feeling very hungry now, and the weaker for it, he flew up to resume his circular tours, only more slowly. As the circles became wider and wider, he had further to fly on each circuit – thereby using up more energy. The sense of panic was returning. His big eyes scanned the area below as he flew. The blue sky was turning grey and the sun was sinking lower and lower.

'What was it about the sun?' he muttered to himself, thinking again of the facts of flight. He didn't know; the other drone hadn't gone into detail. But as he thought about the sun, he became more aware of it as he continued flying his circuits. His wings began to feel as though they were going to drop off, but just then he recognised something about the sun. In some strange way it seemed more familiar to him at one particular part of his circuit, and it didn't matter how wide the circuit was.

'Interesting,' said Twenty-one out loud. 'Next time I'm going to stop when I reach a familiar part of the circuit.'

This he did, and he landmarked the tree on which he stopped in the area which felt familiar. Shortly he took off on a slightly wider circuit and flew until he sensed he had reached the familiar part of the circuit again.

'Yes!' he exclaimed, as he landed nearby and looked back at the landmarked tree he had chosen previously. It was close to where he had stopped this time. 'Same again – just one more circuit.'

The idea did not appeal as far as his energy supply was concerned, but his spirits were boosted. Off he flew, slowly but with some confidence. To his considerable relief he found the same part of this third circuit was familiar in relation to the sun.

Now he had three points marked out in a line, giving him a direction – one he suspected, and hoped, would take him back to the hive. So should he risk it? Should he use this direction as a beeline or continue with the circuits? His stomach answered the question for him. He wasn't going to last many more circuits. He must risk his last reserves of energy on a straight flight.

Slowly, Twenty-one selected the beeline according to his direction finding, set a landmark, and lifted himself up into the air once more. Wings aching with the effort, he set off, carefully scanning the area below him as he flew. Things were becoming desperate; his energy was fading fast. He flew slower and slower. Then his wings faltered and he couldn't help but lose height. He forced himself to keep in the air. Even his sight was beginning to a blur a bit. Surely he hadn't come this far from the hive? But he hadn't appreciated how fast he had flown on the outward journey compared with how slowly he was flying on this return trip.

'Must keep going, must keep flying, must keep straight,' he urged himself, but he was down to his last drops of energy. 'Please, please,' he added in a whisper. 'Somebee help me, give me strength…' and with that, he crash-landed onto something too hard to be a plant.

At first he thought he had flown into a tree trunk, but in fact his landing site was not vertical but sloping. Dragging himself along it, he shortly came to an edge and peeped over. For a moment his vision blurred, then it focused. Below him were…bees, flying into a wall.

'Now what's significant about that?' he asked himself. Being so weak, it took him some time to make the connection. 'The tube! The hive entrance! The tube comes out of a wall – the picture was imprinted.'

So relieved was Twenty-one that he took off without due respect to his condition. Instead of flying gently down to the tube, he flopped straight past it and crashed onto the plant life below. Now the tube was above him!

'Stupid!' he told himself. 'Now how do I get back up there?'

He waited a while to gather his strength – what strength he had left. When he was ready he made one last big effort and took off. He hovered to begin with, and then inched his way upwards to the tube, the hive entrance, and safety. He was just coming up level with the entrance, success in his grasp, when two

COPPICE I

worker bees returning laden to the hive, barged into him as they came in to land in the tube! Twenty-one plummeted back to the foliage below, landing with a thud onto a plant full of bright yellow flowers. He lay there, absolutely shattered, hardly believing the thoughtlessness of those who had knocked him down. All his efforts to get back, beaten by a bee-length!

Feeling sorry for himself, Twenty-one gazed blandly around his final resting place. The yellow flowers, with their tubular bases, were very beautiful. He recalled his efforts to extract food from inside such flowers.

How did that worker bee manage it, he wondered once more? Still, it really didn't matter now, did it? He'd had an exciting short life since emerging – couldn't really grumble.

Twenty-one remembered his emergence; how he thought he wasn't going to make it; the alarm bell that warned him; how he discovered his mandibles could move and how he cut through his cell capping...now that seemed to set something off in his little mind. As he lay there, he applied all the powers of concentration he had left. His physical energy might have gone but he could still think. He looked hard at the yellow, tubular flowers. There was an answer in there somewhere, somehow...

Suddenly, in a flash of insight, he saw it! As a result he edged his way painfully over to the nearest flower and plunged his mandibles into the base of its yellow tube. As soon as a hole was made, he inserted his tongue and located the food. It tasted like honey and he sucked some into his empty stomach. It didn't feel quite right but it had to be food of some sort. When his tongue could find no more, he retracted it and flopped back from the flower, which was now clearly punctured.

Twenty-one waited for the food to take effect. He could no longer see the sun from where he was lying, and it was getting colder all the time. Nevertheless, he waited patiently until he felt sure some of his energy was restored – enough to enable him to fly again. When he felt confident of this, he lifted himself a few bee-lengths into the air, hovering briefly and then landing again. He wanted to be quite certain he had enough power to land in the tube without being knocked over this time!

Satisfied he could do it, he sighted up the target and took off. He came at the entrance from one side and virtually threw himself into the tube, crashing into a couple of worker bees in the process. They briefly applied their antennae to Twenty-one and then ignored him. He crawled off down the tube to the combs. On reaching them he climbed onto the nearest one and collapsed, utterly exhausted – mentally as well as physically – and with a stomach ache for good measure. It wasn't long before other bees clustered around. Heatfall had come again.

4. PIPER

Outside the hive the sun was rising in a clear blue sky. Inside the hive, heatrise came quickly. The worker bees were busy at their tasks and the Queen was laying even more eggs. Twenty-one was still dozing! Eventually he was stirred by the numerous bumps and shoves from passing bees.

After staggering to the nearest honey cell for a good feed, he took stock of his situation. Life had been very exciting, though quite a risky business so far. He'd only just made it back to the hive yesterday. His first task today must be to find his two friends.

Racking his memory for the location of those barrier bees he'd upset, Twenty-one headed back to the hive entrance. From there he worked his way back to where he thought he had met the Queen – although she wasn't around – and then over to the barrier bees, who were still around. He was about to start searching the vicinity when he heard a familiar voice.

'Is that you, Twenty-one?'

'I'm sure it is,' said a second voice.

Twenty-one swung around and grinned at his two friends. 'Great to see you!'

'We thought you'd come back here,' explained Twenty-two, 'but you've taken your time!'

'Well I came here as soon as I could after heatrise, but...'

'Don't tell me,' guessed Twenty-three, 'you were late getting going?'

'Hmm.'

'Anyway, now you're back, tell us what happened,' urged Twenty-three.

That's exactly what Twenty-one did. He told them about the Queen, his first flight and the facts of flight, the drone zone, the scary shadows and how he eventually got back into the hive. His listeners were very impressed. They had done very little during the time their friend had been away, apart from worrying about him.

'And what were the barrier bees guarding?' asked Twenty-two.

'I'm afraid they were so quick to surround me that I didn't get a close look, but it was some sort of large wax cell, maybe more than one cell.'

'So what now?' asked Twenty-two.

'Hmm,' muttered Twenty-one. 'I'm not sure. If we stay in the hive it's "everybee to its task, nothing more nothing less," according the Queen and that drone I met.

'But what *is* our task?' asked Twenty-two.

'That's a good point,' said Twenty-three. 'We don't appear to have a task, do we?'

The trio pondered that for a while, until Twenty-one made a suggestion. 'Look, we don't like the way Shouter runs things in the hive but it looks as if she's under the Queen's control, so we can't do much about it can we? I suggest we do what the other drones do and fly out to the drone zone for the day.'

'But what about those scary shadows?' Twenty-three objected.

'Maybe they were a once off. Maybe they won't come back again.'

'Or if they do,' chipped in Twenty-two, 'we could sort them out!'

Twenty-one wasn't too sure about that but admitted he wouldn't mind finding out more about them. Twenty-three said he'd rather not!

'Oh come on,' urged Twenty-one, 'let's get out there. You'll love flying. Follow me.'

They did – Twenty-two with enthusiasm, Twenty-three with reservations.

Twenty-one picked up the gentle draught that led them to the tube and they crawled along to its end.

'Right,' he announced. 'He we are. Jump off and you'll automatically fly.'

'Really,' said Twenty-three.

'No problem,' said Twenty-two, as he threw himself off and flew immediately.

Twenty-one joined him and they both hovered, facing the entrance, waiting for Twenty-three. Several worker bees were taking off or landing and Twenty-three was in their way.

'Jump!' shouted Twenty-two, but his friend remained firmly rooted to the tube's surface, despite the buffeting he was receiving from other bees. It was like trying to get him out of his cell at emergence.

Twenty-one whispered to Twenty-two, 'I'll keep him talking if you go down and give him a shove from behind!'

Twenty-two dipped an antenna in a gesture of understanding and flew back to the entrance. Twenty-one moved in and hovered directly in front of the reluctant Twenty-three, trying to keep out of other bees' flight-paths as best he could. He adopted a reasoning approach.

'Come on, Twenty-three. When I was first brought here and pushed off, I found I could fly immediately. You see, it's like this…'

At that moment Twenty-two came up behind Twenty-three and barged straight into him, taking them both over the edge and into mid-air.

'I can do it, I can do it!' yelled Twenty-three. 'I'm flying!' At which he turned as if to shoot upwards.

'Hey, hang around a bit!' cried Twenty-one. And he made them both hover in front of the hive to get its location imprinted on their memories. Then he allowed them to start flying around as they wished.

The once reluctant Twenty-three was exuberant. He happily forgave the others for the trick they had played on him. He was now zooming around keenly, along with Twenty-two, who shot gracefully through the air at high speed. Twenty-one allowed them to 'find their wings' before indicating a landing area. They followed him down and landed on a plant with tubular yellow flowers. Twenty-three's abdomen was visibly contacting and expanding as he pumped air into his spiracles.

'Before we fly off to the drone zone,' said Twenty-one, 'I want to show you that little trick I worked out. See these yellow flowers, near the base? You puncture about here.' He pointed with his left foreleg. 'Then you suck out the honey, or whatever it is.'

'Nectar,' said Twenty-three. 'That's something we did find out while you were away. The foragers collect nectar from the flowers and change it into honey.'

'Is that right?' responded Twenty-one. 'But how…?'

'In their stomachs,' he explained. 'Once the nectar's in their stomachs, it begins to change into honey and that's what's stored in the hive.'

'Hmm. Well, so much for that. How about heading off to the drone zone then? I'll lead the way and point out some landmarks. Oh, and keep an eye on the sun's position as well. Ready?'

'No problem,' said Twenty-two.

Twenty-three had just about got his breath back and away they went. It was an uneventful trip apart from Twenty-three's comment that he thought he could detect the force field. The others just nodded and continued on the beeline.

At the drone zone they found several other drones and no signs of any scary shadows. They spent most of the morning trying to engage the other drones in conversation, but failed miserably. They were forced to the conclusion that their fellow drones were an unsociable lot for some reason, and gave up trying to communicate with them.

A scout bee by the name of Piper already knew that the drones in this zone were unsociable, and he had a good idea why. When he saw three drones resting together on a branch and apparently having a discussion, he flew down to investigate.

'Hi fellers! How's it going? Don't mind if I drop in for a chat do yer?'

The trio was so surprised that they were unable to answer for a few moments and Piper thought he had made a mistake. It was Twenty-one who found his voice first.

'Well, er...yes, I mean no. I mean, who are you?'

'My name's Piper,' he replied, guessing that might cause some confusion.

'Your *name* is Piper? You don't have a number?'

'Nope, no number. And you?'

'Um, I'm Twenty-one. These are my friends, Twenty-two and Twenty-three.'

Piper greeted them as they looked him over. He was a trim figure – very fit looking. His wings appeared tough and strong, as though he had done a lot of flying. His eyes twinkled with a slightly mischievous look. Most of all, he came over as a very cheerful, optimistic drone bee.

'Do you belong to our hive?' asked Twenty-two.

'Nope, I'm an intelligence scout. I fly around keeping an eye on things and collecting information.'

'For whom?' asked Twenty-one, now very curious about their visitor.

Piper was impressed with the question, so he told him. 'For sharing with other intelligence scouts. That's how we look after this region.'

'Do we need looking after?' queried Twenty-two.

'Most of the time, nope,' replied Piper, 'but now and again problems arise.' Twenty-one's memory was suddenly jogged. 'Like scary shadows?'

'Explain,' said Piper, so Twenty-one repeated his previous day's experience. 'I'd like to know if they pass this way again,' said the scout bee thoughtfully. Twenty-one nodded. Twenty-three hoped they wouldn't and changed the topic.

'Why are you called Piper instead of having a number? I thought all drones had to have a number?'

'Yep, well I guess that's because I'm such a chatterbox. They reckoned I talked before I emerged from my cell, and that's called "piping". As for numbers, I'm afraid that's typical of aberrant hives.'

Twenty-one looked puzzled. 'What do you mean "aberrant" hives? I was told that aberrations are things made by the giant creatures.'

'Yep. Yer were told right.'

'Are you trying to tell us we come from a beehive not made by bees?'

''Fraid so. Yer workers may have built the wax cells but they sure didn't build the framework, or the outer covering of the hive.' The trio looked stunned. Piper continued.

'What's more, I bet yer've got very strict comb controllers in there who don't allow any funny business from drones. In fact the whole set up is a bit unnatural I'd say – hence the numbers instead of proper names.'

They had to admit that Piper was right. Having had nothing to compare their hive with until now, they assumed they were from a normal home with normal bees, even if many of them were unfriendly.

For some time they shared information on beehives. They learned about Piper's home hive in a hollow where two stone walls met. He learned what Twenty-one and his friends had done in just two days.

'Yer've really put it about a bit,' commented Piper. 'Tell yer what. It's getting late now but I'd like us to meet up again tomorrow. I'll meet yer here at sunpeak – that's the middle of the day. Yep?'

'Yep, er, I mean, yes,' agreed Twenty-one.

Piper grinned and zoomed off.

'Well,' said Twenty-three, 'that was very interesting.'

'Very helpful,' added Twenty-two.

Twenty-one just nodded, as he was still thinking about some of the things Piper had told them.

They stayed in the drone zone well into the afternoon before Twenty-one suggested, 'Time to fly back to our hive – aberration or not.'

With the route properly landmarked, Twenty-one had a simple task leading his friends back. He just wished he'd got it right the day before. As they approached their hive, he was struck by the size of the structure. Surely it was much bigger than it needed to be for the amount of comb inside the hive – or were there parts of this hive they had not yet discovered?

Dropping down to the hive entrance, they were about to set a landing course when Twenty-two cried out abruptly. 'Hold it! Don't land yet!'

They held back, hovering at about fifty bee-lengths distance from the hive. Then they withdrew further back because they saw a mass of bees filling the entrance.

'What's going on?' shouted Twenty-three.

'I don't know, just watch out,' warned Twenty-two. 'There are bees tumbling all over each other.'

'Two different colours of bees in there,' observed Twenty-one. 'Ours and some with very bright yellow banded abdomens.'

'I'm going in closer,' announced Twenty-two, sensing some action.

'Careful!' warned the others, but Twenty-two was on his way. As he left, one of the 'other' bees shot past, flying away from the hive. It made no buzzing noise at all. Very close in now, Twenty-two realised there was a fight going on. The bright yellow-banded bees were trying to force their way into the hive. The defending workers were hanging on to the intruders' wings and legs, trying to keep them out. He joined in fearlessly, helping to block off the tube entrance. He saw a worker bee crawl onto an intruder's back and plunge her sting in. After a few seconds, both of them went rigid and fell sideways. Other workers pushed them over the edge of the tube onto the ground below. Astonished and shaken, Twenty-two flew off to rejoin his two friends. The battle was winding down as more of the enemy flew off, while others were being shoved off the end of the tube onto the ground below. Some of the defending worker bees went with them.

'The hive was being attacked,' reported Twenty-two, 'but we've driven them off!'

COPPICE I

'Well done! You're very brave!' said Twenty-three, who would have been the last bee to fly into the fray.

Twenty-one was concerned about the bees who had been thrown onto the ground below. 'There's something I don't understand,' he said. 'I'm going to check out those bees on the ground.'

Without waiting for the others' agreement, he flew over. They followed. He counted eight enemy bees and seven of their own. All were quite rigid – quite still.

'No sign of life here,' announced Twenty-two.

'Then they're dead?' asked Twenty-three.

'Looks like it,' replied Twenty-two. 'From what I saw, I'd say they were stung. Look – there's a sting protruding from this one.'

'And here,' said Twenty-three, not venturing too close.

'But not here,' observed Twenty-one. 'There's no sting that I can see but...'

'But what?' asked the others.

'Come and see for yourselves.'

They did. One of the workers lay dead with the back end of her abdomen ripped out. The three drones looked silently at the dead worker bee. Then as they surveyed the whole scene, they began to take it all in at a deeper level. It was Twenty-two who first put their thoughts into words.

'We've just witnessed the sacrifice of some of our guard bees in repelling the intruders. Some were stung *by* the enemy; some died because they used their sting *on* the enemy.'

Twenty-one added, 'And the enemy aren't bees, they're something a bit different. We'll ask back at the hive.'

The three drones took a last look at the dead bodies and took off together for the hive entrance. Twenty-two landed first and approached the worker bees now on guard, a double guard by the look of it. As he came up to the nearest guard she cocked her antennae towards him and then moved over to let him pass. The same happened to Twenty-three, and Twenty-one, bringing up the rear. He had just passed the guard when he remembered his question.

'Oh, er, who were those intruders?' To which he received a puzzled look followed by a one-word answer.

'Wasps!'

5. HIVEQUAKE

Shortly after heatrise the next morning, the trio met up to discuss what to do on what was only their third day since emergence.

'We don't need to fly out to the drone zone straight away, do we?' asked Twenty-three. 'I mean, Piper said he'd come at sunpeak so we've got all morning to do something else.'

'Like what?' asked Twenty-two.

'Like fly around the area near the hive.'

'For what purpose?'

'Maybe those wasps will come back.'

'If they do, we'll be ready for them I should think.'

Twenty-one suggested, 'We could look around more inside the hive.'

'Don't we know enough about it already?' asked Twenty-two.

'It's this aberration thing that bothers me,' explained Twenty-one. 'When we flew in yesterday, I was struck by the size of our hive – from the outside. It's so big that I can believe the giant creatures built it. But inside it's much smaller, unless we've not explored it properly.'

'Which we haven't, have we?' said Twenty-three.

'Not unless you had a good look around while I was "away".'

'Not really.'

'So let's do it now. Any objections?'

There weren't, so the trio set off. Twenty-two led the way as usual, his powerful frame protecting the other two as well as providing speedy progress along the combs. Twenty-three kept his antennae twitching while Twenty-one kept his eyes open.

By mid-morning they had discovered rows and rows of honey stores in the upper part of the hive, separated from the lower combs, with eggs and larvae, by a thin piece of very hard material with holes in it. The hive was bigger than they had realised but not big enough to fill the structure as seen from the outside. It was a puzzle the trio could not solve.

'What now?' asked Twenty-three.

'We know our hive from top to bottom and from side to side, I reckon,' declared Twenty-two.

'There's nowhere else to explore…is there?' added Twenty-three.

Twenty-one was thinking, then muttered, 'Hmm, just one place, of course.'

'What do you mean?' enquired Twenty-three, staring at him.

Twenty-one didn't answer. He just waited until it dawned on them.

'Oh, you don't mean those things behind the barrier bees do you?' objected Twenty-three.

'Yes he does,' confirmed Twenty-two.

'But you wouldn't risk being arrested again, would you?' said Twenty-three.

Twenty-one grinned. 'Not if I can help it.'

'Go on,' said Twenty-two.

'Well, I'm not sure how we'll do it but I think we should try and get a closer, longer look at those cells or whatever they were.'

'Count me out!' declared Twenty-three, but Twenty-two was interested, so it was two to one in favour!

They set off to locate the barrier bees on the lower comb. Sure enough, they were still there. Twenty-three picked up the distinctive scent even before they could see the barrier.

'So how are we going to play this?' enquired Twenty-two. 'No point in repeating our last effort is there?'

'Erm, well actually we could,' suggested Twenty-one, 'only this time we swap roles.'

Twenty-two paused while he took in the implications of that. 'I beg your pardon!'

'But all they'll do is make you fly.'

'You hope!'

Twenty-three didn't like the way this was going. 'Do we really need to find out any more about this structure or whatever it is?'

'Do we need to find out about anything?' retorted Twenty-one. 'We could just be good drones and keep ourselves to ourselves – no bother to anybee?'

'OK,' said Twenty-two, 'I'll give it a go. But I'm going to find it a bit harder squeezing through the gap.'

'But you're stronger than I am,' replied Twenty-one. 'Tell you what though; Twenty-three and I will walk into the barrier side by side. That might cause them a few headaches and perhaps make things easier for you.'

'Did I hear you right?' asked Twenty-three.

'Yes! And you're going to do it,' insisted Twenty-one, 'even if I have to drag you up to the barrier bees! Now are you ready, Twenty-two?'

'So for once it was Twenty-one and Twenty-three leading the way, with Twenty-two tucked in behind. They crawled up to the nearest barrier bee who began to deflect them to the right. However, while Twenty-one allowed himself to be slowly deflected, Twenty-three became confused and jumped to the left. Twenty-two came out from behind in a hurry and crashed into him, pushing him through the gap!

'Oh!' exclaimed Twenty-three. 'What a big cell!'

Seeing that there was another cell attached to the first one, he was about to advance a little further when he was halted abruptly.

'Hey you! What do you want?'

Twenty-three cringed but Twenty-two came up along side. 'If that's Shouter, I'm ready for her.'

It was, but she didn't come alone. Half a dozen angry looking worker bees were with her.

'Now we're for it,' mumbled Twenty-three.

'Just stay close to me,' said Twenty-two.

The next thing that happened surprised everybee. Twenty-three, with his twitching, silvery antennae, was the first to pick it up. There arose the distinctive smell of the honeybee's alarm scent. Twenty-three thought that it must be a response to their attempt to cross the barrier – perhaps triggered by the comb controller to alert surrounding workers. Then he picked up a completely alien scent.

'Emergency, emergency!' shouted the comb controller, and the whole situation changed. Everybee started moving in all directions. Panic set in!

'Honey, honey!' was the cry from the workers, and a few drones, as they scurried off to find the nearest supplies. The scent grew rapidly stronger. Twenty-two and Twenty-three also felt the urge to find food. Just a few bee-lengths away, Twenty-one felt the same, but he saw the barrier bees depart and moved in to join the other two.

'We can get a proper look at these cells now,' he said.

'We can get out of here right now!' shouted Twenty-two.

But Twenty-one was already moving in. He found a very large wax structure extending from near the base of the comb. It was a sort of giant cell – too big to fit on the comb with normal cells. Then, to his surprise, he spotted something inside the cell. It was a larva, a very big larva! Twenty-two was by now alongside, intending to drag his friend away. Twenty-one was taking a closer look inside the cell.

'Oh, I think I know what that could be.' But before he could tell his friend, a loud cracking noise came from somewhere above them.

'What was that?' asked Twenty-one, withdrawing his head from the giant cell.

'I don't know, but let's go, *now*!'

Another cracking sound came from above. The trio set off together for the hive entrance. The unpleasant scent was in fact smoke, and it was getting worse. Suddenly, a whole frame of comb moved upwards in front of them. Horrified, they stopped dead in their tracks. A number of thoughts ran through their minds: What could have done that? Was the hive falling apart? What do we do now? Several seconds later the comb came back down again with a thud. Then the comb next to it went upwards!

'Move!' yelled Twenty-two, and they shot off again. When they reached the entrance tube they found it was completely clogged up with bees trying to escape. Twenty-two tried to force his way through, but it was hopeless.

'Let's try upwards,' shouted Twenty-one above the din. The place was in turmoil, and still the smoke came. It wasn't easy ascending the comb as others were mostly descending, loaded with honey, heading for the tube. All the time they kept hearing the loud cracking and grating sounds. The buzz was greater than they had ever experienced.

Approaching the region of the upper combs with the honeystores, they were amazed to see quite a strong light. What was going on? They passed a few bees still gorging themselves on honey and then took to the air. Many bees were flying around in all directions while the unpleasant smell of the smoke continued to pervade the area. Next thing they saw were giant white forms, two of them, moving over and around the hive – or what was left of it! Scared stiff, they dived back down to the cover of the lower combs. Straight down they went, followed by more banging and scraping noises. Suddenly, the light above the hive was extinguished, accompanied by a loud 'thump'. After a final crack or two, no more loud noises were heard.

The frantic buzzing died down and the smoke began to disperse. Some bees were returning to the hive, many had never left. Workers were beginning to take up their tasks again. The trio was still together, in a state of shock, trying to take in what had happened. They wandered aimlessly over the floor of the hive. Shortly they came to a sight that brought back sad memories.

'Oh dear,' said Twenty-three. 'This worker's dead.'

Twenty-two took a look. 'Badly crushed, by the look of it.'

'Not stung, then?' queried Twenty-one.

'Maybe. I can't see any remains of a sting, but then she's so badly damaged I…'

But they weren't in the mood for an analysis. There was still a lingering scent from the smoke so Twenty-one thought about going outside the hive. That jogged his memory and he remembered the appointment with Piper.

'Hey, we've got to meet Piper at sunpeak, remember?'

'Oh, I'd forgotten all about that,' admitted Twenty-three.

'Hardly surprising,' added Twenty-two.

'So let's get out of here,' suggested Twenty-one.

6. STRANGERS

'I reckon those wax structures behind the barrier were Queen cells,' said Twenty-one as the trio flew out to the drone zone. 'The larva I saw was as big as any I've seen but it was only half-filling the cell.'

'Does that mean there can be more than one Queen in the hive?' asked Twenty-three.

'I don't know.'

'And what about the chaos we've just left behind?' asked Twenty-two.

'Your guess is as good as mine,' replied Twenty-one. 'It was as if the hive was being taken apart, bit by bit, and then put back together again?'

'And those massive white things?' asked Twenty-three.

Twenty-one thought about that before suggesting, 'They were big enough to be giant creatures, don't you think?'

'What?'

'Remember what that drone told me on my first flight. He said that "giant creatures" made aberrations and Piper reckoned our hive is an aberration, so maybe it's not so surprising we were visited by some of those giants.'

'Some visit!' said Twenty-two. 'More like they were trying to rebuild the place!'

'Yes, well, let's hope they leave us alone now,' said Twenty-two.

'Let's hope so,' agreed the others, as the drone zone came into view.

After a quick zoom around the area to see if Piper had arrived early, which he hadn't, the trio settled down on the branch of a young silver birch tree, not far from ground level. There were some of Twenty-one's favourite yellow flowers just below them. They were still discussing the morning's events when Twenty-three made an unusual comment.

'Oh, it's cold today, isn't it?'

'Is it?' queried Twenty-two.

'No it isn't,' said Twenty-one, 'it's nearly sunpeak and it's very warm...Are you OK, Twenty-three?'

But Twenty-three clearly wasn't. 'There's something wrong,' he said, 'can't you feel it?'

They couldn't at first, but then they could. 'I can now,' said Twenty-two.'

'Me too,' added Twenty-one, looking worried. 'Keep your eyes open, this reminds me of something.' The others looked at him. 'When those dark shadows scared everybee out of the drone zone!'

'Oh!' said Twenty-three, antennae now twitching in all directions.

'There!' pointed Twenty-two, as two dark shadows shot overhead and landed on the yellow flowers below.

The trio froze.

'They're bees,' whispered Twenty-two, almost in relief.

'They're very dark,' said Twenty-three. 'Sort of brown and black or...'

'Very dark blue,' suggested Twenty-one. 'Their colouring is brown with dark blue, I think – most odd.'

'What are they doing here?' asked Twenty-three.

'*Ssh*! – Just watch,' urged Twenty-one. So they did.

After a short time it became very obvious what they were doing.

'They're robbing those flowers!' exclaimed Twenty-one. 'They know how to do it as well!' The whole episode was really sparking his interest now. He was adjusting to the eerie chill and his curiosity was about to get the better of him. 'I'm going in for a closer look.'

'I beg your pardon?' said Twenty-two. 'Don't even think about it!'

But Twenty-one already had, and so he did! He flew in from the blind side to avoid detection, and landed half a dozen blooms away from the visitors. It felt even more eerie being this close to them and he felt like flying straight back to his friends. However, he clenched his mandibles and hung on. Peering through the petals he could make out the nearest visitor. It was a drone and he did have a very dark blue tinge to his body. He had dark brown and black abdominal bands with this dark blue tinge, and his wings had the same tinge.

Twenty-one wondered if anything else about them was different. He edged forwards for an even closer look, but as he did so, one of the visitors picked up his movements. He looked up and tapped his partner on the head with one antenna. Both of them stared across in Twenty-one's direction. He felt their cold glare and froze. A second later something hit him very hard and knocked him off his flower onto the ground below! He didn't know what had happened but Twenty-two and Twenty-three did. They quickly took off to their friend's aid. He was trying to regain his feet when they reached him.

'What happened?' groaned Twenty-one.

'They rammed right into you,' explained Twenty-two. 'They didn't give you a chance.'

'Are you hurt?' asked Twenty-three.

'No, I'm just groaning for effect!'

'Let's see if you can fly,' suggested Twenty-two.

Twenty-one, back on all six feet, tried to lift off. 'Ouch!' he yelled almost immediately, and fell back down on one side having raised himself barely a bee-length into the air. 'It's my right forewing, I think. Take a look, will you?'

His friends carefully examined the injured wing, managing to straighten out some of its bent sections.

'Now try,' announced Twenty-three, at which Twenty-one tentatively beat his wings and attempted a low hover.

'Ouf!' he groaned as he landed. 'That's a bit better, but I'm still very sore.'

'OK,' said Twenty-two. 'Your right side wing muscles are probably bruised but they will recover in time. If we can just get you off the ground and onto the nearest plant, then we can rest in safety while you recover a bit more.'

With a considerable effort, Twenty-one flew in jerks up to the nearest yellow flower and crash-landed. Only Twenty-two's quick reactions prevented him from falling back to the ground.

Twenty-three congratulated him. 'Well done! Now take it easy, there's plenty of time left before heatfall.'

But the excitement wasn't over yet. They hadn't been resting for long when a voice rang out. 'Hi fellers, how's it going?'

'Piper!' exclaimed Twenty-three. 'What are you doing here?'

'Coming to see yer, remember? But I'm also looking for an odd pair of drones, or a pair of odd drones – seen any?'

'No!' replied Twenty-one, but Twenty-two explained.

'What he means is, he didn't see them coming. They knocked him straight off his flower!'

'No joking?' asked Piper. 'Are yer OK?' Having checked Twenty-one's condition he asked for more information. 'Now describe them to me.'

'Well,' said Twenty-one, 'I was watching from a few bee-lengths away (Piper cringed on hearing that) and I could see they had a very dark blue tinge to their body colouring. Their brown bands were very dark as well, and of course they seem to give off a sort of chilly feeling?'

'No wonder they had a go at yer – yer probably got off lightly. Anything else about them?'

Twenty-three pointed out that they were robbing the flowers.

'You know about robbing flowers? My goodness, yer live in the wrong hive do yer lot. Now show me the flower they were robbing.'

Twenty-two led him to the flower. Piper examined the borehole carefully.

'Right, I've got the scent. Now which way did they go?'

'That way, I think,' said Twenty-two. 'Can I come with you?'

Piper nodded and shot off with Twenty-two in close pursuit, leaving Twenty-three with the injured Twenty-one. They flew rapidly in the direction they believed the blue drones had gone, picking up landmarks en route. Piper then stalled to a hover.

'Still no trace of that scent,' he said, distinctly disappointed. 'We must get back to the starting point and try circling the area.'

Twenty-two obediently followed the scout bee back to the drone zone, whereupon Piper immediately commenced circling. He persisted for several circuits before indicating to Twenty-two that they should return to the others.

'Dash it!' exclaimed Piper on landing. 'I was too late getting here in the first place. These fellers are very clever. They'd have flown off in one direction and then, as soon as they were out of sight, they'd have changed direction. I was taking a gamble that they might not have bothered this time because they'd knocked poor Twenty-one to the ground. Obviously they were taking no risks – they allowed for onlookers.'

'So you know something about them?' quizzed Twenty-one.

'Yep, but not a lot. Early this season a rumour came, through scout intelligence, of a hive being "taken over" by an unusual, unknown strain of bees. The hive's a

COPPICE

long way from here, beyond our day-range – that's the distance a normal bee can fly in one day, yer see. Anyway, early season takeovers aren't unheard of. Sometimes a hive over-winters without enough honeystores. When the next cycle begins, their stores run out before they can replenish them with fresh supplies. At this stage they usually die out, but they could, in theory, be taken over.'

'In theory?' queried Twenty-one.

'Another hive, which had over-wintered particularly well, could send out a very early swarm and use the spare hive as a home for their overflow population. Thing is, honeybees don't usually like having to clear out loads of dead bodies before setting up home. Scouts wouldn't select an expired hive unless really pushed for choice.'

'Really?' said Twenty-three, fascinated by the insights Piper was supplying.

The intelligence scout continued, 'Maybe we'd have thought more about it, or even dismissed it as a false rumour, but then something more ominous happened. We began receiving reports of scout bees being attacked and even killed, in the area of the hive, which had reputedly been taken over. Now that just doesn't happen! But it did. One of the other hives in that area was bright enough to investigate the matter. Their search party was attacked. Only one bee escaped. She said they were attacked by drones! That's also unheard of. As yer know, we drones don't have stings. What these bees did was to barge into or ram their investigators, knocking them to the ground and making sure they never flew again. I guess yer've a rough idea of their methods, Twenty-one?'

'Rough, is putting it mildly,' he replied. 'They were quick, and very powerful.'

'Yep,' agreed Piper. 'Good thing yer not a scout bee or else they might have finished yer off, even in a drone zone! Now the other thing the escaped worker reported was an unusual, dark bluish tinge to the bodies of the attackers. Since them we've nicknamed them "Blues" for convenience. Very recently we've been getting reports of Blues scouting in pairs, spreading themselves over a very wide area, including parts of our region. We have to discover what these Blues are up to. Nothing like this has happened in living memory. We're stumped, and very concerned.'

'Thanks for letting us in on it, Piper,' said Twenty-one. 'You've made our day, after all that's happened.'

'And he doesn't just mean the Blues,' explained Twenty-two, who went on to tell Piper about the morning's 'hivequake' and the giant creatures.

'Good grief!' exclaimed Piper. 'I've got to get yer out of there.'

'What?' exclaimed Twenty-three.

'You mean we don't have to stay in our own hive?' asked Twenty-one.

'When can we come?' asked Twenty-two.

'Nope, yer don't have to stay in your hive, and yer can come as soon as Twenty-one's fit enough to fly the distance. Yer're important eyewitnesses now, so I can easily justify a change of hives. First thing is to get Twenty-one back to yer aberr…I mean, yer hive. Take yer time. Stop as often as yer need to. Now let's say three days to recover from the injury…what do yer think?'

'Make it two,' said Twenty-one.

'OK,' agreed Piper, 'it's yer injury. I'll meet yer here in two days time at sunpeak.'

So it was agreed, and Piper bid them farewell before turning to fly off. But he hesitated.

'Forgotten something?' asked Twenty-two, but Piper was concentrating. After an unusually long silence for him, he made his decision.

'I think I ought to give yer the directions to my hive now, just in case anything happens to me.'

That disturbed the other bee somewhat. 'Like Blues, you mean?' asked Twenty-three. 'We don't want anything to happen to you Piper, please be careful.'

'I will, but I reckon this is a necessary precaution. Twenty-two; fly up with me and I'll tell yer what yer need to know.'

The two drones took off and flew high. Piper gave Twenty-two a directional setting and a list of four landmarks for the route, the first of which was visible from where they were hovering. He made quite sure that Twenty-two had them fixed in his mind before they flew back to the others. On landing, he waited a little longer before testing him again. He'd got it, so Piper said farewell.

'See yer fellers,' and he flew off.

'Let's get you back to the hive,' said Twenty-two.

That proved harder than they expected. Twenty-one had to keep within easy

COPPICE

reach of a landing site, though climbing to any great height was too difficult for him anyway. In the open field they could proceed easily enough but in the wooded area it became quite tricky, and most of their journey was in woods. As they neared the hive, Twenty-one had to stop more often – he was very sore. The thought of soon being able to leave their hive lifted them, though, and they made it back in good time. Three tired, but excited drones relaxed in the cluster at heatfall, dreaming of a new life in Piper's hive.

7. OUT DRONES, OUT!

At heatrise, Twenty-three thought he could detect a slight tension in the hive. The others reckoned he was imagining things. After feeding from the honeystores, they trundled down to the entrance tube and tested out Twenty-two's wing muscles in short flights around the hive. The long rest had helped considerably. If they hadn't already agreed to give him two days to recover, he would have been tempted to make the flight there and then. However, as the day went on he realised the folly of that idea. His right side wing muscle was beginning to ache. It was still quite sore.

'Time to call it a day,' announced Twenty-one.

'You've done well,' commented Twenty-three.

'But you need a good long rest before tomorrow's flight,' advised Twenty-two. So the trio returned to the hive.

Once in amongst the combs, all three of them sensed the tension that only Twenty-three had picked up at the beginning of the day. He was now twitching his antennae constantly, trying to locate the source of the tension. He suspected there was a new scent in the hive but he wasn't certain, and the other two couldn't detect it at all.

'Strange,' said Twenty-three. 'I think I can sense danger.'

'Danger? In here? At this time of day?' objected Twenty-two.

'Do you mean the giant creatures again?' asked Twenty-one.

'No, I don't think so. I mean "bee" trouble. It's more like when we first saw those blue drones.'

'Oh,' said Twenty-one, 'I hope they're not coming here.'

'Perhaps we should stock up with honey, just in case,' suggested Twenty-two

'It's a bit late in the day for flying very far,' said Twenty-one. 'But OK, why not?'

They decided to climb up into the vast honeystores in the upper combs for their feed. Twenty-three wanted to see if he could feel the tension up there as well. In fact it was less obvious to him up there. Down below, however, the tension was rising. More and more workers and drones were returning to the hive as heatfall approached. There were very few still outside when it started.

Without warning, the worker bees turned on the drones! They suddenly went for them! Somebee, somewhere must have started it all off, but in no time at all the thousands of workers in the hive turned on the hundreds of drones. As it began in the lower combs, the trio heard it before they saw it.

'What's happening?' asked a worried Twenty-three.

'Something bad,' replied Twenty-two. 'There's a lot of shouting going on down there.'

'And now it's coming up here!' exclaimed Twenty-one as he spotted workers climbing through the odd piece of material that separated the upper from the lower combs.

'Out drones, out!' cried the leading worker bee, and others took up the call.

'Out drones, out! Out drones, out!'

Twenty-two had thoughts about resistance but dropped the idea when he saw more workers appearing.

'Let's go!' he shouted. 'Follow me!' and off they scurried, upwards towards the top of the hive, with several workers in hot pursuit.

Throughout the lower combs drones were being buffeted and shoved around – pushed in the general direction of the hive entrance. The few drones up in the honeystores had more time to manoeuvre. The trio was giving their pursuers a run for their honey but going up to the top of the hive didn't shake them off.

'Out drones, out! Out drones, out!'

There were even more of them now. The trio reached the inner roof of the hive.

'Good grief!' exclaimed Twenty-two. 'There's another lot coming up the next comb. Let's try the side wall.'

They sped across the tops of the combs to the side wall. Still the cry came.

'Out drones, out! Out, drones out!'

The space between the last comb and the side wall was clear.

'Right, down here!' yelled Twenty-two, and the other two quickly obeyed.

But now they were heading in the direction the workers wanted.
They reached the base of the upper combs and plunged on into the lower combs. A horde of chanting workers was coming up behind them.

'Out drones, out! Out drones, out!'

Twenty-two led them onto the floor of the hive. What a sight! There were bees everywhere, crawling all over each other, pushing and shoving, slowly moving towards the region of the hive entrance. The pursuing workers were right up behind the trio now. Twenty-two boldly placed himself between them and Twenty-one.

'Keep pushing towards the entrance!' he ordered – which again was what the workers wanted.

There were several workers in the melee around them, allowing themselves to be carried along by the tide of worker bees whose chant was getting louder.

'Out drones, out! *Out drones, out!*'

Suddenly a worker pounced on a nearby drone and stung him!

'Horrors!' cried Twenty-three. 'Do they really mean to kill us?'

Twenty-two pushed his friends even harder into the mass of drones, away from direct contact with the workers and their stings. The noise was awful. Workers screamed in triumph, drones yelled in pain and terror. At last they reached the entrance. Drones were piling into the tube; workers were shoving them in, damaging wings, legs and antennae in the process. The trio tried desperately to steer clear of the workers, but the latter were in a very determined mood.

'*Out drones, out! Out drones, out!*'

Twenty-three squeezed into the tube, carried by a cluster of other drones. Twenty-one was next, but a worker bee came at him. Twenty-two lunged out, taking her by surprise, and Twenty-one escaped. The worker attacked Twenty-two instead. He responded, keeping her sting as far a way as possible. He was a well-built drone and the worker wasn't expecting such resistance. Another worker joined in. Twenty-two edged his way backwards, towards the tube, facing his attackers all the time. Then the massed tide of drones took over, pushing him clear of the workers near the edge of the tube, and into the tube itself with all the other expelled drones.

There was no sign of his two friends. They had to be further up the tube, just as squashed up as he was. The workers' chant continued from inside the hive, muffled by the mass of drones in the tube.

COPPICE

'Out drones, out! Out drones, out!'

Twenty-one could still hear it as he squeezed through to the end of the tube. His legs hadn't touched the tube's surface anywhere along its length! Now what? Some drones were flying off, some were just falling off – resigned to their fate. As the pressure of drones in the tube pushed him forwards, Twenty-one jumped off the end of the tube and hovered there, looking back at the awful scene just below. He couldn't see either of his two friends. More and more drones were pouring out of the entrance. Then workers started appearing and the chant was loud and clear again.

'*Out drones, out! Out drones, out!*'

Workers were now throwing dead and injured bees off the end of the tube onto the ground below. A pile of bodies was rapidly accumulating. Shattered drones were crawling over the heap. Workers began taking to the air.

Time to get out of here, thought Twenty-one...but where to?

The drone zone was the only place he knew how to get to, so he flew off in that direction, hoping that perhaps Twenty-two and Twenty-three would be doing the same.

Unfortunately, however, the crush of bees in the hive, and especially the tube, had aggravated Twenty-one's wing muscle injury. He started losing height. He realised he wasn't going to make it to the drone zone. Down he came, near the edge of a field, in a hedgerow. He flopped there for a while, trying to take in the situation. He knew that heatfall was approaching and he couldn't get back to the hive. Then again, he had no doubt that the workers would deal severely with any drones who did try and get back into the hive. There had been a deliberate, organised expulsion – something none of them had anticipated.

Twenty-one had never spent the time after heatfall anywhere other than inside the hive. Now he was about to discover what it was like to be without the comfort of other bees at this time. The temperature was falling steadily. He shivered for the first time in his life. He must find somewhere warmer. He started crawling around amongst the smaller hedgerow plants. Not really knowing what he was looking for, he failed miserably. All the time the temperature was dropping and he found it harder to exert himself as his muscles stiffened up. In fact, his whole body was slowing down. He couldn't even think clearly anymore, and his vision became blurred. Next came the dark, swirling mist, enveloping him. Where had he come across that before? An alarm was triggered – but this time Twenty-one could not respond to it.

HIVE TWO

8. COPPICE

As Twenty-one's body warmed up, his eyes began to function properly. His head cleared and he could see his surroundings. Then he wished he couldn't. Just two bee-lengths away stood the biggest bee he had ever seen!

Twenty-one froze; not that he had moved much anyway. Thoughts raced through his mind: Where am I? How did I get here? Who is that massive bee?

He tried to examine the creature without moving his head. He, or she, was rounder in the body than a honeybee. There was a yellow band at the front of the thorax and the abdomen was yellow with three black stripes, very close together.

As he waited for something to happen, another super-large bee emerged from somewhere. Twenty-one realised he was trapped, yet he didn't sense any hostility from this pair of giants. All the same, he stayed very still. Nothing happened. His thoughts drifted back to his own hive and he recalled the horrific attack by the worker bees. That made him shudder, and one of his hosts noticed.

'Ah, I see our young friend is with us at last. Now please don't be afraid. You're quite safe with us.'

Wisely, neither of the giant bees made any movement towards Twenty-one. He struggled to his feet. They still didn't move.

One of them said, 'Allow us to introduce ourselves. We are humble bumblebees, at your service. My name is Ling, and this is my worker companion, Heather. This is our home – or part of it anyway.' He paused for that to sink in. 'We really are here to help you. There's no need to be afraid.'

Twenty-one plucked up enough courage to respond. 'How did I get here?'

'I carried you,' replied Ling.

'Hmm,' muttered Twenty-one, thinking that Ling was certainly big enough for the task. 'And where exactly are we?'

Heather answered, 'In our underground nest, which isn't so far from your hive.'

'Hmm.'

'Do you have a name?' she asked.

Twenty-one looked at her, thoughts of Twenty-two and Twenty-three in his mind. 'My, er, name is...Twenty-one.'

Ling and Heather exchanged knowing glances. Ling made a suggestion. 'I think it's time you had a proper name.'

'A proper name?' queried Twenty-one.

'Yes. Numbering is the sort of thing that only happens in hives like yours.'

'Hives like mine?'

'Yes. I mean hives made by the giant creatures – aberrant hives.'

'We would like to call you "Coppice",' said Heather.

'Coppice?' repeated Twenty-one.

'Yes,' she confirmed. 'Coppice is a way in which trees sometimes grow – or are made to grow. Near your "old" hive there's a lot of sweet chestnut coppice. Instead of one big trunk, there are several small ones, all shooting up from the ground together. Most of the sweet chestnuts around there are like that.'

'So, am I going back to my, er, aberrant hive?'

'Do you really want to?'

Coppice shook his head but then remembered: 'My friends, my friends Twenty-two and Twenty-three. Do you know what happened to them?'

After a few moments thought, Ling offered some consolation. 'If they were half as determined to survive as you were, then they're probably still alive too... somewhere.'

Coppice didn't react. Ling continued, 'Given your sore wing muscles, the terror of the expulsion and the time of day, you did very well to get as far as you did. Most drones wouldn't have even bothered to attempt an escape flight. You were quite close to the drone zone, you know. Fortunately, I was out on my evening track and spotted you tucked away in the bottom of the hedgerow. I almost missed you because you'd made an attempt to get in amongst the foliage to keep warm, but I'd picked up your scent anyway. I could even tell you were probably injured.'

'That's remarkable,' said Coppice, wondering if super-sensitive Twenty-three could have done the same, 'but how could you fly in that temperature?'

COPPICE

'Ah, good question,' replied Ling, pleased to have the opportunity to explain. 'You see, we bumblebees are very good at flexing our wing muscles without flapping our wings.'

'*What?*' objected Coppice.

'We can uncouple our wings from their muscles if we want to. I've known honeybees who can do it as well, but we're the experts. It allows us to warm up before flying in cold weather. Once in the air, we keep warm by non-stop flying. So, compared with other bees, we can fly out earlier in the day and stay out later at night, collecting food without competition.'

Coppice looked closely at the two large, furry bumblebees. They really were friendly and quite reassuring. There was nothing at all unpleasant about them.

'Thank you,' he said. 'Thank you for rescuing me. What now?'

'How about some food?' asked Heather. 'You must be starving.'

She ambled over to one side of the chamber and grabbed hold of a sort of wax cup or pot. It was like a single cell from a honeycomb. She cut off its capping.

'Here, try some of this,' and she sampled some herself as if to reassure him.

Coppice took his first sip of bumblebee honey. It had a beautiful, rich taste, similar to honey he had eaten before but with something extra. He tucked into the rest of it while his hosts looked on, knowing that their guest would soon be ready to discover what else they had in store for him.

'Feeling better?' enquired Heather as Coppice withdrew his tongue for the last time. She was actually quite proud of her honey.

'Terrific!' he replied. 'Ready for anything.'

'But we won't overdo it with the wing muscles just yet,' Ling advised. 'To begin with you won't need them much anyway. We want to teach you the secrets of our maze, and that means a lot of walking. First we'll show you the way in and out. Follow me!'

Ling led the way out of the nest chamber along one of the four tunnels that fed into it. Coppice followed him with Heather bringing up the rear. The temperature was cool but acceptable. They soon reached a junction in the tunnel.

'Now then,' announced Ling. 'Here's the first parting of the ways. You'll have to remember which way to turn – left this time.'

On they walked, through a second tunnel, just wide enough for two bumblebees to pass and therefore with sufficient space for about five honeybees.

'Did you make all these tunnels?' asked Coppice, his usual curious self once again.

'Some and some,' replied Ling. 'Our maze is based on tunnels left by a field vole. We've developed them into a complicated system known as a "refuge".'

'Refuge?' queried Coppice.

'Yes, a place where you can go to escape from your troubles, or those who trouble you.'

'Hmm.'

They reached another junction and turned right. Ling paused and decided to test Coppice. 'Tell me, what are the three turns we've made so far, Coppice?'

'Whoops!' thought Coppice, racking his brain for a few moments as he recalled their route. Then he came up with the right answer. 'Left, right, right.'

'Good,' said Ling, 'but concentrate please, we're not finished yet.'

The fourth turn was left, after which they came to cross tunnels at which they turned right. After this they began ascending, the temperature rose, and they reached an opening.

'Here we are,' announced Ling. 'The next bit will be familiar to you I think.'

Coppice followed Ling into the air, turned to face the entrance and imprinted it into his memory. After a few seconds, Ling flew up to his key landmark, a massive pine tree.

'Note the severed branch just below half height where lightning struck it. You can see the black stain.'

'I've not seen lightning,' said Coppice, 'but I've heard thunder.'

'Frightening, but spectacular – such vivid flashes of light in the sky, followed by bangs and crackling noises. I was almost caught in it once, on my way back from my late evening track. I stayed just inside the tunnel entrance to watch it for a while – fantastic. I thought the end had come!'

'I'd like to see it someday.'

'Good for you, but for now we'd better get back to Heather.'

They flew down to the hawthorn hedgerow and rejoined Heather.

'Right,' said Ling to Coppice, 'you lead us back to the nest chamber!'

Coppice looked at him, eyes twinkling. 'You might have warned me!'
The first bit was easy enough, no turns as they descended and then levelled out. As he went, Coppice tried to re-live the outward route. The first turn had been a left, followed by two rights, then a left, and finally – yes, right at the cross tunnels. That was it: left, right, right, left, right. Shortly they came to the cross tunnels. He was about to go left when he checked himself. Learning the route out from the nest hadn't been too difficult for him but the return journey posed a problem or two. Ling and Heather waited patiently and watched from behind.

Eventually, Coppice decided that for the return journey he must reverse the memorised order of turns, so it would be right, left, right, right, left. But still he wasn't sure. He concentrated on the cross tunnels. What had they done when they were here before? They had turned right, but now they were approaching from the opposite direction.

'That's it!' he exclaimed. 'Reverse the memory order, then switch the lefts and rights!'

He set off with renewed confidence and led the delighted bumblebees back to their nest chamber.

'Well done!' said Heather.

'Yes,' agreed Ling. 'Not bad for a honeybee! Now practise on your own!'

'What?' said Coppice.

'It's one thing to have us behind you, ready to correct your mistakes, but it's another being alone and having to trust your own judgement. Off you go – while it's fresh in your mind.'

Coppice could see that Ling meant what he said, so he set off, hoping they would follow at a safe distance. He didn't fancy getting lost in this maze of tunnels. At the first junction he listened carefully for any sound of Ling and Heather. Nothing. Well, at least they would come looking for him if he didn't return within a reasonable amount of time – wouldn't they?

He turned left and walked on to the next junction. Perhaps they'd only rescued him to play games with him in their maze? He turned right, and right again at the next junction, followed by a left turn. He reached the cross tunnels where having three choices was more threatening. He wondered what Twenty-two or Twenty-three would have made of all this. At least as a team, they would have been helping each other out.

Why so many turns anyway? Why not a single entrance tunnel, like the tube at his hive? As he thought about it, he realised it must be something to do with security, in which case, why? He recalled the wasps who had attacked his hive. They would never have got in through a maze of passages like this. But what about scent? Twenty-three had such a good sense of smell and Piper had searched for the Blues' scent trail. He'd have to ask Ling about that. For now though, he would have to trust his memory, which told him it was a right turn at the cross tunnels. He was relieved to find this tunnel begin to turn upwards and before long he emerged into the open air.

'No problem,' he declared to the surrounding vegetation. That was a phrase Twenty-two often used. Coppice wondered where he was now. Did he escape, or what? Putting that thought aside, he turned back to the tunnel entrance and made the return journey. Heather was delighted to see him and his taskmaster Ling seemed pleased.

'Well done,' he said. 'Have some honey before you do it a couple of times more, then we'll turn to something else.'

A more confident Coppice topped up with Heather's rich honey and set off again. By the third time he was scurrying through the tunnels and he emerged into the open air in record time, only to be pounced on by a large bee!

'Oh!' cried Coppice. 'Ling! How did you get here?'

'Ah well, you see there are more tunnels than this one. How do you think I made sure you really had completed the route on your first solo attempt?'

Coppice looked puzzled. Ling continued, 'Well, you could have stayed part way down the tunnel for a time and then returned to the nest chamber, or you could have got lost and emerged somewhere else in the hedgerow.'

'You mean you were here each time I emerged?'

'Right.'

'Hmm. So why knock me over this time?'

'Sorry about that. I hope I didn't upset your sore wing muscles, but it was a good way of teaching you another lesson. Never emerge from a tunnel without checking first. You must listen, look and smell, just in case anything's lying in wait for you.'

COPPICE

That reminded Coppice of the question he wanted to ask. 'And, er, what are we looking out for? I mean, why such a complicated entrance to your nest chamber?'

Ling put on his very serious look. 'It is always wise to be alert, young Coppice. Some enemies we know about, others are…unexpected.'

Coppice stared back.

'Now let's return to the nest chamber,' said Ling. 'There's a lot more to learn.'

During the next two days, Coppice learned the routes through two more of the four tunnels leading out from the bumblebees nest chamber. Both of them had five junctions. One was completely blocked off at its end while the other had been recently unplugged. Ling explained that this was the tunnel he had used to get quickly outside to spy on Coppice when he was learning the first tunnel.

The two of them set about replugging the tunnel. They scooped the soil with their legs and then rammed it hard with their heads. On the outside, Ling skilfully disguised the repair job so that even Heather would be pushed to find it.

By the fourth day of his stay, Coppice's wing muscles had fully recovered. Heather's honey was doing him more good than he realised. She was always happy to chat with him, while Ling remained a demanding teacher. In no way was Coppice a prisoner – he could come and go as he pleased.

Coppice learned a great deal from his hosts. They taught him about the various types of wasps, flies, beetles, grasshoppers, mites, ants and spiders. Ants were interesting – living in large colonies like honeybees did. Spiders' webs were fascinating but dangerous. Heather was something of an expert on plants and what you could use them for. Coppice rapidly made up for his previous lack of experience.

On the fifth day, Ling announced the last task. 'We're going to tackle the fourth and final tunnel. It's a tough one because it's a seven junction route and it doesn't lead to the outside.'

'So where does it go?' asked Coppice.

'I think we'll leave that as a surprise! Heather will stay here; she has some honey stores to sort out.'

Coppice obediently followed Ling into the fourth tunnel. They quickly reached the first junction, a cross tunnel. Ling turned right. The next junction was a cross tunnel as well, and they turned right again. To Coppice's surprise, the tunnel now started descending. At the third and fourth cross tunnels they went straight ahead, and the descent continued. Ling made Coppice repeat the details of the route as they proceeded. The tunnel was very dry and crusty. A left turn came next, followed by a right, and now the tunnel showed signs of crumbling. At the final junction they turned left. The tunnel began to narrow until there was only room for one bumblebee instead of the usual two.

At last Ling stopped and turned to Coppice and said, 'We've arrived. We've reached the safe chamber.'

9. THE SAFE

'Be ready for a surprise,' warned Ling. 'This is something of a rarity.' He squeezed himself through the narrow entrance into the safe chamber. Coppice, being a honeybee, had no such difficulty getting inside. Once in, however, he was amazed to find his eyes adjusting to a glow – the source of which he couldn't identify. He was struck dumb by the strangeness of the place. There was no bedding, no honey-pots, nothing at all inside the chamber, yet there was this odd glow.

'Keep looking,' advised Ling. 'The secret of this place is on its walls.'

Coppice gazed at the chamber's circular walls. He walked up to the nearest part of the wall, touched it and smelt it.

'Wax. There's a thin layer of beeswax on these walls – and on the ceiling!' he exclaimed, as he followed the curving wall up over his head and down the other side. The glow seemed to come out of the walls and ceiling, but not the floor. As he peered more closely at a section of the wall, he noticed the markings. There were quite a lot of them. In fact, the walls were covered in them; the ceiling too. They weren't simply careless scratches either – there was a pattern to them. They were spaced out and they began to make some sort of impression on him.

'Getting the idea?' asked Ling. 'Have you worked out what it is?'

'I've never seen anything like it,' replied Coppice, 'and yet there's something familiar about it.'

'What if I suggest the word "landmarks"?'

Coppice added that to his thoughts and then it dawned on him. 'Yes! That's it! I see now – amazing! This is one great big collection of landmarks – only instead of existing in a bee's memory, it's…it's sort of scratched into this wax.'

'Right,' confirmed Ling. 'This way, other bees can learn from it. The remarkable thing is the area it covers.' Ling was now well into his instructor mode. 'First you must appreciate that where the walls meet the floor represents the outer limits of the land covered by this "map" as we call it. So, the centre of the land represented here is in the middle of the ceiling – yes? Take a look, Coppice.'

His willing student examined the highest part of the ceiling. Some of the markings looked familiar. 'Isn't that a spider's web?'

'Correct.'

'Not much good as a landmark is it?'

'Not as a rule, but this one's different.'

'In what way?'

'It glows.'

'What – like these walls?'

'Like these walls.'

'Hmm.'

Ling explained to the bemused Coppice. 'There's a substance mixed into this wax, and into that web, which gives off the glow. It does eventually wear out but it can be renewed. It lasts a very long time anyway. The important thing is that the web marks the entrance to the Caves of Knowledge, and this safe chamber gives the position of the Caves in relation to the surrounding land – up to a distance of a double day-range.'

Coppice had learned from Piper that a day-range is the distance a honeybee could normally expect to fly in one day. So this map covered a vast area. No wonder there were so many scratch marks all over it. You needed plenty of landmarks to cover one day-range, never mind two.

'This is marvellous,' concluded Coppice. 'Who made it?'

'Good question but I'm afraid I can't give you the answer.

'Can't or won't?'

'A bit of each. I can't let you into all the secrets just yet. Suffice to say the only bees with sufficient know-how to construct this chamber live in the Caves of Knowledge.'

'Hmm. OK so where are we on the map?'

'We're not.'

'What?'

COPPICE

'I mean, we do live in the area covered by the map, but our landmark is not scratched into the wax.'

'Why not? What's the point if we can't see where we are?'

'Coppice, why do you think this place is called a safe chamber, and this whole maze of tunnels a refuge? And why is our nest chamber protected by a five-junction maze of tunnels and this chamber by a further seven-junction route?'

Coppice remained silent. Ling continued, 'Access to the Caves of Knowledge is granted only in times of extreme urgency – when great danger threatens the region. The route to the Caves is therefore available but highly protected. There are other safe chambers but I don't even know where they are. I only know about this one – because I'm its guardian.'

Coppice was both stunned and intrigued and admitted he was having trouble taking all this in. He asked, 'Is there anything else I should know about this place?'

'Are you sure you want to know?'

'I'm sure.'

'Very well then, listen carefully. It seems we may be entering dangerous days – a time of evil happenings for bees of all kinds. We're not completely certain but we're preparing for the worst. This means that somebee may be granted access to the Caves of Knowledge and so will need to know the route. Whatever he or she learns at the Caves could be crucial in the battle against evil. Now if – and I emphasise the "if" – it should happen that you, Coppice, ever find yourself in the position of needing to get to the Caves, then you will have to come to this safe chamber and use this map. Do you understand what I'm saying?'

'Yes, but what's this evil? What's…'

'It's not certain, as I said, but if you think about it…'

Coppice didn't have to flick back very far in his memory. 'Do you mean the blue drones by any chance? And if so, how do you know about them?'

'I know a lot more than I've let on up till now, Coppice. In fact, I slipped up once in our earlier conversations, when I mentioned your terror at being expelled from your hive. Had you been more alert at the time, you might have wondered how I knew?'

Coppice looked at his instructor in amazement.

Ling answered his unspoken question. 'Yes. We knew you'd been expelled and we were actually looking for you.'

'We? You mean Heather was out flying as well? I thought you never left the refuge unoccupied?'

'Correct. It wasn't Heather who was helping me, it was Piper.'

'Piper!' exclaimed Coppice, almost rolling over in surprise. This is too much – what next?'

'I think I'm just about through with the revelations for now, but let me just point out that Piper, having spotted the three of you in the drone zone, learned quite a lot about you and decided you should be rescued. That's why he arranged to take you to his hive. Unfortunately, you were injured and the expulsion took place before you could move hive. Piper was flying around the drone zone during the expulsion, hoping you might fly there. I was alerted to search the route between the hive and the drone zone. It was still something of a miracle that we found you in time.'

'And where's Piper now? Have you seen him? Did Twenty-two and Twenty-three get to him?'

'Sorry, sorry, I don't know, and Piper's long since gone off on his intelligence collecting duties. It will be some time before he passes this way again. There are other intelligence scouts – maybe we'll hear something from one of them.'

'I hope so. I do hope so.'

Ling admired Coppice's concern for his two friends – so rare in bees from an aberrant hive. They must have been special bees.

'Now, let me show you a few things about this map,' said Ling. 'As I said, the Caves of Knowledge are at the centre, which is in the middle of the ceiling, and the scratches represent landmarks. Here we have a stream and here, with the wider squiggles, a river. These are hills, these are very tall trees, and these are aberrant structures – they do come in useful for navigation.' Ling was enjoying his teachers' role again. 'Then we have ponds – see here – and a lake, which is much bigger of course, and even the occasional waterfall. All quite straightforward really.'

Coppice nodded. The scratches were simple and generally easy to match up with what they stood for. All the same, it was remarkable idea to a honeybee who could store route maps in his memory, but had never considered recording them in a form that other bees could see.

Ling continued, 'There are one or two oddities that are very important. You already know about the spider's web representing the Caves of Knowledge. Now look at these curved lines – three of them, close together. They represent a fault in the force field.'

Coppice looked him. The force field was one of the five facts of flight. Twenty-three had been close to working it out but Coppice had almost forgotten about it. Ling saw the need to explain further.

'Basically it runs in one direction. Once you can accept this, you can use it to navigate. You should be able to tell when you're flying along the direction of the force field as opposed to when you're cutting across it. Receptors in your brain can even assess the angle at which you're cutting across it.'

'Well I guess mine aren't working properly!'

'More likely you're not taking enough notice of them.'

'Maybe.'

'Anyway, a fault in the force field is a means of defence. The field is mixed up somehow and you get thrown off in the wrong direction. You think you're going north, but in fact you're going north-east, or something like that. So, when you come to one of these faults, assuming you know it's there, use only the sun and landmarks for navigation – understood?'

'Understood,' said Coppice.

'Good, because the Caves of Knowledge are guarded by a fault in the force field. Now I'll show you the mark that I'll scratch onto the map so that it can be read.'

Ling dragged his right front leg through the dusty floor of the chamber twice. 'There you are – the great pine with the burnt out branch.'

Coppice peered at it and nodded his head, quietly admiring Ling's artwork.

Ling then scrubbed it out. 'So that's the key landmark,' he said. 'I'll scratch it onto the map in the correct place at the right time.'

'How will you know when the right time is?'

'I just will – trust me! Next thing – the map must be destroyed after it's been read.'

'What?'

'Damage it in some way so that no other bee can learn the route.'

'But who else…?'

'Don't argue, just remember to do it. Promise?'

Coppice was silent for a few moments, then promised. He did trust Ling, and Heather. They had rescued him after all, but this was a creepy business. He sort of hoped he wouldn't have to come here again, but he was also very curious about these Caves of Knowledge.

'One more thing,' said Ling. Coppice couldn't believe there was more to come. 'There's a bolthole from this chamber. Come over here.'

Ling led him to a point where the wall met the floor. It didn't appear to be any different at first, but on closer inspection Coppice detected a seam in the wax.

'The wall's very thin here,' explained Ling. 'You can push your way through it very easily, into the escape tunnel directly behind it – just in case.'

'Just in case what?'

'Just in case you can't go back the way you came. Simply a precaution. The escape tunnel has no junctions but it does have a plug made of soil at the end. I hope you never have to use it.'

'Me too!'

That was the end of Ling's instruction. He led Coppice back to the nest chamber where Heather was waiting for them as if she'd never moved all the time they were away. But she was no longer alone.

'Did you have a good visit?' she asked. 'Look who's arrived.'

'Ah, good to see you,' said Ling. 'Coppice, this is Fern. He's an intelligence scout – like Piper.'

'Greetings,' said Fern, looking Coppice hard in the eyes.

Coppice just nodded. Fern appeared to be a perfectly normal drone apart from the look in his eyes. He looked even more serious than Ling.

'Any problems?' enquired Ling of Fern.

'No – just putting in an appearance to let you know I'm ready when you are.'

'Well,' said Ling, 'I've not told Coppice yet but I guess there's no time like the present.'

COPPICE

Coppice wondered what he was in for now.

Ling continued, 'Fern's from a hive quite close by. In fact, he's our closest intelligence scout. He's going to take you to his hive.'

Coppice heard that but something more pressing was on his mind, so he asked, 'Does he know Piper and does he know anything about Twenty-two and Twenty-three?'

'Yes and no, in that order,' replied Fern in a firm, no nonsense voice. 'I certainly know Piper but I don't see him very often, so I've no news of your friends. Now, about the transfer to my hive.'

'Why do I have to leave?' objected Coppice.

Fern looked peeved but Heather intervened: 'This isn't the best place for you to over-winter. You need the warmth of a cluster in a honeybee hive. We can stand lower temperatures than you, remember, and we may be called on to rescue other bees before the season's over.'

It hadn't occurred to Coppice that he might not be the only honeybee to come to the refuge.

'So you've had other bees here before me?'

'Er, yes,' admitted Ling, unusually faltering. 'Yes, we have.'

'Hmm.'

Ling and Heather were glad that Coppice didn't pursue the matter.

'OK,' said Fern, 'I'll be off then. Back tomorrow for the actual transfer?'

'Fine,' agreed Ling, and Fern departed alone, obviously knowing his way through the tunnel to the outside.

'We'll be sorry to lose you,' Heather assured Coppice, 'but it's for the best. Now how about some honey?'

Ling and Coppice tucked into a pot each. They spent the rest of the day either practising the route to the safe chamber or flying around outside. This continued the following day until Ling was convinced that Coppice knew all he needed to know, and knew it well.

It wasn't until early evening, near the time for Ling's late track that Fern showed up.

'Greetings,' he said, almost solemnly. 'All set?'

'All ready,' confirmed Ling.

'Listen carefully, Coppice,' said Fern. 'We're going to make things easier by taking a "coldflight" into my hive. I think you've heard about bumblebees and their ability to fly late in the evening. Well, we're going to do the same! The most important thing is to keep flying – fast and straight. No stopping, no hovering, no nonsense – just flat out from here to the hive. When we reach the hive, we fly straight in. Don't zig-zag or hesitate at the entrance – that will arouse suspicion if there are any guards on duty. However, I doubt if there will be any this late in the day – that's why we're going in on a coldflight. Once inside, we still have the problem of your scent not being right until you've eaten some of our food and generally made contact with other bees in the hive. If you're challenged at the hive entrance, or on the edge of the cluster, you must not resist. Just tuck your tail end in and stand quietly – you'll be OK.'

'Got all that, Coppice?' asked Ling.

'Think so. How far do we have to fly?'

'Not very far,' replied Fern. 'Take half a load of Heather's honey and we'll be away.'

'Only half a load?'

'Yes, you don't want to be carrying too much extra weight.'

Coppice took his last feed of Heather's marvellous honey. Fern appeared to be already supplied. Heather looked on wistfully.

'I'm ready,' announced Coppice.

'Right, say your goodbyes and we'll be off,' ordered Fern.

Coppice turned to his bumblebee hosts. In silence his thoughts went out to them. They weren't honeybees but he felt he was sharing his feelings with them and they were reciprocating.

'Thanks for everything,' whispered Coppice, and he turned to follow Fern.

Heather watched Coppice disappear before she turned to Ling and said, 'I wonder if he has any idea at all how important he is?'

10. HOME FROM HOME

Coppice and Fern left Ling and Heather in their nest chamber and silently followed the correct route to the outside. Some distance short of the entrance, Fern paused to explain to Coppice that they would take off while still inside the tunnel and shoot out of the entrance at as near full speed as possible.

'You'll be hit by the coldness of the air when you burst out into the night but it's essential that you don't falter because of it. Instead, you must bring your speed up to maximum and stick close to me.'

Coppice turned once more to look back in the direction of the bumblebees' chamber. It certainly had been a refuge for him. He wasn't sure if he'd really thanked his hosts adequately. Too late now. Perhaps he would be able to make it up to them some day. Fern couldn't let him ponder any longer. The air near the end of the tunnel was already much cooler than in the nest chamber.

'Ready, young friend?' Fern asked. Coppice turned back to him and tried to focus on the task in hand. 'Take off in the tunnel, fly as fast as you can, ignore the shock of the cold air and hit full speed as soon as possible.'

He looked closely at Fern. He hardly knew him, yet here he was, trusting this scout bee wasn't going to lose him in the chill of the night.

'I'm ready.'

'Good. Now start those wings, but hold your ground.'

That wasn't easy but they raised their wingbeat speed as high as they could.

'Stand by, Coppice…*now*!' And off they shot

Fern zoomed ahead with Coppice in very close attendance. In an instant they hit the cold night air. Coppice knew he would certainly have faltered if he hadn't been forewarned. He spent all his time hanging in as close as possible to Fern. Although there was no bright light in the sky, he did notice a much softer light instead, so it wasn't completely dark. After a while the coldflight became quite exhilarating. He was warm in himself while all around him was cold – too cold. Yet he was surviving. A feeling of confidence, even power, came over him. He was doing what bees are not supposed to be able to do. He was different, perhaps one of a select few. He was so enthralled by these thoughts that he failed to detect Fern's slight drop in speed and flew into the back of his guide.

'Coppice! Pay attention!'

'Sorry!'

With that rebuff, Fern swung left and downwards. After winding around some dense bushes they flew up several bee-lengths, straight into a tree – or so it seemed to Coppice. Of course it was the unguarded entrance to a hive that filled a hollow inside the tree trunk. Immediately on landing, Fern insisted they crawl to the bee cluster and settle until heatrise. Coppice complied and soon dozed off, dreaming about his first ever coldflight.

Coppice awoke with a start as he sensed the hive was shaking. In fact it was Fern trying to wake him up.

'Come on, Coppice! There's a simple but urgent job to be done; get moving!' Fern virtually dragged him to the nearest honey cell. 'Get a load of this inside you while I distribute a few globules over your body.'

'What for?' queried the half-asleep Coppice.

'Apart from needing food inside you...'

'Not that bit, the other bit.'

'Because you must have the scent of the hive to be accepted into it. You've gained much of it simply by being here in the cluster during heatfall, but I want to be sure. A few drops of honey will do the job nicely – a little trick I learned from my scout trainer. You never know when these things might come in useful.'

'Hmm,' was the only reply he could get out of Coppice, who was by now well into his honey.

'When you're ready I'll introduce you to some new friends who will happily show you around the hive. They won't necessarily understand how you came to be here but they probably won't ask either, so you needn't worry about it. Now come this way.'

Coppice followed Fern along the comb and over into the next one. It seemed

COPPICE

different to the comb back in his old hive, not as straight maybe. Anyway, he was keen to meet some new friends so he didn't ponder over the matter. For a moment he recalled Twenty-two and Twenty-three. He would have dwelt on them but Fern's confident voice prevented him.

'Coppice, meet Scruff…and this is Spurge, and then there's Sorrell.'

'Welcome,' said Scruff, so named because most of his hairs stuck out at odd angles. He did look as though he could have been dragged through a cell backwards.

'Glad to meet you,' added Spurge. He was a comparatively large drone with very clear bands on his abdomen, although the colours were identical to those of Scruff and Sorrell. Sorrell didn't exactly speak, but his remarkably bright eyes seemed to communicate directly with Coppice. They were both penetrating and accepting.

'So why don't you three show Coppice around and visit the drone zone quite soon?' urged Fern. It was almost an order, Coppice observed.

'Will do,' responded Scruff, and they set off at once.

It was quite unlike Coppice's first hive. For a start, it was in the hollow of a large tree. The sides, ceiling and floor were not regular. They curved a lot but the workers had somehow coped with that. They had made the best use of the space they had to work with. It was some time before Coppice realised there was no hard piece of material with holes in it, separating the brood from the honeystores. There were honeystores, but not as extensive as in his old hive. They saw some brood areas where a few larvae were being fed but no eggs were being laid. It was nearly the end of the season, Sorrell had explained. That was the first time he had spoken.

What really stood out was the attitude of the other bees to the foursome as they toured the place. Many took the trouble to acknowledge them, either by a brief word, a flick of an antenna, or just nodding in their direction. Scruff and Spurge replied verbally, Sorrell usually nodded.

'And the Queen?' asked Coppice, wondering about barrier bees and his previous experiences.

'You'd like to see her?' asked Scruff.

'Well. I'm er, sort of...'

'Curious,' said Sorrell, as a statement of fact, not a question. Coppice nodded.

'This way,' indicated Spurge, and off they crawled.

The Queen was large, as she should be, with several workers in attendance; one of whom was feeding her, and she appeared to be in conversation with another. The drones were not too close, but a distinctive smell was evident. Coppice watched carefully for a while, trying to work out what was different, apart from the absence of barrier bees of course. Then it dawned on him.

'Ah, no blue marking.'

'No what?' enquired a puzzled Scruff.

'No blue spot on the top of her thorax. The Queen in my last hive had a...' And he realised what he was saying. The others went quiet. Sorrell's deep eyes sparkled.

He said,' We guessed you were from another hive. Don't worry about it. Fern's done it before – visitors appearing from nowhere. But what I don't understand is this bit about the blue spot.'

'Me neither,' added Scruff, while Spurge just looked confused.

Coppice explained. 'There was one occasion, not exactly intentional, when I met...was taken before the Queen. The "audience" didn't last very long but it did leave a lasting impression on me. She definitely had a large blue spot marked on the top of her thorax. I assumed all Queens were like that, until now.'

'Quite,' commented Sorrell, his interest very much aroused. 'Tell us about this "audience", as you call it.'

So Coppice told them all about the barrier bees, the wax structures, the comb controller and the Queen's judgement over him.

'Amazing,' said Scruff, when he had finished.

'Not the friendliest of hives,' suggested Spurge.

Sorrell was still thinking about it, then he asked about the comb controller.

'We were given our numbers by her,' explained Coppice.

'Numbers?' queried Scruff. That led to another explanation from Coppice.

Finally, the astute Sorrell said they had heard enough for now and that they should fly out to the drone zone and continue their conversation there. So they did.

COPPICE I

There was no long tubular entrance, just a brief gap between comb and open air, and there were guards on duty. Coppice remembered to hover facing the entrance, then move slowly backwards to imprint a picture of the place. Once assured of this, he flipped round and flew away from the hive behind the other three, who had wisely given him time for the imprinting procedure, knowing now that this was a new hive for him.

Flying in a beeline they reached the drone zone quickly. Coppice picked up two landmarks on the way. He now applied the five facts of flight quite automatically. The zone was sparsely occupied but the drones they did encounter were just as friendly as the bees inside the hive. After zooming around for a time, as drones like to do, they settled in an oak tree together.

'Now tell us the rest of your life history,' requested Sorrell, with a deep but assuring look in his eyes.

Coppice was slightly taken aback at first, but reckoned he owed it to them, so he obliged. The others listened quietly but with increasing amazement as he poured out his exploits; learning to rob flowers, getting lost, meeting Piper, the hivequake, blue bees, the expulsion of the drones and his rescue by bumblebees. He didn't tell them about the safe chamber.

There was silence after he had finished. Eventually Scruff spoke. 'That was some story for a drone who hasn't exactly been around for very long.'

'Too right,' agreed Spurge.

Sorrell was still mulling over what he had just heard, eyes twinkling madly. It was Scruff who continued.

'I'm afraid our life stories aren't nearly as exciting as yours. Spurge and I are only first season drones; Sorrell is in his second. We've always lived in this hive, which I'm told we have occupied for many seasons as a colony – the present Queen being our third apparently. Life has been good, but rather uneventful.'

'Until now!' added Spurge.

'Oh, do you mean because of me?' asked Coppice apologetically.

'No and yes,' said Sorrell, breaking from his meditation. 'You see, we've run into a puzzling problem just recently and you may have shed some light on it.'

'Has he?' asked Scruff.

'Maybe, I'm not certain.'

Spurge said, 'Well, if *you're* not certain, no bee is.'

'Fern may have some idea,' Sorrell answered, 'or maybe this Piper chap.'

'So what *is* the problem?' asked Coppice.

His three new friends looked at each other. Sorrell looked him straight in the eye and spoke. 'You must not spread this around. It could cause unnecessary worry – panic at worst. We're finding it difficult to gather in enough food stores for the winter. Furthermore, we think we're losing more worker bees than we should be. Maybe they're flying further afield in search of honey and too many aren't making it back. There doesn't appear to be any disease problem and the Queen's egg production was up to the necessary level, or so we thought. Somewhere, somehow, we're losing out. Now, if we go into the winter cluster low on food supplies, we shall be extremely reliant on a rapid collection of honey early in the new season. That's a risky business, although we may get away with it.'

'Hmm,' was Coppice's response, 'but where do you think I fit in?'

'You've had such experiences already,' said Scruff. 'You might be able to help us.'

Coppice was taken aback at this but Sorrell explained, 'I don't think Scruff means you can personally solve our problems, but the events you've described do suggest that something is "about" – namely these blue bees that the intelligence scouts are so concerned about.'

'And rightly so,' insisted Spurge.

'Do you think they could be the cause of your troubles?' asked Coppice.

'It's just possible,' replied Sorrell. 'Just possible, though I'm not sure how or why.'

That brought their conversation to a close so they took off and headed back to the hive. Coppice was careful to check his landmarks on the way home. The four drones approached the hive, known as 'Middle Oak' and landed in front of the guard bees who vetted them quickly, but carefully, with their antennae. Coppice must have been fully scented up with the smell peculiar to the hive as he was allowed to enter with the other three. After stocking up on honey, they walked around for a while and agreed a regular meeting place on the lower comb

COPPICE

near the entrance.

They didn't meet for many days however, because winter was close at hand. The workers kept busy until the last minute, raking in as much honey as they could, but the general feeling was that a shortfall existed. The temperature dropped further and the bees remaining in the hive, mostly workers, with a few drones, plus the Queen of course, began to form their winter cluster. No bee was left out. They would be inactive throughout the cold period except for the occasional cleansing flights on warmer days. Coppice joined his new friends in their winter repose, pleased to be in such a friendly hive, pleased to be alive.

11. RAIDERS

There is one secret activity that takes place during the winter months. The intelligence scouts use the off-season period to assess the situation in their region. Through a complicated system of pre-arranged meetings, designed to allow for the unpredictability of the weather, they meet to share information. Each scout normally attends two meetings.

The first one concerns his region, which involves three or four scouts, each covering his own area within the region. A region usually extends to a distance of one day-range and contains lots of hives, each with its drone zone. The intelligence scout must know about all the hives in his area. When they meet up they report on the progress of the hives under their surveillance.

Some time after this meeting, each scout flies to a second meeting that is somewhere on the border with an adjacent region. This provides for the sharing of information on a wider scale. These meetings are harder to co-ordinate but the scouts overcome this by designating a hive close to the border of the two regions where they can stay for several heatfalls if necessary. Only in emergencies are further meetings called.

'I moved Coppice to Middle Oak as late as I dare,' explained Fern, 'so that there would be little or no time for the resident bees to become suspicious of him. I can trust Sorrell, Scruff and Spurge with such a guest, even if they have found about his life history in the little time available.

'I bet yer they did,' replied Piper. 'That Sorrell's not daft for a start. He could be an intelligence scout one day I reckon.'

'It'll be fine,' assured Fern. 'Coppice is safe – that's the main thing for the moment. Now what about our situation?'

'Yer better at summarising than me – go ahead, Fern.'

COPPICE

'Very well. First; still only one contact with blue bees inside our region – that by Coppice. Second; increasing rumours from outside our region about problems with the, er, "Blues" as they're being called. We can learn more about those rumours at our inter-regional meetings, of course.'

'If not before,' interrupted a third member of the meeting, named Dock. He was the eldest in the group, and the wisest. 'We cannot be too careful about these invaders – they're like nothing in bee history…to my knowledge anyway.'

'I'm sure yer right,' agreed Piper.

Fern continued his summary. 'Thirdly; there are increasing problems with food shortages in hives in the northern and eastern areas of our region, for example Upper Beech, Lower Beech, River Bank, Upper Oak and even Middle Oak, I suspect.'

'So where's this leading us?' asked Piper.

'We can't be sure,' replied Dock. 'The enemy is not clearly showing his intent.'

'But we know they've taken over other hives,' insisted Fern.

'Only one for sure, so far,' Dock corrected him.

'So far,' said Piper.

That ended the discussion for a few moments as they considered the implications of the last comment. Then the three of them turned to the fourth member of their group. His name was Fescue.

Fescue was the youngest and newest intelligence scout. He had a remarkable memory and even more remarkable speed. It was said that his day-range was one and a half times that of the average honeybee. Because he was new, he didn't speak until asked. He was a good listener anyway and quite happy to soak up all the information he could. However, he had one important contribution to the present discussion.

'My information suggests that there's a significant increase in the raiding activities by wasps.'

'Interesting', said Dock.

'Puzzling,' said Fern.

'Yer could have a good point there, Fescue,' Piper declared. 'Strangely enough, Coppice's first hive, the aberrant one, has had trouble with wasps.'

'I don't know if this is related to the Blues or something quite separate. We'll just have to be careful and extra observant,' concluded Dock. 'Our inter-regional meetings are going to be particularly important this winter. I'll take the north border if you go east, Fern. Piper west and Fescue south please. I strongly advise that we should meet back here on the seventh heatrise of the new season. That will give you an opportunity to survey your areas after the cluster breaks up. Check out the food situation especially.'

There were a few relatively minor matters to clear up, for example the ages of the Queens in the various hives and which of the hives were likely to replace their Queen in the coming season. After that the four intelligence scouts made their preparations and plans for reaching their inter-regional meetings.

The new season was getting underway in Middle Oak and Coppice was delighted with his new home. The bees, especially the drones, were so friendly compared to those in his previous hive, which was a great blessing to Coppice because he still missed Twenty-two and Twenty-three. He spent much of his time with Scruff, Spurge and Sorrell but did make some other friends.

Briar and Teasel were an inseparable pair of drones who went everywhere together and were very supportive of each other. They were also very good at encouraging other bees, always looking on the bright side. Their physical characteristics were identical – you could only tell them apart by their voices. Teasel spoke with a bit of a squeak whereas Briar was just a little lower in pitch than the average drone.

Coppice also made his first worker friendships. Lavender was a sort of comb controller although she didn't approach the job in the same way that Shouter had done. Instead she moved around quietly and efficiently, without fuss and certainly without shouting. She gently but firmly organised her worker bees. Thyme was a forager who spent most of her day outside Middle Oak. She was a bit smaller than Lavender, with tough, but somewhat worn wings. She had a reputation for locating new sources of pollen and nectar but she covered long distances in doing so. So often it was Thyme who performed the figure of eight dances on the comb surfaces to inform other workers of the location of food supplies. The middle part of the figure eight told them how far to fly and the position of the figure on the comb indicated the direction in which they should fly.

COPPICE

The new season was only a few heatrises old but Lavender and Thyme were already concerned. Food stores were not good and they were struggling to bring in sufficient nectar. The Queen had begun laying eggs before the bees began flying at the beginning of the season but not many new workers had reached the foraging stage of their life yet. In the meantime last season's foragers had to work flat out. This was a dangerous time for the hive, one in which they were vulnerable to raiders. They didn't have to wait long.

Coppice and his friends were returning from their mid-morning exercise in the drone zone. As they approached Middle Oak, it was clear that something was wrong.

'Trouble!' warned Spurge, who spotted it first.

'Wasps!' shouted Scruff.

Coppice had seen it all before. The defending workers would be trying to stop the raiders by stinging them to death, but losing their own lives in the process. The raiders were out to steal precious food stores.

The drones hovered some distance above the battle area. Coppice recalled Twenty-two's bold investigation of the raid at his first hive. Suddenly he decided to do the same thing here. Without warning the others, he flew straight into the scrap. Soon he was weaving, dodging and even colliding into other bees – and wasps. Defenders blocked the entrance – the wasps were not getting in. Bees and wasps were grappling with each other and falling onto the ground below. One or two managed to fly back up and rejoin the fight.

It was all over in a few minutes. The wasps were repelled, the defenders were triumphant. With some relief the drones entered the hive, which by now had extra guards on duty.

'That was very bold of you,' Scruff said to Coppice.

'Or very stupid,' added Spurge.

'It's been done before,' explained Coppice, 'by a friend of mine at my last hive.'

'And did you learn anything?' asked Sorrell, who was quite moved by Coppice's bravery, but didn't show it.

'I don't think so.'

'Anyway, we won,' said Scruff.

'But how many workers did we lose?' asked Sorrell.

That was an important question. Coppice took them down to the ground below Middle Oak to assess the losses. It looked worse than they had thought – the attack must have been going on for some time before they arrived on the scene.

'I estimate over sixty dead bees here,' announced Coppice.

'Plus about forty wasps,' added Scruff.

They flew back into the hive to report their findings. Lavender was sad to hear the figures, and puzzled.

'Not a single wasp made it into the hive then?' she queried.

'Not a single one,' replied Coppice.

'They must have been very disappointed,' commented Spurge. They can't sustain losses like that against our superior numbers, even at this time of the year.'

'But we can't afford to lose too many workers either,' Lavender reminded them.

'Maybe we've taught them a lesson so they won't bother us again,' suggested Scruff.

'Maybe,' replied Lavender. 'Maybe.'

The raid took place on the seventh heatrise of the new season. Dock was on his way to the meeting of intelligence scouts in his region. It was the special meeting they had arranged at the off-season meeting. He had reached his inter-regional meeting on the northern border and met with just one other scout. What he learned filled him with great concern and he was anxious to report back and organise some response to what was likely to happen.

He was flying hard to the rendezvous at Birch Cave – a particularly well-hidden hive in the north-eastern sector. Perhaps it was the anxiety, or just his sheer speed, but he didn't notice the two bees tracking him. They made no attempt to catch up with him but waited until he landed to take on water. As soon as he did so, they closed on him immediately. He barely saw them coming and couldn't avoid being hit hard by the first one. The second followed straight in and smashed Dock's head against the ground. He was stunned but not dead, his tough cuticle saving him, although one eye was seriously damaged. He

COPPICE

wasn't stung either, which was a great relief. But that relief was short-lived. He felt his attackers cutting his wings while they pinned him to the ground! They wouldn't have to sting him – he would just be left to starve to death!

As they completed the job, Dock caught a glimpse of them through his good eye. Their body hair was tinted dark blue – their wings also. He now knew exactly what was going on, but was unable to do anything about it.

The very next morning the wasps launched another attack on Middle Oak. Again the drones were out at the drone zone and many foragers were out as well. This time the scrap was all over by the time Coppice and friends returned to the hive. The wasps had been successfully repelled but with the loss of about seventy-five workers this time. Lavender was very worried.

'Is this going to be a regular occurrence?' she asked no bee in particular.

The following days provided the answer – 'yes'. After seven days of raids, Lavender was desperate.

'Can't you drones do anything? We just can't go on losing workers like this.'

'How long before we have this season's new workers available in good numbers?' asked Coppice.

'Oh, several heatrises yet.'

'At least the wasps haven't reached our foodstores yet,' Briar pointed out.

'And bees like Thyme are keeping new supplies coming in,' added Teasel, looking on the bright side as usual.

'True, but I think we're losing too many foragers out in the fields as well.'

'What do you mean?' enquired Coppice.

'Occasionally a forager fails to return because she's underestimated her energy needs, or the time of day, or she just loses her way, but it's happening too often. That's all I can say.'

'Disturbing, if you're right,' said Sorrell, who had been listening attentively. 'Has anybee seen an intelligence scout yet this season? They should be able to advise us.'

But Fern had yet to put in an appearance as far as they knew. The meeting broke up inconclusively.

Next morning the wasps attacked earlier than usual and the drones were still in the hive. Coppice and friends stayed behind the guards at the entrance for some time, letting the workers get on with it. Suddenly three wasps broke through for the first time. The drones were startled. What should they do?

'Quick!' shouted Coppice. 'We must do something!'

'We've got to get them out!' yelled Scruff.

'Right,' shouted Coppice, with a sudden inspiration. 'We'll barge them out.'

'We'll what?' complained Spurge.

'Get close together and shove then out,' explained Coppice.

'OK, OK.'

So the drones quickly packed close together and rushed at the incoming wasps. They hit them hard, piling into them and forcing them backwards. Two of them immediately flew out of the hive but the third held its ground. Briar and Teasel paired up and flung themselves at the wasp. Briar accidentally sliced off part of its wing while Teasel grabbed the poor creature's head and yanked him – or her – away from the entrance. He then let go and the hapless wasp fell towards the ground way below.

'Well done you two!' yelled Scruff, who grabbed Coppice and went for another wasp who had just dared to land right in the entrance. Spurge and Sorrell made a third pairing and positioned themselves, ready for the next invader. They didn't have to wait long because the workers had become too tied up in the battle in the air. Scruff and Coppice downed their intruder and went after another. Spurge and Sorrell were struggling with theirs but Briar and Teasel were going strong – they worked so well as a pair. When the wasps realised they weren't going to get into the hive, despite creating an opening, they called off the raid and withdrew. The drones were exhilarated. The workers were amazed. Lavender was delighted.

'That was terrific!' she gasped. 'Why haven't you done that before?'

'Never had to, I guess,' replied Scruff.

'Didn't know how to,' added Spurge.

'Whose idea was it anyway?' asked Lavender.

They all looked at each other. In the heat of the battle they'd forgotten how they came to join in.

'Coppice,' said Sorrell eventually. 'It was your idea, wasn't it?'

COPPICE

'Hmm. I think you could say I've learned from experience. Remember that pair of blue drones I told you about? Well, I think their actions gave me the idea in our moment of desperation, and I must say Briar and Teasel set a marvellous example.'

'Hear, hear!' agreed Lavender.

'They certainly did,' said Sorrell, 'and now we must educate as many drones as possible so that we can support the workers. I think we can save many of them from having to sacrifice their lives in the defence of the hive.'

'How?' demanded Lavender immediately.

Sorrell's astute brain had already worked it out. 'Partly by downing the wasps ourselves, partly by showing the workers how to fight in pairs, slicing off wings – like Briar and Teasel did, accidentally at first.'

Lavender was struggling to take it all in. This was such an innovation. But the need was great, and urgent.

'Right,' she said, 'leave the workers to me – you organise the drones. I think we might be able to face tomorrow with some confidence for once.'

She was right. The wasps came at Middle Oak as usual. The honeybees counter-attacked in pairs, going for the wings. Some of the workers couldn't help using their stings and so went down with the wasps, but the majority soon caught on. The drones operated near the entrance at first but soon became bolder and attacked further out. This did allow one wasp into the hive, but it wasn't able to carry away much honey. Not long afterwards the raiders withdrew. This time the hive lost less than ten worker bees, which cheered Lavender no end. Some of the drones were roughed up a bit – which just made them look like Scruff! – but that was all. They had been able to pick their fights as they chose. The wasps hadn't expected them to be a threat so left them alone as a rule – much to their cost.

The next day saw an even quicker and less expensive victory for the bees of Middle Oak and the following day the raids ceased. There was quite a celebration when they realised they had won!

12. THE COUNCIL

Life in Middle Oak was returning to normal after the wasps' raids. Maybe their losses were too great; maybe they were trying their luck at some other hive. If the latter was the case, the scout bees might find out about it and pass on Middle Oak's defence tactics.

New worker bees were now emerging in large numbers and the first of them would shortly be out foraging. Food supplies inside the hive were still low but it would only be a matter of time before the expanding worker force built them up. The Queen was laying eggs at an amazing rate while the drones, rather pleased with their recent exploits, were enjoying their drone zone again.

The hive's Council had met and passed their congratulations to Coppice and company. They now felt their hive would survive the season. The Council consisted of the Queen, three workers and three drones. The worker members did have one minor concern – namely the higher than normal loss of foragers out in the field. The comb controllers were asked to monitor this situation.

Lavender, being a conscientious comb controller, was keen to check out the progress of her foragers. After a few days she was convinced she was still losing more than she should be. She informed the Council, who were waiting for reports from all the controllers before meeting to review the situation. Lavender also mentioned her findings to Coppice one morning as he was about to leave for the drone zone with Scruff, Spurge and Sorrell. He didn't know what to make of it but thanked Lavender anyway.

After zooming around the drone zone for some time, and meeting up with Briar and Teasel, Coppice called them all in for a chat.

'Any ideas why we're still losing too many foragers?' he asked. No replies were forthcoming. 'Hmm. Well then, any ideas as to how we might investigate the matter?'

COPPICE

'Why should we want to do that?' asked Spurge, who could be a bit grumpy sometimes.

'Maybe we could help out – like we did with the wasps.'

'But that was a desperate situation – this isn't.'

'Supposing the loss of foragers worsens?'

'Supposing it doesn't?'

'I think we're doing just fine now,' said Briar, speaking for Teasel as well.

Coppice went quiet for a time. Scruff said nothing but Coppice could sense that Sorrell was sympathetic so he tried again. 'Supposing these foragers are not going missing due to natural means. What would anybee gain by killing them in such small numbers?'

Silence. But then Sorrell suggested, 'Food. It could only be the food they're collecting.'

'But the honey's inside their stomachs,' objected Scruff.

'True, but the pollen baskets are on their legs.'

'Interesting,' said Coppice. 'That means they probably wouldn't be attacked until they've collected a full load.'

'So?' demanded Spurge, who wasn't exactly enthralled by the discussion.

'So we could be waiting and watching over foragers as they return to the hive fully loaded.'

'We could *what*?'

'You don't have to, Spurge, if you don't want to, but anybee who's willing to try it can let me know by heatfall,' announced Coppice. 'I'll ask Lavender where the main foraging areas are at present and we'll go out tomorrow heatrise.'

'I'm definitely willing to help,' said Sorrell, proving his sympathy for the cause.

'We don't mind joining in,' said Briar and Teasel in unison.

Scruff said he'd probably help while Spurge remained silent. However, by heatrise the next day he had grudgingly consented rather than be left out.

Lavender asked Thyme to lead the drones to one of the best foraging areas. It happened to be a dense hedgerow with a variety of early flowers including ground ivy, vetches and violets. A group of about twenty foragers had come out to work the area and others would follow.

Coppice and company watched them for a while, admiring the way they extracted nectar from right inside some of the flowers. In addition, any pollen that stuck to their bodies was skilfully brushed off and packed into wodges on their rear legs. When full, these pollen baskets were visible from a distance.

'A tempting sight to raiders,' thought Coppice. He turned to the others, 'Keep your eyes open for foragers returning with full pollen baskets. We'll take up positions away from the hedgerow, on the beeline back to Middle Oak.'

Sorrell had been working out similar tactics and agreed immediately, the rest were carried along – Spurge only just. They took up positions and began their patient watch over the loaded foragers. Nothing happened. By mid-morning Spurge was all for giving up and Scruff wasn't exactly enthusiastic.

'Go back to the hive then if you really want to,' said Coppice. 'This is only a voluntary job after all. Maybe you could come back later and relieve some of us?'

'Huh, don't think so,' muttered Spurge.

'I'll think about it,' said Scruff. 'Perhaps I'll find some new volunteers.'

'Yes, that would help,' agreed Coppice.

So Spurge and Scruff set off back for the hive. They had travelled about one quarter of the way when Scruff spotted something he didn't like the look of.

'Forager on the ground below us,' he shouted to Spurge, and dived down, his friend in close pursuit.

'Wings severed,' observed Scruff.

'No pollen baskets,' added Spurge.

'But look, there are traces of pollen on her rear legs, I think.'

'So what do we do now?'

'We must go and fetch the others, surely?'

Spurge considered for a moment. He might be grumpy at times but he wasn't callous. 'Yes, you're right. Let's go.'

They reported back to Coppice and the others who were pleased to see them return and happy to have something to show for their morning's efforts. They flew to the scene of the presumed attack.

'Right,' said Coppice. 'Let's spread out in pairs along this section of the beeline and keep our eyes peeled.'

COPPICE

Scruff stayed with Spurge, Sorrell joined Coppice, and of course Briar and Teasel were inseparable. As he waited, Coppice realised how much better this part of the beeline was for an ambush. There was plenty of cover – no wide open spaces like there were near the hedgerow. He would learn from that.

This time they didn't have very long to wait. About a dozen foragers had flown past, not all heavily laden with pollen. Then one came along with both baskets fully packed. She passed Briar and Teasel, then Coppice and Sorrell. She was approaching Scruff and Spurge when it happened.

Suddenly, out of nowhere, two dark bees appeared above the forager and dropped down onto her back, knocking her to the ground. Immediately one of her attackers began slicing off one pair of wings while the other started cutting off the pollen packs from her rear legs. For a moment Scruff and Spurge were dumbstruck, then they responded.

'Quick!' yelled Scruff. 'Let's get out there!'

'Sure, ramming tactics – go!'

When forced into action, Spurge was a different bee. With Scruff just behind him, he shot out of their hiding place, straight for the two dark blue bees who had downed the forager. They rammed the pair, knocking them off their quarry. The Blues were so surprised that they hesitated for a second or two, then they went for Scruff. He shot out of the way and was joined by Spurge. The four drones were zooming around madly. The Blues kept trying to pick off either Scruff or Spurge while that pair did their best to stick together. Round and round, up and down they went, burning up their food supplies in the process. Scruff began to tire first. The Blues sensed this and concentrated on him. Spurge was getting desperate. What could he do? Where were the others? Suddenly he recognised the best course of action.

'Scruff!' he yelled, 'follow me, follow me!' And the pair, under Spurge's guidance, worked their way towards where Coppice and Sorrell should have been hiding. They didn't dare fly in a beeline so they had to weave and circle a lot. Scruff was fading.

'Come on, come on!' urged Spurge.

Just then one of the attackers caught Scruff heavily on his right flank and he fell away from Spurge. Spurge counter-attacked, partly from anger, partly to draw the enemy away from Scruff. He was more successful than he expected. Spurge was a well-built drone, though he was only just beginning to appreciate that fact. He attacked again. The blue drone had to put his full attention to dealing with Spurge. Scruff now only had one opponent to avoid, but even that was proving too much. Spurge zoomed down and rammed Scruff's attacker, knocking him clean away.

'Fly for help, quick! Coppice must be close!' gasped Spurge to the escaping Scruff. Spurge now tried to engage both enemy drones. He flew at one, then the other. Scruff wisely flew off using the cover of nearby foliage.

'Where on earth are they?' Spurge asked himself as he kept up his offensive, but sensing he was tiring fast. For a moment he lost one of the Blues altogether. Next thing he knew, something hit him hard from behind. He spun round, only to be hit in the side. He was caught on the retreat; the Blues were now in control. Spurge began falling. He landed, expecting to be thumped again at any moment…but nothing happened. He looked around, then above. The Blues were being attacked by several other bees! Yes, Scruff had made it! Coppice, Sorrell, Briar and Teasel were in action above him. The Blues didn't hang around for long against these odds; they were tired anyway. Shortly they zoomed off in a beeline, briefly pursued by Briar and Teasel. The chase wasn't continued. They all came and gathered round Spurge.

'Great effort Spurge!' said Teasel, his voice even higher than usual in his excitement.

'Fantastic!' added Briar.

'I'm so grateful Spurge, I'd never have made it,' said Scruff, looking even more bedraggled than usual.

'We've just successfully engaged a pair of Blues, my friends,' announced Coppice, 'and sent them packing!'

'That'll give them something to think about,' suggested Sorrell, 'while we try and work out exactly what they're up to. This will have to go to the Council.'

They checked Scruff's condition but he was only a bit sore in places, as was Spurge. They had just finished tidying him up – as far as it was possible to tidy Scruff that is, when they remembered the poor forager. They found her transfixed to the ground where she had been forced down. They took some time to reassure her she was safe, and only slightly injured. They left her pollen baskets behind so that she could fly more easily, one wing being partly cut, and the whole party flew slowly back to Middle Oak.

Back at the hive, Lavender was waiting for them.

'We've found out what's happening to your foragers,' said Coppice, and he related their findings, with full details of the battle.

Lavender listened carefully, as if already trying to work out what to do. When she had heard the whole story, she gave them her news. 'You've another pair of visitors.'

'What?' said Coppice.

'A pair of scouts is waiting for you out in the drone zone. They said it was urgent.'

'They're not blue are they?' quipped Scruff.

Coppice guessed who one of them might be. He suggested Scruff and Spurge relax while the rest of them flew out to meet their visitors.

'Hi fellers, how's it going?' greeted them on their arrival.

'Piper!' exclaimed Coppice, and then Fern appeared. 'And Fern – I guessed you might be around. What can we do for you?'

Coppice guessed almost as soon as he had finished his sentence, but first he introduced Piper to his friends. Fern already knew them of course, Middle Oak being his home hive. Piper, significantly, was out of his area. Sorrell recognised this and commented on it.

'It's most unusual to see two intelligence scouts together. There must be a good reason?'

'Correct,' responded Fern. 'We need any information you may have on "trouble" in this area.'

'Like Blues, for instance?' suggested Coppice. Fern nodded. 'You've come at a good time – we've just met some.'

'Details please,' demanded Fern, with authority.

'Well, we were watching over some of our foragers to try and discover why an unusually high number of them weren't making it back to the hive. Two of our party – they're back at Middle Oak, recovering – actually saw a forager attacked by a pair of Blues and dived in to rescue her…'

'They did *what?*' interrupted Piper.

'They attacked the Blues.'

'What happened?' asked Fern.

'Well, good old Spurge held them off while his partner Scruff flew off to fetch the rest of us. The Blues didn't like the odds of six to two so they cleared off. The forager survived.'

'Yer did very well,' commended Piper, 'but how exactly did yer fight them?'

Coppice explained the battle tactics they had developed against the raiding wasps. Piper was enthusiastic about their success.

Fern was more thoughtful, then expressed his concern. 'I fear you may have brought more trouble on yourselves.'

'How come?' asked Coppice.

'Because you've stood up to them they will be most curious and keen to do something about it – about you! Let me fill you in with some of the details. Our senior intelligence scout, Dock, failed to turn up for a meeting at the beginning of the season. We've been unable to find him and must presume him lost. He was, in all likelihood, returning from an important meeting on the northern border with a scout or two from the next region. We suspect he had some idea of what these Blues are up to. We also suspect they intercepted him on his way back.'

'You mean they killed him?' enquired Sorrell.

'We can't be sure. Scout bees are very resourceful,' replied Piper.

Fern continued, 'I learned a lot from my meeting on the eastern border but I reckon more is happening to the north. The Blues are attacking wasps first because their nests are smaller than beehives, and there are fewer of them. The wasps are driven to raid the nearest beehives which, when sufficiently weakened, are taken over by Blues. Sometimes they simply lay them waste, sometimes they inhabit them. What you've told us bears out our suspicions that the Blues' scouts can survive in pairs away from their base hive, probably using wasps' nests they've cleaned out. They rob flowers and foragers for their food. Dock probably knows, or knew, where the main threat is coming from, and when. Whatever that may be, I fear Middle Oak will become an urgent target for the Blues after today's events. Those two you defeated were a scout

COPPICE

pair and they will doubtless be reporting back immediately.' Fern paused to let his words sink in.

'So what do we do now?' asked Coppice.

'Go and warn your Council of the danger. You should suggest a swarm to relocate to a new hive, somewhere to the south or west of here.'

'A swarm!' exclaimed Briar and Teasel.

'That's an extreme measure,' commented Sorrell.

'A swarm?' asked Coppice, trying to recall who had mentioned that term before.

Fern reminded him, 'When the Queen takes several thousand bees out of the hive to go and settle in a new one, located by her scouts. A new Queen takes her place in the old hive.'

'Oh yes, I remember now – an interesting idea.'

'Good,' said Piper. 'Fern or I won't be too far away for the next few heatrises. One of us will visit yer drone zone every day until we know the swarm's approved.'

And that was that. Heatfall was approaching, so they all returned to Middle Oak. Fern and Piper had themselves scented up properly before passing the guards.

The two scouts were gone just before heatrise next day. Coppice took Sorrell, Spurge, Scruff and Lavender to find the Council. He wasn't anticipating too much difficulty getting his message through, especially as two intelligence scouts were backing him up. It was a pity they couldn't have met the Council themselves.

The Council's three worker bees were all ex-comb controllers. Their names were Celandine, Fluellen and Juniper. The three 'senior' drones on the Council were in at least their third year and were named Valerian, Erinus and Gentian. The Queen was simply called 'The Queen' and she would have to cease laying eggs for the duration of the Council meeting so they must report as concisely as possible. Sometimes the Queen did not attend the meetings but left the other six to deal with matters and report back to her, or bring her into the meeting if necessary. On this occasion the nature of the threat to the hive was so unusual that she decided to be present from the beginning.

The Council already knew of Coppice from his efforts against the wasps. They listened as he related the encounter with the pair of Blues and then the information and warning from Piper. He concluded with Fern's advice.

'...and so we should seriously consider a swarm with the aim of establishing a new hive to the south-west of here.'

The Council considered the report for a few moments. It was probably the most unusual one any of them had heard.

'Questions,' said the Queen, indicating that now was the time for Council members to clarify anything they weren't sure about.

Juniper addressed Lavender, 'Have you recently checked with other comb controllers regarding losses of foragers?'

'I've asked several, but only four or five thought they might be in my situation. I would suggest that's because of the area being visited. The Blues may not be everywhere.'

Coppice wanted to add 'yet', but it wasn't done to speak out of turn at a Council meeting.

'And just how heavy are your losses?' continued Juniper.

Lavender thought about it. 'About fifteen in every hundred, I should say.'

'Too many,' commented Celandine.

Valerian, the eldest drone, spoke next. 'We successfully defeated the wasps, er, thanks to your battle tactics that is, and it sounds as if you held your own against these, er, Blues. So, er, do we really need a swarm? I mean, isn't it possible to, er, adjust our newly discovered tactics to cope with this new threat?'

Spurge and Scuff were nodding in agreement but Coppice replied carefully. 'I can see what you mean, and if it wasn't for the intelligence scouts' warning I might well agree with you. However, Fern and Piper were extremely concerned for the safety of Middle Oak.'

Gentian asked, 'How do we know these Blues won't follow us to the south-west?'

That was a good question. There was a difficult pause before Sorrell came to the rescue.

'I think we have to assume that Fern, who is responsible for our area, knows what he's doing when he advises us to swarm.'

'When we are into assumptions we are into uncertainties,' replied Gentian.

'The whole situation is uncertain,' retorted Coppice. 'It's a new problem – that's why we should get well away from it. Middle Oak could have been

COPPICE

abandoned already if we hadn't found a way to deal with the wasps. And now we're told the wasps were only being used by the Blues. Whoever heard of wasps being manipulated in that way before?'

'Can we rely on the intelligence reports from the next region?' asked Erinus.

'Why shouldn't we?' responded Coppice.

'It does seem a great shame to have to uproot and move just when things seem to be going so well,' said Fluellen. 'Our numbers are swelling and the food stores are beginning to look sufficient at last.' She glanced at Lavender.

'True enough,' said Sorrell, 'but we would therefore be starting afresh from a position of strength, not getting out at the last moment with depleted numbers.'

'It's going to upset the Queen's egg laying programme considerably,' argued Fluellen. 'By the time new combs are built we could be struggling to raise sufficient numbers for over-wintering successfully.'

Such calculations by a Council worker be are hard to dispute. Their experience allows them the last word on such matters.

'The, er, trouble is,' said Valerian, 'we're quite comfortable at present. There is, er, no obvious cause for swarming. I mean, er, nothing that anybee in the hive would notice. It won't make any, er, sense to them. I would have thought we could, er, monitor the, er, situation for a little while – to see if the, er, threat has in fact gone away. They might even, er, leave us alone.'

Coppice thought to himself how that was wishful and dangerous thinking but he couldn't simply say so. Sorrell's eyes showed he felt the same way. Lavender looked quite agitated. Before any of them could think of a suitable response, the Queen indicated question time was over and she would speak.

'Something most unpleasant has come to our area. So far we have defended ourselves admirably. I believe we have time to ensure that if we do swarm, we will remove the threat for certain. That means locating a safe new hive. I am authorising a search to the south-west in order to find an ideal site. Coppice will lead the search and he may select his helpers. Council is ended.'

13. SEARCH PARTY

The drones and Lavender left the Council meeting with the sort of result they wanted – or did they?

'What did you make of that?' Coppice asked Sorrell.

Sorrell thought for a moment then replied, 'I feel the Queen's decision was against the run of play – if you understand my meaning. Valerian, Gentian and Fluellen seemed to be anti-swarming, Celandine was probably in favour, and I'm not sure about the other two.'

'Hmm, and yet the Queen came down on our side.'

'So it would seem.'

'Are your Council meetings always that short?'

'They're usually short when the Queen's present because of the time she's taking out from egg laying. If she leaves matters to the other six, they always go on longer in my experience.'

'But this one was unusual?'

'The problem's unusual.'

Coppice nodded his agreement. 'Let's go and tell Piper and Fern.'

They flew out to the drone zone with the others and waited around for the two scouts. They didn't have to wait long.

'Hi there fellers, how did yer get on?' Piper called out even before he and Fern had landed.

'Permission to take a search party to the south-west to locate a site for a new hive,' replied Coppice, 'and I'm in charge.'

'Great,' said Piper. 'Who's in yer party?'

'That's up to me.'

'Couldn't be better. So what are yer looking so worried about?'

Coppice and Sorrell passed on their unease about the way in which the

COPPICE

Council had come to a decision. Fern considered what they said.

'Sometimes it's difficult to know just how a Queen is thinking. It depends on how well she knows her Council I suspect. We must accept the decision and act on it, so what about the members of the your party?'

'Well, I'd like to take Sorrell, Spurge, Scruff, Briar and Teasel – as I know them all pretty well now.'

'What about a worker or two?' suggested Piper.

'Hadn't thought of that.'

'Workers can advise on the suitability of the site and assess the potential food supply in the surrounding area. Rather important, don't yer think?'

'Quite right, Piper. I wonder if Lavender would come?'

'She's a comb-controller – she'll have to stay at Middle Oak,' said Fern, 'but you could ask her to recommend some workers.'

'Will do,' said Coppice, glad of the advice. 'I'll go and see her immediately.'

'Hold on a moment,' said Fern. 'There's a bee we want to recommend. The intelligence scout for the southern area is a drone called Fescue. He's a terrific flier, with a day-range well beyond average. We would like you to take him with you. No need to tell the Council though – they can be a bit funny about us intelligence scouts, sort of jealous.'

'I'd be only too pleased to have a scout in the party,' agreed Coppice. 'When can he get here?'

'We'll have him here first thing tomorrow heatrise,' Fern assured him.

So it was agreed. Fern and Piper departed. They were working as a pair all the time now that they knew the Blues were doing so. While Fescue was busy with the search party, they would be patrolling the north-eastern border of their region as that was the direction from which the Blues seemed to be coming. Middle Oak was just inside the north-eastern sector and must be a target, especially after defeating the wasps and seeing off a pair of Blues. Sooner or later they would be attacked again.

Back at the hive, Coppice explained to Lavender what he needed. She immediately recommended Thyme as an expert on food sources. The other choice wasn't so easy. She really wanted to go herself but knew she couldn't leave her combs.

'I'll think about my second choice and let you know first thing tomorrow,' she suggested. 'You've already met Thyme, of course. She was the one who took you out to the hedgerow, remember?'

'Ah yes,' said Coppice. 'Thanks Lavender.'

He was developing quite an admiration for the comb controller. She seemed so capable and responsible – not the sort of job he'd like to take on.

There was little else to do for the rest of the day apart from confirming his search party membership. Briar and Teasel were delighted to be going, Scruff was just pleased, and Spurge said he'd come along for the trip! Sorrell was already signed up of course. All of them settled into a loose cluster at heatfall, with a mixture of excitement and apprehension in their stomachs.

It had been a hot day and it was now a warm night. Bryony was a young worker bee who had just begun her foraging duties. She was under Lavender's charge as it happened. She was quite tired and rested easily for some time. In the early hours of the morning she felt an urgent need for honey, so she made her way to the lower edge of the comb, not very far from the hive entrance. It being night time, there were no guards on duty. Bryony fed from an uncapped honey cell. She took a small amount because she wasn't going foraging or anything. As she turned to go back up the comb, she caught a movement with the side of one eye. Something was happening at the hive entrance.

She stood still and turned her head to get a better view. Yes, she could make out two bees at the entrance, antennae twitching. They edged warily forwards, towards the centre of the hive floor. They passed within about five bee-lengths of Bryony. She remained rooted to the spot, keeping as still as possible, trying to pretend she wasn't observing them. The pair continued, a little faster as they gained confidence. As they passed her, Bryony felt a chill creep right through her body. There was something very unpleasant about these two. A few more seconds and the intruders were beyond her, continuing en route for the centre of the hive floor.

Bryony felt the wave of relief pass through her and she could move again. Her first reaction was to return smartly to the cluster, but she checked herself. Anger took over from fear – anger at these intruders with their cold, evil presence, polluting her hive. What were they up to? Only one way to find out!

She began following at a safe distance. The dark pair reached the centre of the floor space. From there they moved across to one side of the hive and then all the way across to the opposite side. Next they climbed the first comb, Bryony in cautious pursuit. They stopped briefly to sample some honey before continuing up into the partially made combs, which Middle Oak was building as the season developed. She was taking a big risk following them this far because it was a long run back to the cluster.

When the pair reached the top of the comb, they stopped. Bryony stopped. She was barely on the same comb. If they turned and saw her, she would have to run for it. They did turn, and Bryony didn't hang around to see if she was spotted or not – she shot off as fast as her six legs would carry her! Down to the comb below, then the comb below that, and from there into the centre of the hive. She didn't dare waste time looking behind, she just kept going. Reaching the centre, she dived into the loose cluster, burying herself amongst hundreds of other honeybees.

What Bryony didn't know, was that the intruders had pursued her down to the top of the base comb but declined to chase her inwards because they knew it would be hopeless once she reached the cluster. They weren't at all pleased at having been spotted but there was nothing they could do in the circumstances. If they'd caught their observer they would have seen to it that she had no story to tell, and dumped her body outside the hive. Instead, they departed with their information, apparently having no problem flying at that time of night.

At heatrise Bryony woke up from a bad dream, or so she thought. Then it all came back to her and she shuddered. She must report the intruders but wondered if she would be believed. They might think she'd dreamt it. Would they accept the word of a young forager? She decided against it, filled up with honey, and set off for the hive entrance. When she reached it she could go no further in case the intruders were outside waiting for her. That was it – she had to report the matter for the sake of her own peace of mind.

Bryony located her comb controller and spilled the whole story. To her surprise, Lavender listened carefully and didn't interrupt her once.

'Thank you,' she said. 'You've been very brave indeed, if the intruders are who I think they are.'

'You mean you might actually know them?'

'Yes, yes, unfortunately. Now I want you to come with me and repeat your account to somebee, then I may have a special job for you.'

Lavender hid her concern and led Bryony to Coppice's comb, hoping to catch him before he flew out to the drone zone. He was there with Sorrell, having sent Briar and Teasel to collect Fescue from the drone zone. Lavender introduced Bryony and had her relate her late night experience. Coppice and Sorrell listened just as attentively as Lavender had done.

'You did the right thing, Bryony,' said Coppice. 'Your description tells us what they were doing, and we know who they must have been, even though you couldn't detect the precise colouring at that time of night.'

'Excellent!' added Sorrell, appreciating what Bryony must have gone through. 'I'm pleased to hear you were angry enough to overcome your fear and track them.'

'Yes,' said Lavender, 'and that's why I think Bryony should be the second worker bee in your search party?'

'Hmm,' muttered Coppice, thinking that she was only a youngster.

Lavender added, 'I haven't thought of anybee else and I reckon Bryony is well motivated, under the circumstances.'

Sorrell addressed Bryony, 'Would you like to join us? We're flying out to find a new site ready for a swarm. The idea is to get well away from these intruders – we call them Blues, by the way, as they have a very dark blue tinge to their body hair and wings.'

Bryony glanced at her comb controller. Lavender nodded. 'Yes, I'll come.'

Briar and Teasel returned with Fescue. They daubed him with honey from inside the hive and walked him past the guards, who applied their antennae briefly. They met up with the others, including Lavender, who would act as their link bee at Middle Oak. She would hear about their exploits before the Council did, and collect any information at her end. That included keeping in touch with Piper and Fern.

'Right,' said Coppice, 'we're all here. Allow me to introduce Fescue, who's the intelligence scout for the southern area – but keep that to yourselves please – and this is Bryony, our second worker bee member. She's here because she was brave

COPPICE

enough to follow a pair of Blues around our hive last night.'

'She did what?' asked Scruff.

'You heard. We were spied on. They came to assess the size of Middle Oak – that's quite clear from Bryony's description. This all adds to the urgency and importance of our search. Now Fescue has something to say.'

'Thank you Coppice. Up to now you probably thought we would be flying day trips to investigate the south-western area in depth. Well, we may do some day trips but we shall be using "stopovers", as we call them. That means entering a strange hive and joining its cluster for the night. We do this by entering as late as possible, after the guards have turned in, and then coating ourselves with some honey from the hive we're visiting. I think some of you already understand this procedure. Any questions?'

'Why do we need to do this?' asked Spurge, not quite following the plot.

'It will save us having to return to Middle Oak every heatfall,' replied Fescue patiently, 'and extend the range of our search.'

Only Coppice and Sorrell knew the implications of that. The others would have to work it out for themselves.

'Any more questions?' asked Coppice. There were none. 'Fine. We fly in pairs, except for Fescue of course, who will scout around as he sees fit. Sorrell and I will lead, followed by Briar and Teasel, then Thyme and Bryony with Scruff and Spurge bringing up the rear. Now load up with honey and we'll be away.'

It was a glorious day. The search party, directed by Fescue, made its way southwards, carefully noting landmarks as well as the position of the sun. Fescue chose a beeline they could all remember easily. At the end of it he selected a very unusual landmark so that they could all find the beeline back to Middle Oak. The landmark was actually an aberration. It was like a pair of black rivers crossing each other at the edge of a wood.

They stopped once to take water from the edge of a real river – a stream, in fact – and then flew on until sunpeak. It was soon after this that they had reached 'Black River crossing', as it came to be called.

'Note this landmark well,' said Fescue. 'It's the centre of the southern area. Whenever you come south, follow the beeline to this point. Now we're going on to my home hive, Hollybank. Everybee OK?' They were all fine, so on they flew.

Fescue's home fitted its description. It was built into a bank of ground somewhere in the wood they had entered at Black River crossing. There were three holly trees on top of it, along with birch and the occasional conifer. Fescue entered his home hive and came out with some honey, which he daubed on Thyme and Bryony. He took the two workers back inside Hollybank to fetch more honey. They could collect large amounts and regurgitate it – a good reason for having worker bees in the search party. Very soon all six drones were 'scented up' and ready to enter Hollybank.

It was unusual to have walls of hard, dry soil after Middle Oak's wood, but they soon adjusted. Coppice had, of course, encountered such conditions at the refuge. After a good feed they familiarised themselves with Hollybank and its locality. It was a lovely wood with a fair amount of ground cover plants as well as trees. The hive entrance was partially hidden by brambles and nettles – no problem for honeybees. Inside, the combs were extensive and the stores plentiful. They learned from Fescue that Hollybank was very old, although the original hive was in a different part of the bank. Apparently there were some tunnels running to the old site and 'other places'. Coppice was reminded of the safe chamber and wondered if there was something like it here. Maybe he would have an opportunity to find out later. For the moment though, there was work to be done.

The search party joined the cluster for heatfall. For some of them it was quite a novelty, and at heatrise they weren't exactly sure where they were. For Bryony it was the second successive exciting night. Coppice and Sorrell gathered them together after they had filled up with honey and the party set off behind Fescue, continuing due south.

'We can start looking for suitable sites from now on,' Fescue told them, 'so we won't be travelling quite so fast.'

And so it was. From time to time they descended, usually into wooded areas, and looked around for likely sites. Hollow trees were the favourite, but so often bird's nests already occupied them. Others were in leafless trees and Fescue warned them off those – 'Too dangerous,' he insisted. Another consideration was the size of the entrance. It mustn't be so large that it couldn't be defended. They were, therefore, looking for a small opening which led into a big space –

COPPICE

big enough for sufficient combs to support a complete hive of bees.

Then there were underground sites. They had to have soil that wouldn't collapse. That usually meant finding a raised area that didn't suffer from serious flooding. Another good site was in a dense hedge, such as hawthorn, of which there was plenty around. The hive would take a bit of building but it would be well protected. Some bees simply built their combs where large branches joined, fairly high up in a tree. Occasionally, bees would use part of an aberration in which to build their home, but there had been some sad endings to some of those hives, according to Fescue.

They searched for most of the day, finding one or two possible sites but nothing that really grabbed them. They returned to Hollybank for heatfall. Before they clustered for the night, Fescue took Coppice to one side.

'Tomorrow we'll try something different,' he whispered. 'I intend flying due south without searching for sites, and then…Well, we will have to let Piper and Fern know because we shall be flying out of our region.'

'Go on,' urged Coppice.

'I want us to make the crossing!'

14. SQUILL'S ISLAND

'Making the crossing?' queried Coppice, expecting an explanation. 'It's like flying over a very wide river,' said Fescue. 'The problem is the non-existence of landmarks, but it can be done. I'll show you, don't worry. Now you must choose a pair to report back to Middle Oak and bring back any information from Fern and Piper. That means they'll be away overnight. Who do you recommend?'

'Hmm. If it's a pair you want then it ought to be Briar and Teasel. Spurge would probably argue with Scruff and we need the others with us.'

Fescue would have made the same choice but he wanted the search party leader to come to his own decision. Coppice went off to inform the inseparable pair who were a bit disappointed but looked forward to rejoining the party in two days time.

The team was out promptly at heatrise. Briar and Teasel flew off northwards while the search party headed south. Coppice had decided to wait until they reached the 'wide river' before telling them what they were going to do. They flew for most of the morning; Fescue indicating various landmarks until they arrived at the border of their region, although only Coppice and Fescue knew that. The others were startled by what they saw ahead of them.

'What's that!' exclaimed Scruff.

'A gigantic river?' asked Thyme.

'That, my friends, is the sea!' announced Fescue.

'Even Sorrell was moved to exclaim – 'Amazing!'

'Now we fly over it,' said Fescue.

'You're kidding,' objected Spurge.

'You're right,' countered Coppice. 'If we can find a site across there, we really shall be safe because this "sea" must be a natural barrier. What puzzles me is how you made the first crossing, Fescue?'

'It wasn't me who crossed over to them – they came to me. It's easier that way round anyway.'

'Could have fooled me,' grumbled an unhappy Spurge.

Fescue explained, 'We're on a vast piece of land while they're on a small piece – they call it an island. If they want to cross over to us, they only have to set off in roughly the right direction and they'll come to land, which is exactly what happened a long time ago. However, for us to reach them, we must carefully line up our landmarks on this side and then maintain our direction by very accurate use of the sun.'

They were all astounded at first but Fescue took them to the three landmarks he had used in the past. It reminded Coppice of the time he got lost on his first day out flying. He had eventually used an idea that bore some resemblance to what Fescue was now doing. The party lined up behind the landmark furthest inland, a tall pine tree, and then headed for a damaged oak, after which they flew over the spot where a river entered the sea. Then they held their direction using the sun. Before long there was no land in sight. They were completely surrounded by water – most unnerving for honeybees.

'Fescue had better know what he's doing,' Spurge said to his flying partner Scruff.

'Well there's no way we're turning back without him, is there?'

They flew over open water for nearly an hour, then Bryony cried out, 'Land! I can see land!'

Sure enough the island loomed up ahead of them. It was most impressive, with big green hills and plenty of trees. Fescue brought them in to land just beyond a sandy seashore.

'There you are,' he said, 'your first over-water navigation successfully completed.'

'Brilliant!' said Scruff.

'I hope we can get back,' grumbled Spurge.

'Right,' said Coppice, 'we're going to the hive of a scout friend of Fescue's. He'll accommodate us while we carry out our search.'

'Do they mind us searching their island?' asked Thyme, fully aware of rivalry for food sources.

'Good question,' replied Coppice, turning to Fescue for an answer.

'The island's big enough for all of us as long as we don't try and settle too close to one of their colonies. Now follow me, it's not far.'

Fescue led them to 'The Beacon' hive. There they met Squill himself. He was a very neat and tidy looking drone; not a hair out of place – the exact opposite of Scruff! Even his body colouring seemed to be ultra precise somehow, but a shade or two lighter than that of his visitors. He was very polite and obviously pleased to meet up with Fescue again.

'Welcome to our island, friends,' he said, and he appeared to twitch one antenna sufficiently enough to bring out some workers with honey supplies. Once scented up they entered the hive. It was high up in the branches of a beautiful cedar tree. The arrangement of the branches provided good protection for the combs built into the forks between them. It was an immense hive. In fact, Sorrell wondered whether he wasn't looking at more than one hive.

'How did you build such a large hive?' he asked, 'and how do you maintain it?'

'Without boring you with all the details just now,' replied Squill, 'just bear in mind that we have no problems with aberrations, wasps or hostile bees and there's a tremendous food supply here – the flowers are marvellous.'

'The whole place is marvellous,' commented Thyme.

'Too good to be true,' muttered Spurge.

'*Ssh!*' hissed Scruff. 'You should be grateful.'

'Come on you two,' ordered Coppice. 'Fill up with honey and we'll fly out to get our bearings. Tomorrow we shall find our site.'

The next day, after heatrise, Squill took his visitors on a guided tour of The Beacon. It was a splendid hive – or hives? Squill called it a 'colony'. Coppice thought it was more like a multi-colony and Spurge thought it was headache trying to work out where they were in the maze of tunnels that linked up the different parts of the colony.

From talking to Squill, they gained the impression that the island was a place where anybees in need of a safe home could come. The Beacon was a sort of headquarters, which received incoming bees and directed them to suitable sites on the island. Squill was the senior of four intelligence scouts who ensured

COPPICE

regular contact with the mainland. That's how Fescue came to know about the island. Coppice and Sorrell now suspected that Fern and Piper had planned this visit because they knew the island was the best place to escape to.

'Just one problem,' Coppice whispered to Sorrell. 'How do we get a whole swarm over here?'

'I can see that will take some doing but I should think we could stopover at the edge of the mainland and cross over the following day.'

'Easier said then done. Will a swarm actually fly over the sea?'

'If we can persuade the Queen to cross, the rest will join her, I'm sure.'

'Hmm.'

They asked Fescue about it and he reassured them it could, and would be done. Then he urged them to find something for the swarm to fly to, so the search party was reconvened.

Squill led them out in an easterly direction, collecting landmarks en route. They flew a suitable distance from The Beacon before Squill left them with permission to search the locality. He was sure they would find several good sites.

Briar and Teasel had an uneventful flight back to Middle Oak. They located Lavender and told her all about the search party's progress. She had no news from Fern and Piper but promised to pass on their report.

Next day they were keen to rejoin the search party so they were away shortly after heatrise. They flew up to the landmark indicating the beginning of their beeline to Hollybank. In their eagerness to get on with it, they didn't notice much of what was going on around them. If they had been more observant they might just have spotted a pair of Blues slip out from the undergrowth close to Middle Oak and follow them to the beeline. Once Briar and Teasel started at speed along this beeline, the Blues were able to follow at a much safer distance. When Briar and Teasel stopped for water the scout pair overflew them by a short distance and hid in a nearby tree. When Briar and Teasel set off again, the Blues followed them all the way to Hollybank, picking up a number of landmarks on the way.

Squill's search area was excellent. It was mostly birch and oak in a hilly region. There were possible sites in banks but also plenty in the hollows of oak trees. Not all of them were occupied by birds or squirrels. Thyme was more than satisfied with the flowers in the area. The wood wasn't dense so there were open spaces which provided light for a wider variety of plants than you might expect. She had to make some estimates as to how long the flowering season was likely to be, but she could also ask Squill's advice. Bryony was learning a lot from Thyme.

The search party's task had been made easy. They settled on three possible sites, one of which they marked as their first choice. It would be called 'High Oak', for obvious reasons. Even if it didn't work out, there would be plenty of other options nearby. Their mission accomplished, a very satisfied search party returned to The Beacon before sunpeak. They would be able to get back to Hollybank by heatfall.

Coppice thanked the immaculate Squill and hoped to see him again very soon. The party stocked up on honey and Fescue led them to the three landmarks for the return crossing. It was still an eerie experience flying over water, but they were all more comfortable about it this time, except Spurge of course, who thought it wasn't 'natural'.

With Fescue as their guide, the return crossing was accurate. They soon reached the mainland and continued on to Hollybank where they found Briar and Teasel waiting for them. Amid much excitement they told the pair all about the crossing, Squill's Island and High Oak. Briar and Teasel congratulated them enthusiastically while quietly wishing they had been there. After that it was time to cluster for the night.

Next morning the whole party set off confidently along the beeline to Middle Oak. They would only need to stop for water en route. Fescue selected a small stream that looked shallow enough for bees to walk into for a drink.

All nine bees were quietly drinking when it happened. About a dozen Blues appeared from nowhere and landed on the soft ground just behind the drinking bees. Fescue was the first to realise.

'Don't make any sudden movements,' he ordered, 'just turn slowly round and face them.'

A mixture if surprise and fear spread through the search party.

'What do we do now?' whispered Coppice.

COPPICE

No answer. The two sets of bees were eyeing each other up.

'Nine against twelve isn't so bad,' suggested Scruff.

'I'm ready to have a go at them,' volunteered Spurge.

'Look above you,' said Sorrell.

Spurge shifted his head slightly and saw that a large number of Blues were hovering in the air several bee-lengths above them.

Then one of the Blues spoke. 'There is no escape. You will come with us. You will fly inside the cordon we set around you.'

'Get lost!' muttered Spurge.

'*Ssh!*' hissed Fescue. 'Do as they say but try and fly close together. That's probably what they want anyway.'

The Blue leader gave Spurge a withering look and spoke again. 'Hover at ten bee-lengths until we are all around you.'

They obeyed. Only Thyme and Fescue had not seen Blues before, but to be surrounded by about fifty of them was scary for all of them.

'Why haven't they attacked us?' Coppice asked Fescue.

'And how did they know we were here?' added Sorrell, who had already been thinking things through more carefully than the rest of them.

The Blues encircled their prisoners, then their leader spoke once more: 'Now we fly.' And they set off at a steady pace.

It was easier to talk now. Fescue tried to answer the questions asked earlier.

'They may have stumbled across us but more likely their scouts have been looking out for us.'

'Do you think they know about Squill's Island?' asked Coppice.

'Very unlikely, but I fear Hollybank might be known to them now.'

'Where are they taking us?'

'Your guess is as good as mine.'

'We have to do something!'

'Don't do anything rash, Coppice. Think carefully. Pick up a few landmarks so we can work out where to fly if we get the chance.'

Scruff edged alongside Coppice and Fescue. 'If just one of us could escape and sound the alarm…'

'Maybe,' answered Coppice.

'Who's the fastest flier in our party?' asked Sorrell as he drifted alongside.

'Fescue is,' replied Coppice.

'How do you know?'

'Piper and Fern told me he had an exceptionally long day-range, so he must be quick.'

'Then he must go,' said Sorrell.

'But he might need some help if he's to make a clean break.'

'How about a diversion?'

Coppice realised Sorrell was right so he drifted over to Fescue and told him what they wanted to do. Fescue was impressed with their attitude. It was a difficult decision however, because his escape might cause them to be hurt – or worse. It seemed to him though, that the Blues were keeping them alive for a purpose. If they lost just one of their prisoners, would it bother them much? He mulled it over for a little while.

'Very well, Coppice. It's a brave plan – let's try it. Pass the word carefully to the others so they know what's coming. You and Sorrell distract the Blues on the left flank and I'll make a break through any space that becomes available.'

They took their time passing the message, so as not to raise suspicion. When they were all informed, Fescue looked out for the next open area. He needed a straight flight path with nothing to slow him down. He reckoned he might be able to outfly the Blues but he couldn't be sure until he actually tried it.

They came to some meadowland. Fescue gave Coppice the nod. Sorrell closed up on Coppice and the pair suddenly shot downwards together, hitting the nearest Blues in the process. There was absolute pandemonium! The Blues went frantic! About half of them shot after Coppice and Sorrell. Immediately Fescue shot upwards with ferocious acceleration! That threw the remaining Blues into more confusion and most of them, including their leader, set off after Fescue. The remaining six members of the search party suddenly found themselves virtually unattended! Scruff reacted first.

'Quick, this is our chance! Briar, Teasel, take Thyme and Bryony and fly off to the north. Try and get back to Middle Oak if you can.'

'What about you?' asked Thyme.

'We'll try for Hollybank,' replied Scruff. 'Now go!'

COPPICE

The foursome shot off. The remaining few Blues flew after them but they weren't really sure if they were supposed to or not. They were lost without their leader.

The Blues chasing Coppice and Sorrell had their orders and maintained their pursuit, only to find themselves returning to where the rest of the party should have been. Having only intended a simple diversion, Coppice and Sorrell were flying back to the others. They had some difficulty finding anybee, but Scruff and Spurge were free to look out for them and soon zoomed in to join them.

'Where's…?' began Coppice.

'Don't worry,' yelled Scruff, 'just keep going. We'll wing it in that direction – the four of us together – go!'

So the foursome flew for their lives with about twenty Blues in hot pursuit. They kept to a tight beeline. Any curving or swerving could allow the Blues to close the gap. Their direction, as far as they could estimate, was west or southwest. Spurge flew just behind the other three. He might be a bit grumpy at times but not when it came to a good scrap – he would be the first to tackle any blue drone who dared to catch up with them.

In fact, the Blues were not closing the gap. They were still in pursuit but they were not closing the gap.

'I think we're outflying them,' shouted Spurge.

They flew on in hope. It was a long chase but it was the chasers who tired first.

Spurge passed the message to the three just ahead of him, 'They're a long way back now.'

Coppice dropped back alongside Spurge and glanced behind.

'You're right. We've enough of a lead to make a dive for cover.'

Sorrell and Scruff were informed and Coppice took the lead. The next wooded area would do.

It soon arrived, although it was different somehow from most woods they knew. Coppice thought he might have seen something like it before but hadn't the time to work out where.

'Stand by!' he yelled.

A few seconds later he began to descend. When they neared the first tree tops he dropped smartly into their cover, out of sight of the pursuing Blues. The foursome weaved in and out amongst the trees – mostly sweet chestnut and not very tall. After a short time they found a resting place, protected from the open sky. The Blues could only guess where the foursome had hidden so they began a systematic search. They couldn't do it in their usual pairs because they had four bees to deal with. Instead, they split into two groups of ten. The foursome remained hidden, the Blues persevered.

'Sooner or later they'll come this way,' whispered Scruff.

'Maybe,' replied Coppice, 'but they've a lot of wood to search.'

'I wish I knew where they were,' said Spurge.

'Over there,' pointed Sorrell with one antenna.

'Some of them,' whispered Coppice.

'Supposing we follow them?' suggested Sorrell.

'*What?*' objected Coppice.

'*Ssh*! What I mean is – if we keep behind them, they'll never actually find us.'

'Hmm. I see what you mean. Very clever.'

Scruff and Spurge agreed so the foursome moved out of cover and began tracking the Blues at what they hoped was a safe distance. They found they could do it. After a while it almost became fun! However, the Blues weren't giving up yet and the foursome was in danger of losing its concentration. Sorrell was leading when he suddenly stopped and the others crashed into him, causing a minor disturbance.

'Grief, they must have heard that!' complained Coppice. 'Get ready to wing it.'

'Hang on,' said Scruff, 'they've stopped but they're not looking in our direction.'

'So where are they looking?' asked Spurge.

'I can't make out from here, not without breaking cover,' replied Scruff, then he added, 'They're going! They're flying upwards – up and away.'

They all edged out to see.

'It's not a trick is it?' asked Coppice. 'I think we should stay under cover for a while just in case.'

'Wise,' said Sorrell, so they did.

Had they been able to observe the Blues they would have seen them contact

the other half of their search party and fly away from the wood altogether.
When the foursome were sure it wasn't a trick, they left their hiding place.
'Now let's see what they were looking at,' said Coppice.
The foursome flew cautiously to the spot from which their pursuers had departed. There was something there, and Coppice recognised it!

15. GIANTS

Coppice hovered in mid-air, staring at the hive entrance which was the first one ever to be imprinted on his memory. The large aberrant hive stood starkly in front of him. The entrance tube was clearly visible, as was the blue mark to one side of it. It was an eerie feeling. He had never expected to see this place again.

Of course the memories were still there, and now they came to the surface with a mixture of emotions: the horror of that last day when the workers had expelled the drones, the routine emergencies, the unfriendliness of the other bees. But there were the better memories of Twenty-two, Twenty-three and the exploring they did together. Were either of them still here, he wondered?

He was jolted back to the present by the observant Sorrell.

'Something wrong, Coppice?'

No reply.

'Are we going to hover around here all day?' grumbled Spurge.

'What exactly are we looking at?' enquired Scruff.

Coppice relaxed a little. 'It's a beehive – built in an aberration, with a tube for an entrance.'

'How do you know that?' asked Scruff.

Sorrell had already guessed and asked, 'Coppice, is this where you came from?'

Spurge and Scruff stared in amazement. Coppice just nodded and explained, 'I need to land somewhere and think this out.' So he led them onto the nearest sweet chestnut three. It was all sweet chestnut around there, as Heather and Ling had explained.

He watched the bees coming and going from the hive entrance. What was he doing here? Why had the Blues flown off? Was it something to do with the aberrant hive? What should he do next? He just didn't know.

Wise Sorrell helped him out. 'Coppice, do you reckon we could make a stopover in this hive? Time's getting on and we aren't going to find our way back to Middle Oak today, are we?'

Coppice realised Sorrell was right, but could he face re-entering his old hive? He looked around at his three companions and knew he must do it – for their sakes.

'Right,' he said, You're right, but we'll have to wait until heatfall when the guards have gone to the cluster.'

'Is there no other way?' asked Scruff. 'Can't we get some of their scent from somewhere?'

'Only if you can persuade one of the workers to feed you some honey and I doubt that somehow.'

Spurge suggested, 'But if you lived here, maybe they would feed you?'

'I'm scented up for Hollybank at the moment.'

'So we have to hang around until heatfall,' concluded Scruff, 'but we could do with some food after all the energy we've burned up today.'

'Well, I can show you some flowers worth robbing but don't blame me if you get a stomach ache!'

'No thanks,' said Scruff, 'I'll just hang around!'

Coppice would have liked to fly out to the drone zone on the off chance that Twenty-two or Twenty-three might still be there. Still, that could wait until tomorrow. So the foursome rested as patiently as they could, pleased at least to be free of the Blues but wondering what had happened to Fescue and the others.

Fescue was a truly magnificent flier. His break from the Blues' escort party, made possible by Coppice and Sorrell's diversion, had worked like a dream. The chasing Blues were rapidly left behind in his wake. Although they soon lost sight of him, a group of four continued along his beeline when the rest turned back to where the break had been made. When they returned they were puzzled by the complete absence of anybees of any kind, so they just waited for somebee to come and give them some orders.

Meanwhile, after recognising enough landmarks to correct his course, Fescue was approaching Middle Oak. He went straight to the drone zone to look for Piper and Fern. They weren't there so he flew to the hive and found Lavender.

'We must get hold of Piper and Fern,' he gasped, short of air after his exertions. 'We were captured by Blues but Coppice and Sorrell set up a diversion to let me get away. I've outflown my pursuers but I don't know what's happened to the others. We must try and find them.'

Lavender was very shocked by this news but couldn't see what they could do until the next day. Fescue decided he could at least scout around the local area in case any of them had made it back. It was rather a long shot but he had to do something. After stocking up with honey, he flew out.

Fescue's course corrections on the way to Middle Oak had thrown the Blues off his track. They gave up their pursuit at heatfall and looked around for a suitable stopover hive.

Coppice could no longer see any guard bees at the entrance of the tube. The temperature was falling steadily but they waited a bit longer in case the guards had simply retreated to the inner end of the tube.

'Right, follow me,' he said at last, 'and don't be surprised by the length of the tube.'

The four visitors flew over to the tube and landed cautiously just inside it. Peering into it, Coppice seemed satisfied and led them in. The awful memories of his last journey through this tube returned. Then it had been packed with drones being forced out by workers, now it was dark and empty. They moved a little faster. Near the inner end of the tube, Coppice stopped and waited. No guards appeared to challenge him. Much relieved, they entered the combs and searched out the nearest honey cells.

'Take a short feed and then smear some honey over each other,' he whispered.

'The inside of the hive seems OK to me,' said Scruff.

'You haven't met the inhabitants yet,' replied Coppice.

Once scented up, the foursome located the cluster and settled down for the night. Coppice was the last to relax into the warmth of the mass of bees.

Heatrise saw the hive surge into activity and the four visitors were able to roam freely – well, they were once they'd managed to wake Coppice! He warned them not expect too much from the hive but they were still taken aback by the general indifference to them, especially when they tried greeting other

COPPICE

bees. After checking what had been his original home comb and one or two other places, Coppice took his friends out to the drone zone. There the unfriendliness of the drones disappointed them all, including Coppice.

'So what happens now?' asked Spurge, after they had landed on a nearby sweet chestnut tree.

'Obviously we have to get back to Middle Oak,' said Coppice.

'Obviously,' replied Spurge, 'go on.'

Silence, until Coppice said, 'I can only think of one way out – wait for the intelligence scouts to find us.'

'Explain,' demanded Spurge, who was feeling more pessimistic even than usual.

'Assuming Fescue's made it to Middle Oak, he'll tell Piper and Fern who will start a search. What we must do is ensure that at least one of us is in the drone zone at all times during the day – that's where they'll look. They'll check all the drone zones in the region if they have to.'

Sorrell had been thinking as well. 'There's something else we could do,' he suggested. 'We could make exploratory flights in various directions to see if we can find any landmarks familiar to us.'

Coppice perked up, 'That's a good idea, Sorrell. Two of us could do that while the other two stay in the drone zone.'

'Yes,' added Scruff,' at least we would be doing something useful.

Sorrell continued, 'And, depending on where we are, it shouldn't take Piper or one of the others very long to find us.'

'True enough,' agreed Coppice. 'Middle Oak wasn't far from the home of my bumblebee rescuers I told you about, and I couldn't have got very far from the hive after the expulsion. So, that only leaves the distance from my crash landing to Heather and Ling's nest. I don't suppose Ling could have carried me a particularly great distance that late in the day.'

'From what you've said,' Sorrell deduced, 'we aren't very far from Middle Oak.'

'So let's start,' urged Scruff, eager for action. 'I volunteer for the first exploration. Spurge, you come with me – keep you busy!'

'Fine,' agreed Coppice. 'Which area will you start with?'

Sorrell suggested, 'Not south – that would certainly take us away from Middle Oak. We thought we escaped in a west or south-westerly direction so we don't want to continue that way either. I guess it's north and east we need.'

'Sounds good to me,' said Coppice, impressed with Sorrell's reasoning. 'Scruff, you and Spurge start due north and work your beelines a little to the east each time you start a new one. You would be wiser to return here to begin each beeline – agreed?'

'Will do. Let's go Spurge.' And away they flew.

Coppice and Sorrell watched them zoom off and then settled down to see if Piper and Fern would come looking for them that day.

In the Middle Oak drone zone, Fescue had been waiting for Piper and Fern since shortly after heatrise. It was mid-morning before they arrived. As soon as they saw Fescue, they knew there would be lots of news. It was, however, much more than they had bargained for. Fescue related the whole story of the search party, ending up with the fact that he hadn't a clue where the other eight members were. The only thing he could do was to show Piper and Fern where he had made his break for freedom.

'I don't think that will help us much,' said Fern, looking quite glum for once.

'But we have to do something!' insisted Fescue.

'Yer dead right we do,' said Piper, 'but we'll think it out carefully. Now then, Fescue, Fern and me know all the hives in our area and a few of those in Dock's area. If any of the search party's still alive, they'll have to be using a hive somewhere. They know all about stopovers so they can survive, and even travel from hive to hive.'

'Which might be a problem,' said Fern.

'Yer right, but we'll have to take that chance. Anyway, if they're moving from hive to hive they probably know where they're heading, so maybe they'll make their own way back to Middle Oak.'

'But if they stay at one hive, we'll be relying on them visiting the drone zone I presume?' queried Fescue.

'Correct,' replied Fern.

'But what if they've been captured?'

COPPICE

Piper looked at him but said nothing. All three bees fell quiet for a time, sharing silent thoughts. They came out of their silence with the conviction that it really was worth searching for their lost friends.

Piper spoke at last, 'We'll search by sectors. Fern, yer go east, Sorrell to the south and I'll go west. We'll leave the north until last and search it together because it's the most dangerous sector. I reckon we can visit every drone zone in three or four days. Let's get cracking!'

While Piper began his search of hives beginning with the three closest to Middle Oak and working outwards, Scruff and Spurge were completing their first half dozen sorties to the north and east. Each time they reported back to Coppice and Sorrell. So far they had seen nothing they recognised.

'Let's leave it for today,' said Spurge, 'Heatfall isn't so far away and I could do with my fill of honey.'

Scruff was game for one more beeline but let it rest.

'We'll continue tomorrow then,' agreed Coppice. 'Sorrell and I could do alternate flights with you two maybe?'

Scruff nodded. He looked ready for a rest as well.

'I'll wait here a little longer,' said Sorrell, 'just in case the scouts are working late. You never know. I'd hate to miss them. I'll meet you near the inside end of the tube at heatfall.'

'Sure,' replied Coppice, and he flew off with Scruff and Spurge.

Back at the hive they took some honey and a little pollen. They had some time to kill before Sorrell rejoined them and the bees went into a cluster for the night. They were just wandering into level two near the hard, thin piece of material with bee-sized holes in it.

'What's this for?' asked Scruff.

'Haven't a clue,' replied Coppice, who vaguely remembered it from his first time in the hive.

'Must be here for some reason,' said Scruff.

They were just about to continue upwards when they were stopped dead in their tracks by a loud cracking noise from up above. Scruff and Spurge peered up ahead but Coppice was frozen with horror.

'Now what's that all about?' asked Spurge.

'Wow, I thought I felt the whole hive vibrate,' said Scruff. 'Any ideas Coppice? Coppice? What's wrong, Coppice?'

Then the smell reached them.

'Ugh!' exclaimed Spurge. 'What's that strange scent?'

'I feel hungry again,' said Scruff.

'Crack!' – another sound from above. Coppice was still speechless and unmoving.

'Speak to us, Coppice!' demanded Scruff. 'What should we do? Is it dangerous?'

Spurge, seeing they were getting nowhere, walked up to Coppice, took hold of him with his front pair of legs and shook him. That had the desired effect. Coppice came to.

'Sorry, I, er,...was just remembering. Now, um, we should be careful. Down to the entrance, I think.'

Another cracking noise came from above. Then, to the horror of all three of them this time, level two moved in its entirety!

'Quick, out of the way, follow me!' yelled Spurge, taking the initiative.

Scruff nudged Coppice and they flew up with Spurge, only to be confronted by two gigantic white shapes in the newly made opening above level one of the hive. They seemed to move slowly, like clouds in the sky – maybe faster, but a lot closer! The trio flew away from the white giants but discovered they couldn't go very far before they came to a sort of ceiling. Baffled by this, they flew sideways but found walls. It was like being in a massive, empty hive.

'Now what?' shouted Scruff, as they hovered together.

'Just keep away from those things, whatever they are,' replied Spurge. 'Are you OK Coppice?'

But Coppice was trying to take it all in. He was watching the white giants as much as he dare. 'They're moving the hive!' The giants are moving pieces of the hive.' He broke off as the scent drifted into their corner.

Spurge led them to a safer place. He observed the giants as they moved around what he took to be their hive. They seemed to be putting the beehive back together again. Eventually they moved away, leaving traces of that scent and thousands of very upset bees, most of them gorged with honey. A few other bees remained in their vicinity but most of them had flown out of the tube or remained in level one.

'Now what?' asked Scruff.

'We must get back inside the hive and find Sorrell. If he's lucky he'll have missed this.' So Coppice led them down to the hive in order to re-enter – but they couldn't! It was covered over – hidden away. They flew round to the other side. No openings, no nothing. Completely stumped, they landed on top of the hive, though they hardly realised it, and considered their situation.

'We're completely shut out from our hive,' announced Coppice.

'*Our* hive?' queried Spurge.

'You know what I mean!'

'And heatfall's approaching,' added Scruff.

'And heatfall's approaching,' echoed Coppice.

There was silence for a time before Spurge noticed something was missing.

'What happened to the other bees who were in this area a short time ago?'

Coppice looked up and answered, 'Gone! But if they've gone, we can go too!'

'You mean there's a way out?' asked Scruff.

Well, I don't think they could have flown directly back into the hive, not all of them anyway, and they haven't vanished into thin air have they? So there must be a way out of here.'

'Circular search,' suggested Spurge.

'Good idea – lead the way,' said Coppice.

It wasn't long before they found a remarkably large opening that led into the fresh air. Flying through it, they recognised the plants that grew near the entrance of the hive and quickly located the tube. There were quite a few bees returning to the hive, both drones and workers. They waited for the congestion to ease, but before it did they spotted Sorrell flying in from the drone zone.

'Hey Sorrell, over here!' shouted Scruff.

He heard the call and veered over towards them.

'Been out for a late zoom around?' enquired Sorrell.

'That's one way of putting it!' replied Scruff.

16. BETRAYED

Coppice did his best to convince Scruff and Spurge that they could settle down into the cluster without fear of further disruption to the hive. Having missed the frightening experience, Sorrell wasn't a problem. Coppice and Sorrell decided to put Scruff and Spurge between them as an extra comfort but they still only rested fitfully. Their restlessness kept Coppice more alert than he should have been and he found himself mulling over the day's events.

How strange that the Blues had left the area like they did. How odd that he should find himself back at his first hive. He began to wonder if he was being given the chance to help them in some way – like a long lost hero returning to lead them to a better life! No, that didn't seem quite right. Then again, he did know a better way of life. He also knew that the Blues were a serious threat. So he pondered. By heatrise he had decided on a definite course of action.

As soon as they had taken their early morning feed, he announced to the others, 'Wait here for me. I've an important message to deliver before we fly out to the drone zone. It could be my only opportunity if Piper or Fern finds us today.'

'What important message?' asked Scruff, trying to smooth out the hairs on his rear legs.'

'I'm going to speak to the Council.'

'You're *what*?' objected Spurge.

'I intend to warn them of the danger they're in and recommend a swarm.'

'You're kidding!' replied Spurge.

'Are you serious?' asked Sorrell.

'No, I'm not kidding and yes, I am serious.'

'And how do you intend to find the Council?' asked Scruff.

'I shall simply walk around shouting out for an audience.'

The others looked at him with a mixture of surprise, puzzlement and dismay.

'Well, um, you don't mind if we don't join you?' asked Scruff.

'Like I said, I'm quite happy to go on my own.' But he would have appreciated some moral support.

Coppice set off up the nearest comb. Plucking up his courage, he called out, 'Take me to the Queen. I want to speak to the Council.' It didn't come out very loud at first though several heads turned in his direction. He pressed on. 'Take me to the Queen. I want to see the Council.'

No positive response on the first comb, so over into the next. 'Take me to the Queen. I want to warn the Council.'

By the fourth comb he was beginning to wonder if this was really such a good idea. Perhaps they wouldn't listen to him anyway. Another comb, then another. At last he received a response.

'Who are you?' demanded a worker bee.

'A drone with an important message for the Council,' he replied, being careful not to give his name.

'A drone with an important message – humph! Very unlikely.'

'The hive's in danger. I must warn the Council!'

The worker was a comb controller but comparatively new to the role and not completely certain of herself. Coppice didn't notice a drone bee, situated a short distance behind him, gesture to the worker bee with his antennae.

She responded, 'Oh, very well, come with me…but don't expect them to want to hear you.'

She led Coppice along the comb with the mysterious drone following three or four bee-lengths behind. Two combs further along, she told him to wait. He knew she was going to ask the Council if they would give him an audience. He wasn't going to take no for an answer so he followed her to where the Queen and Council were situated. She had barely begun to speak to the nearest Council member when Coppice burst into their presence.

'Hey! What do you think you're doing?' objected the novice comb controller, afraid she would now be in trouble.

'Sorry, but this is too serious to miss – you're all in danger!'

That had the desired effect of gaining their attention. A large worker member of the Council glared at him and said, 'This had better be good. Wasting the Queen's egg laying time is a serious matter too! Who are you, anyway?'

'My number is Twenty-one. I come from this hive but I've also lived elsewhere.' The Council members pricked up their antennae at that. 'I've come to warn you that a vicious strain of bees, with a deep blue tinge to their body colouring, are attacking bees and even hives not so far from here. The intelligence scouts are recommending swarming to distant parts to escape this peril.'

He stopped there, hoping he had been concise enough to get the point over. They were silent for a moment. They didn't know what to make of it. Was he just an idiot or was he genuine?

Another Council member spoke up, 'How do you expect us to believe that? This hive's existed for many seasons with nothing more than a few raiding wasps to deal with.'

'These "Blues" as we call them, are much more dangerous than wasps,' insisted Coppice.

'Why are they attacking other hives?' asked a third Council member.

'They want to take over the whole region.'

'We've not seen any around here, have you?'

'Yes – the day before yesterday, in fact.'

'But they haven't attacked us.'

'Not yet.' Coppice was bit worried here because the Blues had flown off as soon as they had discovered this hive. He hoped the Council wouldn't pursue that line of questioning. As he awaited the follow up, a different voice spoke up. 'Permission to speak?'

The Council turned to look at the bee who had addressed them. One of then replied, 'The elder drone has permission.'

'I believe this drone has been before the Council previously. If you would care to think back to last season you may recall a newly emerged drone who burst through the barrier bees guarding the Queen cells?'

The Council racked their brains. Coppice was staring hard at the elder drone. The Queen remembered and that brought her quickly to a decision.

'Yes, as I recall, you were made to fly immediately as punishment for your curiosity. You were fortunate to survive I think. Now you're being very presumptuous again and must be punished. Had you been a complete stranger you would be killed. However, as you come from this hive, you will simply be expelled – but if you come back again you shall be killed! Take him away!'

Coppice missed most of the Queen's judgement because he was still staring at the elder drone. He was sure he looked like Twenty-three. Next thing he knew, worker bees were shoving him along. The elder drone accompanied them. When they had left the vicinity of the Queen and her Council, the elder drone took over.

'Wait a moment please, escorts – I'll deal with this now. Just stand by in case he turns nasty,' he said, looking firmly into Coppice's face.

Coppice stared back. He decided to risk it. Quietly he asked, 'Twenty-three?'

He thought he detected the faintest flicker in the elder drone's eyes but the reply was disappointing. 'I am the elder drone. I have no need of a number. Now listen to me,' and he too spoke quietly now. 'Find your friends and leave quickly. Do not return.'

That shook Coppice. The elder drone knew about the others, and he seemed to have more than a trace of concern for them. Scruff, Spurge and Sorrell were not from this hive so they were in some danger.

'Yes – right you are,' whispered Coppice, still looking him straight in the face. He badly wanted to ask again if he was Twenty-three, but the elder drone spoke again.

'Please go now.'

Very reluctantly, Coppice turned to leave, but thought of one last thing. 'I'm called Coppice now,' and with that he departed.

He went and found the others and simply told them he had been unsuccessful. They commiserated and asked for details.

'I think I've been betrayed,' was all he would say. 'Now let's get out of here – it's not safe.'

Several days later, one of the worker bee Council members died. The elder drone was appointed to take her place. He was being rewarded for his wisdom in the recent case of the 'prophet of doom' as they referred to Twenty-one. He was also the first drone to reach the position of Council member in that particular hive.

The four friends flew out to the drone zone where Scruff and Spurge commenced searching along beelines in a north-easterly direction. Coppice, somewhat upset, remained on the outer branches of a larch tree with Sorrell for company.

'I just don't know if it was Twenty-three or not,' confided Coppice. 'I thought I saw something in his eyes but...'

'You hadn't seen him for a long time. He would have matured – changed quite a lot,' Sorrell pointed out.

'True enough – his physical appearance would have altered. Mind you, that elder drone was on the small side, just like Twenty-three was...is? I think I told you how we had to help him out of his cell. I'm sure he wouldn't have survived otherwise.'

'Which makes his betrayal even more disappointing?'

'Yes, and that's the point. How many drones could have known that I'd been before the Council the previous season? There were no drones on the Council. They had to be reminded by the elder drone. It must have been Twenty-three.'

'Or some drone who knew him well. Twenty-two maybe?'

'No, Twenty-two was a big drone. Anyway, how could either of them have survived the expulsion and regained the hive?'

'I've no answer to that.'

'I guess we're rather short on answers at the moment.'

'Perhaps we shall understand one day,' suggested Sorrell wisely, 'but for now we have more pressing needs. If the scouts don't find us today we'll have to stopover in another hive and that will complicate their efforts to locate us.'

'You mean moving to another drone zone – one they may have already checked out?'

'Exactly.'

'Well, two of us could find another hive while the other two stay in this drone zone, then one comes back to tell the other two who are still here, who then stay here until heatfall and then join the other two who stayed in the other drone zone, after which we make a coldflight into the new hive.'

'Pardon?'

'I don't think I can repeat it!'

Sorrell tried to work out Coppice's idea while Coppice returned to his thoughts about Twenty-three. Scruff and Spurge returned from their first beeline and set off on their second. So far they hadn't seen a single familiar landmark.

It was shortly after sunpeak when the break-through came. Piper was on a south-westerly beeline beyond the hives closest to Middle Oak when he realised that the aberrant hive was his next call. How strange it would be if that was where he found them. Then again, these were strange times. He flew into the drone zone and looked around. Spotting a pair of drones close together, high up in a larch tree, he approached them carefully, not wanting to alarm them.

'Hi yer fellers, good to see yer!'

'Piper!' yelled Coppice.

'Fancy finding you here, of all places.'

Sorrell glanced at Coppice and cautioned Piper, 'Yes, but that's a bit of a sore point I fear.'

'Who else is with you?'

'Scruff and Spurge are out searching. We thought we might pick up a landmark we recognised and then make our own way home.'

'And the others?'

'What others?'

'I mean Thyme, Bryony, Briar and Teasel of course.'

Coppice just looked at him while Sorrell shook his head.

'Oh,' said Piper. He thought for a moment. 'Well, the good news is that Fescue made it back to Middle Oak. He didn't know what happened to the rest of yer.'

'We guessed he might have made it,' said Sorrell. 'That's why we were half expecting you or Fern.'

'Great, so let's find Scruff and Spurge and get ourselves back to Middle Oak. Maybe Fern or Fescue has found the others.'

In fact they sensibly waited until Scruff and Spurge returned from their latest beeline before flying back home in a north-easterly direction. The trip was uneventful but Coppice was surprised how far it was. Given that the bumblebees' refuge was quite close to Middle Oak, then surely his original hive must be reasonably close by, because he certainly didn't get very far after the expulsion. Surely Ling hadn't carried him any great distance – had he? But if he had, then what was he doing so far from the refuge? Another puzzle to add to his collection.

The party arrived at Middle Oak to be welcomed by a delighted Lavender, and later on by Fern and Fescue. Fern took charge and ensured that everyone was fully briefed, then he suggested two courses of action – both obvious. Firstly, before heatfall, some of them would report to the Council and recommend a swarm to High Oak on Squill's Island, as they now called it. Secondly, the search for the four missing bees would continue, using the same procedure as before, until all known hives had been checked out. That would take another two or three days. After that they would have to let the matter rest, although the scouts would always be on the lookout, of course. There was some dissension about ever giving up the official search, but the scout bees insisted. It was possible that the four were out of the region even now. No bee suggested they were dead.

Coppice, Lavender, Sorrell, Scruff and Spurge went off to find the Council while the scouts had their own little get together. There was some delay while Lavender made the appropriate contacts but eventually they were brought to the Council. The Queen wasn't present this time – apparently she was too busy.

'That could be a good sign,' whispered Lavender. 'The decision may be so straightforward that she doesn't need to attend.'

'I hope you're right,' said Coppice.

'Humph?' grunted Valerian. Gentian and Erinus were either side of him.

'Erm, yes,' said Coppice. 'I have the outcome of the official search party, directed to locate a suitable new hive site to the south or west of here.'

He described the site on Squill's Island in some detail, giving it the agreed name of 'High Oak'.

'What exactly is this "island"?' enquired Valerian.

'And how long does it take to get there?' added Erinus.

Coppice explained briefly.

'But how wide is this "river"?' Gentian asked.

'Oh quite wide, but quite crossable. We did it in both directions – no problems.'

'Humph,' grunted Valerian. 'Could a swarm really reach this High Oak place in one day?'

'Yes,' stated Sorrell, before Coppice could answer. Coppice gave him a quizzical look. It probably was asking too much of a swarm in one day, but Sorrell was trying to avoid complications.

'And did you encounter any of the so-called "Blues" during your search?' asked Gentian.

There was a slight pause before Coppice answered, 'Yes – a few.'

'Go on.'

'Well, we were intercepted on the way back and…'

'And that's why some of your search party aren't with you?' suggested Valerian.

'Er, yes. That's right. Four are missing – but the scouts are looking for them.'

'Indeed,' commented Erinus. 'Now these Blues you encountered. If you were on your way back here, then clearly they are to be found between High Oak and us?'

'Erm, yes,' admitted Coppice, who didn't like the way things were going.

'So isn't there some risk in swarming off in that direction? Wouldn't we be better staying where we are?' suggested Valerian, with Gentian and Erinus nodding their agreement.

'Isn't there a greater risk in staying here?' chipped in Scruff.

Coppice gave him a short, sharp stare.

Valerian turned to Fluellen, 'I gather our loss of foragers has subsided in the past three or four days?'

'Quite correct,' replied Fluellen on cue.

'Not that all the comb controllers had reported losses in the first place,' added Juniper.

Celandine said nothing.

Coppice turned to Lavender. 'Have your losses stopped?'

'Er, as far as I can tell, they have fallen away since the search party left.'

That rather took the comb from under their feet. The loss of foragers was the one thing that had concerned at least some of the Council members from the beginning. Now it appeared to be over. What's more, the Council were hinting that this cessation was connected in some way to the search party.

Coppice was worried and tried to get back to the need to swarm. 'So can the Queen be told about High Oak now please?'

'I hardly think that will be necessary,' replied Valerian. 'It's quite clear to us that we no longer need to risk a swarm, especially to such a distant site – involving what you call a "water crossing". Thank you for your efforts. That will be all. Heatfall beckons, I believe.'

The Council withdrew. Presumably one of them would inform the Queen. Coppice and his friends were at first speechless – then very angry.

'They never had any intention of leaving this hive!' announced Sorrell.

'Right,' agreed Scruff, 'they're just a bunch of old...'

'They also happen to be the Council around here, and their word's final,' pointed out a frustrated Coppice. 'We did think our first audience with them went rather too well – didn't we?'

'Yes,' agreed Sorrell, 'but the Queen wasn't present this time and she was the positive one originally.'

'I just don't know what to think,' said Coppice. 'I give up.'

'No way!' said Spurge, thinking about those Blues and the threat they posed. 'We have to think of a way around this. We must swarm!'

'Well said, Spurge,' added Scruff.

Sorrell nodded and asked, 'What about you, Lavender? It's your home hive. What do think?'

She thought for a few moments before speaking, 'I think those Council members have had it easy here. They wouldn't want to give up their comfortable hive if they could possibly avoid it. They've not encountered any Blues themselves, but then neither have I, yet I can see the effect they've had on some of you. And didn't you notice how the drones were controlling the Council this time? They would go for the easy option if at all possible. However, I think Celandine might just be on our side.'

'How does that help us?' asked Coppice.

'Because if she will support us, we might still be able to swarm!'

17. REARING A QUEEN

Lavender beckoned the others to follow her and led them to her home comb. Once in the centre of her two comb faces, she explained her idea.

'I think you know we've just the one Queen in the hive and that she lays all the eggs.' A quick scan of the drones' faces told her she assumed correctly. 'But you probably don't know that the Queen issues a scent that's passed round the hive by touch and food sharing. This "Queen scent" somehow stops the worker bees from making Queen cells.'

'So how do you get a new Queen?' asked Coppice.

'Well, as I understand it, either her scent wears a bit thin when she gets old or the hive grows so big that her scent can't cover all of it. In the first case it's time to replace the old Queen; in the second it's time for the hive to divide into two colonies.'

'Interesting,' said Coppice – and he meant it.

Lavender continued, 'The key to our problem lies in the fact that comb controllers like myself are not influenced by the Queen scent as much as the workers are. That wouldn't normally matter because we're supervisors and we don't do any of the routine jobs. However, we haven't lost the ability to do those jobs. For example, I can still produce wax.'

She paused there, to ensure they were still with her.

Sorrell's eyes twinkled as he cleverly suggested, 'So you could build a Queen cell – if you wanted to?'

'Exactly! Not only that, but in my official capacity as comb controller, I could organise the feeding of the Queen larva. We simply select an egg laid three days ago, which is due to hatch into a larva. I then build up its cell into a Queen cup, at first, and into a full-length Queen cell later on. My nurse bees will provide the right food – lots of it – for five days, after which the larva will spin a cocoon around itself and pupate.'

'Pupate?' queried Scruff.

'Sorry, I mean change into an adult. It takes seven or eight days, so the Queen should emerge sixteen days after the egg was laid.'

'Only sixteen days for all that to happen?' asked Coppice.

'Yes, but don't forget we're starting on day four, when the egg has already hatched. That means we could have a new Queen ready in twelve or thirteen days.'

'Amazing!' exclaimed Coppice. 'Is it really as simple as that?'

'Not quite. We have our present Queen to consider – she's the one who will fly out with the swarm.'

'What?' objected Scruff. 'You mean this new Queen won't come with us?'

'No, she will stay behind in charge of the hive, and she will fight any other Queens she finds in a fight to the death –including the old Queen if she's still hanging around!'

The listening drones were astounded.

'OK,' said Coppice, 'but the old Queen won't like it, will she?'

'True enough, and that's the tricky bit. She will have to be warned a short time before the new Queen emerges, so that she can escape with the swarm. Up until then we shall have to keep the new Queen cell secret. We cannot tell the Queen ourselves but that's where Celandine comes in. I can tell Celandine and she, as a Council member, can tell the Queen.'

'What if she won't?' asked Coppice.

'Oh, she'll tell her all right, for the sake of her own safety. The question is – will she tell the other Council members as well?'

'Hmm,' muttered Coppice, 'but would they dare try and stop the new Queen from emerging?'

'I just don't know,' replied Lavender. 'I've never heard of Queen cells being destroyed so late in a new Queen's development but I suppose it's a possibility. If Celandine does tell them, we shall have quite a fight to cope with.'

'This is a brilliant idea,' said Sorrell, looking deep into Lavender's eyes. 'You may just have saved the hive – or a large proportion of it anyway. We shall do everything to make this plan succeed.'

'We certainly will,' added Coppice. 'When do we start?'

COPPICE

'At heatrise tomorrow!' declared Lavender.

Coppice, Sorrell, Scruff and even Spurge were eager to locate Lavender immediately after heatrise. She was glad of their support but also had to ensure they didn't obstruct the work that had to be done.

'Now then,' she said, 'there are some eggs over by the far wall. They'll be out of the way because the comb is sealed to the wall just beyond them, so there's less chance of unexpected visitors. You can gather round and watch the first bit if you like – in fact, that might be a good idea.'

She selected a cell with a newly hatched larva and began producing wax from the glands in her abdomen. She blended the new wax with that at the rim of the cell and carefully worked it upwards and outwards. It was a painstaking task and the drones looked on in admiration. Before too long the lower part of a cup-shaped structure could be seen. It was already mid-morning when Lavender stopped her building.

'So far so good,' she announced. 'I think the nurse bees can make a start now. Keep an eye on it, will you please?'

She wandered off to collect a couple of worker bees whose special job was the feeding of young larvae. All she had to do was place them in front of the partially built Queen cup and let them get on with it. The drones had to back off a bit to allow room for the nurse bees, who began feeding the larva – continuously. They just kept going while the drones looked on in bewilderment until the larva was swimming in food!

'It can't possibly eat all that!' exclaimed Scruff.

'Is this really going to work?' asked Coppice.

'Yes,' replied Lavender. 'The Queen will, as you know, be much larger than a drone or a worker, yet she will be the quickest to emerge, so her growth has to be rapid. The only way to do that is to have as much food as the larva can eat, available at all times.'

'Right,' mused Sorrell. 'So a larva can never actually overeat?'

'I guess that's true,' agreed Lavender, 'but it's not just the quantity that counts, it's the quality as well. We're feeding royal jelly here. It's richer than the bee-bread we feed to other larvae. So, all I have to do now is to keep adding wax to the Queen cup until it becomes a Queen cell and the nurse bees will do the rest – for the next five days. I must carry out my comb controller duties between cell building though, in case I'm missed and a Council member comes to investigate.'

'Fine,' said Coppice. 'What can we do to help?'

'I think it might be worth two or three of you being sort of "on duty" here, just in case anybee gets any ideas.'

'What sort of ideas?' asked Scruff.

'I don't know – I've never done this before. There might be a reaction I don't know about.'

'What about a barrier?' Coppice suggested.

'A what?' asked Lavender.

'A barrier of living bees around the Queen cell. I've seen it done, in my first hive – didn't I tell you? I investigated it and found myself arrested but the barrier was pretty effective.'

'Until you came along!' said Spurge.

'It might be a useful idea later on,' said Lavender thoughtfully. 'We could use some extra protection as soon as we've told Celandine what's going to happen.'

'Hmm,' replied Coppice. And that was that, apart from telling the scout bees what they were up to.

Briar, Teasel, Thyme and Bryony had taken a direction similar to Sorrell at the split up, hoping to reach Middle Oak themselves. Fortunately there were only six drones left to chase them after Coppice and Sorrell's diversion and Fescue's dash for freedom had attracted about fifty or so Blues. Unfortunately though, they didn't have Fescue's knowledge of landmarks so they were unable to make the flight corrections needed to bring them on line to Middle Oak. Instead they passed some distance to the east of their hive, into the comparatively dangerous north-eastern sector.

'We've lost them!' yelled Briar.

'Let's make quite sure,' replied Thyme. So they zoomed on for a while longer.

'Time to find cover,' shouted Teasel, indicating the approaching hills with conifer woods.

'Better if you could find us a spot with some flowers,' suggested Thyme.

COPPICE

'We'll need to feed soon.'

'Fair enough,' agreed Teasel. 'Follow me.'

He dived down towards the nearest wood but skirted the edge of it until he came to a meadow of grass with plenty of cinquefoil, daisies and groundsel. As they dived in, Bryony caught a glimpse of something odd at the opposite end of the meadow. She didn't mention it until she and Thyme had collected nectar and pollen from certain flowers and shared it with Briar and Teasel.

'Now what?' asked Thyme.

'Any idea where we are?' asked Bryony.

'Not a clue,' replied Briar.

'Me neither,' added Teasel. 'Mind you, given the sun's position and the time of day, I think we might be, I should say…I should say…'

'We're lost!' suggested Briar.

'Not exactly. We're just a long way from home.'

Thyme tried to reason things out. 'If we had set out in the same direction as Fescue, we should be at Middle Oak by now, I would have thought. But we're not, so I reckon we've flown past it. We're too far north.'

'If you say so,' said Teasel.

'I'll go along with that,' added Briar.

'Excuse me,' interrupted Bryony, 'but what are those things at the other end of the meadow?'

'Hang on, Bryony,' replied Teasel, 'we're trying to work out where we are.'

'And why are honeybees flying a beeline in that direction?' added Bryony.

'Never mi…What?' asked Briar.

'Two bees have flown past in that direction since we landed. They were flying straight towards those things.'

'Ah, right you are,' admitted Teasel. 'Well spotted. Now, er…I suppose we should take a look. How about it, Briar?'

'Do you think they might be…?'

'Let's take a peek.'

The four flew off towards the opposite end of the meadow, keeping high up to avoid established beelines. They hovered above the structures and watched for a while. Bryony was right. Honeybees were flying up to them and disappearing from sight. There were six of the things, in two rows of three.

'There has to be an entrance,' said Thyme.

'Obviously,' agreed Briar, 'but what are these things they're flying into? They look nothing like hives.'

'They look nothing like anything,' said Teasel.

'Oh!' exclaimed Thyme, 'I think I can guess what they are.'

The others looked at her.

'Well?' said Briar.

'Aberrations,' said Thyme. 'They're aberrations in which some bees have chosen to build their hives – but don't ask me why.'

Teasel and Briar thought about it for a while. Bryony just listened carefully.

Then Thyme added, 'Didn't Coppice once live inside an aberration of some sort?'

Briar looked at her, 'Yes, I think he might have done – and he's survived to tell the tale.'

'Only just, if I remember his story correctly,' added Teasel.

'So, do we risk a stopover in one of these hives?' asked Thyme.

'I guess so,' replied Briar.

'Agreed,' said Teasel, 'but what about getting scented up? We've no bee who belongs to one of these hives like Fescue did at Hollybank.'

That caused sufficient consternation for the foursome to fly into a hedgerow to consider the matter. It was Thyme who came up with the answer.

'What if I spot the type of flowers their workers are feeding on, collect some myself and try entering the hive? If I make it, I can bring out some of their honey to smear over you three.'

Briar congratulated her. 'Brilliant idea, Thyme. Now why didn't I think of that?'

'Probably because you're not a worker bee,' suggested Thyme rather cheekily.

There was no answer to that, so Thyme flew out to pick up the first forager she could find, flying away from the hives. She shot after her for some distance and was led over the nearest conifer wood to some rough looking heathland beyond. The forager alighted on one of several gorse bushes and began collecting food. It wasn't yet mid-season so the gorse was still in flower. Thyme sucked up a load of nectar into her honey stomach and then had to wait while the worker brushed pollen off her head and body into the pollen baskets on her rear legs. At last she was ready to return to the hive, duly pursued by Thyme.

As they approached the hive entrance, Thyme tucked in just behind the forager and made a point of brushing against her body as they landed. It was very nerve-racking because of the guard bees. They applied their antennae to both bees for several seconds. This was longer than normal and brought Thyme close to panic, but she held on. The guards turned aside and let her pass. What a relief!

Once inside the hive it was easy enough to find a honey store and fill up with a supply to take back to the others. Thyme first unloaded what was already in her stomach and then reloaded with stored honey. Without paying much attention to the hive and its bees, she departed for the hedgerow where the others were patiently awaiting her return.

'Did you make it?' called Briar, even before she had landed.

Thyme nodded and began to regurgitate the honey. The four worked together to smear it over each other.

'I can't wait for a good feed,' said Bryony.

'Me too,' agreed Teasel.

'Won't be long now,' declared Briar.

'I wonder if we should wait?' said Thyme.

'Why?' demanded Bryony.

'Because the guards seemed extra careful to my mind. I wonder if they've had trouble with "visitors"? If we waited until heatfall we could be more certain of a successful entry.'

'You got in, Thyme, and you didn't have honey from the inside of the hive as part of your scenting up,' argued Teasel.

'True, but I'd been working the same flowers for some time.'

'Yes, and I thought you'd got lost. Anyway, I say we go for it,' said Briar.

Teasel and Bryony supported him so Thyme gave in and led them off to the hive she had entered previously. The four of them went in together, giving the guards more to deal with, thus hoping they would work a little faster and not linger over any one of them. Thyme would go last as she had already been accepted. Briar and Teasel went in side by side and the three guard bees checked them out. Again they prolonged their duties but eventually allowed the two drones to enter. Bryony stood as still as she could in a submissive posture. They let her pass, shortly to be followed by Thyme.

Once inside, they made indecent haste to the nearest food supplies and feasted to their hearts' content. It had been an exciting day and they were still alive and well. They wondered what had happened to the others. Had Fescue escaped and found his way back to Middle Oak? Had Coppice and the others also escaped?

'Tomorrow we can think about finding our way back to Middle Oak,' said Briar, 'but for now we'll just have a look around this hive, I think.'

That seemed like a good course of action so off they went. When they looked carefully at the combs, they realised how uniform they were. All the combs appeared to be identical in shape and size. There was plenty of brood on the first combs they investigated. They were just crawling underneath one of them when Bryony froze. Thyme bumped into her. Briar and Teasel were ahead of the two workers.

'Keep going, Bryony,' ordered Thyme, to no effect. 'Bryony, what's wrong?'

Thyme came alongside her and called Briar and Teasel.

'What's up, Thyme?' asked Briar.

'It's Bryony. Something's frightened her, I think.'

'What is it, Bryony?' Teasel gently enquired.

'I…I think I saw one of them.'

'One of who?' asked Thyme, but she guessed the answer even as she spoke. 'Oh no, not in here. Have the Blues caught up with us?'

'What?' demanded Briar. 'Blues? In here!'

'*Ssh*,' insisted Thyme. 'We mustn't give ourselves away.'

'But what do we do about it?' asked Teasel.

'Bryony, how close were you to the Blue?' Thyme enquired.

'V…very close.'

'Did you make eye contact?'

'Y…yes, on one side.'

'And the Blue didn't recognise you?'

'Er, no – I guess not.'

'Good! We don't need to panic then.'

'But we can't stay here,' complained Briar.

COPPICE

'We probably could,' replied Thyme, 'though I suppose you'd feel safer in one of the other hives.'

'Too right I would,' responded Briar, 'and I think Bryony would as well.'

'Fair enough,' said Thyme, 'we can switch hives at heatfall, as soon as the guards have retired.'

So it was decided. In the meantime the four friends stuck close together and made their way nearer to the hive entrance. They looked around very cautiously now, and actually spotted three more Blues in the hive. Apparently they were accepted as normal drones, so they must have been properly scented up.

At last heatfall arrived. Briar made a recce flight to the nearest hive to see if its guards had retired. They hadn't. A little later, Teasel flew out and this time the guards had gone. The foursome waited a little longer still, until most bees had joined the cluster for the night, before crawling to the entrance together. From there they made the short trip to the next hive, entering unchallenged. They walked to the nearest honey supply to get scented up before joining the safety of the cluster, hoping for better things the next day.

18. REUNION

Thyme was first into action the following morning. She went to feed and returned to the others who were just stirring.

'Oh, been out already, Thyme?' enquired Briar.

'No, just taking a good feed.'

'Good idea, especially after last night's exploits. I think we should move on from here pretty smartly – I don't like being so close to those Blues. Come on, Teasel, let's stock up with honey.'

While Teasel joined Briar, Bryony trundled off in another direction to find her early morning feed. She had sucked up less than half a stomachful when something made her look up. There was a Blue just two bee-lengths away!

'Oh no,' she thought. 'They've followed us to this hive!'

For a while she was unable to do anything. Then, as she calmed herself a little, she withdrew from the honey cell, turned her back on the feeding Blue, and gently moved away to tell the others. Thyme was looking out for her.

'What's wrong, Bryony? You look like waking up was a mistake!'

'Maybe it was. Maybe it's the last time I shall ever wake up. Maybe that was my last feed, maybe…'

'Bryony! What are you on about?'

'Blue bee.'

'Oh no!'

'Oh yes.'

'Oh dear, where?'

Bryony indicated. Thyme edged over to investigate and quickly returned. Briar and Teasel also returned to hear the bad news from Thyme.

'What?' exclaimed Briar.

'You're kidding!' added Teasel.

COPPICE 1

'I'm not. Go and look for yourself.'

'Then let's get out of here, double quick!' decided Briar.

The others needed no second invitation so they bustled along to the entrance. In their haste they failed to spot the danger. Briar, leading the way, was the first to run into trouble.

'Hey you! Where do you think you're going?' shouted one of the guard bees, and he moved to obstruct Briar's departure.

'We're going out for...' but Briar's words froze in his mouth. The guard had a blue tinge to his body hair and wings! Another Blue came alongside, and another! Teasel, Thyme and Bryony piled up behind Briar and were surrounded by Blues in an instant. It hadn't occurred to them that the guard bees might be checking departures as well as arrivals.

'Right!' yelled a Blue who had just flown in to investigate the minor disturbance. 'Take 'em back inside and seal 'em off. I'll send a message to Yarrow.'

'Sure thing, Bugle,' replied one of the guards, and they marched their captives into the hive.

In fact, the Blues had now set guards on all six hives and they had spies inside as well. The tale of the bees who had dared to try and escape from the raiding party had spread rapidly amongst the Blues in the area and Bugle, being responsible for the infiltration operation, knew he would have to do something about it before his master found out. He had about fifty Blues spread through the six hives. Some of them were scout pairs, responsible for intelligence work in the region, so they couldn't make the trip back to headquarters. Bugle decided he would need reinforcements if he was going to deliver his four captives to Yarrow without further incident. Knowing that a raiding party of about fifty Blues had failed to hold the nine bees they had originally captured, he wanted to have a good hundred Blues to escort these four back to his master. No doubt Yarrow would be very pleased as long as the mission was completed. Then again, now that he had sent the message informing Yarrow of the arrests, he had to deliver the goods or...But Bugle put that thought aside. He *would* succeed – he *had* to.

He flew over to the next hive, entering unchecked past his own guards, and located a suitable pair of Blues, whom he dispatched immediately. They had a long way to go, up to two days journey each way as a rule, possibly one and a half. Meanwhile, the captives had to be carefully imprisoned and Bugle knew exactly how to do that.

The miserable foursome were pushed and shoved along the floor of the hive to one of the back corners. The Blues then called up a number of worker bees who were ordered to produce wax in the shape of an enclosing wall around the terrified prisoners. It was one thing to be captured in the open air but entirely another to be imprisoned inside a hive.

'That'll keep you quiet,' said one of the guards, as he watched the workers sealing them in. 'We'll leave you one or two breathing holes – as long as you behave yourselves! Oh, and don't eat all your honey supply at once – there won't be any more!'

There was absolutely nothing the captives could do. They were angry at being caught in the way they were but also frightened of what might happen to them. It did sound as if they were being kept alive until somebee else was told about them. For the time being they had to concentrate on getting enough air through the tiny holes in their prison wall. They were already too hot in such a small space. Eventually Thyme and Bryony did some fanning with their wings, and that helped. However, they couldn't keep it up for long because they were burning up precious food supplies and they had no idea how long they would be in their tiny jail. Not until heatfall approached did they get some relief from the cooler temperature.

The following day they had no visitors whatsoever and no idea of what was happening. Young Bryony found the confinement hardest and had to be calmed by Thyme. The two drones found it easier to be inactive, but still rather boring. Wisely, they rationed their honey supplies. Their captivity entered a third day.

Back at Middle Oak, the scout bees had completed their systematic search of the east, west and south sectors, and were meeting to decide how to tackle the more dangerous north sector. It was fairly obvious that they should begin on a north-eastern line and work their way to the north-west. Coppice reckoned their missing friends were most likely to have passed to the east of Middle Oak, assuming they had got that far. The truth was that they could be anywhere by now, but there must always be hope.

Before joining the cluster for heatfall, they went and took a peep at the Queen larva being reared by Lavender and her nurse bees. The little white grub was swimming in bee jelly, guzzling away as though it didn't have a care in the world, which of course it didn't – yet! Piper briefed Coppice and Sorrell on their plan of action. They would send for help if and when they needed it. Little did they know that their four friends had been captured and hidden away in the back of a distant hive, and an aberrant hive at that!

Shortly after heatrise the next day, Piper, Fern and Fescue set off on a north-easterly beeline. They didn't enter the hives they wished to check out but visited the drone zones instead. One of the important tasks of a scout bee was to establish good contacts in every drone zone in his sector. They were at some disadvantage in this respect because this area belonged to Dock, who had sadly gone missing, presumed lost. However, with three of them on the job they should be able to find suitable informants reasonably quickly. The only exception would be where aberrant hives were involved. The drones from those hives were usually less communicative, as Piper knew well enough from his experience with Coppice's first hive.

The scouting party soon reached their first port of call, the hive known as 'The Mound' because it was built into a steep riverbank, about three hundred bee-lengths above the surface of the water. It was a large, old colony of honeybees, which had survived peacefully for as long as anybee could remember. The top of The Mound was covered in brambles and thus difficult to penetrate by anything of size. The entrance was set on the riverside of the colony, where The Mound rose vertically out of the water.

They flew over the hive towards its drone zone where they began sounding out the locals, but they had no information about Briar and company. There had been some sightings of Blues in the area but not inside the hive.

Fern decided they should move on to Lower and Upper Beach hives. Here they heard that the Blues were quite active in the area, usually in scout pairs. One drone from Upper Beach thought a group of six or seven Blues had flown through their area recently. Fern felt that could be significant and urged the others to fly on to the next drone zone, which was a tricky one because it belonged to aberrant hives. They should reach it just after sunpeak.

Just *before* sunpeak, a large number of Blues arrived at 'Six Hives' in the field near the orchards. It was the largest raiding party to date; the previous one being that which had intercepted Coppice's search party on its return from Hollybank. As the Blues had control of Six Hives, there was no problem distributing the visitors amongst them. Blues remained in charge of guard duties. The prisoners were now in their fourth day of captivity, wondering why nothing was happening. No bee came to talk to them. They just remained in their waxen jail, becoming more and more depressed – and running very low on food.

Fern and his scouting party reached Six Hives after the arrival of the Blues' reinforcements. They were fortunate that the drones from all six hives shared the same drone zone. As usual though, for aberrant hives, the drones were generally uncommunicative. They approached several individuals without success.

'This is very frustrating,' concluded Fescue, after his tenth failure to extract any information from the locals.

Fern was thoughtful. 'There must be a way round this,' he said. 'We have to be certain they're not here.'

'One drone admitted to seeing a couple of Blues,' reported Piper,' but we already know, thanks to Dock, that they frequent this area.'

'Yes, and what else does – *did* – poor Dock find out?' pondered Fern out loud.'

Piper continued, 'There must be somebee here who'll tell us something.' His thoughts wandered back to his first encounters with Coppice. After a few seconds he perked up. 'Now what sort of drone do yer think we should be looking for?'

'What do you mean "what sort of drone"? They're all the same aren't they?' retorted Fescue, while Fern waited in anticipation – he knew Piper better than Fescue did.

'Yer must be joking! There are old drones and young drones, experienced drones and inexperienced drones. Now, I reckon we'll have more luck with a young, inexperienced drone, who may well blurt out what he knows and who

COPPICE

isn't yet too depressed by living in an aberrant hive.'

Fescue stared at him – Fern waited for more.

'Y'see, I first spotted Coppice and his pals when they were newly out of the hive. They were lively and only too happy to chat to me.'

Fern nodded, 'Very good, Piper. We should be looking for a very young drone. Look out for the tell-tale sign of fluffy body hair.'

And with that inspiration they renewed their search. Fern was first to spot a likely candidate. 'Hello there. How's life? Exciting out here in the drone zone isn't it?'

'Sure is,' replied the enthusiastic youngster.

'Yes,' agreed Fern. 'In fact, life's very exciting these days I find.'

'Oh yes, it certainly is!'

Fern then took a gamble, 'These Blues are livening things up, aren't they?'

'You mean our dark blue visitors? Yes – lots of them back at the hives today.'

'Really? More than usual?' Fern was hedging a bit.

'Didn't you know?'

'Know what?'

'Just before sunpeak today!'

'Oh, er, I've been in the zone most of the day actually.'

'Well then, let me tell you. A big group of those, er, Blues, flew in to join us.'

'Join us?'

'Yes, they've come for a special visit – to look at our orchards, according to the guard bees.'

'Ah yes, of course – our orchards are rather special aren't they?'

'Sure thing.'

'Well, thanks for the update. See you again sometime,' concluded Fern before buzzing off to locate Piper and Fescue to report his find.

Piper congratulated him, 'Yer did well there. Now what would a large party of Blues be doing out here? And how come we've not seen any of them in the drone zone?'

'Only one way to find out,' said Fern.

The others needed no further encouragement so they zoomed over to Six Hives. They hovered above the beelines and observed the nearest of the six.

Piper spotted something he'd not come across before.

'Excuse me if I'm seeing things, but aren't those guards drones – and blue drones at that?'

'Well, well,' said Fern. 'Let's check the other hives.'

Sure enough, all six had Blues on guard duty. The trio retreated to the nearest hedgerow.

'What does this mean?' asked Fescue.

'Trouble,' replied Piper and Fern in unison.

'So what do we do now?'

'Stop and think carefully,' said Fern tersely, which put a stop to the questions. Then he said, 'I think we may have found our friends, but we can't prove it without assistance. We have to get inside the hives to check them out and we can't do that without removing the Blues on guard. I suggest one of us stays here while the other two fly back to Middle Oak for help. If we can muster a hundred or so fighters and bring them out here immediately after heatrise tomorrow, then we can go straight into action.'

Piper nodded his agreement and Fescue offered to fly back on his own.

'Safer if two of us go,' said Piper. 'The other bee can find a snug hiding place somewhere around here, I'm sure – rob a few flowers for food, no problem.'

It was Fern who stayed.

Piper and Fescue arrived back at Middle Oak well before heatfall. They went directly to Lavender's home combs where they knew they would find at least some of their drone friends. In fact, all four were busy observing the Queen larva, now in its second day of feeding. What had drawn their attention was the fact that it was already moulting. It was growing so rapidly that it had to shed its present skin and expand into a new one, which had grown beneath it. The new skin was elastic for a while but soon hardened. The workers held back while the 'little wriggler' changed skins, so the drones were able to get a good look. It was only Fescue's voice that drew their attention away from the cell.

'Fescue!' exclaimed Coppice, 'and Piper! Where's Fern? What's happened?'

'Don't panic,' Fescue reassured him. 'Fern's fine and we think we've located the others.'

'That's great!' said Scruff. 'Where are they?'

'Some distance to the north-east of here.'

'Have you actually seen them?' asked Sorrell, guessing there was a complication.

'Ah, yer see, that's the catch. They're hidden away in one of six hives guarded by Blues,' explained Piper. 'Fern's staying close by while we round up a raiding party – about a hundred if possible.'

'Raiding party? A hundred?' queried Scruff.

'Yes, and we must get back there as soon as possible after heatrise tomorrow,' urged Coppice, 'because we've also discovered that a large party of Blues arrived at Six Hives earlier today.'

It took a while for Coppice and the others to grasp the situation. They were actually going to attempt a rescue which involved attacking the Blues! That was both encouraging and worrying. Only Scruff and Spurge had launched an attack on the Blues to date.

'What about the Queen larva?' asked Coppice.

'Lavender shouldn't need drone support until near emergence time,' Piper reminded him. 'Unless you'd like to stay, Coppice?'

'Hmm, I guess you're right, and I don't want to miss out on the rescue bid.'

'So let's get recruiting,' said Piper, 'but not from these two combs. Have yer volunteers meet in the drone zone first thing after heatrise. Good luck.'

They quickly realised they would have to rely on bees who had memories of the early season skirmishes with the raiding wasps. Bees who had emerged after that time showed little or no inclination to go out and fight anything, let alone Blues. At heatfall they met up to compare tallies.

'I've found about twenty,' said Coppice.

'Fifteen for me,' added Scruff.

Spurge thought he'd recruited ten, while Sorrell had reached twenty-five. The two scout bees were unable to help of course.

'That's about seventy,' reckoned Coppice. 'Not quite what we'd hoped for.'

'Let's see how many of them turn up in the morning,' mused Spurge.

Piper and Fescue were in the drone zone first, awaiting the arrival of the recruits. Sorrell and Scruff were doing a quick round up of those they had contacted the previous evening while Coppice and Spurge were checking out the little wriggler, now into its third day of guzzling. When all of them had congregated in the drone zone, Fescue could only count about fifty bees in total.

'I guess some of our volunteers had second thoughts,' said Scruff.

'Or they're not fully active yet,' suggested Coppice hopefully.

'We can't hang around,' Piper reminded them. 'We must fly out to Six Hives now.'

Without more ado, Piper led them off in a north-easterly direction, with a mixture of apprehension and excitement.

Fern was also out early, keeping a wary eye on all six hives. He didn't have to wait long for some action. Several Blues were gathering in the air around one of the hives. Their numbers grew steadily until there were at least a hundred of them. They then descended like a small blue cloud on the entrance of the hive and just hung there.

'Very odd,' thought Fern. 'What are they up to?'

He watched carefully as even more Blues joined in.

'I wonder, I just wonder if they might be collecting their prisoners?'

He flew in as close as he dare but couldn't be certain his four friends were in there. After quite some time he saw the blue cloud began to drift away from the hive and pick up speed.

'Dash it, they're leaving, and our reinforcements haven't arrived yet.'

Now he had a difficult decision. Did he wait for the others or follow the Blues? Being an accomplished scout he calculated the time it would take his friends to reach Six Hives. He then worked out how long he could track the Blues before having to return to meet up with Piper and company. Satisfied with his sums, Fern flew after the Blues, following at a safe distance of course.

The Blues escort party hadn't made an early start because they had to remove the wax walls from their captives' prison and allow them to stock up with honey after four days of rationing. Because of their full honey loads and their recent lack of exercise, the four captives were not able to fly very quickly at all. This had the effect of slowing down the escort party's progress. The Blues weren't too worried about that because they would soon be out of this somewhat troublesome region, and they had plenty of fighting Blues on the wing. Fern was pleased because their speed suggested they were indeed escorting prisoners.

Not very long after the Blues flew out, Piper and the reinforcements flew in. Fescue went off to try and locate Fern who tracked the Blues as long as he dared before turning back to Six Hives. He found Piper first and observed the recruits.

'Is this all?' he asked.

''Fraid so,' replied Piper. 'About fifty of us.'

'But they've over a hundred and—'

'Shh…you'll scare them off!'

'What's up?' asked Coppice, as Fescue joined them, nodding at Fern as he landed.

'We're outnumbered,' whispered Piper.

'Too bad. We'll have to manage with what we've got.'

Scruff and Sorrell nodded their agreement. Spurge was thinking, 'Here we go again, but I might as well join in!'

Fern said, 'Let's get on with it, shall we? I have their beeline. Piper and Fescue can scout ahead so that most of us can keep well back from the Blues.'

The bees from Middle Oak set off, continuing in a north-easterly direction as it happened. Piper and Fescue soon made eye contact with the Blues and so ensured the pursuit was on line.

'What happens now?' asked Fescue.

'Not sure. They'll have to stop for water at some time. We might get a chance then.'

'But there aren't enough of us, surely?'

'That doesn't mean we can't beat them, does it?'

There was no answer to that because Piper was much more experienced than Fescue, and so must know better! Piper, however, was just as stumped but he wasn't letting on. Something would turn up, if his experience was anything to go by, and when it did, the important thing was to take full advantage of it. What happened next was certainly unexpected.

One second Piper and Fescue were flying steadily along in pursuit, the next second they were surrounded by a mass of bees! Even Piper was rattled.

'What the…?'

'Don't panic,' ordered one of the interceptors, 'we're friendly. Tell your following party not to attack us.'

Piper and Fescue hesitated. Fescue was already considering making a break.

'Look! We're not blue, are we?' insisted their spokesbee.

Piper looked them over. They were quite normal in colour and they didn't actually look as though they wanted to fight. He nodded and turned to meet the Middle Oakers coming up behind them. The interceptors made room for him and Piper flew back the short distance to meet them and prevent any panic.

'What's up?' asked Fern.

'Not sure. We've got visitors – but they seem friendly.'

The Middle Oakers were puzzled. The interceptors' leader flew over and introduced himself.

'My name is Trefoil, from the Birch Cave hive. I'd like you to come back with me.'

'But we have to chase these Blues,' insisted Coppice. 'They have four of our friends and…'

A light turned on in Trefoil's eyes. Now he understood why a group of ordinary honeybees was being audacious enough to pursue a crowd of Blues.

'Don't worry,' he replied, 'my scouts are tracking them and they're not travelling very quickly, and now I can guess why. It will be much more sensible for you to come to Birch Cave and meet Madder. He's probably the only bee who can help you.'

'Madder?' What sort of a name's that?' asked Scruff.

There is plant called by that name,' answered the knowledgeable Fern. 'Yellowish flowers I believe – grows in rocky areas, like cliffs I think.'

'That's right,' added Fescue, 'I've seen it on the south coast.'

'Are you coming to Birch Cave or not?' asked Trefoil.

'Do we have a choice?' asked Coppice.

'Yes you do. We'll not stand in your way if you prefer to continue your pursuit, but you must realise you're outnumbered. You'd do better to accept our offer of help.'

Coppice looked to Fern, Piper and Fescue for advice. Piper, relying on his instinct and hoping he wasn't leading them into a trap, made the decision. 'Lead the way, Trefoil.'

Trefoil turned immediately and led them down to ground level. He had surprised Piper and Fern by dropping smartly down on them from out of the sun. Now he was taking an undercover approach to Birch Cave in order to preserve its secrecy. He had to be extra careful with so many bees to bring in. Coppice and company were intrigued by the devious route into the hive, which was accessed through tunnels amongst the rocks. They eventually reached a cleverly disguised entrance. After being accepted by the guards on Trefoil's orders, they entered the hive.

'You must feed first,' ordered Trefoil, 'and then send your leaders with Clover here. He'll bring you along to meet Madder.'

It was a coolish hive, the comb being built between the rocks. Piper was the only bee who didn't find it strange because his home hive, Stonewall, was amongst rocks where two stone walls met, leaving a useful space in the middle. Somebee, seasons ago, had found a way in and a swarm made good use of it not long afterwards.

When they had all taken their fill of honey, which tasted very good, the scout bees, along with Coppice, Sorrell, Scruff and Spurge reported to Clover. He led them to a distant comb where a group of bees was awaiting them. Trefoil was there, standing next to a rather powerful looking drone.

Trefoil stepped forward, 'Friends, meet Madder.'

Piper introduced his party. Coppice had gone very still and quiet.

'And this is Coppice...'

Madder's gaze stopped at Coppice, although Piper had moved on to Sorrell and Scruff.

'Something wrong?' enquired Piper.

Coppice was beginning to shake. Madder stepped closer. The two of them were now face to face and they were both trembling now. Piper had stopped his introductions. Trefoil and Clover looked equally puzzled.

'Twenty-two?' whispered Coppice.

'TWENTY-ONE!' shouted a delighted Madder.

19. A ROLLING AMBUSH

The two honeybees were uncontainable in their delight. Piper soon caught on and Fern wasn't far behind, but everyone else was baffled. When at last they simmered down, Coppice explained:

'This is my long lost friend from my first hive. I knew him then as Twenty-two.'

'And you were Twenty-one. Where have you been all this time?'

'But what about you? How did you survive?'

'I might ask you the same question but we haven't time right now – we must get after those Blues.'

'Oh yes, Briar and Teasel and…I'd almost forgotten. How can we rescue them?'

Madder turned to Trefoil and Clover and whispered something to them. Turning back to the others he suggested, 'If we bring about a hundred of our drones, I reckon we shall match their numbers.'

'Only match them?' interrupted Scruff. 'Surely we need to outnumber them – by at least two to one?'

'Three to one actually,' said Madder, 'and that's what I intend for the final attack.' His visitors looked truly puzzled as he announced, 'We shall use a rolling ambush!'

'What's one of those?' asked Spurge, wondering what he was in for now.

'The best way to find out is to take part. I assume you want to come along?' responded Madder.

'Yer bet we do,' said Piper. 'Let's get on with it!'

Madder dispatched Trefoil and Clover to round up a hundred or so of Birch Cave's experienced drones. He took Coppice and his party to the hive's outer entrance, or rather a little way around the corner from it so as not to give away any secrets. The recruits were quick to appear and the ambush party set off towards the beeline taken by the Blues. They hadn't been flying for long before a Birch Cave scout called Milfoil met up with them.

'They're holding the beeline and you're closing fast,' he reported. 'For some reason they're travelling at about two-thirds normal speed.'

'That's because they're escorting prisoners,' explained Madder. 'Fly ahead of us until you make visual contact again, then whiz back to bring us up into range.'

'Will do,' replied Milfoil, and he shot off.

Some minutes later he was back. Without speaking, he indicated that the ambush party should follow him as he dived down at full speed and led them a few degrees off course, close to the ground, winding through the trees wherever possible. Piper and Fern found this most intriguing. Coppice and Sorrell looked at each other in amazement. They flew like this for some time. Piper thought they might have edged back towards the Blues beeline but he wasn't quite certain. Suddenly they reached some caves, flew through a narrow entrance and landed in a crevice.

'What's this in aid of?' grumbled Spurge to Scruff.

'How should I know?'

'*Ssh*!' insisted Fescue. 'Patience!'

Madder turned to explain, 'This is our first ambush site. Trefoil will take a dozen drones to act as decoys while the rest of us wait here. Position yourselves above the entrance, in groups of three. Clover will fly out to spot their approach. When he returns you must stand by, ready to pounce. Each triplet will attack one enemy bee. Twenty of our party must block the entrance as soon as they're all through, so they can't fly back and warn their party. That's the key to this tactic – we have to take out the entire group of Blues which enters our ambush. Understood?'

'Yes,' replied Coppice, 'but I don't see how this rescues Briar and the others.'

'By repeating the exercise until their numbers are depleted enough for us to attack the main party, preferably on a three to one basis.'

'Brilliant!' exclaimed Piper. 'How did yer think that one up?'

'Necessity, is the simple answer. Now, Trefoil, select a dozen and go. Clover, follow on as usual.'

Coppice and friends could only admire Madder's control of the situation. The rolling ambush sounded as if it could work, but would it? Would the Blues fall for it?

Time to get into triplets. Madder insisted that his visitors mix in with his own bees. He took Coppice aside to be with him as he oversaw the operation. While they waited for Clover's signal, there was time to do some catching up.

'So how did you survive that terrible evening when we were thrown out of the hive?' asked Coppice.

Madder explained, 'You recall that Piper had told us how to find his hive, just in case anything happened to him?' Coppice nodded. 'Well, after I lost you and Twenty-three...by the way, any news of him?'

'Maybe, I'm not sure.'

'Meaning?'

'I'll explain later. Carry on with your story first.'

'OK, so I lost sight of you and Twenty-three and found myself pushed out of the tube into the open air, with hundreds of other drones buzzing around in ever decreasing circles, or so it seemed to me. I looked around frantically for you and Twenty-three but it was so chaotic and the light was fading. I didn't know what to do until I asked myself where on earth I could go. Then I remembered Piper's instructions, so I set off for the first landmark. I was successful and flew quickly on to the next one. As heatfall came I reached open fields divided up by stone walls. I spotted the likely site of Piper's hive and tried to fly in but the guards were still on duty and they attacked me! I didn't know then about having to be scented up before entering a strange hive!

'Anyway, I was horrified and buzzed around in the cool night air, my energy fading as the temperature fell. I had to get into that hive and the warmth of its cluster somehow. I decided to try again, determined to barge my way in if necessary. I approached cautiously at first and, to my surprise saw that the guards had gone. I still edged my way in carefully, in case they were lying in wait for me but they weren't. I was so relieved and settled quickly into the cluster, hoping I could escape early in the morning.

'At heatrise I was into the honey supplies and off to the entrance. The guards didn't challenge me but I left at some speed, just in case! I actually flew back

COPPICE

to our home hive. The pile of dead drones under the hive's entrance deterred me from any further investigation, and I flew off to check out the drone zone – not a soul around. Thoroughly depressed by then, I flew off in no particular direction. To cut a long story short, I eventually came across Birch Cave's drone zone where I was actually welcomed and recruited!'

'That must have been a pleasant surprise after our home drone zone.'

'Certainly was, but Birch cave was already having some bother from the Blues. Having had a little experience of them made me all the more acceptable. Winter soon arrived and then the new season, with me settled nicely in my new hive, helping more and more with defences against the Blues.'

'Amazing!' said Coppice. 'But you appear to be in charge of these defences – and offences?'

'Yes, that's probably down to my…'

At that moment Clover flew in. 'Stand by!' he shouted. 'Stand by!'

Everybee was ready. About ten seconds later the Birch Cave dozen flew in, followed two seconds later by a load of Blues. Immediately the Birch Cavers dropped on them. They were so quick and decisive that Coppice's bees were left lagging behind. The Blues found two opponents on each wing and a third cutting the wings off. Coppice almost felt sorry for them. In fact he did feel sorry for them – they never had a chance. Did they really deserve this?

Madder was flying around, overseeing the ambush. There were no hitches, no bee escaped. The last of about twenty Blues was de-winged and grounded. The ambushers congregated back on the crevice.

'Well done! Madder congratulated them. 'How about joining the next decoy, Coppice?' He could see that his old friend was upset and wanted to keep him busy. He moved close to him, 'I know it's easier to kill when you're defending your hive than it is when you go onto the offensive, but if you want your friends back…?'

Coppice nodded, 'OK. I'll do it.'

'Good, but first we must all move on some way so as to keep up with the Blues.'

Away they went, Clover and Trefoil out in front with Fescue, who assured them he would have no problem keeping up with them at their top speed. They tried him out and were suitably impressed.

Some time later they located their second ambush site and called in the rest of the party. Milfoil had gone down with them to a dense fir tree copse. He indicated the position of the Blues' beeline so that Trefoil, Clover, Coppice and a dozen drones, could take off for the intercept.

Coppice was happier to be doing something instead of just watching. As they flew, Trefoil explained the tactics.

'We fly in very close formation, coming at them from underneath as fast as possible. We fly very close to the leading edge of the Blues and immediately dive down towards the ambush site. They won't be able to resist sending an attack party after us, hopefully about twenty to twenty-five bees – they like to outnumber their opponents!'

'Don't we all?' thought Coppice.

'Ready? There they are! Tight formation – go!'

The interceptors shot up towards the Blues, clipped their leading edge – Trefoil actually touched one of them – and dived down again. It was very daring and Coppice felt quite exhilarated, but his attention was quickly focused on the business of keeping the tight formation with the other interceptors and reaching the ambush ahead of the Blues. Clover flew in to warn the ambushers and the interceptors shot into the fir tree copse shortly afterwards. About twenty-five Blues were caught this time – another massacre. It was sickening. How long would the Blues keep falling for this?

As if guessing his thoughts, Madder told Coppice there would be one more ambush site, but this time with a double intercept – a bit trickier as two groups of Blues would arrive in quick succession. Away they flew.

High up above them, Bugle was scanning the sky for his second chasing party. The first one still hadn't returned and he'd let a second one go as well. He was just a little bit disturbed, but then no bee had ever challenged them seriously in this particular region, or any other region for that matter. The chasing parties were probably making sure of their prey and raiding somebee's honeystore as a reward. His confidence was more or less restored when two groups of bees hit his party simultaneously, one on each side!

Automatically the Blues gave chase, as they were trained to do, but Bugle watched them depart with some anxiety. Something wasn't right. He wasn't used to dealing with extraordinary events. He had always called the tune as the Blues' plan steadily unfolded. His master, the mighty Yarrow, had predicted most accurately how their campaign would develop. Success was assured.

With much effort he came to the conclusion that he couldn't afford to let his party fall any lower in number. A brief scan suggested it was now only half its original strength. There must be no more pursuits until some of his chasers returned. He issued the relevant order and hoped that his drones could cope with it.

Far below, the rolling ambush continued as the latest Blue pursuit groups were taken out.

'At this rate there soon won't be any Blues left,' exclaimed a triumphant Scruff.

'They'll guess what's happening sooner or later,' said Madder. 'Perhaps they already have. However, that's not our problem. We have to make a direct attack next because we're getting too far away from our home territory and can't rely on finding a friendly hive to stay in, especially if there are blue scouts in every hive.'

'What do yer reckon the odds are?' asked Piper.

'I think we've reduced them to two against one.'

'Is that enough?' queried Coppice.

'It'll have to be.'

Madder consulted briefly with Trefoil, Clover and Milfoil, who had just flown in. The others waited expectantly.

'Right,' announced Madder, 'this is how we'll do it. Coppice; you and your bees, plus Milfoil, will concentrate on locating and freeing your four friends. As soon as you've separated them from the Blues, you'll set off back to Birch Cave with Milfoil as your guide. Don't hang around waiting for the rest of us. We shall take out as many of the Blues as possible though I doubt whether we can remove the whole party. When I judge we've done enough damage, we'll break off the engagement and return home – with some detours if time allows. Is that clear?'

There was no dissension so Milfoil took them up and away in their final pursuit. They flew higher and higher until they were well above the Blues' beeline. Milfoil then shot off to locate the enemy. He was soon back, and then Madder took his party into a position such that they would drop onto the Blues from out of the sun. That should give them the initial advantage. The Middle Oakers sensed the increasing tension as they prepared for this last stage in the remarkable rolling ambush. Up until now they had kept full control of their attacks, but this time they would be fighting in the open air. Anything could happen.

'Stand by,' shouted Madder. 'Close formation. *Dive!*'

They zoomed down, out of the sun, onto the unsuspecting Blues who were so shocked that they were paralysed for a few seconds. That gave the ambushers the advantage they needed in order to knock out several Blues and locate the captives. Bugle then gathered his wits and screamed for action – which he got. The Blues were fighting for their lives and they weren't going to give in easily. Bees were zooming and tumbling around all over the place, many in groups of two or three, dropping down to earth as the attackers hung onto Blues and attempted to de-wing them. The odds of two to one weren't quite enough and there were some spare Blues shooting around, making life difficult. Coppice and Sorrell were the first to locate Briar and the others who were too shocked to react at first.

'Come on!' yelled Coppice, 'follow us!'

Fescue and Piper helped usher them away in the right direction, Milfoil leading the way. Behind them, the battle continued. Birch Cavers who had successfully debilitated their enemies flew back up to help those who were struggling. Bugle was taking stock of the situation. He grabbed the nearest two Blues.

'Follow me!' he snapped. They hesitated to leave the battle. 'Now!' he ordered, and he took them clear of the fighting. 'Names?'

'Crowfoot, Master Bugle,'

'Figwort, Master Bu—'

'Now listen very carefully. You two are to fly to The Glade immediately, with as short a stopover as possible. You will report to Master Yarrow that we've been attacked by hordes of bees and been robbed of our prisoners.'

'Er, hordes, Master Bugle?' queried Figwort.

COPPICE

'Yes, hordes!' insisted Bugle. 'I trust you have that quite clear! When I next see our master I shall check the accuracy of your report – understood?'

'Understood, Master Bugle,' replied Crowfoot.

'Right, now get out of here!'

The pair zoomed off, glad but surprised to be out of the battle. Bugle flew around the area, observing from a safe distance. No sign of his captives. He now realised that his party had been deliberately reduced in number before the final attack came. There had been a clever plan to rescue the four prisoners, but by whom? This could be serious. Then he became angry as he realised he'd been outwitted. They'd made a fool of him – Bugle, the great field commander!

Madder judged it was time to break off the engagement. Milfoil and company were would be well clear by now and he didn't want any more casualties. He zoomed around issuing instructions and the Birch Cavers were away, heading into the sun initially. Bugle spotted their manoeuvre and watched for the descent that followed, it was designed to collect any stragglers before heading home.

'And where is "home"?' thought Bugle. 'I must find out. I must have something to tell Yarrow.'

His remaining Blues were hovering around aimlessly. None of them showed any inclination to pursue the departing bees. Bugle rounded them up. He counted only nineteen of them! Some defeat! He could never tell Yarrow what really happened here – it would be more than his life was worth.

'We shall follow at a safe distance,' he ordered his remnant. 'If you can't keep up, I'm not waiting for you. Now follow me.'

Well out of Bugle's reach, Milfoil, Coppice and company were soon closing on Birch Cave. It had been a long day and they were hungry. Briar, Teasel, Thyme and Bryony saved their stories until they entered Birch Cave hive. They were well into their account when Madder arrived back with his bees. He had lost eleven of his party, some of them Middle Oakers.

'I'm so sorry we've lost that many,' said Coppice.

'Look at the wider picture,' suggested Fern. 'There's what amounts to an invasion by these Blues, and they don't tolerate anybee who gets in their way.'

'Remember, they've almost certainly killed Dock,' Piper reminded him.

'Dock – dead?' asked Trefoil.

'We think so,' said Piper. 'Did you know him?'

'Of course, we're in his area – just. He's visited our drone zone a few times and passed on useful advice about the Blues. He seemed to know quite a lot about them.'

'Too much,' muttered Fern.

'Pardon?'

'I guess he knew more than most. He was on his way to meet us at the beginning of the season when he went missing.'

No bee felt like adding to that and the whole group fell silent. Shortly they crept into the cluster for the night, hoping for a more peaceful day to come.

Bugle had only half a dozen of his company left with him by the time his pursuit came to an end. He saw his quarry fly into some caves and followed them in very cautiously. But he lost them.

'They're in here somewhere,' he grumbled to no bee in particular. 'Search in pairs and meet me back here, only quickly – it's nearly heatfall.'

They did so without any success, after which Bugle decided to fly to Six Hives for the night and return in the morning for a closer look.

COPPICE

20. SWARM FORCE ONE

In Birch Cave at heatrise there was a sense of achievement after the previous day's successful rolling ambush. Madder's tactics had worked again. It was his ideas that had eventually put him in charge of the resistance, although he was the first to admit that Trefoil, Clover and Milfoil were most capable assistants. The hive's Council had been very supportive and even suggested the careful concealment of the hive's entrance.

'You must stay for a guided tour,' Madder urged his guests.

'Certainly,' replied Coppice.

'What about the Queen rearing back at Middle Oak?' Sorrell reminded him.

'Hmm. How far on will they be now?' wondered Coppice.

Sorrell thought about it for a few moments, then said, 'By my reckoning they'll be on the fourth day of feeding the larva, which is the seventh day since the egg was laid, which means nine days to go before the Queen emerges.'

Coppice was impressed, 'Very good – I'll take your word for it.'

'Thank you.'

'May I ask what you're on about?' said Madder.

Coppice hadn't told Madder about his problems with the Middle Oak Council and their apparent change of mind over swarming. He did so now, and then explained about Lavender's secret Queen rearing in order to force a swarm.

Madder's eyes nearly popped out of his head. 'Incredible! I'd never have thought of that.'

'And I'd never have dreamed up the idea of a rolling ambush.'

'Oh I don't know. When you put your mind to it, you can usually come up with an answer.'

Piper, Fern and Fescue arrived at that point and learned of Madder's invitation.

'That's very kind of yer, but we must get back to our scouting duties,' explained

Piper, 'and we need to check out the Queen rearing, I think.'

It was agreed that the scouts would take Briar, Teasel, Thyme and Bryony back to Middle Oak while Coppice, Sorrell, Scruff and Spurge stayed on at Birch Cave for the day.

'Right then,' announced Coppice, 'that's fixed. Tell Lavender we'll be back in time to see the little wriggler pupate tomorrow, I think?' He turned to Sorrell for confirmation.

'Pupation late tomorrow or the day after.'

'Thank you.'

Crowfoot and Figwort had made their stopover in a hive controlled by Blues, and set off again promptly after heatrise. They reached The Glade close to sunpeak. It was an eerie place – as dark as the dark blue colouring of its occupants. Being located in a vast forest of evergreens, it was impossible to find without knowing the precise landmarks.

Knowing they had an important message for Yarrow, the two messengers zoomed straight up to the master hive – The Glade being a collection of hives, all linked together.

'Halt!' called the multiple guard in unison.

'We've an urgent message for Master Yarrow!' blurted Figwort, without being asked. 'We've been sent by Bugle, the commander of the infiltration forces and—'

'Enough!' demanded a voice from behind the guards. 'Let them in.'

Kale was captain of the guard in Yarrow's hive. He was an extremely well-groomed drone, not a hair out of place. His body was sleek and it almost glistened with energy. His job was to vet all visitors – by clever questioning if necessary. The mention of Bugle's name by these unexpected and somewhat anxious messengers told him something wasn't quite right. He didn't want any bad news spilling out to the local population if that was possible.

'Follow me!' he ordered, and he led the now even more worried Crowfoot and Figwort to a waiting chamber and turned to face them. 'Now tell me your message and I will pass it on to our Master.'

Crowfoot turned to Figwort, who hesitated before saying, 'Um, we, er, that is to say, Bugle told us to report to Master Yarrow and...'

Immediately Kale lunged and struck him hard in the right eye! Figwort reeled back, terrified.

'Who do you think you are?' roared Kale, smoothing down the hairs on his right foreleg. 'Do you think anybee can just crawl in here and chat to the mighty Yarrow! Now tell me what the message is or I'll attend to your other eye!'

'W-w-we were bringing some captive bees back for interrogation when we were attacked by hundreds, no, *thousands* of bees. We – er, *Bugle* – led us in terrific battle, but there were too many of them. We were hopelessly outnumbered. Realising we couldn't hold the prisoners, Bugle selected the two of us to carry a message back to Master Yarrow.'

'How many captives?'

'Er, pardon sir?'

'How many captured bees were you escorting?'

'Oh, um, four.'

'Just four?'

Figwort nodded. Crowfoot did the same. Kale looked angry, but inside he was puzzled. He didn't believe this story. He knew about the reinforcements recently sent in response to Bugle's request, but why did he want so many to bring in only four prisoners? Now he appeared to have failed in that simple task? Yet up until now Bugle had done an excellent job, unless he'd been fooling them all the time? No, that wasn't possible. Yarrow had his spies who checked up on these things.

'Wait here,' he ordered Figwort and Crowfoot.

Kale walked off deeper into the hive. He eventually entered a peculiar wax passage, which led to Yarrow's private chamber. There were four guards at the entrance and several attendants inside. Kale wasn't challenged as he walked into the sumptuous chamber. It had strange etchings on the walls and a large collection of honeypots, containing a variety of foods – not all honey and pollen. Yarrow was peering at one of his wall etchings. He was a magnificent, dark blue drone. His body glistened even more than Kale's.

Without turning round he asked, 'And what can I do for you, Captain Kale?'

'Master, I need to talk to you in private.'

Now Yarrow did turn around and he peered at Kale. 'Do you mean what you just said?'

Kale held his gaze, so Yarrow knew he did mean it.

'Leave us!' he ordered his attendants, and they scurried past the guards into an adjoining room. 'Now, tell me what's happened.'

Kale related the message and commented on the attitude of the two messengers.

Yarrow pondered the matter for a time then said, 'You've acted wisely Kale, as usual. Kindly "dispose" of the messengers, would you? We don't want their story spread around The Glade, do we? However accurate or inaccurate it may be!'

Kale nodded and departed to deal with the hapless Figwort and Crowfoot. Bugle had known very well, when he had chosen them, that they wouldn't survive, but there was no way he was going back with that sort of news.

Back in his chamber, Yarrow was mulling over his course of action. Ambling over to the chamber entrance, he ordered his guards to make sure he was undisturbed until further notice. He then went over to the far side of his splendid accommodation and began tracing over the etched pattern on the chamber wall. Locating the two key marks with his two front legs, he pushed firmly against the wall until the secret panel opened up. Yarrow crawled through and entered the gently glowing passage behind it. He crawled deeper and deeper into the depths of The Glade. Only two bees, as far as he knew, were aware of the secret passage and the chamber to which it led.

He arrived at the chamber and entered a sort of anteroom. There was a thin wax wall separating this anteroom from the chamber proper. Yarrow had never been into the actual chamber. Apparently there was no way through the thin wax wall. He could however, with the help of the glow in the wax, just make out the shape of a honeybee on the other side of the thin wall. That was as close as he ever came to the 'Overlord'.

Yarrow had been specially chosen by the Overlord for his present task. The Overlord had great knowledge, which enabled Yarrow to direct the takeover of surrounding regions, using the strain of blue bees of which he was the leader.

Three seasons ago Yarrow had come to The Glade – he would say he had been 'led' there – and taken part in a mating flight with the Queen bee of the hive. Many of the drone bees produced thereafter were of the strange, blue-tinged colouring. These bees had taken over the hive and had it extended to immense proportions. Yarrow discovered the remains of an ancient hive nearby, in which he discovered the glowing passage and secret chamber. He had The Glade extended further so that his personal chamber backed onto the secret passage. The first time he visited the secret chamber he was addressed by the Overlord, who seemed to have been waiting for him. It was his destiny, Yarrow believed. He was indeed chosen to lead a new, stronger, more powerful strain of honeybee, which would take over the land and ensure the future of his kind.

Yarrow crouched down, facing the thin, glowing, wax wall. He did not speak – he waited in silence. After some time a shadow appeared on the other side of the wall. The Overlord had come – as he always did. Yarrow looked up.

'Share your request if you will, my chosen one.'

'I have received a report from my captain, who is one and a half to two day ranges to the south-west. I am not convinced of its accuracy, but he does seem to have encountered serious opposition.'

The Overlord asked him what he knew of the area. Yarrow passed on all the information he had, after which the Overlord fell into silence for some time – longer than usual, Yarrow thought.

At last he spoke, 'This opposition proves you are succeeding, my chosen one. You are nearing a most important hive, one which contains a Queen who must be taken alive and brought to The Glade. She is to take over from our present Queen, and she will produce the perfect blue honeybee as long as you, my chosen one, are the only drone taking part in the mating flight.'

He paused there, so that Yarrow could take it all in. This was, after all, the revelation of the most crucial part of the plan. The Overlord had at first thought that Six Hives might hold the Queen he was looking for, but it didn't. Now he sensed he wasn't far away from finding the correct hive.

He continued, 'There are two things you must do now. Firstly you must personally take Swarm Force One to the area and crush all opposition – fly today and you'll be there by heatfall tomorrow. Six Hives will suffice as your base.

Secondly, you must investigate all the hives you can find in the area beyond the trouble spot, up to a distance of one day range, including aberrant hives. I believe you will find what we're looking for.'

The Overlord then told Yarrow how he thought the right Queen might be recognised. Yarrow was overawed and excited. At last he could fly out with his drones. At last he would be in the centre of the action. Soon the great plan would come to fruition. He had been patient in the early stages while his Blues had gradually taken control of all the hives within a day range. Next they stretched their control towards the two day range. Now it seemed that Bugle's little problem had indicated the direction in which they should concentrate. This would be the very first swarm force to go out from The Glade – in fact it was most likely the first swarm force in bee history!

Yarrow lowered his head, 'I understand and readily obey. I will return with the Queen you are looking for.'

On the opposite side of the thin, glowing wall, the shadow moved. The Overlord had departed. Yarrow turned and headed back towards his chamber. He accelerated as he thought about leading out his swarm force!

Bugle had returned at heatrise that day to continue his investigation of the caves into which those annoying honeybees had disappeared the previous day. He had about twenty Blues with him. They had been flying around in pairs, checking out every passage they came across and watching for any foragers returning to the hive with honey and pollen. There had to be a route in somewhere!

The search proved fruitless, but tracking incoming bees was more successful. For some time every forager they followed seemed to know they were there and just led them around in circles. Bugle was annoyed but impressed. There was a hive here somewhere and these bees were protecting it very carefully. However, he reckoned somebee would get careless sooner or later.

He was right. Shortly after sunpeak one of the younger foragers zoomed in rather too quickly, excited with her news of a new nectar source. She was already performing the figure of eight dance in her mind and failed to notice she was being tracked. Sadly, she led a pair of Blues, albeit by a devious route, right to the main entrance of the Birch Cave hive.

COPPICE 1

The happy pair marked a spot near the entrance and flew off to tell Bugle, who would surely reward them. In their eagerness they failed to learn the route thoroughly enough and were very embarrassed when they could only re-trace the first half of it with Bugle and the rest of the squad! A seething Bugle put his Blues to search the area but it took them until early evening to find the mark left by the pair. After that they carefully marked the whole route.

The increased presence of Blues was reported to Madder who sent his scouts out to investigate. He wondered what they were up to.

Next morning the Birch Cavers waited for something to happen – but nothing did. Coppice, Sorrell, Scruff and Spurge decided to stay on for another day, in case there was trouble. It was early evening when Milfoil arrived with an urgent message.

'Madder, there's swarm approaching!'

'And?'

'And it's travelling too fast for a normal swarm.'

'Anything else?'

'We think…we think it's a swarm of Blues!'

Madder stared at him while the implications sunk in. 'A swarm of Blues heading this way?'

'That's what it looks like.'

Madder went into action mode. 'Right, let's get out there smartish and check it out. Clover, you make the initial preparations for the hive's defence – show Scruff and Spurge what you're doing. Coppice and Sorrell, join Trefoil and I if you will.'

Milfoil led them out of Birch Cave and away to the north-east. After just a few minutes he took them up into the sun and turned them around.

'Coming up behind us and below us,' indicated Milfoil.

They all peered downwards. There it was – a swarm flying in a beeline in the direction of Birch Cave.

'How many?' asked Coppice.

'I can't be too accurate on that without making a pass,' replied Madder.

'Oh,' said Coppice, wondering just how close they would have to fly to so many Blues. Swarms weren't usually interested in what was going on around them – but this one might be different!

'Here's what we'll do,' explained Madder. 'We all tuck in behind Milfoil and Trefoil and grab a close look as we fly past. The next thing you'll know is that we're undercover and winding our way back home. No second chances on this one!'

The scouting party closed formation, lined themselves up, and dived. They zoomed past the rear end of the swarm to lessen the risk of detection. Such was their speed that anybee who did happen to be looking behind would have had doubts as to what exactly had flown past. The close formation made them look like a large insect.

Once they reached the safety of a sitka spruce near Birch Cave, they shared impressions.

'Definitely Blues,' said Sorrell.

'About ten thousand,' added Madder.

'Not such a big swarm then,' Coppice pointed out.

'Big enough to be a whole bundle of trouble,' said Madder.

'Were they all drones?' asked Trefoil.

'Couldn't tell for sure,' replied Madder, 'but if they are, it's the first swarm of its kind, to my knowledge, so we must be prepared for the worst. Milfoil, keep us informed. The rest of us will go and help Clover with the defences.'

Milfoil and his regular scouts watched the incoming bees very closely. The first thing they noticed was that the swarm did not lose height as it approached. The next thing they realised, was that the Blues were not quite on line for Birch Cave. When he was certain they were going to fly over, Milfoil sent a message to Madder. He then tracked the swarm, knowing it couldn't have far to go at that time of the day. He wasn't surprised to see it descend onto Six Hives. Milfoil and his scouts watched in amazement as ten thousand bees – all drones as far as they could tell – distributed themselves efficiently amongst the six hives.

There was much relief in Birch Cave when Milfoil reported in. Madder, though, was troubled by the whole scenario.

'Look!' he said sternly, what have we got here? We rescue four bees, knocking out their large escort party in the process. The very next day there are Blues

COPPICE

hanging around Birch Cave from heatrise to heatfall almost. The following day we have a swarm of ten thousand Blues, landing a few fields away in hives which are obviously acting as a base. Now don't tell me all that doesn't add up to big trouble!' He brought everybee back to earth.

'You're right,' agreed Coppice. 'These events may very well be linked.'

'And even if they aren't,' added Sorrell, 'we should be ready to defend ourselves in case they choose to come our way.'

'They'll come – I'm sure of that,' said Madder. 'What I'm not sure of, is their main objective.' He turned to Coppice and his associates. 'You may prefer to get back to Middle Oak while you can – first thing after heatrise?'

'That's not fair on you,' responded Coppice. 'We got you into this fix.'

'But the Blues were already here, don't forget, and we've given them some stick ourselves. It was probably only a matter of time before they hit back.'

'Hmm,' muttered Coppice. 'We stay!'

'Thanks – see you at heatrise. I think Clover has completed his preparations. I just hope we don't need to use all of them.'

Soon after heatrise everything changed! A few workers had time to leave in search of nectar and pollen but that was all, apart from the early morning scout bee who was sadly taken by surprise. A mass of Blues filled the area leading up to Birch Cave. No bee could get past them, in either direction. Yarrow had sent Bugle in with the whole of Swarm Force One. The leading Blues flew directly into the hive's entrance, meeting the guards head on and knocking them over. The hive's inhabitants had barely realised what was happening before the first attackers broke through into the hive. Madder and Trefoil shot over to the entrance, shouting for back up as they went.

'Quick!' yelled Madder. 'Quick as you can! Form a wedge and drive into the entrance – never mind the Blues who are already inside.!'

Under his command the Birch Cavers sprang into action. Coppice, Sorrell, Scruff and Spurge arrived on the scene to see Madder already directing the defences. They also saw, to their dismay, that some Blues were inside the hive.

'Let's sort them out!' shouted Coppice, leading his friends into the melee.

The dozen or so Blues inside the hive were trying to interfere with the wedge as it tried to secure the entrance. Spurge piled in first and yanked out the nearest Blue. Scruff joined in. Sorrell encouraged some Birch Cavers to help out, while Coppice went to help Madder and Trefoil.

'Harder, harder!' yelled Madder. 'Push harder! Ram the entrance. We must push them back!'

Because there was more space inside the hive entrance than just outside, the Birch Cavers were able to get more bees into their wedge than the Blues could put against it. The defenders were slowly succeeding.

'Just a bit further,' Madder urged them. 'That's it, that's it! Well done! Now keep plenty of bees on hand to support the back of the wedge, Trefoil. I'll go and see what's happened to the Blues who did get inside.'

He turned to find Coppice close by.

'Spurge and the others are tackling the intruders already,' Coppice told him.

'Great! But I'm afraid they'll have to be stung – not much point in clipping their wings inside the hive, they'll just crawl into the fight and carry on, I'm sure they'll fight to the death.'

A number of worker bees turned their attention to the task and soon there were no Blues moving around inside Birch Cave hive. Outside was a different matter. The problem was that Madder couldn't see what the Blues were doing. He watched the wedge very carefully. It was holding, but he called in more reinforcements just in case, then he called Trefoil to bring Clover and Milfoil over. Coppice and companions were also invited.

Madder began. 'Right, we're holding them OK. Now we have to discover their ultimate intention and whether can they possibly succeed. Clover, you can start the arrangements for withdrawal to Little Birch. Milfoil, take your best scouts and depart through the Little Birch entrance. Fly round to the main caves and try and estimate the enemy's strength – but be very careful! Trefoil, you remain here in charge of the wedge. Any questions? Right, go to it!'

'What shall we do?' asked Coppice, quietly admiring Madder's command of the situation.

'Thanks – you've done a good job already. Hang around if you wish, or escape to Little Birch if you prefer.'

'Certainly not! We got you into this, we're not deserting now.'

'Thanks again, but like I said before, they'd have come after us sooner or later.'

The situation seemed to stabilise for a time. On the other side of the entrance Bugle was furious that his rush entry had been foiled. 'Very well,' he thought to himself, 'we can do it the hard way as well!' So he ordered his bees to attack the front row of the Birch Cave wedge and drag them out. This they did but because of the lack of space they could only remove four or five defenders at a time. They passed them back and then moved them right out of the way, before clipping their wings and dumping them outside the cave. Bugle sat back to watch.

Watching outside, hidden in the undergrowth, were Milfoil and his scouts. They had half flown, half crawled through the foliage to get near enough to see what was happening. They had been unable to fly in the open air anywhere near the cave because of the large numbers of Blues milling around. Sadly they observed the dumping of Birch Cave defenders onto the ground just beyond them. Milfoil was horrified. He left two scouts in place, carefully hidden, and took the others back to Little Birch's secret entrance. They flew three diversions before entering the hive, just in case anybee had spotted them.

Milfoil reported to Madder who had noticed that the wedge was moving well into the entrance. Trefoil was adding more bees on the inside. He wasn't sure if the wedge's progress was a good sign or not. Milfoil answered that one.

'They must be continually taking our bees from the front of the wedge, Madder,' explained Milfoil. 'I'm sure they have the numbers to stay at it as well.'

'That swarm we saw last evening. How many thousands did we say?'

'About ten thousand.'

'And how many of us are there in Birch Cave do you reckon?'

'About twenty-five thousand?' suggested Milfoil.

'Maybe, but not all fighters. Did you spot any enemy worker bees out there?'

Milfoil thought for a moment, 'No, I don't believe we did.'

Madder was very troubled. He looked at the wedge, then at Milfoil. 'I wonder how long we can hold the entrance?'

'For a long time, maybe all day,' suggested Milfoil. 'Let me go and ask

Trefoil.'

He did so, and came back with a less optimistic answer. Madder wasn't sure what to do, but didn't say as much. He said to Milfoil, 'Have Trefoil put somebee else in charge and come over here.'

So Madder gathered his two experts, along with Coppice and friends, to help him decide what they should do. He outlined the position and then went quiet. They all did for a time.

It was Sorrell who spoke first. 'I don't believe this hive can survive, now that those Blues have found it. You have to withdraw.'

'I agree,' said Madder, 'but there are two ways of doing that.'

'Wouldn't we just leave through the Little Birch entrance?' queried Coppice.

'Certainly we could, but what about Little Birch itself?'

'We should try to save it,' said Trefoil.

'I agree,' added Milfoil.

'How?' asked Coppice.

Madder explained, 'We already have a way of blocking Little Birch off from Birch Cave. The passage can be filled in with bits of rock, which then has soil packed up against it on the Little Birch side. The idea is that a number of our bees retreat into the smaller hive, then block the passage such that no bee would suspect it had ever been there.'

'Sounds good to me,' said Coppice.

'There's one catch to this plan,' added Madder. 'We can't take our Queen into Little Birch.'

'Why not?' demanded Trefoil.

'Because if the Blues do capture Birch Cave, they'll expect to find a Queen inside. If they can't find her they may well suspect we had an escape route and start searching for it. If they look hard enough they might find our filled in passage.'

'Hmm,' muttered Coppice. Madder was very smart, and the implications of what he said were daunting.

'So how does our escape group survive without a Queen?' asked Milfoil.

'I don't know for sure,' replied Madder, 'but I think we could survive if we had the right worker bees and some eggs.'

'Eggs!' exclaimed Coppice. 'Eggs, yes. Now wait a moment.' Sorrell caught on, followed by Scruff and, eventually, Spurge.

Coppice continued, 'Queen rearing! That's what we're doing at Middle Oak.'

Madder looked at him. Coppice had already told him about Lavender's brilliant scheme but only now did Madder see that the Birch Cavers could do the same.

'Let's do it!' declared Madder. 'Trefoil, back to the wedge. Keep it going as long as possible. Milfoil, withdraw your scouts – no point in risking showing the Blues there might be another way out of the hive. I'll go and tell Clover exactly what we're going to do. Coppice, could your team help us move out sufficient eggs, and even get the Queen rearing underway, please? Any questions? No? Good – let's get moving.'

For the next few hours they worked feverishly. Clover completed the preparations for blocking off the connecting passage, while large quantities of pollen and honey were moved into Little Birch, followed by the precious eggs and nurse bees. In all they transferred about two thousand bees to the smaller hive, without the knowledge of the Council, who stayed close to the Queen as she continued laying eggs, despite the crisis. Trefoil stuck to his demoralising task of feeding bees into the wedge as fast as the Blues were removing them on the other side. Hundreds of bees were lost. It was an appalling waste. Trefoil would never forget it as long as he lived.

Bugle was so confident of his eventual success that he took time out to make the short trip back to Six hives to report to Yarrow. A robust looking Blue, by the name of Scabious, was left in charge. Bugle explained to Yarrow what Swarm Force One was doing, and that he expected completion of the task by heatfall. Yarrow asked to be present when the final entry was made.

Not long after sunpeak, Madder was ready to begin plugging the passage between Birch Cave and Little Birch. That posed a problem however. He didn't want to leave Trefoil behind, but then who would oversee the wedge in his place? Somebee had to do it, otherwise the Blues could break in before the passage was properly blocked.

'Coppice,' he said, 'I think I've made a stupid mistake. Trefoil is ensuring the wedge works, but I can't leave him behind, can I?'

'Hmm, I see what you mean.'

'I must do it.'

'What?'

Madder set off towards the wedge. Coppice shot after him and pulled him back. 'No, no, you mustn't! They need you in Little Birch!'

'Clover will manage there, and you can help him. I must stay here.'

'*No!*' A scuffle broke out between the two bees.

'Hey! What's going on?' called Sorrell, returning from his last egg carrying trip. 'Break it up!'

He only succeeded when Spurge arrived on the scene to help him.

'What's all this about? Isn't there enough fighting without your own private scrap?' demanded Spurge.

Coppice explained the problem. The others saw the difficulty. 'I'm sure we're doing the right thing,' said Coppice, 'so there must be an answer to this. There must be somebee who can do the job – or a group of bees, perhaps?'

'Yes!' said Sorrell. 'A group of bees – the Council!'

Madder looked at him.

'If we tell them what to do, and how essential it is, they would probably see to it – or least some of them would. We can say that Trefoil has to go off and do another important job.'

'Very good, we'll try it,' agreed Madder. 'You go and warn Trefoil he might be due for a break. I'll go and see the Council.'

It worked. Two of the Council came over to the wedge. They listened to Trefoil, then took over from him. He retreated to the passage with Madder and the others. They scurried through, except for Madder, who turned and gave his adopted hive one last look. He had no doubt it would fall to the Blues. With much remorse he walked through the passage into Little Birch, nodding to Clover as he passed him. Then he went off to a quiet spot to be alone for a time. What they had done may have been the means of survival for some, but it also felt too much like running away.

Clover began the skilful job of blocking the passage. The first stage was especially important, as the rocks they put in first had to look natural. After the first two or three bee-lengths, he and his team rammed in a single piece of rock,

COPPICE

carefully chosen for the task last season when they first thought up the whole idea. Smaller pieces were used to wedge the big one in place, then they started packing in the soil, ramming it in with their heads. This continued for about ten bee-lengths. That put a total of about fifteen bee-lengths between them and Birch Cave.

In the main hive the wedge began to falter. The two Council members were not as efficient as Trefoil had been, and they allowed the bees to pack too loosely. On the other side, Bugle detected this weakening and sent for Yarrow. By the time he arrived, victory was in sight. The wedge became too weak and at last collapsed. The Blues rushed through in numbers and established their position just inside the hive. The remaining Birch Cavers fled from them. Bugle crawled through and took stock of the situation. He turned to call to Yarrow.

'Swarm Force One has accomplished its first task, Master Yarrow.'

A delighted Yarrow entered Birch Cave hive and surveyed the scene before him.

'Congratulations, Captain Bugle, you've done well. Let me know when you've found the Queen – alive, please. And check the place for escape routes, just in case.'

Bugle, humiliated by the loss of his four prisoners a few days back, was about to take his revenge in full. 'Right!' he ordered. 'We're not taking over this hive – it's too close to the six we've already got in this area, so you can clear them all out. Just bring me the Queen alive!'

It didn't take long. Bugle showed the Queen to Yarrow who looked her over carefully, seemed disappointed, and ordered her execution. Bugle then gave the hive a quick check for escape routes and left. He was looking forward to working with Storm Force One again.

21. ONE FORCED SWARM

At heatrise the survivors in Little Birch were wandering around aimlessly inside the tiny hive. Their leaders were still badly shaken after the terrible events of the previous day. Their thoughts were for the thousands of honeybees left behind, most of them dead. The big question now, was whether the Blues had occupied Birch Cave hive or not. If they had, they would probably discover the concealed link to Little Birch sooner or later.

Madder eventually called the leaders together. He seemed weary and burdened but he knew he had to get things moving.

'I suggest there should be no foraging flights at all today. First we have to find out whether the Blues have occupied Birch Cave or not. Milfoil, I'll leave you to answer that. Please be careful and take your time.' Milfoil nodded and Madder continued, 'The other thing we can get on with is our Queen rearing.' He looked towards Coppice, 'Any ideas?'

Coppice thought for a moment then said, 'Some of us must return to Middle Oak and ask Lavender's advice. Couldn't you come and talk to her, Madder? You could leave Trefoil or Clover in charge here.'

'Couldn't Lavender come here?' asked Trefoil.

'I doubt that,' said Sorrell. 'As comb controller she must stay in the hive. Her absence would raise suspicion and be investigated.'

'True enough,' agreed Coppice.

'No problem,' decided Madder. 'Trefoil and I will come with you as soon as we're sure it's safe to do so. Clover will be in charge in our absence.'

So it was agreed and they settled down to wait patiently while their scout bees cautiously investigated Birch Cave.

Milfoil was using ground search methods again. His team crawled or flew in little hops, using plants as cover. They soon came across bodies of worker bees littering the ground. At the cave entrance they had to adopt riskier tactics. The fastest flier entered alone, covering a short distance only. When he remained unchallenged, the next scout flew forwards to join him. When the first scout set off on his next short hop, a third scout moved up to join the second, and so on. By the time they had done this six times, the actual hive entrance was in view, as were the bodies of more dead workers. Not a single bee had flown past them from the hive so they feared the worst. However, there might still be some Blues lying in wait for them.

The lead scout went back down the line to fetch Milfoil and the two of them flew right up to the hive entrance. Milfoil edged forward. He listened very carefully – not a sound. He sensed the temperature – not warm enough to indicate active bees. He beckoned his lead scout to stay back, just in case. Milfoil crawled into his home hive.

Birch Cave was as silent as death. There were many dead bees, including the occasional Blue, but he estimated that the majority had been removed from the hive. He checked out the concealed entrance to Little Birch – it looked untouched.

'Time to go,' thought Milfoil. 'Maybe one day we shall return and restore it to its former life.'

Madder received Milfoil's report with great sadness, yet he took some comfort from the fact that the Blues had gone. It was still only mid-morning so there was plenty of time to visit Middle Oak. Clover was put in charge of Little Birch, with Milfoil responsible for security. Madder then set off with Trefoil and the four Middle Oakers.

They took a southerly route initially, in order to keep well away from the Blues' base at Six Hives and that awful swarm. Just beyond Upper Oak they steered due west, reaching Middle Oak without incident.

There was quite a reunion with Briar, Teasel, Thyme and Bryony, plus the introductions of Madder and Trefoil. The intelligence scouts were all out flying so Lavender took them to see the Queen pupa – as it was now.

'Magnificent!' declared Scruff, observing the full size Queen cell.

'What's happening inside?' asked Coppice.

'Just a gradual transformation from the big fat larva we last saw, to an adult

Queen ready to emerge,' explained Lavender.

'Amazing!' said Coppice, trying to recall life as a pupa – but he couldn't.

'Can this happen in my hive?' asked Madder.

Coppice briefly explained the situation to Lavender, who said, 'I don't see why not. In fact, I suspect your worker bees may have already begun. It's natural to try and replace a lost Queen. If you go back and look for the beginnings of a Queen cell, then you'll know the matter is being addressed. I'm assuming some of the eggs you rescued were three or four days old, in which case they will have hatched today. Your problem will be the food supply. It's essential that the nurse bees have unlimited supplies.'

Madder nodded, 'Got that Trefoil?'

'I have indeed. How long before the new Queen emerges?'

'About twelve days,' replied Lavender. 'Once she's out, her scent will unite the hive. After a few more days she should go on a mating flight and then start laying eggs. Your problem then will be the amount of space available for the eggs, bearing in mind what you'll need for over-wintering.'

This was quite a lot for Madder's brain to cope with but Trefoil was taking it all in. He commented, 'Well, I guess we'll have to tackle each problem as it comes. I reckon Little Birch can accommodate five thousand at a push – which should be enough for the winter, shouldn't it?'

'Maybe,' said Lavender, 'as long as your food supplies are good.'

'Fair enough,' said Coppice. 'Now what?'

'I think we should return to Little Birch and go looking for Queen cells,' said Madder.

'Mind if I join you?' asked Coppice, not wanting to leave Madder so soon after finding him again.

'No problem!'

With a stomach full of honey and the latest intelligence on the Blues' activities, Coppice, Madder and Trefoil set off for Little Birch on the same roundabout route they had used on the way in. This time, as they approached Upper Oak hive, they could see that something was amiss.

'Slow up!' warned Madder.

'What's wrong?' asked Coppice.

'Not sure yet, but I don't like the look of it.'
'That number of bees can only mean one thing,' suggested Trefoil.
'Yes,' agreed Madder, 'it has to be a swarm.'
'Of what colour, dare I ask?' said Coppice.
'I don't think we're going to hang around here to find out,' Madder decided. 'We'll fly further east to avoid them, before turning northwards.'

Coppice looked at him with some surprise. Madder continued, 'Little Birch takes priority for the moment, we can check out Upper Oak later.'

'If they are Blues, I've had enough of them for the time being anyway,' said Trefoil.

Without further discussion, the trio selected a new course and continued their journey. They reached Little Birch safely but entered carefully to ensure they weren't spotted. Trefoil went off in search of Queen cells while Madder and Coppice caught up with Milfoil's latest news. The Blues hadn't been seen all day, apparently.

'I think they must be up to something,' said Milfoil.

'And maybe we know what,' said Madder. 'We spotted a large mass of bees around Upper Oak on our way back. We didn't go close enough to identify them, but…'

'But we reckon it was the Blues' swarm,' added Coppice. 'So what are they up to? They had a reason for attacking us, but what's Upper Oak done wrong?'

'Nothing, I'm sure,' suggested Madder.

Milfoil pointed out, 'Upper Oak is the nearest hive to Six Hives apart from Upper Beech perhaps. Then there's Lower Beech, and The Mound, with River Bank and Pines to the east. They might be starting some sort of invasion?'

'You're very well informed,' said Coppice, 'and that's and interesting theory.'

'We need to find out just what was going on at Upper Oak before we adopt Milfoil's theory,' suggested Madder.

'You're right,' agreed Coppice, 'and the sooner the better!'

'Trefoil can manage here; I'll come with you,' said Madder.

After informing Trefoil, the pair zoomed off southwards.

As they approached Upper Oak they were relieved to see no signs of a swarm. When they reached the great oak tree itself, however, they noticed a large number of bodies on the ground below, including a few Blues. Up at the hive entrance there were still guards on duty.

'That's encouraging,' said Coppice. 'They obviously haven't been wiped out.'

'So what happened to the Blues?' asked Madder.

'We could ask in the drone zone?'

'Yes. I think we should. Let's go.'

There were a few Upper Oak drones in the zone. Madder approached one of them carefully.

'I see you've had visitors back at the hive today?'

The drone glanced at Madder's body, as if to satisfy himself that he was the right colour. 'We did indeed.'

'And you managed to send them packing – well done!' added Coppice.

'Not until they'd taken our Queen!'

Coppice looked at Madder. They didn't know what to make of that.

'Oh, um, sorry to hear that,' said Coppice. 'There must have been quite a scrap then – inside the hive, I mean. I suppose you'll be able to rear a replacement though?'

'I suppose so.'

That was his last word before flying off.

Coppice puzzled over what they had heard. 'Very odd. Very odd indeed. What would they want with a Queen?'

'Well, what are Queens for?' posed Madder.

'Yes, but I didn't think you could just steal one like that!'

'Must be another explanation. Perhaps the intelligence scouts can shed some light on the matter. Let's move on. Upper Oak will survive without us.'

Madder and Coppice had an easy trip back to Middle Oak where they reported their day's experiences. They found Scruff and Spurge guarding the Queen pupa, accompanied by Thyme and Bryony. Lavender thought their Queen rearing was right on course, with just six days to go. She was beginning to think about when she should inform Celandine. Madder wanted to hear from the intelligence scouts so decided to stay until they turned up.

The following day was uneventful. Madder took a turn guarding the pupa,

COPPICE

now only five days from becoming an adult Queen. It would be quite something, if Lavender could pull it off. He hoped the same process was continuing at Little Birch. Trefoil had indeed located a Queen cup so the rearing was underway. Of course they had no opposition to their Queen rearing – it had to happen if the remnant was to have any chance of survival.

Towards heatfall, Fern flew in with bad news.

'Lower Beech was attacked today,' he announced. 'The Blues forced an entry by a mass attack after taking the guards by surprise.'

'Did they find the Queen?' asked Coppice.

'How did you know they were after her?' replied Fern.

'Madder and I discovered what happened at Upper Oak yesterday. We wondered if one of the Beech hives would be next.'

'I see. So you already know that Upper Oak's Queen is dead?'

'Well, missing at least.'

'No, they've found the body I'm afraid.'

After a short silence among his listeners, Madder then pointed out, 'So, Upper Beech next? They'll go for it tomorrow?'

Fern just nodded his agreement.

'Is there anything we can do about it?' asked Sorrell.

'Piper and Fescue are already over there trying to warn them.'

'Good,' said Madder. 'Maybe they'll set up some sort of defence.'

'Or maybe they won't listen to him,' suggested Fern.

'Why ever not – if they've heard about Lower Beech?' asked Coppice.

'I'm afraid the two Beech hives are keen rivals. They don't go in for helping each other. I believe there was an upset many seasons ago and they've never forgiven each other.'

'Not good,' said Sorrell.

'Plain stupid,' added Spurge.

Sorrell continued, 'And it certainly doesn't help us. If you think about it, we're now on day eleven out of sixteen in our Queen rearing. Suppose the Blues spend tomorrow dealing with Upper Beech...' he paused.

'Go on,' insisted Coppice, wondering what was coming.

'Erm, that would be day twelve. Then, assuming the Blues are attacking the hives nearest to their base first, and working outwards – if you see what I mean – where would they go after Upper Beech?'

Fern answered, 'Probably over to River Bank and Pines, followed by The Mound, or possibly the other way around.'

'Right – and if they only tackle one hive each day, that's three more days accounted for – thirteen, fourteen and fifteen.'

'So what?' asked Scruff, who wasn't following at all well.

'So which hive would be next on their hit list? Which hive would they be targeting on day sixteen of our Queen rearing?'

'You're right!' Fern congratulated him. 'Middle Oak would be the next in line!'

As the implications of Sorrell's clever analysis spread through the assembled company a silence fell, until Fern said, 'Somebee fetch Lavender, please.'

Scruff obliged and quickly found her.

'Is anything wrong?' she asked on arrival, and Fern explained the situation.

'Is there anything we can do to get our Queen to emerge a day earlier?' Fern asked.

Lavender hesitated the answered, 'Not that I'm aware of. These things can't be forced. All we can do is listen in carefully so that we know more accurately when she's about to emerge.'

'Listen in?' queried Coppice.

'To the Queen's piping noises.'

'Ah yes, Piper's the bee for that job!'

Lavender looked puzzled. The others were trying to imagine what would happen if they didn't get away before the Blues arrived, or if the two swarms met in mid-air – that would be an absolute disaster!

'As it's the old Queen who'll be coming in the swarm, couldn't we leave earlier?' asked Scruff.

'Yes…I mean, no,' replied Lavender. 'I mean, normally yes, we would leave earlier, even a few days earlier, but we're Queen rearing in secret. We would have to tell the Council what we've done in order to swarm early and they'd just come and destroy our pupa.'

Scruff thought about that for a time.

Madder was already thinking tactics. 'We have to help at least one of those

COPPICE

hives against the Blues in order to set the Blues back a day. Which of Pines, River Bank and The Mound will they hit last, Fern?'

'My honey would go on The Mound, but we may have to wait until tomorrow to know for certain. Pines and River Bank are fairly close together and some way from The Mound. If they go for either Pines or River Bank tomorrow, then they'll take the other one the following day. That would give us an opportunity to do something about The Mound.'

'That sounds reasonable to me,' said Coppice, looking at Sorrell for his response.

Sorrell nodded but asked, 'And how shall we know which hive they attack first?'

Fern explained, 'I'm meeting up with Piper and Fescue tomorrow heatfall. They'll have been watching Upper Beech during the day. I'll suggest that they watch River Bank and Pines the following day while I watch The Mound. If we then all return to Middle Oak, we should have a better idea of our options – agreed?'

They did – and the meeting broke up. Some of them wandered over to the Queen cell to take their minds off the problem. It was a magnificent structure. Briar and Teasel were keeping an eye on things. Lavender had suggested they now enlist the help of some worker bees to form a barrier round the cell. Coppice had shown them how to do it, and even tested its efficiency. Inside the cell was their best hope of escape. The sad thing was that the new Queen would stay in the hive – it was the old one who would fly out with the swarm. Coppice admired the wax structure, thinking to himself what a pity it was that they couldn't leave the old Queen behind.

The following day, Upper Beech was attacked by Swarm Force One. There was little resistance. Piper and Fescue reported to Fern that heatfall and agreed the duties for the next day – Piper and Fescue to observe Pines and River Bank, while Fern watched The Mound. On day thirteen of Middle Oak's secret Queen rearing, the Blues attacked the River Bank hive. Now the scouts knew it was The Mound they needed to help.

On day fourteen the three scouts, plus Coppice, Madder, Sorrell, Scruff and Spurge, flew out to The Mound's drone zone. Making contact was no problem because the locals were very sociable. They knew of the Blues – they had observed them several times, but only in small numbers, usually scouting pairs. The news of full-scale attacks on other hives in the area upset them considerably. The details of the defence of Birch Cave hive they found astonishing and they readily agreed to take Fern into The Mound to meet their Council. Fern was the official intelligence scout for the eastern sector so he was quite acceptable to most, if not all the hives in that area.

He soon returned to inform his friends that the Council had agreed to try the wedge defence system and they would welcome a demonstration. The friends didn't need asking twice and they zoomed over to the hive. It was covered with dense brambles with its entrance facing the river. That made for slightly easier defence because the entrance was in the sheer wall rising directly out of the water. There was nowhere to land nearby.

Madder directed the demonstration. Afterwards he asked if they had a secret escape route from the hive – but they hadn't. He suggested they make one, but they didn't think they could do it in time because the soil was very difficult to tunnel through as you moved away from the bank, and that was the direction their escape route would have to take. They reckoned The Mound's population was far too large for the Blues to wipe out, and as the Blues seemed interested in Queen bees they decided to build a hiding place for her within the hive. Madder offered to stay to direct the defences the next day but the residents felt their own leaders could control their own bees best. Madder had to admit they were probably right. Coppice thought they were a good crowd and earnestly hoped they would succeed in resisting the Blues, who at that time were busy attacking the Pines hive.

Day fifteen of the Queen rearing saw Fern, Fescue, Coppice, Madder and Sorrell fly out to observe The Mound. Piper stayed behind in order to try and communicate with the pupa inside the Queen cell. Lavender had decided to wait until Piper had positive results before she told Celandine what was going to happen.

The five selected a suitable observation post in a tree across the river from The Mound. There was plenty of activity around the entrance so Fescue zoomed up for a scout around. Soon enough he spotted a small, dark cloud moving their way. It grew larger and larger. Scouts from The Mound had also seen it and

COPPICE

flown in to report. Foraging was halted. The defences were put in place. Fescue rejoined his friends and everybee waited.

The first thing they observed was a stream of Blues shoot out of nowhere into The Mound's entrance. As they hit the wedge of bees just inside, there was a sudden pile up, followed by confusion! They regrouped and tried again. The wedge held. A third time they blasted the entrance but still they couldn't get inside. They retreated, and nothing appeared to happen for some time. Then they came again. This time they tried to land in the entrance and begin pulling bees out from the wedge. This proved very difficult because of the steep wall and lack of space. They did manage to set up a tiny platform from which they could attack the wedge. Inside the hive, the defenders were pleased at the way the wedge was holding – they had very little filling in to do. This was the position throughout the morning.

By sunpeak Bugle was a troubled bee. This was the first problem he'd encountered since dealing with that troublesome hive in the caves, and he wasn't pleased. At this rate the hive would easily last out the day. Coppice and company had come to the same conclusion. They were beginning to feel confident that they had secured the extra day they so badly needed.

Everything changed about two hours after sunpeak. Yarrow had received progress reports; some of which he began to doubt as the day wore on with Bugle still apparently outside the hive. He decided it was time for him to flex his wing muscles, not to mention his mandibles. Calling for his personal guard, he set out for the hive. On arrival he summoned Bugle and extracted the truth from him. Yarrow was furious, and he showed it! He became transformed from the smooth, controlled bee he normally appeared to be, into a seething, vicious creature, bent on destruction. He flew into Swarm Force One and screamed at them, drawing a few hundred of them to himself as he zoomed around in figures of eight. He whipped them into a frenzy and shot downwards. As each drone reached the hive entrance he flew onto a guard bee, and sunk in his mandibles. Another Blue, or pair of Blues, then pulled out the pair of them and threw them to one side. The mandibles remained in the victim as the wings were cut before releasing the defeated bee into the river below. This continued as long as Yarrow persisted in his screaming flight.

Madder was first to spot the change of tactics. Coppice eventually realised that one bee seemed to be making the difference. The figure of eight pattern could at times be picked out above the hive's entrance. Inside The Mound they realised something had changed. They were now filling in the wedge quite rapidly. Matters deteriorated. Outside, Yarrow continued to spur his drones into even more frenzied attacks.

Within an hour of Yarrow's arrival, his bees had forced open the wedge and poured into The Mound. They searched the hive systematically for the Queen bee. They were surprised at the size of the hive as they penetrated deeper and deeper. Yarrow began to think this might be the hive he was looking for, and entered himself. Catching up with the search party, he added some urgency to their efforts. At last they came across a large group of guard bees who were obviously there for a reason. The Blues steamed right into them, smashing them out of the way. Behind them was the entrance to a small wax chamber – inside which they found the Queen and her Council.

Yarrow had the Queen dragged forward. He peered at her closely, then in disgust issued the fatal order. His guards followed him out and the Blues withdrew. Outside the entrance Swarm Force One was gathered in, after which it flew away to the north-east.

Madder turned to Coppice and shook his head. 'There's nothing we can do here. The hive will survive. They'll rear a new Queen without any difficulty.'

'You really think the Blues succeeded then?' asked Coppice.

'I should say it's definitely a matter of "mission accomplished". I don't know if they took the Queen away or not, but they've certainly found her.'

'We can check that out later with the locals in the drone zone,' said Fern. 'More important to get back to Middle Oak and see what we can do for our own hive.'

So the disappointed group made their way home, wondering if they were going to suffer the same fate as The Mound – only there would be two Queens to lose!

'Piper's made contact!' Briar shouted, as Coppice returned to Lavender's home combs. 'He's heard the Queen piping and he's tried tapping on the outside of the cell in reply. Oh, and Lavender thinks we should tell Celandine now.'

'Right,' said Coppice. 'Spurge, can you strengthen the barrier, just in case?

COPPICE

We'll find Celandine a short while before heatfall so that there will be very little time for the wrong sort of reaction.'

Lavender arrived at that moment and explained, 'We don't want Celandine to warn the present Queen until the new one is just beginning to emerge.'

Coppice agreed. 'Now what about you, Madder?'

'What about me?'

'If you're going to return to Little Birch, you'll have to do so first thing in the morning. You've been a great help to us over the past few days but I can't expect you to stay any longer.'

Madder considered for a moment. 'I'll decide in the morning. If I see you can escape with your swarm, I'll return to Little Birch. You can send a scout to let me know when you reach Squill's Island, can't you?'

'Certainly. Now let's have a look at our Queen cell, then we can think about locating Celandine.'

Lavender was the one to make the contact. Shortly before heatfall she approached the Council worker bee as a comb controller with something to discuss. This drew Celandine away from the other Council members. Coppice and some of the drones placed themselves within easy access in case Celandine went berserk or something. She didn't. She was, after all, the one Council member whom they suspected might be sympathetic to their cause. She was that, but she was also shocked and amazed at what had been done. It took some time to talk her through it but eventually she was satisfied – as long as she could see the proof! That bothered Coppice and the other drones but Lavender was confident by now that Celandine was on their side.

They took her to see the Queen cell and Celandine listened in for any piping. Turning towards Lavender she nodded her head, and then departed. Coppice organised a guard around 'their' Queen cell. They had an uneventful night.

Day sixteen was overcast but not actually raining. Coppice wondered if the Blues' swarm could operate in pouring rain. The drones maintained their guard around the Queen cell while Piper continually listened in, trying to encourage the occupant to emerge by talking her out! Fern and Fescue flew out on watch.

Celandine waited until the Council had taken their fill of honey before approaching the Queen. She was absolutely stunned. The other Council members reacted slowly at first and then with increasing anger.

'When did you find out about this?' screamed Valerian.

'Why didn't you tell us sooner?' demanded Fluellen.

'We must stop it immediately!' declared Gentian.

Celandine composed herself and replied, 'I was only told last heatfall. The new Queen is due to emerge anytime now. I think it's too late to stop her.'

'Not if I have anything to do with it,' insisted Valerian. 'I assume it's on comb controller Lavender's patch?'

Celandine didn't answer. Valerian set off with the other four, leaving Celandine to attend to the Queen. When they reached the comb they searched systematically until they came to a suspicious looking group of drones who were obviously hiding something.

'Out of my way!' shouted Valerian.

Coppice and company held their ground.

'Did you hear what I said?'

Still no reaction.

'Very well. Juniper, collect a band of workers and remove these drones!'

Behind the barrier, Piper thought he felt a movement under the capping. He warned Coppice and the others. 'I think she might be on the move! Can we hold out against these workers?'

Coppice thought back to when he and all the other drones were expelled from his first hive. He shuddered, but answered Piper. 'We have to! Lavender, go and tell Celandine we think it's time!'

As she scurried off, Juniper was returning with her crowd of workers. They came face to face with the drone barrier, and hesitated.

'Well? Get on with it!' yelled Valerian.

Juniper glanced in his direction and ordered her bees, 'Throw out those drones!'

Meanwhile, Lavender found Celandine, delivered the message, and shot back to rejoin the others. Celandine looked at her Queen. The Queen nodded, came close to Celandine, and covered her with an extra dose of her scent. Celandine then took off as fast as she could, scampering across the combs. Workers were immediately aroused and drawn to her. Over into the next combs she went, alerting more bees to what was coming. The Queen began to make her way to the hive entrance as Celandine continued her run. On Lavender's comb she, Thyme and Bryony, had taken a position directly opposite Juniper's workers. This had the effect of adding to their hesitation.

'There's a hole in the capping!' shouted an excited Piper.

'Throw them out!' yelled Juniper, and her bees edged forward.

At that moment Celandine reached Lavender's home comb and went scurrying past. All worker bees in the vicinity were attracted to Celandine, including Juniper's. They pulled away from the Queen cell and followed the throng. Lavender breathed a sigh of relief.

'We'll be all right now,' she told the drones. 'Nothing can stop the swarm. Are you coming or staying?'

They suddenly remembered they had to desert the new Queen if they were to leave with the swarm. Piper, for once, was in two minds, until he recalled the Blues' swarm and what it had done to other hives. Would this new Queen be killed? Yes, she surely would – and he couldn't cope with that.

'Come on,' urged Coppice, 'we have to go!'

Piper didn't move. He felt he already knew this new Queen.

'Now!' insisted Madder, grabbing Piper's foreleg. 'Scruff, Spurge, help me get him out of here!'

They half dragged, half pushed Piper away from the emerging Queen.

The old Queen reached the entrance with a mass of bees on her tail. She took to the air and flew in tight circles around Middle Oak as her workers joined her in ever increasing numbers. There were thousands of them, and they were noisy! A few drones joined them – on the fringe of the swarm. Celandine had done her job well. It was a good sized swarm, probably as big as the Blues' swarm, or even bigger.

As Coppice and friends circulated around the edge of the swarm, Fern and Fescue flew in and tried to locate them. They eventually succeeded.

'Blue swarm on its way!' cried Fern. 'Can we get our swarm away from here?'

Coppice looked at him. 'And just how are we supposed to do that?'

No bee was going to move the swarm except the Queen herself, and she was waiting until the swarm had reached its full size. In the meantime the Blues were approaching. In the relative darkness of that overcast morning, Swarm Force One was difficult to spot at a distance.

'We've got to do something!' yelled Sorrell.

'We have to find the Queen,' shouted Madder. 'Follow me.'

Sorrell, Madder and Coppice made their way into the centre of the swarm where they expected the Queen might be, along with Celandine, and perhaps Lavender? They found Celandine first and shouted at her. No response – she was too involved in the swarm. They moved and located the Queen. Same problem – it was useless.

Bugle was leading Swarm Force One up to the target of the day when he saw the mass of bees around the oak tree.

'What on....?' After the previous day's upset he shuddered to think what would happen if he faltered in any way today. Then he realised his luck. That was a swarm he was looking at! That meant the target hive was completely vulnerable! But he needed to catch the escaping Queen as well. Not so easy, but at least that would be an open-air situation. A rejuvenated Bugle led the swarm force forward.

Coppice, Madder and Sorrell withdrew from the centre of the swarm and rejoined the other drones on its fringe. Thyme and Bryony were with Lavender somewhere in the swarm's centre. The Blues came ever closer. Still the Middle Oak swarm hung around the entrance to its mother hive.

'This is madness!' exclaimed Coppice.

'We have to try something,' insisted Madder, 'but I don't know what!'

'We can't take on a whole swarm, can we?' asked Scruff.

'I've a good mind to,' said Piper, thinking of the Queen they'd left behind.

Sorrell said, 'No, we can't deal with every single problem. This one's too big for us. This time we're completely powerless. There's going to be a terrible massacre very shortly.'

A streak of bright white light shot across the sky. Some seconds later a loud rumbling noise was clearly heard. The drones looked in the direction from which the noise had come – more or less to the south-east.

COPPICE

'What was that?' asked Coppice.

'Lightning, followed by thunder,' replied Fern. 'Remember the pine tree with the severed branch, by the refuge?'

Coppice did remember. 'So what now?'

Before anybee could reply, another flash of lightning lit up the dull morning sky. The thunder followed quickly, then the first rain drops. Bugle reacted badly. More problems – a delay at least. He wondered if he could reach the target hive and use it as a shelter? If not, he would have to find some dense foliage as cover for his swarm – and quickly.

The arrival of the thunderstorm also had an effect on the Middle Oak swarm. The Queen stopped her circling and flew off in a north-westerly direction. Fescue noticed first and called to the others, 'Look, they're heading off in the wrong direction!'

'Quick,' shouted Fern, 'get in there and draw them to the south. Now the swarm's moving, it will listen to its scouts.'

The Queen had simply taken the direction opposite to that of the approaching thunderstorm. There were two problems with this: firstly it was no good for Squill's Island, secondly there was little or no cover from the rain if it caught up with them.

Then Coppice had an idea. 'What if we take the swarm into the woods and fly low, under the cover of the branches?'

'Yes,' said Fescue, who knew the area, 'we could travel in a south-westerly direction for some distance.'

Enough said, time was short. The drones became the scout bees for the swarm, with a clear idea of the direction the swarm should take. They shot into the swarm and found the Queen. She accepted their guidance and away they went, just as the rain became seriously heavy.

Bugle noted the swarm's departure to the north-west and decided to make a quick dash for the hive. He didn't see the swarm change direction. The Blues found little opposition at the Middle Oak entrance and piled in. They kept on piling in as the rain became heavier and heavier.

There was something of a fight back inside the hive as the thunderstorm came right overhead. Big, heavy drops of rain were now seriously hindering the Blues still queuing up to get inside the hive. Bugle was inside, directing the fighting and desperately trying to keep the entrance clear for the rest of his swarm force. The Middle Oakers, encouraged by the few bees in their hive who knew something about fighting Blues, were now resisting like heroes. The emergence of the new Queen, with her fresh, strong scent, seemed to unite the colony in a special way. Swarm Force One was in some disarray because one half was inside the hive while the other half had flown into the nearest undergrowth for cover. The heavy rain was grounding many of them. There was no way they would be pursuing the Middle Oak swarm, which had now made good its escape.

COPPICE

HIVE THREE

22. FOOD IS POWER

The scouts, Fern Piper and Fescue, directed the Middle Oak swarm as best they could in the circumstances. They had moved off prematurely, in very poor weather, to avoid the Blues. It was most unlikely they would have swarmed at all that day if they hadn't been forced to. Even the overcast conditions of that morning should have been enough to deter them from leaving the hive in numbers. Now they were weaving their way through the woods, using tree cover to avoid being flattened by the large raindrops. Not all the bees survived.

They were now in Fescue's territory, heading towards the coast opposite Squill's Island, hoping the rain would let up before they ran out of cover. It didn't. They had travelled about half way to the coast when they reached the southernmost point of the woodland. The scouts reluctantly called a halt, knowing that the swarm would have to cluster around the Queen, expecting only a short flight to a new hive.

'How far are we from our target area?' asked Fern.

'About the same distance we've already travelled,' replied Fescue.

'That's something,' said Piper. 'I guess we'd better start looking for a new site.'

'What about a temporary hive?' asked Fescue.

'Good try,' replied Fern, 'but Queen bees just don't do that – as far as I know. She would have to swarm again to move on, and nothing's going to make her do that in a hurry!'

'Maybe later on in the season?' queried Piper.

Fern considered that for a moment. 'Er, yes, in theory. But not too late because of building up food supplies for the winter.'

'OK, so let's get on with it,' urged Piper. 'Let the Queen form her cluster. I'll fetch Coppice and the others to help find a new site.'

That's exactly what happened. The swarm was halted and the Queen formed a cluster on a sheltered, low-hanging branch. Her scent held the bees together while the scouts organised their search. They concentrated on the area just inside the woods so that they would have easy access to the flowers in the fields beyond. Madder wanted somewhere that could have escape tunnels built into it. That rather did away with hollow tree trunks, so his team examined banks and mounds of earth.

It was well past sunpeak when Madder found what he was looking for. He showed Coppice first, then the others. It was a mixture of soil and rock, which formed a gentle mound along the edge of the wood. At its higher end the mound became solid rock. Part of the way along, Madder had discovered some small tunnels, possibly made by bumblebees in the past. They led to a number of small chambers before ending in one large one.

The scouts examined it carefully and compared it with other possible sites they had found. Madder pointed out that escape tunnels could be added quite easily. He also suggested that the entrance should be on the side facing into the woods so that it could be hidden from anybee flying by in the meadow. The abundance of bracken and bramble around the mound, added to its concealment.

After some discussion the intelligence scouts agreed, as long as the new entrance was made immediately.

'Name?' asked Scruff.

Fern said, 'I suppose we could call it "The Mound" in memory of the other hive of that name.

'We must have a new name,' insisted Fescue, 'which is in some way fitting to the site – that's the honeybee way.'

'Well, if it's not a mound, then it's a bank,' said Sorrell.

'And it's covered in brambles and bracken, added Scruff.

'Bramble Bank then?' suggested Coppice.

'Or Bracken Bank?' said Scruff.

Madder was troubled by this 'naming ceremony' and voiced his fears. 'Doesn't anybee think we're giving the opposition a clue as to our whereabouts by naming our new hive to match its location?'

There was a short silence before Scruff said, 'But there must be lots of mounds – I mean banks – like this one.'

'That's right,' added Coppice, 'and with bracken and brambles all over them.'

'We must have a suitable name,' insisted Fescue, 'it's our tradition.'

That just about summed it up. All the drones bar Madder were too conditioned to be able to break the tradition and they plumped for 'Bracken Bank'.

A short time later, a somewhat bedraggled swarm of bees followed the Queen into their new home. The workers started comb building immediately, but filling them with food wasn't so easy. The nearby meadow was out of bounds until the rain ceased, but a little emergency foraging was undertaken in the woods. The drones organised the beginning of the construction of a new main entrance. Everybee was busy, but heatfall came as a welcome relief after such a difficult day.

Next heatrise was met by the warmth of a clear blue day – there wasn't a cloud to be seen. The new occupants of Bracken Bank sprang into action, with Thyme in charge of the foraging. There was still some hawthorn in flower on the edge of the wood, with celandine and wild strawberry, also reaching the end of their flowering season, below it. Coming into flower was the blackberry, white deadnettle and thistle. The best source of food, however, was the clover in the meadow alongside the wood. Thyme even found some flowers of the plant going by her own name.

The foragers began near the hive to save time. The food being so close, they used the round dance to tell other workers where the food was, along with the scent of the food source itself. Using this method they soon had all the available foragers bringing in food. Inside the hive the 'house bees' were supplied with food as they built the comb using wax made by the glands under their abdomens. It was fascinating to watch them but the drones didn't have much time to spare – if any.

The intelligence scouts had to re-establish their patrols. Given the recent turn of events, they opted for two bases. To the north, Piper and Fern would operate together from the Stonewall hive – Piper's home. They would be a safe distance from the Blues, who were to the east – they hoped. Fescue would work from his home hive, Hollybank, which was in the middle of the southern area. He asked for Sorrell to join him whenever possible. Coppice wasn't surprised – he reckoned Sorrell would make a very good intelligence scout, but he hoped he wouldn't be away all the time. Bracken Bank would receive regular reports from both pairs and act as a link up post.

In addition, a local patrol was set up. Coppice and Madder would work as a pair, as would Scruff and Spurge, and of course the inseparable Briar and Teasel. There would always be one of these pairs out on local patrol. For their base they would use Lavender's home comb, when she had one – it was still being built!

Madder had decided he would be more use where he was because of his knowledge of tunnel building – something he would oversee when not on patrol duty. When, and if, he felt Bracken Bank was safe, then he could return to Little Birch. Tunnel building was slow at first because no workers could be spared, but he did persuade a few drones to help out. Most of them had been with him on the rolling ambush and understood the need for the safety precautions.

Bryony was helping Thyme. With the nectar flow now underway, they began checking out sources beyond the nearest meadow. The fields spread to the south and the woods to the north, roughly speaking, although there were some woods further to the south-east. Thyme instructed Bryony as she surveyed the plant life.

'It's most important,' she explained, 'that you appreciate how long each plant can be in flower. For example, the hawthorns are full of flowers for a short span of time, then they're finished. Things like white deadnettle and dandelion seem to flower nearly all the time we're around, but they're not enough to keep a big hive going. Now clover's different. That's quite recently come into flower and it will go on for the rest of the season. A meadow with a lot of clover is a great asset – and that's what we've got here, along with vetch, poppy, hawkbit and plenty of thistles. Along the edge of the woods we shall be getting blackberry for some time, ground ivy, violets, wood sage and wood anemone. How many of those did you spot?'

'Er, not too many,' admitted Bryony. 'You'd better point them out to me – one at a time, please.'

'Indeed I will. It really is very important that you understand the importance of assessing the food supply. You see, if you think about it, food is power. Our hive can only expand if it has the food supply to do so. If we can't set up a really strong food flow, we're in trouble.'

'If we worked very hard, do you think we might be able to swarm again this season – and make it to Squill's Island?'

COPPICE

'That depends on how much support we could get from Squill's bees. We would need help with our food supplies if we started a new hive later this season, or perhaps we could over-winter in his colony.'

'With our Queen?'

'Not normally, no, but Squill's hive was so large I'm not sure one Queen could control it.'

'Why not?'

'Because the Queen's scent holds the bees together and it would become too diluted in such a big colony.'

'Then what happens?'

'Er, I'm not sure. I'd have to ask Lavender. What I'm trying to say is that there's a limit to the size of a hive, and Squill's colony is well beyond it. I think he had more than one Queen at The Beacon.'

'Ah, so there might be room for another one?'

'Very good Bryony! But I'm only guessing.'

Inside Bracken Bank the wax combs were taking shape as worker bees laboured with only occasional breaks. As soon as some cells were complete, two things followed. Food supplies were stored in some, and the Queen laid eggs in the others. The hive was underway.

They were just as busy on day two. The local patrols didn't spot any Blues while Fescue and Sorrell reported that all was quiet in the southern area. Piper and Fern were probing cautiously to the east of Stonewall, and they did encounter Blues as they approached the river, which ran between Middle Oak and River Bank. They only heard about, or saw, enemy scouts in pairs. It was as if hostilities had been halted and they were re-establishing their lines. This came as something of a relief and the news was taken to Bracken Bank. They also took some sad news back. Although The Mound hive appeared to be alive, with a new Queen, there were no drones in the Middle Oak zone. Piper badly wanted to visit Middle Oak itself but he and Fern both knew it was too risky for the time being.

The Blues had suffered a major setback and Bugle knew he would be the scapegoat. Yarrow, having stayed at Six Hives after his previous day's exertions, would bear none of the responsibility. He, Bugle, had allowed Swarm Force One to be split in two. The half that had entered the enemy hive had escaped the rain but not the counter attack. In a belated attempt to save the hive, the Council had made a big effort to protect the new Queen. The Middle Oakers resorted to stinging and the Blues found it difficult to use their wing cutting tactics inside the hive. They found themselves retreating to the entrance area of the hive, where they more or less held their ground.

The other half of the swarm force was sheltering in the nearby woods, waiting for Bugle to come and tell them what to do. Eventually the thunderstorm passed, although the rain continued. Bugle decided to quit the hive and join the other half of his force. This he did. He then held the swarm force undercover until he reckoned they were running out of time as far as getting back to Six hives before heatfall was concerned. To stay in the woods would lose bees due to lack of food. To fly back to base would lose bees due to the rain. He chose the latter option but had no intention of completing the journey himself. He gathered up his depleted force and led it off in the right direction, using the cover of wood whenever possible. Unfortunately for his bees, the trees were often thinly spread on their route back and many of them were struck down by the continuing rain.

As they neared their destination, weary and wet, Bugle appointed an unsuspecting drone by the name of Cudweed to lead them in and report to Yarrow. He was to say that Bugle had been killed fighting valiantly inside the enemy hive. The unthinking Cudweed duly obeyed and delivered the message, along with barely half the original Swarm Force One. Bugle zoomed away to the secret hiding place he had prepared for just this eventuality. Yarrow was absolutely furious!

23. THE MESSENGER

Bracken Bank was beginning to look like a proper beehive – on the inside anyway. The available space in the main chamber was already half filled with wax combs. The first eggs had hatched into larvae, moulted four times and pupated. The first workers would emerge twenty-one days after egg laying began. The future of the hive was looking good.

Briar and Teasel were out on patrol while Coppice and Madder worked on the tunnelling. The new entrance had been completed in the first three days. There was quite a fuss as the foragers had to learn the new beeline from the hive, but Thyme and Lavender sorted them out. Madder organised the building of two escape tunnels to the meadow side and one to the wood side of the hive. Both of them had their entrances carefully concealed and plugged. Coppice and Madder were inspecting the completed tunnels.

'You know,' said Coppice, 'this reminds me of the refuge.'

'I beg your pardon?'

'The refuge, remember? Ling and Heather's home with its complex tunnel system.'

'Ah yes.'

'Their chamber was very cleverly protected by the series of tunnels leading into it. There were so many choices to make. Now, what was it?'

'What was what?'

'Erm, left, right…um…right again I think it was, then left and…ah, the cross tunnels…right. That was it: left, right, right, left and right.'

'What are you on about?'

'The route into…oh no, that was the route out of the refuge, so it must have been left, right, left, left and right to get in. Good, I've remembered.'

'Remembered what exactly?'

Coppice decided it would be easier to give a local example. 'Supposing we linked up our two escape tunnels going to the meadow side of Bracken Bank. You could then take more than one route to the outside couldn't you? And suppose you sealed off the beginning of one tunnel and the end of the other? You could still escape by starting from the remaining opening, following it to the link tunnel, crawling along that until you met the other escape tunnel, and following that to the outside.'

Madder pictured in his mind what Coppice was describing, then he exclaimed, 'Why didn't I think of that?'

'It wasn't my idea either – I just happened to end up with Ling and Heather in their maze of tunnels. In fact, the tunnel system leading to the safe chamber is even more complicated.'

'Safe chamber?'

'Oops! That slipped out. Promise you'll keep it a secret.'

'What secret?'

'Just that it exists.'

'That's not much of a secret.'

'So don't worry about it. If we need it, I'll tell you more.'

Madder was confused, but didn't press the matter. He turned his attention back to his tunnels.

'So how about linking our tunnels – and building a few more?'

'Why not?'

Yarrow wasn't being idle either. When the depleted Swarm Force One returned after their near disaster, he went berserk. Cudweed took the initial blame and wondered what had hit him. Yarrow had to take it out on somebee, and Cudweed was the nearest one connected in any way to the foul up.

When he had calmed down, Yarrow considered his options. The main problem was the weakening of the storm force. It had, as expected, lost some bees in the routine attacks on hives in the area. That old hive by the river had taken a heavier toll than usual, but nothing like what had happened on the latest outing. The hive in the oak tree, plus the bad weather, had combined to knock out at least a third of his swarm force, so it was getting down to about half its original strength. As he had only dealt with an estimated one quarter of the hives in this region, he clearly

COPPICE

had problems. How many more hives would he have to raid before he found the Queen he was looking for? He paced around the hive for a time before coming to his decision. It was still not yet mid-season. There was time to return to The Glade and bring out reinforcements. He needed a replacement for Bugle as well. In addition, he could ask the advice of the Overlord – as long as he wasn't too upset by what had happened.

Yarrow and fifty Blues set off next heatrise and reached The Glade a day and a half later. The Blues at Six Hives were left leaderless because that would prevent them from doing anything at all – which was what Yarrow wanted until he returned.

On arriving at The Glade, Yarrow made his way to his personal chamber, acknowledging only Kale on the way. Once inside he began to sample the tempting foods in his wax pots. Some of them were like honey or pollen, others were definitely not! They had the effect of reducing him to a dull stupor, followed by a deep sleep.

He didn't fully come to his senses until the following heatrise. After cleaning and feeding, he threw out his attendants and opened the secret door at the back of his chamber. Into the narrow passage with its glowing walls he crept. It was both eerie and inspiring. Deeper and deeper he went. At last he reached the anteroom where the thin wax wall separated him from the chamber of the Overlord. Yarrow crouched down and waited, silently contemplating his calling. It seemed longer than usual before the dark shadow appeared on the other side of the wall.

'Share your request, my chosen one.'

'Master, I have need of your advice in light of the latest opposition.'

'Opposition? Do tell me all that has happened.'

'An old hive by the river seemed to know we were coming. It had set up the same sort of defence as that hive in the caves we dealt with some time ago. Bugle was struggling to overcome them so I flew in personally to stir the swarm force to success.'

'Well done, my chosen one.'

'We did lose more drones than normal.'

'Never mind, we have plenty more.'

'The following day, Bugle went to a hive in an oak tree. The weather wasn't too good, but...'

'Do continue,' said the Overlord, as Yarrow hesitated.

'They swarmed just as Swarm Force One approached.'

He waited for his master to comment. No response, so he added, 'And before we could go after them, a thunderstorm broke out!'

Yarrow thought he detected movement on the other side of the thin wall. Still there was silence, so he continued, 'Swarm Force One was split in two. Half entered the hive; half were left sheltering in the wood. There was stout resistance from inside the hive and Bugle was killed in the fighting. A drone called Cudweed brought the swarm force back to Six Hives, losing many on the way. Swarm Force One is now barely half its original strength with only a quarter of the region subdued.'

Another short silence and then the Overlord spoke at last, 'Listen carefully, my chosen one. The root cause of our opposition lies in that swarm which escaped from the oak tree hive – it must be traced. You will take Swarm Force Two back with you, and be its mission leader. Now go over to the caskets to your right.'

This was something new. Yarrow had been aware of them on his visits to the chamber but assumed they were something to do with his master's personal food supplies. He found there were six of them.

'The very small one is the one you need. Don't open it until it's needed. You should use it against that hive in the oak tree.'

'How, master?'

'Bring it a little closer to the partition and I will explain.'

There was great excitement in Bracken Bank as the time arrived for the first bees to emerge. It was twenty-one days since the first eggs had been laid in the new hive. Once a hive produces its own bees, it is considered to be established or 'on the map'. Fescue, as the intelligence scout, had to know all about the hives in his area, including new ones. He and the other drones, apart from Scruff and Spurge out on patrol, were there to witness the occasion – along with Lavender of course. They were delighted when the first bee pierced her cell capping and began squeezing herself out onto the comb surface. It brought back memories for Coppice and Madder, who couldn't help thinking about Twenty-three. They looked at each other.

Madder asked, 'Do you really think Twenty-three's still alive, back in our first hive?'

Coppice paused, 'Yes, I think it was him – and he was quite important in some way, so he's even more chance of surviving.'

'You mean he won't get thrown out of the hive in late season?'

'I'd like to think so.'

'Maybe we could try and contact him.'

'Maybe. Piper tells me the aberrant hive's on the beeline from here to Stonewall. They check it out each time they fly that way – just in case.'

'Just in case what?'

'Just in case…well, just in case anything unusual happens, I suppose.'

'Wouldn't surprise me,' commented Madder. 'I wonder if the Blues will go for it?'

That reminded Coppice. 'Ah,' he said, 'I told you, didn't I, about those Blues who chased us when Fescue made his break after we were captured?'

Madder was trying to remember, so Coppice continued, 'We actually managed to get behind them and we saw them discover the aberrant hive – and that was when they flew away!'

'Is that so?'

'Hmm.'

The pair turned their attention back to the emerging worker bees. Over a dozen were now finding their feet on the comb surface. Very soon they would be put to work as house bees – a honeybee colony was very efficient.

A few days later, very close to mid-season, Fern and Piper were scouting as close as they dared to Middle Oak. The Blues were still not advancing past the line of the river between Middle Oak and River Bank. What was happening behind their lines, they had no way of knowing, unless somebee like Milfoil could get a message out from Little Birch, but he had to put the safety of his hive first.

The two scouts ventured into the Middle Oak drone zone, just in case.

'Nothing,' announced a disappointed Fern.

They were just moving away from the zone when Piper warned Fern, 'Wait!' They hung in mid-air.

'I don't detect anything,' whispered Fern.

'OK, let's fly on slowly.'

They did so until Piper again thought he heard something. 'I'm sure we're being followed.'

'Blues?'

'Dunno.'

'Let's try and force them to break cover,' Fern suggested.

Piper knew what he meant and flew quickly forwards with Fern. Suddenly the pair dived for cover and remained hidden, watching for any pursuers. No bee appeared and they were about to move off again.

'Wait!' came Piper's warning. 'Here they come!'

What actually emerged was a solitary bee, a drone by the look of it, but he was so bedraggled it was hard to be sure. Fern peered carefully. Piper checked to see if this loner really was alone. He was.

'Intercept!' ordered Piper, and they immediately did so.

The poor bee was quite frightened at first and would have shot off had he the strength. It was a drone, and they knew him, but it took a while before Fern could name him.

'Is it you, Gentian?'

'Yes, yes it is! Wh-who are you?'

'Intelligence scouts Fern and Piper.'

'Oh, erm, yes, I think I recognise you, Fern.'

'What's happened to yer?' asked Piper, picking up an unusually strong scent from Gentian.

'Er, well, um, we, er…Oh dear me.'

'Take your time,' said Fern.

'Well, we, er, survived the attack on that terrible day, er, when the swarm left – what a shock that was.'

Piper and Fern exchanged knowing looks.

'Those Blues left us – didn't come back. Thought we were in the clear. The new Queen went on her mating flight a few days later and the hive was returning to normal.'

'Why are there no drones in the drone zone?' asked Piper.

'Oh, we moved our zone.'

'Where to?' asked Fern.

'To the west – the opposite direction to where the Blues came from, you see. But you won't find many drones there now.'

'Why not?' demanded Fern, anxious to get to the bottom of this.

'Because the Blues came back a few days ago.'

'What!' exclaimed Piper and Fern in unison. This was the first report of renewed activity against a hive.

'I didn't actually see what happened but I was told that about two hundred Blues attacked our workers as they returned to the hive.'

'Then what?' asked Fern.

'Then they just flew off.'

'How very odd. So what are you doing here?'

'Looking for help.'

'We'll help yer,' said Piper.

'No, it's not just me – it's the whole hive. There's something wrong. Bees aren't too well and...well, stores are running low.'

Piper and Fern drew aside from Gentian.

'What do you reckon?' asked Fern. 'We can't risk taking him back to Bracken Bank in this state, can we?'

'Nope, we can't, his illness might be catching.'

'How about the refuge?'

'Now that's an idea. Heather and Ling would know what to do.'

'Agreed then – let's try it.'

They turned to a rather worried Gentian and explained what they wanted to do, promising they would ask the bumblebees if they could help the Middle Oak hive. Gentian nodded his acceptance and flew gently up and away with the two scouts.

It was only a short distance to the refuge but Gentian's laboured flying meant it took twice as long. On arrival, Fern entered alone while Piper and Gentian hid themselves. Shortly Fern reappeared and led the others in along several passages, which left even Piper quite baffled. At the end they reached a small, cosy chamber with a honeypot and some sort of soft material on the floor.

'You can relax now, Gentian,' said Fern. 'One of our hosts will be along in a moment.'

It was Heather who next entered the little chamber, causing Gentian to cower a bit.

'Ah, good to see you,' she reassured him. 'And what have we here?'

She paused to sample the scents that filled the chamber. If she was troubled by any of them, she didn't show it.

Piper said, 'This is Gentian, from Middle Oak. They've had some bother with Blues and some sort of illness in their hive.'

'I see. Well I think you can leave him with me for now. He'll be quite safe in this chamber.'

She didn't say it was an isolation chamber, well away from the main part of the refuge, though Fern had a pretty good idea it was because of the route he had taken to get there.

'Thanks Heather,' said Fern. 'Is Ling around?'

'Not at the moment -tomorrow perhaps, when you return?'

'Fine, we'll come back tomorrow. Are we OK to return to our hive – we're not infected or anything?'

'No, I'm sure you're safe, but you were wise not to visit Middle Oak hive.'

Fern nodded to Piper and they departed, Piper trying hard to memorise the route. At the entrance, Fern took the precaution of peering out carefully before emerging. Once assured there was no danger he led Piper up and away, back in the direction of Bracken Bank.

It was nearing heatfall when they arrived. They waited until Coppice and Madder came in from the last patrol of the day before reporting their findings to the friends at Bracken Bank. Only Fescue and Sorrell were absent. After hearing the news, there was much sadness among those who had once lived at Middle Oak, and sympathy from Madder.

'We must find out exactly what happened,' declared Coppice.

COPPICE

'And whether anybee else has survived,' added Scruff.

'What about the Queen?' enquired Lavender, who had been responsible for raising her.

'And just what are those Blues up to now?' asked Thyme.

'Up to no good!' Spurge answered.

'Probably a correct assumption,' said Coppice. 'They must be up to something – some change of tactic or…'

'We'll keep an even closer watch,' Piper assured them, 'and let yer know as soon as we know anything.'

'But we could check out the Middle Oak hive,' suggested Coppice. 'After all, it is – *was* – our home hive.'

Fern interrupted, 'I don't think that would be wise, not yet anyway. I want to know what Heather and Ling make of Gentian first of all.'

Coppice persisted, 'But there's no harm in taking a closer look – keeping an eye out for survivors, surely?'

'We can do that,' responded Fern, speaking for the scouts.

The debate continued for some time. It was so hard for them not to do more for their old hive. In the end they retired to the cluster without complete agreement.

At heatrise, Fern and Piper made a quick tour of the hive, filled up with honey, and set off back to the refuge. Coppice was disgruntled.

'Why do we have to follow the scout's advice all the time?' he complained to Madder. 'Are they really that expert?'

'They do travel about a lot, so they learn a great deal.'

'So why don't we travel more?'

'Well, I guess that's what scouts are for!'

'So you're saying we have to become scouts if we want to know so much that we can tell others what to do?'

'Something like that, but not everybee can become a scout – there are other jobs to be done.'

'Yes, but not so exciting.'

'Don't you think life's been quite exciting so far?'

'Hmm, maybe that's the problem. Life *has* been exciting – so why stop now? I'm flying out to Middle Oak, coming?'

'I beg your pardon? No, I'm not coming!'

'Then you'd better get somebee to take my place on our patrol – try Bryony.' And with that parting comment, Coppice flew off, leaving Madder angry and upset.

Coppice was enjoying flying solo for a change. He knew he could do the return trip in a day quite comfortably. He flew east to the black rivers landmark, and then northwards towards Middle Oak. He even flew by the spot where the Blues had caught him and the search party on their way back from Hollybank. He arrived in the vicinity of Middle Oak well before sunpeak and found a hiding place close to the hive's entrance. He watched carefully for a time but spotted no bees, Blues or otherwise. Eventually a single worker bee flew into the hive.

'Still life in there!' thought Coppice. Now he was eager to go in. 'I'll just wait for one more worker then I'll go in.' But his patience couldn't hold out. He hovered above his hiding place, looked all around, and then flew in. There were no guards at the entrance. He crawled cautiously through the opening in the oak tree. As soon as he was inside the hive, he knew he had made a terrible mistake!

COPPICE

24. PLAGUE

The scent was overpowering. Coppice's spiracles reacted automatically by closing up, thereby restricting the flow of foul air into his body. It was a stench the like of which he had never previously encountered. He had to force himself to allow the slightest relaxation in his body so that a little air could enter.

Edging his way forward into the hive, out of sheer curiosity to find out what had happened to his old home, he peered into the first cells he came to. There was still some honey around. There was even the occasional movement from a worker bee, but in slow motion. Then he noticed something odd about the cell cappings. They were sunk in the middle instead of being dome-shaped. Others had perforations in them. Coppice reckoned the occupants had tried to get out but failed. He looked around for larvae. Inside the cells where there should have been greedy, white wrigglers he found only motionless brown lumps, sometimes yellowish brown. Nearby, a worker bee had died in the process of trying to drag a dead larva from its cell. The larva's shape was unrecognisable. It was just a gooey mess.

Coppice shuddered and turned away. He crawled back the short distance to the hive's unguarded entrance. He was so sickened by what he had seen that he just flew out to the nearest cover and rested there, trying to take in all in. Something had destroyed Middle Oak but it wasn't the Blues. It had to be some sort of illness, but he knew next to nothing about diseases which attacked honeybees.

Then it occurred to him that maybe he could have caught the disease. He knew his body had reacted strongly against the scent inside the hive. So what should he do now? If he returned to Bracken Bank, would the disease go with him? He was confused and stayed where he was for some time, not knowing what to do. He began to realise he may have acted rather foolishly in visiting Middle Oak.

Eventually it dawned on him that he couldn't be too far from somebee who would know exactly what to do. Ling and Heather's refuge was in this area. That was where Fern and Piper had taken Gentian, so it must be the place to go. Thinking back to the night flight he had made with Fern when they flew from the refuge to Middle Oak, he recalled that it was only a short trip. He also knew the large pine tree with the lightning-damaged branch, which acted as the key landmark for the refuge.

Somewhat encouraged, Coppice set off. His memory of his previous flight gave him a rough idea of where to start looking for the landmark. He didn't have to search for very long. There it was, with its blackened branch partly removed. He flew down to examine the ground, seeking out the entrance to the refuge. That didn't take long either. The next bit, however, had to be spot on first time. Coppice had to remember the correct route through the tunnels in order to reach Ling and Heather's nest chamber. Fortunately he had revised the route when discussing the Bracken Bank tunnels with Madder so he didn't have to think back very far.

'Now then,' he said aloud as he entered the tunnel, 'the first turn was...left. Ah yes, here we are – the cross tunnels, it's coming back to me now. Right next, followed by left, and left again.'

He continued with some confidence and reached the fifth junction. 'And finally, right. *Aagh!*'

As he turned the last corner he was accosted by two bees!

'What the...?'

'Coppice!'

'What are yer doing here?'

'Yes, what are you doing here?' demanded Fern, as Piper let go of a shaken but relieved Coppice.

Before he could answer, Fern noticed, 'Your scent! Where did you get that from?'

Piper guessed, 'You've been to Middle Oak, haven't yer?'

Without waiting for an answer, Fern ushered Coppice away from the route into the bumblebees' nest chamber. 'Get moving!' he ordered in his sternest voice. 'Turn when and where I tell you to.'

COPPICE

Fern and Piper followed a few bee-lengths behind the trembling Coppice as he obeyed the instructions, which took him through a maze of tunnels to a small chamber. There he met Heather, who looked up in surprise.

'Oh dear me! What are you doing here, Coppice? I mean, I mean it's good to see you again but, but rather unexpected.'

'He shouldn't be here at all,' explained Fern. 'He's been stupid enough to fly out on his own to visit Middle Oak!'

'Against all good advice,' added Piper.

'Oh surely not, Coppice, I thought…'

'No, he obviously doesn't have as much sense as you thought,' interrupted Fern. 'I suggest we show him what's happened to Gentian. This way, Coppice.'

Fen led him towards the back of the chamber to a wax cell built into the floor. It was partially capped. 'Take a look in there!'

Coppice peered in. He could see the form of a drone bee, bedraggled and motionless.

'Is that Gentian? Is he still alive?'

'Yes to both questions,' replied Piper, 'but he's dying. The illness was already severe when we found him. There's nothing Heather, or we, can do for him now. In fact, he's done well to last this long.'

Coppice's depression returned. He glanced at Heather, who shook her head.

'What is it?' Coppice asked. 'What is his illness?'

'The plague,' replied Heather. 'As I understand it, the larvae are attacked first, by some sort of tiny living creature which eat them up from the inside. The larvae die and the plague is spread as the worker bees attempt to clean out the dead ones from their cells.'

Coppice's stomach was churning over. 'But where does this plague come from? How does it get inside the larvae in the first place?'

'Fair questions,' replied Heather, 'but I don't know the answers.'

'What about Coppice's condition?' asked Fern, concerned because he had been inside Middle Oak.

'Did you touch any dead larvae?' Heather asked.

'No.'

'Did you eat any food in there?'

'No, the terrible scent put me on my guard. It was bad enough being in there, let alone doing anything else.'

Heather looked relieved. 'Very well then, that leaves your feet. Did you fly here directly from the hive?'

'No, I rested in a nearby tree, wondering what to do. I feared I might have exposed myself to the disease by entering the hive.'

'You certainly did, but you're probably OK, except for the scent, which could take some time to wear off completely. You must stay here for a day or two, until I'm quite certain you're not infected.'

'Yes, and Ling will want a word,' Piper pointed out.

Coppice cringed; Ling would not be pleased!

'One last thing before we leave you in Heather's care,' said Fern. 'Are you certain you've seen no Blues at anytime during your little exploit?'

'Quite certain.'

'I hope so, I do hope so.'

Fern and Piper departed. Heather fetched some bits of green leaf, which Coppice didn't recognise, and began to crush them in her mandibles. She then rubbed them all over Coppice's feet and lower legs. He didn't ask why, he just assumed this was something to do with combating the plague. When she was satisfied with her work, she took Coppice to another chamber just around the corner. It contained a couple of honeypots and some bedding. Coppice was left to help himself to some of Heather's delicious honey after which he settled down for heatfall, hoping that Ling would leave the telling-off until the next day.

At heatrise, Coppice topped up with honey and crawled round to the next chamber to see how poor Gentian was faring. To his surprise, Gentian's cell was completely sealed. The he realised what had happened. Poor Gentian indeed.

'It's better that you stay in your own chamber,' advised Heather as she appeared at the entrance. 'I've cleaned this place up, but you can't be too careful with the plague.'

Coppice acknowledged her wisdom and retreated to his own chamber.

'Ling will be along shortly,' she added.

'Oh, dear,' thought Coppice, 'trouble!'

But it wasn't Ling who arrived; it was Fern and Piper.

'Come on, Coppice,' called Fern, 'we've got to get you away from here.'
'Er what? Um, I can leave? I mean, am I clean and everything?'
'You'll have to be. We can rely on Heather anyway, so let's go!'
'Why the sudden hurry?'
'Blues!' hissed Fern. 'We've spotted a pair of their scouts in the area for the first time since we escaped from Middle Oak!'
'Oh!' was all Coppice could say to that, and he followed Fern while Piper said something to Heather.

At the entrance, Fern practised his 'listen, look and smell' routine before beckoning the others to follow him outside. The 'smell' was a bit marred by Coppice's comparatively strong scent, left over from his Middle Oak visit. They took a southerly beeline rather than set a direct course for Bracken Bank, just in case anybee was watching.

A group of four Blues watched them go. They had followed Coppice from Middle Oak the previous day, knowing full well that he would be heavily scented after his contact with the plague. It was, after all, part of their master's cunning trap. Finding Coppice's overnight stopping place was something of a bonus for them. They had seen a bumblebee use the entrance as well as three honeybees. There weren't at all sure what was going on in there, but Yarrow would no doubt be pleased to hear of it!

All four Blues flew off in pursuit, but a long way back from their quarry. The scent from one of them was enough to guide them along the correct route. They stalled when the scent trail dropped towards the ground. Two Blues flew on while the other two dived down to search for the three honeybees. Fern, Piper and Coppice had stopped for water at a stream near the black river crossing. They would be turning west when they resumed. The searching pair of Blues tracked the route of the stream as soon as they saw it, guessing correctly that their quarry had stopped somewhere along it. Their accomplices had flown on some way on the beeline south before landing close to the top of a tall tree, from where they scanned the sky for a trio of bees flying south. Meanwhile, the first pair observed carefully until the trio took to the air. Piper zoomed up first to check out the area above them before fetching the other two. The Blues stayed hidden. They were well trained, and they were deliberately relying on scent before sight. As soon as they deemed the trio were out of sight, the blue trackers shot up to where they had been. Circling around, they located the new direction, discharging a scent of their own for the other pair of Blues to pick up.

The trio flew westwards, thinking they were unobserved. The blue pair who had flown further south doubled back, picked up the marker scent and zoomed off westwards. They caught up with their mates well before Coppice and company reached the vicinity of Bracken Bank. Piper then put one final decoy into operation. He flew beyond the hive before stopping. The Blues repeated their previous manoeuvre in response. This time their quarry had landed in a wooded area. The scent, however, was still traceable, and they located the trio in a young birch tree. They waited patiently.

'Right,' said Piper, 'can yer find the drone zone from here, Coppice?'

'Er, yes, I think so. Aren't you coming too?'

'Yes, later. We're trying to make sure no bee's following us.'

'Have you seen anybee?'

'No – no Blues, that is.'

'So why all the precautions?'

'Because of those Blues we spotted early this morning.'

'But if they've been following us we'd know about it by now, wouldn't we?'

'Normally, yes,' agreed Fern, 'but that scent you're carrying poses a problem. It's just possible they could use it to track us without coming into view.'

'Really!' exclaimed Coppice.

'Yes, but our turn at the stream should have helped throw them off. Also, they work in scout pairs, so if we split up now, they can't follow all three of us, can they?'

'And none of us goes to the hive until heatfall,' added Piper. 'Yer can go to the drone zone and set up a group of drones to keep an eye on the area. Whoever's on local patrol will fly through there regularly so yer can involve them straight away.'

'Hmm,' mumbled Coppice, 'all this bother because of my private trip to Middle Oak. And where are you going to be?'

'Scouting the wider area until we're sure it's clear. We'll let you know before heatfall.'

COPPICE

They sent Coppice off to the drone zone but followed at a distance without telling him, to see if he was being tracked. He wasn't, so they left to commence scouting the wider area.

The Blues watched the trio split up and realised what they were doing. They were amazed at the precautions they saw taking place and decided their quarry must harbour suspicions about being followed. They now had a difficult decision to make. Did they finish the pursuit here and return to Six Hives, thus avoiding detection, or did they continue in order to get a closer fix on their quarry's destination? They decided to withdraw, on the assumption that the three honeybees' hive was somewhere in the vicinity, and they could find it later on when the invasion force reached that area. So they flew off into the sun, a tactic they had recently been taught by Yarrow's new storm force commander, Kale.

At heatfall Coppice was safely inside Bracken Bank after Piper and Fern had given the all clear. Briar and Teasel had been on local patrol so they had come across Coppice earlier and organised a local search. There had been no sign of any Blues, much to everybee's relief. That made it easier for Coppice to apologise profusely to his friends and colleagues. Despite his foolish journey they were still safe and he could tell them something about Middle Oak's fate – not that it cheered them up at all, but it did seem to help to know what had actually happened.

The four Blues made it back to Six Hives shortly after heatfall. On arrival they requested a meeting with Yarrow. Kale demanded a good reason, and was given one. He led them through to Yarrow's private section of the hive.

'This had better be good,' he said, glaring at them.

'It is worth hearing,' Kale assured him.

'Speak then,' demanded Yarrow.

The four looked at each other.

'You!' cried Kale, pointing at one of them, and the scout delivered a reasonably concise account of their day's work.

When he had finished, Yarrow declared, 'So my little trap worked, did it not? It would be beyond their comprehension to even guess that the hive in the oak tree had been deliberately infected by those "spores" I brought back from The Glade.'

He had reckoned that, sooner or later, somebee would come back to that hapless hive to find out what had happened to it. The extra strong scent would permit the visitor to be tracked. He had expected a group of visitors rather than one individual, but his trackers had done well enough. They had also discovered that a bumblebees' nest was in some way involved. That was interesting. What could they have to do with honeybees, especially honeybees who had something to do with that hive in the oak tree and who had caused Bugle so much trouble? Yarrow felt he was making progress at last.

He turned to the four scouts, 'Excellent job! Tell me your names.'

The spokesbee took it upon himself to do the introductions, knowing it was a great privilege to be named in front of the master. 'My name is Flixweed. This is my partner Foxtail, and these two are Scurvy and Ragwort.'

'Good. From now on you will be members of my personal guard with special responsibility for scouting. When we reach the area where those bees split up, you can lead the search for their hive, or hives.'

With that, Yarrow dismissed them and turned to discuss certain matters with Kale, including what he knew about bumblebees.

25. SIEGE

Coppice was suffering no physical after-effects from his visit to plague-ridden Middle Oak but he still felt a bit embarrassed by the inconvenience he had caused Piper, Fern and Heather. He also felt he had let down his friends at Bracken Bank, but they'd forgiven him and life went on. The hive's population was growing fast with the Queen laying hundreds of eggs each day and the food flowing in nicely, thanks especially to Thyme. The scout bees had control of the hive as there was no Council as yet. Madder had completed a basic escape tunnel system but continued to develop that system. Fescue and Sorrell now had a good picture of the area to the south and east while Piper and Fern kept a watchful eye to the north.

About ten days after Coppice's return, Piper and Fern picked up reports of Blues' activity. The strange thing was that the Blues were now working in double pairs or 'quads'. Piper felt uneasy about this development. What were the advantages of operating in this way? Why the change of tactics?

Then they heard that the Blues had crossed the river, a little way south of the Pines hive, and attacked High Orchard with a full swarm force. That meant Lower Orchard or Aspen was next in line – if the Blues had indeed resumed their invasion. After a quick stop at Piper's home hive, Stonewall, the pair flew over to Aspen. Nothing doing – so they flew on to Lower Orchard where they observed complete pandemonium around the hawthorn hedge in which the hive was built. They didn't hang around but flew back to Aspen to warn them.

Next day, Piper and Fern watched from a safe distance as Aspen came under attack. Most worrying was the size of the swarm force. It seemed to be twice the size of the first one. The other disturbing observation was the ease with which the blue hordes broke into Aspen hive. Despite the warning, something seemed to have gone wrong with their defences. Perhaps the Council hadn't taken the scouts' warning seriously enough.

Two very worried intelligence scouts left the scene. Piper insisted on visiting Stonewall to advise them over their defences. He set up extra patrols with instructions to engage any Blues they encountered. He also stopped all foraging for the rest of the day, in the hope that he could hide Stonewall from the enemy.

In mid-afternoon a pair of Blues wandered into the Stonewall drone zone. To their surprise they were attacked and de-winged. Piper and Fern were called in and were puzzled to find only two Blues.

'Where are yer two mates?' demanded Piper.

No reply.

'What are you up to?' shouted Fern, unusually upset.

Still no reply and further questioning proved futile.

'What shall we do with them?' asked one of Piper's drones.

'What do I care?' replied Piper.

But Fern suddenly had an idea. 'Drop them into the hive at Middle Oak – the one with the plague!'

'No, no!' pleaded one of the Blues.

'Oh I think you probably just about deserve it,' said Fern.

'I'm sure they do,' added Piper.

'Anything, we'll do anything!' whimpered the same captive, but his partner remained silent.

Piper asked, 'Where's your next attack? What are you after? Why do you kill Queens?'

'I don't know about the Queens but I do know we're going to invade the whole region and—'

That was as much as he could get out before his partner pounced on him and sunk his mandibles into his neck. Piper dragged him off but it was too late. The first Blue was dying, the second fought to the death. The Stonewall drones carried him away and dumped him out of sight. They hid the expiring body of the first Blue and resumed their patrols, disgusted by what they had seen. The question now was whether the Blue pair had really been on their own.

COPPICE

It seemed they had because no Blues troubled Stonewall next day. Piper had managed to get another ban on foraging – the Council respected his advice. This saved the hive – at least for the time being. Instead the Blues had found and hit Bramble hive, to the south-east of Stonewall. The Blues' quads were now surveying the area to the south of Middle Oak. The pair that Piper's drones had arrested had been based at the Pines. They had the less urgent job of checking out areas beyond the Blues' immediate targets for attention later on.

As the Blues' swarm force had moved south, Fern and Piper decided to fly down to Bracken Bank and operate from there for a while. On arrival they called a meeting of drone patrols and briefed them.

'The Blues have attacked four hives in the last four days as far as we know,' reported Piper. 'They've done High Orchard, Lower Orchard, Aspen and Bramble.'

'Bramble's not so far from here,' Coppice pointed out.

'So they're coming in our direction?' asked Madder.

'Looks like it, but we can't be certain. We don't know where they are today – could be after Copse, or Firs?'

'Or even your original aberrant hive,' suggested Fern, 'though that's as far west as Stonewall is, and they've left that alone so far.'

'And we're further west than Bramble,' said Scruff hopefully.

Piper nodded his agreement, 'Yep! We could be OK for a while yet, and don't forget, our hive's a new one. They don't know we're here.'

Coppice hoped Piper was right because if he wasn't, it was almost certainly his fault for visiting Middle Oak and being followed back. 'So what now?' he asked.

Fern replied, 'We need to hear from Fescue and Sorrell and then help them scout the area west of Bramble hive – their last known target.'

'They're due to report in the day after tomorrow,' said Coppice.

'Pity it's not sooner,' said Piper. 'OK, we'll check out Copse hive first. You lot keep up yer local patrols. Make sure somebee's out there all the time – and make sure yer foragers fly in carefully!'

Fern and Piper discovered Copse hive was still intact and it remained so the following day, after which Fescue and Sorrell turned up. They also had heard about Blue quads – around the Upper and Lower Larch hives this time.

'We're just going to have to check out all the hives in this area, starting tomorrow,' decided Fern, and no bee argued with him.

The three intelligence scouts plus Sorrell, who was learning the job quickly, flew off after heatrise. They found the Copse hive was still untouched, likewise Lower Larch. However, they found the Upper Larch drone zone almost deserted. They didn't bother to stop and talk to the odd remaining drone; they just flew over to the hive. Once again they encountered the deadly blue swarm force.

'Not much point in watching this,' said Fescue. 'We might as well check out some more hives while the Blues are busy here.'

Piper and Fern thought they might learn something from observing the attack but Fescue had a point, so they flew on. During that day they discovered that Dark Oak, Highbank, Firs and Bramble hives had all been attacked, and their Queens removed. The new information was that the Blues had left a contingent of their own bees in each of those hives – something they'd not done before apart from at Six Hives, their base. Fern wondered how they managed to do that. How did a comparatively small group of Blues survive later counter attacks? What would happen when a new Queen emerged?

Back at Bracken Bank that heatfall, scouts, drones, Lavender, Thyme and Bryony were discussing what to do. Only Lower Larch and Copse stood between them and the Blues' swarm force. Assuming the Blues attacked only one hive each day, then they had two days to do something! So far their best hope was that Bracken Bank was new enough to avoid detection or attention.

Piper told them about Stonewall's escape and how he had managed to halt all foraging for over a day. With no Council to persuade, Bracken Bank could easily do the same thing, but for how long?

Madder insisted they must survive somehow. He had escaped the Blues so far and he wasn't going to be caught now – thank you very much! 'If those Blues knew it was us who'd caused them so much trouble this season, they'd really go for us if they thought they'd found us.'

'Hmm,' muttered Coppice. 'We do seem to keep getting in their way, don't we? It's as if we can't avoid confronting them.'

Madder remembered something he learned from Birch Cave. 'Somebee once

COPPICE

told me the best form of defence is attack, you know.'

'How can we attack all those Blues?' complained Scruff.

'But there must be something we can do, rather than just sitting here waiting for them to find us.'

'Maybe there is something,' said Sorrell, eyes twinkling. 'What about these Queens the Blues are taking out? Can we learn something from it – something that would show us what to do?'

They all looked at Lavender – the expert on Queens. 'Um, well, um, I admit it is a bit puzzling. As you know, a Queen can be replaced quite easily. If the workers start feeding a newly hatched egg immediately, they could have a new Queen in twelve days. She would be ready for a mating flight a few days later, so let's say a total of twenty days before egg laying recommences. Any reasonably strong colony should survive the temporary setback.'

'So what do the Blues gain from it?' asked Coppice.

'Not a lot,' commented Spurge.

'Is there nothing else you can think of Lavender?' asked Fern.

'Not really, except of course that a change of Queen means a change of scent. The Queen controls the hive with her scent. Ah, now if there's no Queen for a time…'

'Yes!' exclaimed Madder. 'That's it!' If there's no Queen you might be able to establish an alien unit inside the hive, one which would be scented up correctly when the new Queen arrived! Clever stuff. The initial acceptance would be by forced entry followed by scenting up with honey.'

'They don't even need to force an entry,' Bryony reminded them. 'They can fly in shortly after heatfall and scent up.'

'Good point,' said Coppice. 'So we need to guard our entrance after heatfall.'

'Just how do we do that?' grumped Spurge.

Madder explained, 'It's warm enough at this time of the season for at least part of the colony to cluster close to the entrance.'

'Clever idea,' said Fern, impressed with Madder's thinking.

'We could also reduce the size of our entrance,' added Coppice. 'Less space to defend.'

The ideas began to flow and they felt a lot more confident by the time they fell quiet for the coolest part of the night. Sorrell wasn't quite sure they had fully explained the Blues' tactics but he was happy that the defence of Bracken Bank would begin in earnest the next heatrise.

Next day Lower Larch was attacked by Swarm Force Two and the Blues' scouts appeared in the vicinity of Bracken Bank. Yarrow had dispatched Foxtail, Flixweed, Scurvy and Ragwort to the area in which they had tracked the bees who had visited the hive with the plague. They brought three other quads with them and searched the area systematically. Eventually they came across a drone zone. The quad who found it split in two, with one pair staying in the zone ready to track a drone back to his hive, while the other pair hid themselves and watched.

Fortunately the Bracken Bank drones were alert to the danger and informed Briar and Teasel, who were on local patrol at the time. Briar organised an immediate attack and the two, unsuspecting scouts were suddenly set upon by about fifteen drones who had, up to that moment, been peacefully buzzing around their zone. The watching pair unwisely shot out to assist but soon wished they hadn't. All four Blues were cut down and left to crawl away into the undergrowth.

The Bracken Bankers were jubilant – they had actually beaten the Blues, but were there more of them around? Briar reckoned not because he knew they were scouting in quads. All the same, he returned to the hive to inform Coppice and the others. The intelligence scouts were out, as usual, but the others flew out to the drone zone with Briar.

'I recommend three local patrols,' said Coppice.

'Agreed, but how many bees in each?' asked Briar.

'Steady on,' said Madder. 'If we go looking for them we might give the game away. We would do better to wait for them here. I'm sure they'll come looking for their missing quad.'

'I suppose you're right,' said Coppice, 'but shouldn't our local patrols continue?'

'Yes – Briar and Teasel still, isn't it? So carry on and only come to the drone zone when you're due to be relieved.'

Slightly reluctantly, Briar and Teasel departed. The others spread themselves

COPPICE

around the drone zone, trying to behave as normally as possible.

Flixweed and his team had flown well to the west before encountering a hive called Ivy by the locals. Pleased with their find, but surprised they had to fly so far to discover it, they zoomed back to their rendezvous with their other scout teams. Two quads were waiting for them, the other was late.

'Where've they got to?' grumbled Flixweed.

'How should we know?' complained Scurvy.

'Which area were they searching?' asked Foxtail.

'Erm, south-west of the last hive, wasn't it?' replied Flixweed.

'You should know,' argued Scurvy, 'you sent them!'

'Oh shut up!'

'Excuse me, but shouldn't we go and find them? They might have flown into trouble,' suggested Ragwort.

Flixweed glared at him for even suggesting that Blue scouts could fly into any sort of trouble. He felt like swiping him but thought better of it. There had been some odd stories circulating the scout teams recently – probably all highly exaggerated.

He came to a decision, 'Yep, it's getting late, so you two quads return to Six Hives. My quad will find the others and stopover somewhere nearby. Got that?'

The others nodded. Flixweed wondered how long it would be before the swarm force adopted a base nearer to the centre of operations. 'Comin' you three? We haven't got all day, or even half a day. Let's get a move on!'

The quad searched in vain, finding neither their colleagues nor a drone zone. As heatfall approached they headed for the hive that Swarm Force Two had invaded that day. That would do for a stopover. The next day they would wait for the swarm force to return to that area and inform Yarrow of the missing quad. As they settled down for the night in Lower Larch, a party of about thirty Blues flew out to the Copse hive, which was the swarm force's target for the next day.

At this time in Bracken Bank there was some confidence after the day's events. They had dealt with the Blues and there had been no follow up.

'Perhaps they'll miss us altogether now,' suggested Scruff, trying smooth down the hairs on his left midleg.

'Too soon to tell,' cautioned Madder. 'We must continue our extra patrols tomorrow. If Lower Larch fell today, it'll be Copse tomorrow. The day after that it should probably be us. If it isn't, we might have escaped.'

'I agree with that,' said Coppice, 'unless they go out to Ivy hive first.'

'And just where are our intelligence scouts?' asked Spurge.

No bee knew for sure, but Coppice guessed, 'I bet they're at Copse, trying to set up some sort of defence.'

He was right. Piper, Fern, Fescue and Sorrell were doing their best to persuade the Copse Council that they were almost certainly going to be attacked the next day. It was hard work. All they succeeded in doing was to have extra scouts sent out at heatrise to watch for the so-called 'swarm force' that the intelligence scouts were going on about. Yes, they had heard stories of bad happenings to the north and east of them but no, they didn't think their hive was in danger of being wiped out – which it probably wasn't, but…

Fern called off the audience as politely as he could and the four of them departed. They had permission to stopover, which sounded risky, but the swarm force had a long way to come and so couldn't get there until around mid-morning, assuming they were flying in from Six Hives. Heatfall found them still discussing the defence of the hive.

'I don't think there's anything else we can do,' said Fern.

'Yer right, I guess,' agreed Piper. 'Pity, though.'

'Except…'

'Except what?'

'Except keep an eye on the entrance here.'

Piper looked puzzled but Fescue remembered, 'You mean what that Madder fellow was suggesting – about the Blues flying in after heatfall to spy out the hive?'

'That's right. If Copse is tomorrow's target, they should be checking it out now.'

'So they could be here already?'

'Why don't we find out?' suggested Sorrell.

The others looked at him, as if hardly expecting this newcomer to their ranks to direct their actions.

COPPICE

Fern had to agree, 'Very well then. Stick close together.' And he led them off towards the entrance.

It was a warm night and the temperature hadn't dropped enough to inhibit reasonable activity. The foursome edged their way closer to the entrance. They came to a halt when they were close enough to observe it from a safe distance – if that was possible. There were some other bees around.

'That's odd,' whispered Fescue. 'Copse bees guarding the entrance during the night?'

'*Ssh!*' urged Fern, 'look closely.'

As their eyes adjusted to the dim light around the moonlit entrance, they realised what they were looking at.

'Blues!' gasped Sorrell.

'*Ssh!*' insisted the others in unison.

'How many?' whispered Fern.

'About ten,' Fescue reckoned.

'More over there,' said Fern.

'More like twenty,' Piper calculated. 'Why so many?'

They thought about it and then Piper realised, 'I bet they're here to take out the guards when the swarm force arrives! That explains how they took Aspen hive so easily, remember?'

Fern nodded his agreement.

'Shouldn't we warn Bracken Bank about this?' asked Sorrell.

'First thing in the morning,' replied Fern.

'But will we be able to fly out so easily if these Blues are in guard?'

'They might not interfere with the hive's activity until the swarm force arrives,' said Fern, 'but we're not going to take that chance.'

'Yer mean a night flight?' asked Piper.

'Correct.'

Even Fescue, an intelligence scout, hadn't actually made a night flight, or a cold flight as it was also called. Sorrell had only heard about it from Coppice.

'Don't worry,' said Fern. 'The important thing is to concentrate on flying hard and fast, ignoring the sudden temperature drop, which hits you when you first leave the hive. Now let's slip away and get some honey.

They did so, and then returned to the entrance.

'Tuck in close behind me,' ordered Fern. 'Piper, you bring up the rear.'

The foursome started their wings until they were close to take-off speed, then they half ran, half flew at the entrance, past the resting Blues. As they shot by, one or two of the Blues reacted but thought they must be dreaming. One of them did go and peer out of the entrance but the four bees were well out of sight by then.

'This is great!' exclaimed Sorrell, after he'd overcome the shock of the cool air.

He had that 'doing what we're not supposed to be able to do' feeling, like all honeybees on their first night flight.

They reached Bracken Bank in their close formation and entered unopposed.

'We'll have to do something about this,' thought Fern. 'We must have some sort of guard tomorrow night.'

In the meantime the four bees stayed as near to the entrance as the temperature would allow, just in case.

At heatrise the regular guard came on duty and the intelligence scouts went to find the others on Lavender's comb. They reported their experiences and sent out three, reinforced patrols while Lavender and Bryony set about the task of guarding the entrance. They continued to have it made smaller, using a thick wax wall carefully constructed by the worker bees. They also recruited extra guard bees for duty after heatfall.

Swarm Force Two passed over Lower Larch on its way to Copse shortly after mid-morning. As it did so, Flixweed's quad flew up to report to Yarrow. They were worried because there was now some doubt as to the following day's target hive, and Yarrow didn't like uncertainties. Fortunately for them, it was Kale who received their report, as Yarrow wanted to lead the day's attack.

'You've got until mid-afternoon to sort this one out!' he rasped. 'Take the drones stationed at the hive we took much further west – and Yarrow won't believe you either. Now be off with you!'

The scouts were relieved to get off so lightly, and pleased to be given a couple of hundred drones for their task. They shot off to Lower Larch and collected them. From there they flew to the edge of the woods and started searching in ten groups of approximately twenty bees. The four scouts went to four separate landmarks to await news – good news they hoped.

It was around sunpeak when one of the groups of Blues came across the Bracken Bank drone zone. The locals called in the nearest patrol, Scruff and Spurge, who hesitated for a few moments before ordering an attack. The Blues were taken by surprise and several of them were caught – but not all. Their orders were to escape if attacked, not fight back. Spurge and company were chuffed, if a little puzzled by the lack of resistance. When the news found its way to Coppice and Madder they weren't so pleased, realising that some Blues had escaped to report the location of the drone zone.

'You should have chased them,' complained Madder. 'How many do you think escaped?'

'Well, er, four or five,' guessed Scruff, nervously smoothing his jagged hairs.

'Four or five too many,' said Coppice. 'Now what do we do?'

'Quit our drone zone for a start,' said Madder. 'In fact, we'll get all our drones back to the hive.'

Madder's experience wasn't questioned and the Bracken Bankers called in all their drones and set extra guards as fast as they could. Then they waited. Only the intelligence scouts flew out on patrol. As foragers returned to the hive they were banned from leaving again. Coppice just hoped none of them would give anything away as they flew in.

Foxtail received news of the attack from the four survivors. He informed the others, who rounded up their teams and flew to the offending drone zone, only to find it deserted.

'Are you certain?' hissed Flixweed.

'Um, well, um, yes,' replied a confused drone.

Flixweed swiped him out of the way. 'Find them!' he yelled. 'Watch everybee. Find their hive. It's around here somewhere.'

The two hundred Blues spread out behind Flixweed's quad and filtered their way through the wood. They arrived at a meadow without success.

'Now track any worker bees you come across,' ordered Flixweed, with Foxtail's back up. So the Blues spread out again and this time they had more success. Several laden foragers were spotted leaving the meadow and flying into the wood. When the Blues followed, they lost them as soon as they entered the wood. Puzzled by this, they went and told Flixweed. He gathered Foxtail, Scurvy and Ragwort and flew over to the area that was causing concern.

'What if two of us wait inside the wood and the other two track the next worker?' suggested Ragwort, who was a bit smarter than the other three.

'What?' grumped Flixweed.

'Sounds OK to me,' said Foxtail quickly, before Flixweed could dismiss the idea.

So they tried it. They cleared the two hundred out of sight and waited for the next forager headed for the woods.

Sundew was one of the very first foragers to emerge at Bracken Bank, as opposed to flying in with the Middle Oak swarm. She was returning with her pollen baskets laden and her stomach full of nectar. She knew the hive needed as much food as it could get, so she felt very pleased with her latest load. Being more concerned with delivering her goods safely, she was less than observant and failed to scan around properly as she entered the wood and dived into the bracken. Ragwort and Scurvy watched her disappear. Shortly afterwards, Flixweed and Foxtail flew into the wood. They hadn't seen where the forager had gone.

Ragwort intercepted them, 'It's very clever. Follow me.'

The four Blues searched the bracken on the nearby bank until they spotted the entrance. Immediately Madder's guards shot out to attack them. The Blues were caught by surprise and lost the initiative. Flixweed and Scurvy were caught but Ragwort and Foxtail made off for the meadow. Foxtail was clobbered but Ragwort was that bit faster, and he flew straight into the two hundred Blues hidden at the far end of the meadow. The Blues rallied to his screams and counter attacked. The Bracken Bankers were now taken by surprise. They spun round quickly and headed back for the hive. Two of them were caught before they reached it. Madder was just inside and closed off the entrance with a wedge of his bees. The Blues flew straight at them but the wedge held. Ragwort called

COPPICE

them off. This was a job for Swarm Force Two.

Ragwort had done his bit. Pity about the others – fallen in the line of duty he'd have to tell Kale, which is exactly what he did say later that day at Lower Larch. Kale was both pleased and puzzled. Why should this hive prove so awkward? And if they were the lot who'd escaped Swarm Force One, then it was even more of a puzzle.

Yarrow returned from a successful day's campaign and dispatched Swarm Force Two back to Six Hives with Kale, after hearing his report. Then taking Ragwort as his guide, Yarrow went out on his own scouting mission to investigate this 'hive in the bracken'. The pair found a suitable, concealed observation point and waited.

As he watched, silently and patiently, Yarrow sensed the importance of this hive. Was this where he would find the Queen he was looking for? Unlikely, surely. This was almost certainly a new hive, formed by the swarm that had escaped Bugle earlier in the season. Yet he still felt there was something special about them. He even felt a bit uneasy, though he hid it from Ragwort. If this really was to be a problem hive, then he'd better not rush into anything. He could bring his storm force to a closer base though, then they'd be close at hand. Yes, he would arrange for them to occupy the hives in the larch trees and maybe one or two others. Then he would use a different tactic against the hive in the bracken. He would besiege it! He would starve them out if he had to!

26. FLIGHT FOR HELP

Thousands of Blues were pouring out of Six Hives and congregating in the air above. By the time Kale flew to the head of Swarm Force Two there was something like eighteen thousand of them – all drones. They were Yarrow's final invasion force and they meant business! About five thousand were left over from Storm Force One and there were several hundred more spread through the most recently invaded hives to the south-west.

They set off for Lower Larch where Yarrow was waiting. He had decided to move his base that day and when Kale arrived, around mid-morning, the order was given. Because of the numbers and the delay that was now expected, Yarrow spread his Blues among seven hives, namely Bramble, Firs, Highbank, Dark Oak, Upper Larch, Lower Larch and Copse. He had to ensure that the workers in each hive could keep up with the extra food supplies needed for his extended campaign. Of course he didn't expect to be held up for too long. When all eighteen thousand drones were settled in, Yarrow told Kale what he wanted him to do and then retired to Lower Larch for the rest of the day.

At Bracken Bank they awaited the Blues' attack. The wedge was ready but nothing happened. By sunpeak there was still no sign of the enemy. The Intelligence scouts decided to take a look around just outside the entrance. They spotted nothing, nor were they attacked. By mid-afternoon it was decided to risk sending some foragers out into the meadow under the watch of the drones. Coppice, Madder, Briar and Teasel took the first stint.

A couple of hundred worker bees flew out, delighted to be back among the flowers. Still no sign of any Blues so another two hundred foragers were sent out. They had been collecting for several minutes when it happened. Out of nowhere, so it seemed, a mass of Blues dropped on them! There was utter confusion as the workers fled back towards Bracken Bank. There was nothing the drones could do except try and get back to safety themselves. They weren't far from the hive but the Blues outnumbered them by about five to one and the workers were being badly mauled as a result. The four drones and about half the workers made it, including Thyme fortunately. The Blues rushed the entrance but didn't persist once the wedge was set in place. It wasn't their intention to break in anyway, but it was worth a try in the circumstances. Kale called them off and they returned to the seven hives they now occupied.

Inside Bracken Bank they were trying to work out what had happened.

'Where did they come from?' squeaked Teasel.

'We were looking out in all directions, weren't we?' asked Briar.

'Hmm,' muttered Coppice. 'Except upwards.'

'Well,' added Madder, 'at least not upwards into the sun. They used the old trick and dropped down directly on top of us.'

'I can't imagine a whole swarm doing that,' said Briar.

'But was it a whole swarm?'

They considered that for a moment and decided it only felt like a whole swarm but had in fact been a much smaller number of bees.

'So,' concluded Coppice, 'Madder's right. They took us by surprise with a small force, having lured us out into the meadow in the first place, I suspect.'

'But why aren't they attacking in their usual way?' asked Teasel.

Madder suggested, 'I think they've shown us what will happen if we go out foraging, and if we can't collect food…'

'If we don't collect food we become powerless,' said Coppice. 'That's it, isn't it? They intend to starve us out – or at least weaken us before a head on attack.'

Madder nodded, 'But why are they treating us differently to other hives, I wonder?'

'Maybe we've got them a bit worried?'

'That would be something, I suppose. Let's tell the others anyway.'

The second day of the siege, as it became known, saw the Blues attempt the same tactics. They kept well away from Bracken Bank to encourage them to risk sending out a foraging party. Inside the hive, Madder came up with an idea.

'Supposing we forage in the wood instead?'
'Not so many flowers,' Coppice pointed out.
'True, but better than nothing.'
'And they couldn't drop on us from directly above, of course.'
'Of course.'

The more they thought about it, the more they liked the idea. The intelligence scouts were asked to take a quick look, and they saw nothing. In mid-afternoon fifty foragers left the hive in dribs and drabs. They weren't challenged, so fifty more slipped out. The Blues, meanwhile, reduced their watch in the meadow and Kale dispatched some of his bees into the wood, just in case. They soon came across the Bracken Bankers, who fled to safety. Most of them made it this time, using the cover of the foliage.

Some food had been collected but not nearly enough. On day three they discovered that the Blues had learned their lesson and had set large squads of watchers in the wood, as Fescue and Sorrell found out when they flew the first recce of the morning!

'No good,' reported Fescue, 'they're everywhere now.'

'So we're definitely under siege,' concluded Madder. 'Now what do we do?'

They consulted Lavender and Thyme. Lavender said she would explain matters to the Queen and try and get her to reduce her egg-laying. Thyme said they had to find food from somewhere. Next they assessed their existing stores of pollen and honey. Being a new hive, it wasn't that well stocked up, though they had tried hard once they knew the Blues might be coming their way. Also, being a young hive, the numbers weren't very high and as it was past mid-season the Queen's egg-laying was on the decline. This all meant that the number of adult bees was just about at its peak, so although they could cut back on egg-laying, they still had a lot of adult mouths to feed.

Rationing was introduced before the end of that day. It was easier said than done because worker bees don't normally think twice about feeding. If they don't get enough from incoming foragers, they simply go to the nearest honeystore and help themselves. To control this, Lavender had to put guards on the main storage areas! No worker bees left the hive, and the Blues made no attacks.

By sunpeak of day four nothing had happened so a party of workers was taken

COPPICE

out under heavy drone escort. The Blues attacked within minutes. Fern and Piper were dismayed because they hadn't spotted any enemy bees in the area beforehand. They presumed they must have been very well hidden. This also worried Madder, who thought back to his Birch Cave experiences. What would Milfoil have done? If only his chief scout was with him now. Could he go and fetch him? No, that would be too risky, and unfair to Little Birch – they needed him. So Madder tried to think like Milfoil.

At that moment Coppice joined him. He was going to ask about the escape tunnels but saw that Madder was deep in thought, so waited until he was noticed.

'Ah, Twenty-, I mean Coppice.'

Coppice nodded, 'Any ideas on how we get out of this one?'

'I was just trying to think how Milfoil would approach the situation.'

'Your chief scout at Little Birch?'

Madder nodded. 'You know, we've had more experience of dealing with these Blues than anybee else I reckon – I mean those of us here at Bracken Bank, between us, if you see what I'm getting at?'

'Yes, and no.'

'Well, if anybee's going to stop these invaders, it will probably have to be us.'

'We don't look like stopping them at the moment, do we?'

'Maybe not, but we're still here. There's still hope.'

Coppice considered that for a few moments, 'Yes, there has to be hope.'

'Good. So what are we going to do?'

'Hmm. Now what do we know that could help us crack this? For one thing, we're sure we can outfly the Blues. They're tougher and heavier than we are, but a bit slower in the air.'

'Agreed,' said Madder, 'but that's it, isn't it?'

'I'm not so sure. Remember when we watched them attack The Mound hive? They really struggled until some bee came along and changed the tactics – the drone who flew the figures of eight, assuming it was a drone.'

'Drone? Figures of eight?'

'Oh, I hadn't thought about that, I just presumed...'

'OK, it probably was a drone, given that we've never seen a blue worker bee – have we?'

Coppice thought about that one. 'Er, no. I don't think we have – yet!'

'And that's why they have to harbour in other hives, relying on the workers to feed them.'

'Agreed, but what are they after in the end?'

'The whole of our region I should think. That's what Fern and Piper found out from that scout they captured.'

'Yes, but I don't see the point if they're not bringing in their own workers.'

Madder couldn't see it either but suggested, 'Perhaps they'll fetch them in when they've conquered the whole region?'

'Too many questions, not enough answers. What else do we know?'

'I think we could use some of Milfoil's methods to crawl out of here.'

'We could what?'

'He had this way of crawling, mixed with some very low flying. He does it where the vegetation allows it. If we headed into the wood, we could do it.'

Coppice raised the obvious objection, 'But that would take too long.'

'Not if we knew when we were safely through the Blues' lines. After that, we could take to the air.'

'Fine, but how do we know where the Blues' lines are?'

'Judging by their speed of reaction today, their forces are very close.'

'And their scouts closer still!'

'As you would expect.'

'I suppose we could create a diversion as well,' Coppice suggested, 'like when we fixed up that break for Fescue on the way back from Hollybank. Remember, I did tell you about it.'

'Indeed you did. Caused a lot of confusion you said.'

'Certainly did. The Blues made a right mess of it.'

'Good, so what if we sent Fescue and some others out to draw their scouts away, while some of us slip out into the undergrowth?'

'Fine,' agreed Coppice. 'But hang on a minute, where are we going?'

Madder had been so concerned working out an escape route that he hadn't thought where they were going to escape to. 'Um, how about Hollybank? Or Stonewall? Then there's our old aberrant hive?'

'You're kidding!'

'Twenty-three?'

'Ah, I see, and that gives me another idea. We could go to the refuge and ask Ling and Heather what to do.'

'Are you sure?'

'They're the only bees – sorry, *bumble*bees – that I can think of who could help us.'

'Very well, but the refuge is close to Middle Oak, isn't it?'

'Yes, but to the west – only just in Blues' territory I reckon, but they're busy down here, aren't they?'

'Hopefully.'

So Coppice and Madder called in the others and discussed in some detail what they had come up with. By heatfall they had a plan of action ready.

Fairly early next day, the Bracken Bank drones escorted a party of fifty foraging worker bees into the woods. They didn't venture too far and when the expected attack came, they zoomed back to the hive. That was their effort for the day, or at least that's what they wanted the Blues to think. In fact, most of the Blues did very little thinking at all. Kale was in overall charge while Ragwort took particular care of the wooded area by the besieged hive.

All was quiet until sunpeak. Briar and Teasel led Fescue and Sorrell down one of Madder's escape tunnels – one that exited to the meadow side of the hive. They carefully removed the plug and let them out. The two scouts crawled away from the escape tunnel, through the bracken, so that when they took to the air it could not be assumed they had arisen directly from a secret exit. They were also giving Briar and Teasel a little time to begin replugging the hole. Actually, they would do more than that; they would fill in the whole of the tunnel leading up to that exit.

Fescue turned to Sorrell, touched one of his antennae with his own, then nodded. Up zoomed the pair, straight towards the sun. Nothing happened for a few moments and they thought no bee had spotted them. Fescue slowed his ascent and scanned the area below him.

'Here they come!' he yelled to Sorrell. 'Let's get out of here!'

The pair headed off at full speed in a southerly direction. They would adjust their beeline to head for Hollybank later. Meanwhile, Coppice and Madder crawled out of another escape tunnel, opened up for them by Scruff and Spurge. This one led into the bracken on the wood side of the hive. Simultaneously, Fern, Piper and a few worker bees, including Bryony, made an appearance just outside the main entrance to the hive – anything to draw the Blues' attention. That worked as well. After a short time, a horde of them emerged from the trees and flew at the entrance. The Bracken Bankers shot back inside and quickly re-established their wedge defence.

Coppice and Madder were crawling, hopping or 'flitting' along, according to the density of the undergrowth. It was a slow business, which soon became very tedious. Coppice longed to make a dash for it but they had already agreed that any sort of pursuit should be avoided, especially as they were heading towards the Blues' territory and not away from it.

Well to the south of them, high flying Fescue and Sorrell were out of sight of the fifty or so chasing Blues. Only a scent track could upset their escape now. To overcome that, the pair dived down to a field of bright red poppies, which had only recently come into bloom. They dusted themselves in the pollen and then crushed some of the petals, doing their best to smother themselves with the scent. This was Thyme's idea. There were several flowers that would have done the trick, but the poppies were the easiest to spot. Duly 're-scented', the pair flew back up and took the beeline for Hollybank. The Blues completely lost them.

When they reached Hollybank they searched out one of the food sources being collected by the foragers and spent a long time smothering each other with as much of the pollen as they could get hold of. The poppy scent took some masking but they eventually gained entry to Hollybank without being set upon by the guard bees. Once inside, they immediately contacted the Council to find out whether any Blues had been sighted in the locality or even visited the hive. Yes, there had been the occasional sighting; no, the Blues hadn't entered the hive as far as anybee knew. With that reassurance, Fescue set about explaining to his Council all that had happened and how they should prepare their defences, and then...

The afternoon dragged on as Coppice and Madder necessarily made slow progress northwards, at last they reached the edge of the wood and turned north-

COPPICE I

west to follow the tree line. It was too early to risk flying across open land to the woods further north; they had to keep undercover until heatfall approached.

Eventually the time came for them to make their break. They'd gone over the landmarks several times with Fern and Piper so they zoomed out of the woods with some confidence. Passing over a stream and a single 'black river', they followed the edge of some woods until they reached an area of sweet chestnut, which Coppice recognised. He led Madder on to the vicinity of the aberrant hive.

This was the second time Coppice had revisited the hive of his emergence, but for Madder it was the first. He was now remembering the last time he'd been here – the terrible expulsion by the workers and his flight to freedom. It was an unnerving experience.

'Do you really think Twenty-three's still here?'

'I don't see why not, assuming he is indeed the "elder drone".'

'Let's hide up until the guards retire to the cluster, then we'll go in.'

Madder was insisting they try to locate their old friend, despite Coppice's objections. The idea was to make a stopover in the aberrant hive, with Coppice making an early exit at heatrise while Madder did a quick search for Twenty-three.

The first part of their plan went smoothly, or so they thought. Several minutes after the guards disappeared from the entrance, Coppice and Madder flew in, smeared themselves with honey, and settled down for the night. They stayed as near to the entrance as possible. What they didn't allow for was their tiredness after all that crawling, and the elder drone's vigilance!

A little while after heatrise, Madder was trying to shake Coppice into action. 'Come on – if you want to get out of here alive!'

Coppice stumbled over to the nearest honey cells, accompanied by his ally. His stomach filled, he looked up, only to find a pair of drone eyes which did not belong to Madder.

'Oh, hullo,' mumbled Coppice.

No reply. He glanced at Madder as if to say, 'Shall we get out of here?' but Madder was staring at another drone. Coppice followed his gaze. It was the elder drone. How did he know they were in the hive? Coppice decided to play dumb. At last the elder drone spoke.

'I-I don't think you should be here.'

Coppice looked across at Madder.

'You should depart immediately,' came a more assured voice from the elder drone.

Madder was still staring. Coppice waited. Everybee was getting uneasy.

'Yes, we're just leaving,' said Madder, 'and you're coming with us, Twenty-three!'

Coppice was shocked by Madder's presumption. He waited for a response. The elder drone was clearly shaken. One of his silvery antennae twitched a little.

'What do you mean?' he said.

Madder was ready. 'I mean you're the honeybee who wasn't going to emerge from his cell aren't you? And we're the two who dragged you out, aren't we?'

The elder drone was now trembling. The drones escorting him were looking very puzzled. He ordered them to go, 'Leave this to me!' Then he edged forward. 'What do you want?'

'We want you to come with us,' said Madder. 'We need you. The whole region's under threat and we're trying to do something about it.'

Coppice was even more surprised. Madder must have had an idea he hadn't discussed. They waited for the elder drone to decide. In the end he said nothing but just crawled past them to the entrance. They followed him in silence and expectation as he flew out to the drone zone, where all three settled in Twenty-three's favourite hiding place.

None of them spoke for a time, then Coppice put the question he just had to ask, 'Why did you betray me when I came back before?'

'I'm-I'm not entirely certain. I think it was for your own good...and mine. You see, it gave me the opportunity to reach a position in which I could survive the next expulsion. I couldn't tell what would happen if I left, or you stayed. It was, well, much simpler if I stayed and you left. I...'

'OK, OK,' said Coppice. 'I think I follow you.'

'But how did you survive the expulsion?' asked Madder.

Twenty-three thought back to that awful evening. 'I was thrown out and half-buried in a heap of dead and dying drones on the ground outside the entrance. I was so frightened, I didn't dare move for a long time. I suppose I must have looked as good as dead. When darkness came, I burrowed deep into the pile for warmth.' He shuddered at the memory. 'Some time during the night I passed into unconsciousness but in the morning I came round. At first I was too shocked to think clearly, but I eventually plucked up enough courage to crawl out from the mass of bodies. Too scared to fly back to the hive, I robbed some of those yellow flowers to get some energy. All day I hung around, wondering what to do. At last it occurred to me to fly out to the drone zone to see if either of you were there. Of course you weren't, so I became depressed. I almost left it too late to return to the hive again that heatfall, but when I did get back I decided to fly straight in and take the consequences. No way was I going to spend another night in a pile of dead bodies. Well, to my surprise the guards ignored me and I was safe. I survived the winter, and the next season, being a rare second year drone; I became quite influential, believe it or not. Then you called on us, Twenty-, I mean Coppice. I think they liked my advice. Yes, I am Twenty-three!'

'Yes!' shouted Coppice.

'Great!' roared Madder, and there was an official reunion for the next few minutes, after which Coppice and Madder related their stories.

'So what now?' asked Twenty-three when the trio had caught up with each other's exploits.

'We're on our way to visit the bumblebees,' explained Coppice, 'because they're the ones most likely to be able to help us.'

'Where do they live?'

'Not far from here, in a place known as the "refuge".'

Without more ado the three friends set off to find Ling and Heather. It was a shortish trip, and easy to locate the pine tree with the lightning damage. Coppice led the others to the main entrance. He crawled straight inside and along the passage to the first junction before stopping to explain.

'I didn't want to hang around the entrance, just in case. Now we have a series of junctions to negotiate. Just give me a minute to remember.'

'Remember what?' asked Madder.

'*Ssh*, I'm thinking! Now then…left, then right, then it was right again, no…left and left again, followed by a right. Hang on…'

'We are!' commented Madder with some sarcasm.

'So that's left, right, left, left, right. Follow me!'

By this time Madder had remembered what Coppice had told him about the refuge's tunnel system. After all, Bracken Bank now had something similar, only less complicated.

Coppice led them triumphantly into the main nest chamber. 'Ling! Heather! Anybee at home?'

There was no reply.

'Hmm,' muttered Coppice, crawling into the chamber. 'I'm surprised one of them isn't around here somewhere.'

'It looks a bit deserted to me,' said Madder.

'It *smells* a bit deserted to me,' added Twenty-three, antennae twitching rapidly.

Coppice looked worried, then he heard a noise back down the tunnel. 'Ah, here they come,' he said, with some relief, turning back down the tunnel. But he was stopped dead in his tracks. As he began to make out the approaching shape he realised it wasn't big enough to be a bumblebee…then he realised it was the wrong colour!

27. TO THE CAVES OF KNOWLEDGE

In the next instant Madder burst past Coppice and barged straight into the Blue intruder, smacking him against the tunnel wall and dazing him.

'Quick, take care of this one while I go after his partner,' he ordered.

Coppice sprang into action, shortly followed by a less than enthusiastic Twenty-three. Madder stormed along the passage in hot pursuit until he reached the first junction. He tried to pick up his quarry's scent but it seemed to fill the whole area. Then he realised he didn't know the way out either. Doubling back to the others, he dragged the injured blue drone, with their help, along to the first junction. Coppice indicated the way out and Madder shoved the hapless Blue about twenty bee-lengths down the wrong passage.

'That should throw them for a while,' he said.

'Even if they get this far,' added Coppice.

Twenty-three pointed out, 'That's all very well, but aren't we trapped now?'

Madder gave a knowing look and Coppice explained, 'No, there are other ways out of here, but there's something I must do before we make our escape.'

'What's that?' asked Madder.

'Something I've kept very much to myself.'

'Well come on then, let us in on the secret!'

'Just follow me if you will,' and Coppice led them back to the nest chamber. From there he took them into the seven-junction system, turning right at the first junction and right again at the second. They were all cross-tunnels so you could go straight ahead if you wanted to, and that's what he did at the next two junctions. Madder noticed they were descending. Just ahead of him, Coppice paused.

'Right, right, straight on, straight on…then, yes…the turn you've not yet made. So it's left, right and left again.' And away he went, his friends hoping he knew what he was doing.

As they neared their destination they saw the tunnel was crumbling in places. It was very dry down here, and dusty. 'This stuff could clog your spiracles in no time,' thought Twenty-three, trying not to breathe in too deeply.

The tunnel narrowed and Coppice led them into the safe-chamber. His friends were dumbstruck for a time. Twenty-three was enthralled by the glowing walls. He moved closer, reaching out his antennae, feeling for any sort of sensation. Nothing registered, but he was full of awe for this place.

Madder was taken aback at first but soon directed his attention to the markings covering the walls. 'What are these?' he asked.

'What do you reckon?' replied Coppice, testing him out.

Madder looked a little further. The markings stopped where the walls met the floor. As he stared, so he realised. 'I think…I think this is a collection of landmarks.'

Coppice was impressed. 'Very good, Madder. How did you know?'

'I didn't exactly, but I recall Milfoil making marks in the dust once – he called it a "map". He was showing us how to reach a hive a long way from Birch Cave.'

'Hmm,' muttered Coppice, 'quite somebee is that Milfoil.'

'Who made this?' asked Twenty-three, finding his voice at last. 'It's beautiful!'

Coppice turned to face the elder drone. 'I hadn't quite thought of it as "beautiful", but I guess that's one way of looking at it. To me it's mysterious, but also very practical.'

'Yes, I can appreciate that,' said Madder, 'but what's it telling us?'

'Nothing.'

'What?'

'Nothing, unless the key is added.'

'Explain please.'

'You can't use a map unless you know where you are on it, can you? When I came here before, with Ling, he told me that if I ever needed to use this map, the key would be added to it.'

'And the key is?' asked Madder with limited patience, aware that the Blues may not be all that far away.

'A single downstroke with a shorter stroke coming off it at a right angle, just below halfway.'

'Which means what?'

'Guess?'

'This is no time for games!' complained Madder, already scouring the map.

'Sorry, it's the pine tree with the lightning damage.'

'Very clever,' said Twenty-three, 'and there it is!'

'What? Where?' cried the others.

'Just here – look.'

'Brilliant, Twenty-three!' said Madder, but then realised he didn't know what they were supposed to do with the map now that they knew where they fitted into it.

'See those marks up there,' said Coppice, pointing with his right foreleg. 'That's where we're headed – the Caves of Knowledge.'

'Knowledge about what?' asked Twenty-three.

'I'm not sure,' admitted Coppice, 'but I know it will help us. Ling wouldn't have gone to all this trouble otherwise, and the fact that he's put the key on the map is most significant.'

'What was that?' said an alarmed Twenty-three, antennae twitching.

'What was what?' replied Coppice, but Madder was already moving over to the entrance. He listened very carefully for a few seconds.

'Can't hear a thing,' he said, but Twenty-three persisted.

'I thought I picked up something. Maybe I was imagining it.'

'Surely the Blues couldn't have followed us down here that quickly?' argued Coppice.

'If there were enough of them they might have,' reasoned Madder. 'If they sent one bee down every turn at every junction?'

'Oh,' said Coppice, 'I see what you mean. Right then, Twenty-three; you keep listening, Madder; you find the bolt hole.'

'The what?'

'The bolthole. There's an escape tunnel where the wall meets the floor.'

'Where exactly?'

'I don't know! Start scratching around. We can't leave the same way we came in, can we?'

Madder set to work while Coppice began learning the landmarks from the map. There was the western edge of an orchard, a copse of fir trees set out a short way from a forest, then a fork in the stream. After that came the three semi-circular lines of a fault in the force field as you approached the hills, followed by a waterfall, then the web! Orchard, copse, stream, fault…'

'Listen!' urged Twenty-three.

This time they all heard it – a distant scraping noise was travelling down the tunnel towards them.

'We've got to find that bolthole. How far round the wall are you, Madder?' asked Coppice.

'There,' he indicated. 'Now let me guard the entrance while you two search for it.'

'Yes, I mean, no. I mean, I have to destroy the map.'

The other two looked aghast for a moment then realised the wisdom of it.

'Right you are,' said Twenty-three, and set about finding the bolthole while Coppice attacked the portion of the map around the refuge.

Madder was getting worried. The noises were coming closer.

'Found it!' cried Twenty-three, ripping his way through the wax.

'Great!' exclaimed Coppice. 'Let's go!'

Madder followed Coppice and Twenty-three into the bolthole. It wasn't very long so they soon reached the plug. The tunnel was wide enough for a bumblebee so they had plenty of room in which to work. Madder and Coppice attacked the dry earth with vigour.

At the same moment, the first of the Blues entered the safe-chamber. Seeing he had obviously reached something of importance, he hesitated. Then he spotted the bolthole. Should he follow on his own? How many of them were there? He decided to call in reinforcements and shot off back down the tunnel to the last junction, where several Blues were waiting.

Coppice and Madder were struggling with the hard, dry soil.

'Come on!' urged Twenty-three.

'We are, we are!' replied Madder, 'but it's tough.'

The Blues were returning to the safe-chamber. They entered and peered at the glowing walls.

'Now what have we here?' asked Spleenwort, their leader. He examined the walls more closely, noticing various scratch marks, then the damaged areas. 'Confound them!' he declared suddenly. 'They've done this! They've deliberately damaged this…whatever it is. It must be important then – let's get after them!'

Back inside the bolthole, Twenty-three detected the noise from the chamber. 'They're coming after us! Please hurry!'

'I'm through!' yelled Coppice a moment later.

'Quick, widen the opening,' urged Madder.

The Blues were closing fast.

'OK, you first, Twenty-three,' insisted Coppice.

'You next,' ordered Madder, as he turned to face the oncoming Blues.

Madder began edging his way backwards through the unplugged exit, with some pulling and tugging from his two friends. It was a bit like trying to emerge from a cell the wrong way round. He just had time to see the glint in the eyes of the first Blue before he completed his escape. The trio turned and flew off. Spleenwort scrambled through the exit and watched them go, noting their direction carefully. Then he was out into the open himself, quickly followed by other Blues. As soon as there were six of them, he led them off in pursuit.

Coppice and Madder were used to outflying blue drones but Twenty-three, as an 'elder drone', didn't fly a great deal. Although they had a good start, Coppice found to his dismay that they were not pulling clean away.

Spleenwort was on the scent trail but just a bit puzzled that he wasn't catching them. However, he had them in his sights as they reached the edge of an orchard. By the time the trio reached the fir tree copse, Spleenwort and his pack were virtually ignoring the scent trail.

'They're catching us!' yelled Madder.

'Can't you fly any faster, Twenty-three?' pleaded Coppice.

His friend simply shook his head as he concentrated on flying as fast as he could.

'What's the next landmark?' shouted Madder.

'A fork in the stream. We take the left one. Then watch out for a waterfall.'

Spleenwort was still closing on them as Twenty-three tired. Just past the fork in the stream, Coppice veered to the right.

'Hang on!' cried Madder, 'I thought you said take the left fork?'

'Oh, yes, um…'

'It's the force field,' said Twenty-three. 'There's something odd about it just here.'

'Of course – we've reached the fault!' said Coppice. 'It messes up your direction-finding somehow.'

'Great, so let's make the most of it,' said Madder. 'Follow me!'

Madder dived down towards the nearest trees. Spleenwort saw the change in direction – downwards, and to the right. Once in the trees, Madder continued on a route parallel to the wrong stream to begin with. When he was certain they couldn't be seen, he turned sharply west and forced the trio to cross over to the other stream, regardless of what their senses were trying to tell them. It felt very odd, but they made it. Spleenwort continued in the wrong direction for some time before realising he'd lost his quarry. After circling for a while, he had to admit defeat and he took his drones back to the refuge.

'I think we've lost them,' said Coppice.

'Phew!' was all Twenty-three could say, as he tried to recover from his exertions.

'You're out of shape,' complained Madder. 'We'll have to do something about that.'

Coppice said, 'Not just now, please. We're not there yet.'

The other two turned their attention to the Caves of Knowledge and looked out for the next landmark – a waterfall. They flew low down over the stream which led them directly to a small, but attractive waterfall.

'Now what?' Madder asked Coppice.

'Start looking for a web.'

'Any old spider's web?'

'Hardly, it's supposed to guard the entrance to the Caves of Knowledge. It must be special.'

The trio explored the area – nothing doing.

'Suppose we'll have to sweep further out,' suggested Madder.

'Guess so,' agreed Coppice. 'What do you think, Twenty-three?'

The elder drone was thinking and sensing the air around him with his silvery antennae. The waterfall did something to the air – sort of soaked it with a fine spray which hid the usual smells. He flew up to the waterfall for a closer look.

COPPICE

'Careful!' warned the other two.

Their friend hung in the air for a few moments...then disappeared!

'Twenty-three!' yelled Coppice.

'Where are you?' shouted Madder.

Suddenly, Twenty-three reappeared, laughing. 'Come on, follow me!'

He waited for the others to join him before leading them through a narrow space between the waterfall and the rocks. They were absolutely staggered.

'We're behind the waterfall!' exclaimed Coppice.

'What a brilliant idea,' added Madder.

'And I reckon the web's along there,' indicated Twenty-three.

All three of them peered in the appropriate direction. They could just make out a gentle glow some way ahead of them. Slowly, with a great sense of expectation, they flew along the wide tunnel between the rocks. As they approached, they realised the size and beautiful glow of the web. It was just like the glow in the safe-chamber, only stronger.

'Careful,' warned Twenty-three, antennae twitching feverishly. 'When were spider's webs ever friendly?'

The others nodded their agreement. Coppice went up for a closer look. He was about to risk touching the nearest silky strand when Madder grabbed hold of him with both forelegs and yanked him back.

'Coppice!' he complained. 'Sometimes you're just too curious for your own good!'

'Sorry, but what do we do now? How do we get to the Caves of Knowledge? Are we actually in the right place anyway?'

'Yes you are,' came a voice from behind the web. Slowly, two strands of the web were sort of unfolded and a drone honeybee with a glowing body was revealed. The trio was too stunned to speak. 'Welcome to the Caves of Knowledge. Please come this way.'

28. THE SAGES – BREED AND FEED

Coppice, Madder and Twenty-three stepped very carefully through the opening in the silver web, and followed the strange drone as he walked rather slowly along a winding tunnel. It led them to a medium sized chamber containing various honeypots, and some bedding material. There were all sorts of markings on its walls.

Their host turned to face them. 'I am the Historian and it is my responsibility to see that you find what you are seeking. Please don't be alarmed by this "glow" – it's rather necessary here.' He then politely awaited their response.

Coppice couldn't help noticing how old he looked. This was surely the oldest bee he had ever met – by a long way. 'Erm, well, thank you, but we're not sure what we're looking for.'

The Historian made no comment so Coppice continued. 'That is to say, er, we're having problems back where we come from, with, er, a particular strain of bees. They're rather a vicious lot – trying to take over the whole region we think…'

'And we don't know how to stop them,' chipped in Madder.

The Historian nodded, his ancient, silvery head glowing even more in the darkness of the chamber. 'Good, I'm pleased to hear you're so concerned. If you have the will, there must be a way. Somewhere amongst the sages here, you will find your answer. Now correct me if I'm wrong, but you don't have a lot of time to spare, have you? So this is what we'll do. You will visit each sage in turn, asking whatever you will of each one. When you've seen all of them, you will return to me to complete your quest.'

'How many sages are there?' asked Twenty-three.

'Seven including myself. Now come this way please.'

He led them through a short tunnel to the next chamber. 'Please meet Helleborine, the forager sage. She will answer any questions to do with food.'

COPPICE I

The Historian departed and the trio left facing a comparatively large worker bee, glowing just like the Historian. They didn't know where to start.

'Lost your tongues?' joked Helleborine kindly.

'That did the trick for Coppice. 'Tongues – yes. Now what about the length of our tongues? How come workers have longer tongues than drones?'

'I think you know the answer already. Workers have to collect nectar from inside the flowers. Drones simply receive it from the workers or help themselves from the honeystores. So drones don't need long tongues.'

Coppice wasn't satisfied. 'But why not give drones the same length of tongue in case they need it – in case they find themselves without workers – without foodstores? If I'd had a worker's tongue I wouldn't have needed to figure out how to rob flowers.'

Helleborine saw that she was dealing with no ordinary drone. 'Very good. You're right in one way, but you must realise that we honeybees are organised to share the jobs between us, instead of everybee doing everything. I would say that's a more efficient and therefore a more successful way of living. Honeybees certainly are a successful group of creatures, don't you think?'

'Hmm,' muttered Coppice. 'I did get a stomach ache from the food I robbed.'

'That was because you took raw nectar which hadn't been converted to proper honey in a worker bee's stomach.'

'Anyway,' interrupted Madder, 'I don't see how this is helping us find out what to do about the Blues taking over our region?'

Helleborine waited for the next question. Twenty-three had been taking a closer look around her chamber. He could smell a remarkable variety of honey, pollen, and something he couldn't identify. He asked his question. 'Food is power, isn't it?'

'What is a honeybee without food? What happens to a hive without its winter stores? Yes indeed – food *is* power.'

'And that's why we get raids from those who are short,' commented Madder. 'We've had more than usual this season – from wasps. Something to do with those Blues, we think.'

'You must ask the protector sage about that,' said Helleborine. 'He's the sixth sage. Do you have any more questions for me?'

'Yes,' replied Madder. 'Is there any way the food requirements of the Blues could be different from those of, er, a normal honeybee?'

The forager sage considered that for a moment. 'That depends on whether they have any other features which are different and which might require different foods or quantities of food.'

'You couldn't enlarge on that, could you?' asked Coppice.

'Without a thorough knowledge of these Blues, no. But if they're as warlike as they sound, they may well need bigger winter stores than normal bees do. Again you'll have to check with the protector sage, but I understand that fighting bees may need an early start to the season, which means plenty of winter stores.'

'Interesting,' said Madder. 'We'll certainly remember that.'

'Well, I guess that's about it?' said Coppice, looking at his two companions.

'You do have a marvellous collection of foods here,' said Twenty-three by way of a parting compliment. 'There are so many flowers that honeybees can use, aren't there? I was wondering if some are better than others?'

Helleborine liked this question. 'Yes indeed! Every hive needs its flower expert – a worker, of course. The key is to forage each flower when it's at its best, then move on to the next type of flower when it's at its best. Don't waste time dragging the last tiny globules of nectar from a flower well past its peak. Move on to the next variety. That will make you more efficient, bring in more food, and of course…'

'Food is power!' chimed the three drones, and that was a good note on which to depart.

Helleborine led them through another short tunnel to meet the next sage, who was also a worker and who also glowed, but her chamber was very different. There were wax structures everywhere – all cells of some sort or other. Many were the regular hexagonal worker cells and there were some slightly larger drone cells, but the interesting ones looked like Queen cells of various designs.

Helleborine introduced her. 'This is Chamomile, the breeder sage. Now if you'll excuse me.' And she departed.

Chamomile waited patiently as her visitors eyed the cells in her chamber. The drones were soon recalling their very first memories.

'Why is emergence such a difficult business?' asked Coppice.

COPPICE

'It shouldn't be for a fit and healthy bee. If the bee hasn't the strength to break out of the cell, he or she probably wouldn't last long anyway.'

'Oh!' exclaimed Twenty-three.

Chamomile looked at him closely, waiting for an explanation. She got it.

'Well, I only emerged because Coppice and Madder pulled me out!'

'Remarkable,' commented Chamomile. 'You owe them a great debt.'

Coppice and Madder looked embarrassed, their antennae twitching. Coppice moved on to another question.

'Erm, why can't we remember anything about when we were larvae – before we pupated?'

'Because the changes that take place during pupation are considerable. The larva is simply a feeding creature, with minimal brains and memory, if any. It doesn't think about anything except keeping the food coming in! The adult, however, is a thinking creature. Thinking creatures have memories which they can use to make decisions in new situations.'

Coppice understood. He thought back to Lavender's Queen rearing and Madder's brilliant rolling ambush. The more he thought about it, the more he realised that the more new experiences you encountered, the better your ability to cope with the next problem that came along. That led him to an interesting conclusion. 'It's almost as if, as if…knowledge is power, just as food is,' he suggested.

Chamomile was quite taken aback by his thinking. 'Er, yes, I believe there's a lot in what you say.'

Madder brought them back to practicalities again. 'Now what about these blue bees? They're taking out the Queens from all the hives they attack. Our worker friends have pointed out some of the implications – like the lack of Queen scent making it easier for the Blues to infiltrate or take over the hive, but what do you think?'

'Describe these "Blues" to me please.'

Madder described the blue drones.

'And the blue worker bee?' she asked.

'We've not seen one yet. We don't think there are any in our region.'

'Yet!' added Coppice.

The breeder sage thought for a while then spoke. 'This could be very significant, you know. These Blues are clearly a particular strain of honeybee. They could even have arisen from a Queen and one special drone – almost a "freak" result, but one which has produced a powerful, aggressive drone. Now then, if they're clearing Queens from the hives, they could simply be wanting to set back the food supply, which could have a knock-on effect as far as winter stores are concerned – though I would have thought there was sufficient time left in the season to correct that. More likely then, is the intention to put their own Queens in those hives.'

'But won't those hives already be replacing the lost Queens themselves?' objected Coppice.

'Normally yes,' agreed Chamomile, 'but if these Blues have forces inside the hives, as you suggest they have, then they can destroy any new Queen cells until they're ready to start their own.'

This was a new idea to the three friends and the implications worried them a lot.

'What about workers to rear the blue Queens?' asked Twenty-three. 'Would the Blues have to bring in their own workers or could they use the existing ones in each hive?'

'I think they could succeed either way.'

There was a pause for thought, then Coppice spoke up. 'There's something else I must ask you about Queen bees. Have you ever heard of a Queen with a blue spot on the top of her body – thorax region?'

'A Queen with normal colouring otherwise, do you mean?'

'Yes.'

'That sounds very odd. Where does this Queen live?'

Coppice glanced at Twenty-three and answered, 'In an aberrant hive.'

Chamomile let a deep breath out through her spiracles. 'Then anything is possible. If there's been aberrant interference, who knows what could result from it.'

'Aberrant interference?' repeated Coppice.

'Yes. The giant creatures who make aberrant hives – you ask the next sage about them – seem to be able to mess about with the breeding in the hive by...by changing the Queen in some way.'

'What?' exclaimed Madder. 'That's outrageous!'

'I agree,' responded Chamomile, 'but it's a difficult one to deal with.'

'So I've one last question,' said Coppice. 'Is there a connection between the blue spot on that Queen in the aberrant hive and the blue bees?'

'I don't think I can give you the answer to that one. It's down to those of you who live and fly out there. They could well be linked, but I can't say for sure – it might be a coincidence.'

'Thanks for your help,' said Coppice. 'I guess we'd better be moving on now.'

Chamomile duly obliged and led them off down yet another tunnel to find the third sage.

When Coppice and the others were flying out to the Caves of Knowledge, Ragwort had been flying to Lower Larch to report to Yarrow on the latest, puzzling development at the hive in the bracken.

'What is it?' grumped Yarrow, who was gradually losing his patience.

Ragwort explained, 'I thought you ought to hear what happened at sunpeak.'

'Humph! I hope it's worth your trip!'

Ragwort hoped so too, and continued, 'Well, not long after heatrise they made an effort to take some workers foraging in the woods and...'

'What's surprising about that?'

'Nothing, er, I mean that's not the surprising bit...'

'Then get on with it!'

'Yes, yes. Well, we soon dealt with that little foray and thought the action was over for the day. Then, at sunpeak, they tried again – or at least some worker bees appeared outside their hive entrance. But, at about the same time, two bees made a break. They shot up from nowhere and headed south. Some of our drones chased them but could only keep scent contact and eventually lost it.'

'What do you mean, "lost it"?'

'It just disappeared – gone!'

'Rubbish! Scents don't just disappear – unless your drones were so far behind!'

'I don't think so.'

'Not good enough. Is that it?'

'Er, yes Master.'

'Fetch Kale in here.'

Ragwort went and found Yarrow's captain and had to repeat his account to him.

'So what do you make of that, Kale? What were they up to?'

Kale considered the options then suggested, 'Gone for help, most likely.'

'Indeed,' responded Yarrow, 'but to whom? Who could possibly help them against us?'

'No bees I know of, that's for sure.'

'Whatever they're doing, it sounds like it was intentional and quite clever, so they're up to something Kale. I think it's time for a quick check up on the hives in the south-western area. They're our next targets anyway. We might as well get on with it and maintain the siege at the same time, especially with the whole of Swarm Force Two down here.'

Kale added, 'And if that hive in the bracken's sent for help from that area, we might find out about it.'

'And hit them hard for their cheek! Good. Ragwort; you take full responsibility for the siege and inform me of any other strange manoeuvres by that lot! Kale; you get your scouts out quickly and report back to me before heatfall. I want to work out tomorrow's plan of action. I'm fed up with squatting around here. The storm force needs some exercise too!'

The Blues' leadership was thus prompted into welcome action. Ragwort was chuffed to be in complete control of the siege – no Kale to interfere and give unwanted advice. Kale was pleased to get the invasion going again and dispatched ten sets of quads into the south-western area with instructions to report back as soon as possible – by heatfall at the latest.

He was very concerned about the sunpeak episode at the hive in the bracken. There were too many unanswered questions. How had two bees zoomed into the air from a spot away from the hive entrance? Had they slipped out unnoticed or was there an escape tunnel? And although he knew one or two tricks for changing your scent, it looked like the opposition did as well – unless that incompetent Ragwort has been telling fibs. Mind you, telling fibs to Yarrow was a big risk to take. He had the uncanny knack of spotting lies with surprising ease, and the liar usually came to a sticky end – a very sticky end!

COPPICE

That reminded him of the occasion Yarrow had dealt with Figwort and Crowfoot and the message they brought from Bugle about the 'massive' ambush and stolen prisoners. Kale had doubts about that report but Yarrow had immediately ordered the messengers disposal on the grounds that such stories were bad for morale. But did he disbelieve Figwort and Crowfoot, or was it Bugle who was at fault, or was it just a matter of morale? He thought about that while he awaited the return of his scout quads.

29. THE SAGES – BUILD AND FLY

The chamber of the third sage bee was the most remarkable yet. Chamomile may have had an interesting collection of wax cells but what the trio saw now was quite overwhelming.

It was a large chamber, necessary to accommodate the fantastic variety of wax structures. They set about exploring them, partly from curiosity and partly because the third sage had not yet appeared. Chamomile had warned them this might happen. There were some regular cells, in small groups, but they were built in all sorts of places and in unusual positions. Madder was enthralled by a series of wax tunnels which connected some of the cell groups. Twenty-three was examining the slight differences in the types of wax used. One was surprisingly flexible; another was almost rock hard. Coppice stood back to try and take in the overall picture, but couldn't really find one. He had just said as much when the sage appeared from one of the wax tunnels.

'I see you're interested in my combs, so you're welcome to my chamber.'

The trio turned in the direction of the voice to see a neat, compact, glowing worker bee. She continued, 'Allow me to introduce myself. I am Saxifrage, the hive sage – as you may have guessed. What can I do for you?'

'You've given me a few ideas already,' replied Madder.

'You're welcome.'

'How do you get these different types of wax?' asked Twenty-three.

'By mixing different chemicals in with the wax that I produce naturally.'

'Where do you start with a structure like this?' enquired Coppice.

'That depends on where you want to finish. You see, a good hive builder considers first what she's intending to finish up with. Once she knows that, she can work out the best place, or places to begin.'

Coppice followed up; 'Does that mean there's one worker in charge of the rest?'

'Correct. An experienced worker will take on the role of "hive builder" and direct her team – which may be a very large one of course.'

Coppice just nodded and muttered, 'Amazing.'

'What about aberrant hives?' asked Madder.

'Oh my word!' was Saxifrage's reaction. 'I'm afraid they're something of a disappointment. You see, they rather stifle the initiative of the hive builder. I understand that most of the planning is done for you. There are certain pieces of wood installed which direct where the comb has to be built. Worse still in some cases, the comb foundation is already in position as well! I really don't know what the world's coming to!'

'Quite,' agreed Madder, remembering the hive of his emergence.

Coppice asked, 'Er, do you have any knowledge of – I mean you obviously do, but – what about tunnel systems?'

'Limited only by the ability of the honeybees who use them. I've heard of tunnels which run for hundreds of bee-lengths with lots of junctions, but I've also heard of workers getting lost in their own tunnels! What you don't come across so often is the wax tunnel, such as I have here. They're very useful in multi-colonies where you're connecting the individual colonies together.'

'Oh, like The Beacon on Squill's Island,' said Twenty-three.

'Er, yes, I think that may be a good example.'

'Interesting,' thought Coppice. 'She's well informed – but then these *are* the Caves of Knowledge.' He posed the next question carefully, hoping to gain more than the obvious information. 'What do you know about the wax which glows?'

'As in the safe-chambers?' she replied.

Coppice noticed from her answer that there must be more than one, and replied, 'Yes.'

It's a most unusual feature and quite hard to produce. Without giving away the entire secret, let me tell you that it involves chemicals taken from the glow-worm.'

'Glow-worm?' queried Madder. 'I've not come across one of those.'

'Not surprising really, but if you did, you'd know what I mean.'

'I'll take your word for it.'

'Thank you. Any more questions?'

'Yes,' said Coppice. 'We all lived in an aberrant hive once…'

'Oh, I'm terribly sorry,' Saxifrage sympathised.

'…And the worst part about it was when large chunks of the hive moved, causing chaos and a number of deaths when the "chunks" fell back into place. Have you any idea what was going on?'

The builder sage paused. She looked very sad as she explained, 'I'm afraid the giant creatures are responsible. They make the aberrant hives – at least the main structures of the hive – and then induce honeybees to build their combs inside. Unfortunately they're not content to let the bees get on with the job; they have to keep opening up the hive to see what's happening. Worse still, towards the end of the season, they actually remove most of the honeystores!'

'You mean they rob the hives?' exclaimed Coppice.

'They do indeed. They usually leave enough for over-wintering but they don't always get it right. I've heard of colonies dying out because of this treatment.'

That seemed to put an end to their questions until Coppice thought of one more. 'Oh, and who built the safe-chamber at Ling and Heather's refuge?'

'I did,' replied Saxifrage, surprising the trio, who had presumed she never left the Caves, 'with the help of the next sage, of course, he drew the map!'

With that she led them into one of her wax tunnels, one which twisted and turned until it reached the next chamber. There the next sage was staring at something on the wall of his chamber.

'May I introduce Rowan, the navigator sage,' and with that she disappeared back down her fancy tunnel.

This chamber didn't contain much at all but the walls and ceiling were covered with maps. Rowan glowed but the maps didn't. He turned to greet them.

'Ah, hello there, come to see my maps, have you? Very good, very good. What are you looking for?'

'Well, er, we're not sure,' replied Coppice.

'Not sure, not sure? Ah well, never mind, just come and have a peek at some of these.'

So they did.

'Which is our region?' asked Madder.

'That one,' indicated Rowan.

COPPICE

'And the other maps?' asked Coppice.

'Other regions we're responsible for.'

Coppice thought he could see about a dozen in all. The maps were smaller than those in the safe chamber in order for them to all fit into Rowan's chamber. They spent a little time perusing the mass of landmarks and trying to imagine what these regions looked like.

Eventually Coppice asked, 'Is that Squill's Island?'

'Now let me see – er, yes, it certainly is.'

'So what's all that empty space below it?'

'That's the Great Sea. No bee has ever crossed it, to my knowledge.'

'But some of us have crossed to Squill's Island.'

'And why not, why not? You've only to line up three landmarks on the coast and follow them out towards the island, even though you can't see it.'

'That's exactly what we did.' And that opened up questions on flight and navigation.

Twenty-three asked something he had long wanted to know about. 'What exactly is the force field please?'

Rowan grinned. 'Ah, tricky one that, but I'll do my best. I understand that this force, which is quite invisible, runs more or less from north to south, or south to north if you like. Now, inside your head there are some special receptors that can pick up this force, or at least recognise when you cut across it, as when you change direction. To cut a complicated story short, this gives you another navigating factor, in addition to the light from the sun that is.'

The trio tried to take that in. Twenty-three asked, 'But what about the faults in the force field that we encountered on our way here?'

'Warps, you mean?'

'If you say so.'

'Ah, now even I am at a loss to explain those. All I know is that the force field is disturbed at certain places. The amount of disturbance can vary, but it rarely disappears completely. That makes it a very useful protection device. The Caves of Knowledge were deliberately sited here because the warp acts as a shield. You can't find us by normal navigation methods -we're actually inside a warp! The waterfall is a second line of defence, more against other sorts of creatures that might want to trouble us.'

'Staggering!' declared Twenty-three. 'Quite staggering!'

The others nodded in agreement and moved on to another question. Madder asked if Rowan gathered his information from the intelligence scouts.

'Yes, and no. There is a system of such scouts, usually four to a region, one of whom is the senior scout. He will meet up with the senior scouts from bordering regions once a cycle, to share information. One of the drones at that meeting will report back to me, as a rule.'

'So what about these Blues?' asked Coppice.

'Yes indeed, indeed. They're from this region over here.' He pointed at his maps. 'They come from a place called "The Glade" according to my information. It's somewhere in this extensive forest – just here, you see. No regular intelligence scout has been there and returned!'

'Has anybee tried?'

'I'm afraid so – say no more.'

They didn't.

Madder had one more question. 'These Blues – the drones, that is – they're very clever at tracking and they've taken to working in quads. Any ideas about that?'

Rowan looked worried. 'Hmm, that's very advanced, very advanced indeed. I've not heard of that for many cycles. You see, it gives them a selection of tracking routines and tricks because they can split into pairs when it suits them.'

'So what can you do about it?' enquired Coppice.

'The best thing is to change your scent frequently and never assume you've shaken them off your trail. You have to try and stay one step ahead of them, or even two, in case they do go into pairs. Do you see what I mean?'

'I get the general idea, thank you,' replied Coppice. 'Oh, by the way. Have you ever come across a rolling ambush?'

'A what?'

'A rolling ambush.'

'No, I don't think I have. It sounds more like the protector sage's field to me, you'll have to ask him.'

'Will do,' replied Coppice, inwardly smiling to himself and wondering what Madder was thinking.

COPPICE I

'Ah well then, I suppose it's time to move you along. I hope I've been of some help.'

Rowan took them to a tunnel that would take the trio on to see the fifth sage, after which he returned to his maps.

Fumitory led his quad of Blue scouts out from Lower Larch, one of the seven hives occupied by Storm Force Two as well as being Yarrow's headquarters. Kale had delivered the orders and the scouts were only too pleased to be back in action. They reckoned it must be urgent because it was already past sunpeak – an odd time to begin a day's work. What's more, they'd have to get a move on if they were to report back before heatfall. As all ten quads had been sent out, they should manage the job.

His accomplices were Mustard, Stinkweed and Runch – all seasoned scouts. There would be no problem splitting into pairs with this experienced team. They had been allocated the northernmost part of the south-western area, beginning due west of Bramble hive. They quickly reached it and turned west. They would fly in beelines to and fro across their patch, looking out for drone zones or any other indication of honeybee hives.

They were only halfway across their first sweep when Runch cried out, 'Drone zone below!'

The quad descended and Fumitory saw more drones than he expected. Only a few were buzzing around; most were settled in the foliage, lazing around. They landed in a young sweet chestnut tree and watched for a departing drone. They didn't have to wait long and the quad followed at a discreet distance.

'Dead easy,' said Fumitory, 'must be our day!'

The drone led them to the hive, but it wasn't the sort of hive Fumitory expected. He signalled to the others to land and wait.

'That's an aberrant hive, isn't it?' asked Runch.

'I thought Six Hives were the only aberrants in this region,' added Mustard.

'That's what Yarrow suspected,' replied Fumitory, 'according to Kale anyway. Let's take a closer look.'

All four flew over to the entrance and hovered there, outside the regular beelines.

'Odd entrance,' commented Mustard.
'Odd hive,' concluded Stinkweed.
'Let's try an entry,' said their leader.
They knew it was a simple test run with minimal risks. They flew into the tubular entrance and landed in front of the guards. The response was rapid – they were attacked!

Beating a hasty retreat to a more distant sweet chestnut tree, Fumitory reviewed the situation.

'Now I wonder if this should be reported immediately or not?'
Stinkweed offered his view. 'I think so, especially with that blue marking.'
'What blue marking?' demanded Fumitory.
'The one by the entrance. Didn't you see it as we went in to land?'
'No, I was too busy watching those guards.'
'Wait here while I check it out.' Fumitory was cross with himself for not spotting it himself. He flew over for a closer look. Stinkweed was right – the sneak! There it was, to one side of the entrance – a blue marking of some sort. Very odd. He tried scratching it with his foreleg and feeling it with his antennae but he could make no sense of it, except that it was definitely blue. Returning to the others, he deliberately avoided giving Stinkweed any credit for keeping his eyes open.

'Right, Mustard; you and I will report back to Kale immediately. Runch; you and Stinkweed continue the search until we return. We'll be at the eastern end of the sweeps. Now go!'

Stinkweed was particularly peeved not be reporting 'his' find back to Kale, but there was nothing he could do about it. 'Typical Fumitory' he thought to himself as he and Runch zoomed off.

Kale was surprised to see two of his scouts back so soon and wondered what had happened. As Fumitory made his report though, he couldn't help but feel they had come across something important.

'You're quite sure about this?' he double-checked.
'Positive sir,' replied Fumitory.
Kale looked to Mustard for confirmation, an action that indicated the importance of their find. Mustard nodded.
'Very well then, take me out there. I want to see this for myself!'

30. THE SAGES – INTERPRET AND PROTECT

'Come along in, please. My name is Sedge and I'm the one to ask about bee behaviour. They call me the "interpreter" sage. What would you like to know?'

The trio was a bit taken aback by this abruptness, compared to the other sage's attitude.

'First question?' asked Sedge.

Coppice found his voice. 'Er, right then, anything at all about behaviour… including that of the blue bees?'

'They're honeybees, aren't they?'

Coppice nodded once and continued, 'Yes, but why are they so aggressive?'

'They're made that way – a feature of their strain.'

'Do they *have* to follow their features?' asked Madder.

'They can't help it.'

'So we're stuck with them?'

'It looks like it.'

'So do we let them take over our region?' asked Twenty-three.

'Not necessarily. Of course, the sixth sage can advise you on that, but I would point out the obvious.'

'Which is?'

'That as honeybees, they can be assimilated.'

'Meaning what, exactly?' enquired Coppice.

'Meaning you could learn to live together, if necessary.'

None of the three visitors could imagine living in harmony with the Blues.

'Hmm,' muttered Coppice, 'and in such a "living together", who would be on the Council?'

Firstly, you don't necessarily have to live in the same hive but, secondly, if you did, then the Council positions would be shared – three each.'

'Plus the Queen, of course,' added Coppice.

Sedge didn't reply to the obvious.

The trio racked their brains for other questions. Twenty-three eventually came up with one. 'Why did the workers expel us from our first hive?'

'When the season draws to a close, and there are too many drones in the hive, the workers remove them. If they didn't, the hive would run out of stores during the winter.'

'It doesn't happen in all hives though, does it?'

'It depends on the amount of honey stored – that's what the workers react to.'

'Is it more likely to happen in aberrant hives?' asked Madder.

'Correct, because large amounts of honey are taken from aberrant hives late in the season.'

"Yes, we've heard about that,' confirmed Coppice, 'and there's one more thing. We've seen many worker bees die in the defence of their hive. Is that really necessary when other tactics can be used?'

'What other tactics are you referring to?'

'Ramming and wing-cutting.'

'Where did you get that idea from?'

'It sort of happened by accident to begin with, then we realised how useful it could be. We even taught worker bees to use it.'

'Did they learn?'

'With practice, yes. It didn't come naturally, of course.'

Sedge seemed to soften a bit. 'I congratulate you. I think you've developed a new form of bee behaviour there. However, the stinging response has the element of sacrifice and that's important to the survival of the hive. The members must put the survival of the whole hive before their own. You could apply that to the expulsion of the drones as well, if you like.'

Coppice didn't really like to, but didn't say so.

They were just getting Sedge to loosen up a bit, and Coppice was just wondering whether to slip in another question about the Blues, when the interpreter sage called the meeting to a close.

'Good to meet you. Let me take you through to see the sixth sage. He's called

COPPICE

Tormentil and he's the protector sage. This way, please.'

Unlike Sedge's chamber, this one was full of all sorts of interesting things. There were wax pots of various shapes and sizes, most of them smaller than honey cells. Then there were some odd markings on the wall, and even some odd structures along the sides of the chamber. On closer inspection they recognised some of them.

Tormentil welcomed them and showed them around. 'Yes, that's our common enemy the wasp – what's left of him anyway; it's only his outer casing, there's nothing inside. And here we have a dragonfly, yellow and black you notice. Next to him, the greater and lesser wax moths – they really mess up the comb. Now, inside this pot,' he said as he lifted the lid, 'is the bee louse – a fly really, only with pathetic wings! Actually, they don't do a great deal of damage but they do tend to weaken the cell cappings. In the next pot – mites! They get into your spiracles and upset your oxygen intake. Now we come to the "unopenables". These little pots contain different types of brood disease. In there is foul brood, caused by a germ which gets into the larva and eats it from the inside – leaves rather a gooey mess, very serious…'

'I think I've seen it,' interrupted Coppice.

'Have you now? I hope you were disinfected afterwards?'

'Well, Heather the bumblebee tended me so…'

'So you'll be fine.'

'Do you know her then?'

'Of course, she's one of my healers.'

That surprised the trio, but Tormentil was moving on. 'Now pay attention. In here we have the sac brood germ which also kills larvae, and in here are the spores of a fungus that produces chalk brood, if eaten. That pot has a similar but much rarer fungus. This one has some dormant spores of a tiny, tiny organism which can live in your gut in such large numbers that your life span is reduced by half! So, if you would now care to view my chamber walls, I've etched on some pictures of our larger enemies.'

'This is a swallow, look, and here's a marten, and this one's a blue tit…but *that* – that's a bee-eater! Fortunately he's a very rare bird. Over on this side we have the green woodpecker, who can break into hives in the winter, and the mouse, who likes the warmth of a hive in winter. So, that's a quick run through. It would take all day to cover everything in detail – and you haven't got all day, have you?'

'Amazing!' gasped Twenty-three.

'Impressive, said Coppice, admiring the etchings in particular.

'How do we protect ourselves from this lot?' asked Madder, sensibly moving on to practicalities.

'Cleanliness is one essential, and an efficient guard system is another. Get those two right and you're three quarters of the way there. After that, it's robbing that causes most problems.'

'We've seen a lot of that,' said Coppice.

'Then you have to sacrifice more workers, assuming you have them, especially early in the season.'

Madder told him about the barge and cut tactics, and Tormentil was as impressed as Sedge had been. Then they raised the matter of the Blues.

Madder explained, 'These blue tinted honeybees attack other honeybees with barge and cut tactics. Who taught them to do that?'

Tormentil paused, then said, 'Yes, I've heard about their war-like tendencies. At least it seems you've learned to defend yourselves.'

'And fight back,' added Madder.

'Pardon me?' said Tormentil.

'Haven't you heard of a rolling ambush?' Madder asked.

'I've heard about the ambush tactic, but I'm not sure about the rolling bit.'

Madder explained the process. Tormentil soon understood the principle.

'That's a very clever adaptation,' he pronounced. 'Well done! Now how else can I help you?'

'Helleborine thought that the Blues, being so war-like, might need more food, including bigger winter stores, so that they could become active quickly at the beginning of the season?' suggested Twenty-three.

'That might well be the case,' replied Tormentil, 'but there's a better reason. I understand from our intelligence that these Blues are good at coldflights – know what I mean?'

'Warming up the muscles inside the hive and then shooting out through the cold on a short, sharp bee-line,' responded Madder.

'Yes indeed, and that requires rich energy supplies if done regularly.'
Twenty-three nodded.

Coppice had been thinking about the little sealed jars with the nasty things hidden away inside, which led him to ask, 'Are your specimens safe in those pots?'

'Which ones?'

'The spores and fungi and stuff.'

'As long as they stay sealed in their pots, yes.'

'What if they get out?' challenged Twenty-three.

'Very dangerous.'

'So why keep them at all?'

'To use for identification and healing purposes. You see, if a new illness is discovered, I receive a sample and my healers look for a remedy. It's a tricky business but the healers are committed to finding an answer – and so am I.'

'Good for Heather,' thought Coppice.

'It seems to me that you've omitted one important enemy,' suggested Madder.

'Which is?'

'The giant creatures.'

'True, and they cause so many problems or "aberrant diseases" that they need a whole chamber to themselves. They're also rather difficult to study, being so large. One day, perhaps, I'll get around to making a closer examination of them.'

'I shouldn't get too close if I were you,' warned Coppice.

'Have you?'

Coppice nodded.

'My word, you are an experienced trio!'

'Thank you, Tormentil,' said Coppice. 'We still have to talk to the Historian so I think we should move on.'

'Tell Heather to drop in when she's free,' requested Tormentil, as he led them out of the chamber.

'Heather, here?' queried Coppice on behalf of the trio.

Kale ordered Mustard to stay at Lower Larch to receive any incoming reports, while he and Fumitory zoomed off to the aberrant hive. On arrival, Kale flew right up to the entrance to take a look at the blue marking. Having confirmed his quad's find, he hovered above the entrance and watched for a while. The incoming workers were of normal coloration. He waited for a drone to appear and found exactly the same coloration. Was he expecting something else? A hint of blue would have been encouraging. Still, it was an aberrant hive, and in the right region. It would be worth disturbing Yarrow with this information.

The pair flew back to Lower Larch. Fumitory rejoined Mustard while Kale went to see his master.

'What the…? Oh it's you, Kale. Come in.'

Yarrow had much respect for Kale because he was extremely efficient and never bothered him unless it was really necessary.

'Found something interesting, then?'

'I think so.'

'Try me.'

'Not far to the north-west of here is an aberrant hive.'

'An aberrant? On its own or in a group?'

'On its own, and with a blue marking by its entrance.'

That silenced Yarrow for a time. Kale waited patiently until Yarrow eventually spoke. 'Why has this never been mentioned before?'

'Before when?'

'I mean when we had scout pairs doing the initial explorations – before Swarm Force One arrived.'

That was a good point but Kale came up with an answer. 'If it was spotted then the report would have gone to Bugle, and he's dead – the knowledge went with him!'

'Humph! Not good!' He pondered a little more. 'Describe the surrounding trees to me, Kale.'

'Nearly all sweet chestnuts, I believe.'

Yarrow became noticeably excited, 'And their height?'

'Quite small on the whole.'

Yarrow's excitement abated. 'What, all of them?'

'Yes. In fact, some are very new trees if I remember correctly.'

More silence before Yarrow spoke again. 'This is puzzling. I have this continued resistance from the hive in the bracken and now I hear of an aberrant

COPPICE

hive we didn't know about, and it's got a blue marking on it. Does it have the Queen I'm looking for, I wonder?'

At that moment there was a kerfuffle outside the chamber.

'Excuse me a moment,' said Kale, and he slipped out into the passage. 'What's up? Can't you see I'm with the master?'

'Sorry,' apologised Fumitory, 'but we've had reports from our scouts in the north and they say it's important.'

'Go on then.'

'They report honeybees visiting the bumblebee nest they were watching. When they followed them inside they discovered a secret chamber with a sort of map on its wall.'

'Sort of?'

'It was damaged – very recently though.'

'What happened to the honeybees they were pursuing?'

'They escaped and flew northwards. Our scouts lost their track eventually.'

'Not another tracking failure! And what about the bumblebees?'

'Nowhere to be seen.'

'OK, leave it with me.'

Kale returned to Yarrow's chamber and told him about the events at the bumblebee nest.

'Right!' he exclaimed. 'There just has to be something going on and we must act. I'll visit your aberrant hive first thing after heatrise tomorrow, and then make a final decision on that hive in the bracken. As for the bumblebees, I think we've seen the last of them.'

As they rounded a corner in the tunnel and reached the next chamber, the Historian was waiting for them, with Ling and Heather on either side.

"Heather!' cried Coppice. 'And Ling! What are you doing here?'

There followed a reunion, which the Historian cut short. 'Let me explain; you can ask questions afterwards. Aberrant hives are always a concern to us here in the Caves of Knowledge. If we suspect problems, like interference in the breeding of the bees in the aberrant hive, then we have a pair of bumblebees act as watchers. Their base is called a refuge and from time to time they "rescue" bees from the aberrant hive.'

This was already beginning to make some sense to Coppice.

The Historian continued, 'About three cycles ago, they rescued an unusual drone from an aberrant hive to the south-west of their refuge. He had a dark blue tinge to his body.'

Coppice was astounded; Ling and Heather looked rather sad.

The story continued, 'This bee, now known as "Yarrow" according to our sources, left the refuge of his own accord and ended up in a hive a very long way from here – well outside of your region. The next thing we know is the arrival of a strain of blue-tinted bees in our area. We're sure Yarrow is with them, and that they're looking for something in particular.'

'A Queen bee,' suggested Madder.

'Oh indeed,' said the Historian, 'and very probably the Queen from Yarrow's home hive.'

The three friends were fighting all sorts of feelings by this time. Coppice managed to splutter out, 'He's from the same hive as us then!'

'Indeed he is, but this is no coincidence. Once Yarrow was known to be a potentially serious threat, Ling and Heather were asked to find somebee from the same hive to challenge him.' He paused to let that sink in. 'If the bumblebees succeeded, the challenger would need help, so the safe-chamber was installed with its map – and that's why you're here now. I'm only too pleased there are three of you instead of just one.'

Coppice walked round the chamber, staggered by the implications of what he'd just learned.

'Why did you choose me?' he asked eventually.

Ling answered, 'Because you showed curiosity and determination. Piper picked that up and told Fern. We knew there would be an expulsion of drones so we arranged for you to go to Piper's hive. However, that injury of yours delayed matters and the timing of the expulsion caught us out.'

'This is truly remarkable,' muttered Coppice, 'a truly remarkable revelation. Does the "challenger" have to be from the same hive a as Yarrow himself?'

'It offers the best chance of success, we believe,' replied Heather in her gentle, encouraging tone.

COPPICE

'Success,' repeated Coppice. 'We're a long way from success, aren't we?'

'Are you?' asked the Historian.

'I guess so. We've spent most of the time escaping from these Blues rather than challenging them...if that's what we're supposed to be doing?'

'You don't have to do anything if you don't want to,' replied the Historian. 'It's entirely up to you.'

Madder responded to that, 'But if we do nothing, the Blues will take over the whole region, won't they?'

'I think so, and there's more. We suspect Yarrow is intending to mate with the Queen from his aberrant, home hive and then breed Queens for many of the hives in the region. This will lead to the strain of blue bees taking over.'

'Yes,' agreed Coppice, 'we'd worked out something like that with Chamomile.'

'Good. I suspect you've picked up quite a lot from the sages that will help you in the days to come. That's our job here; to provide knowledge. It's up to you what you do with it.'

'So what now?' enquired Madder.

'It's nearly heatfall, although it's hard to tell in these caves. You've had a long, demanding day and you need to rest, and think over what's happened. At heatrise you may ask more questions if you wish, then you may go.'

'Go where?'

'Wherever you want to.'

'Come with me,' invited Heather, 'I've prepared a comfortable nest chamber for you.'

'Sounds like just what we need!' said Coppice, and the trio followed her out.

31. SHOWDOWN

Coppice rested only fitfully that night – hardly surprising after the day's revelations. He kept churning over in his mind what the sages had said. Seeing the fuller picture for the first time was a big shock. You thought your life had been rolling along from one event to the next, more or less by chance, then you discover it's all 'arranged'. He began to wonder if he could have any effect on the future at all, but then recalled that the Historian had said it was up to him whether he played his part or not. What part? And how did Madder and Twenty-three fit in? *Did* they fit in? When he thought about it, their coming together again after starting out in the same aberrant hive did look like more than sheer chance.

Madder and Twenty-three were also struggling with their thoughts, so heatrise came as something of a relief. By then Coppice had one thing clear in his mind. After the trio had filled up with honey he expressed his thoughts.

'I can't stand by and let those Blues take over our region.'

Madder and Twenty-three nodded their agreement.

'So let's tell the Historian, shall we?'

He arrived on cue and Coppice spoke up. 'From what we've learned, the key appears to be the Queen in our aberrant hive, so we must get to her before the Blues do. I don't think they've invaded that area yet, so we still have time on our side, plus the fact that Twenty-three is a Council member of that hive.'

'What do we do when we reach her?' asked Twenty-three. 'Can we protect her from the Blues and this Yarrow feller?'

'I don't know yet, maybe we can take her away somewhere. What do you think, Historian?'

'I think it's one step at a time, but I agree that she's the key. Yarrow must not be allowed to mate with her at any cost.'

COPPICE I

'Of course, we could "remove" Yarrow instead,' suggested Madder, but the other two looked at him as though he was asking the impossible. The Historian said nothing.

'I think we should get flying,' said Coppice. 'We might have delayed the Blues at Bracken Bank but they won't ignore the unconquered hives forever. Thank you, Historian, and your sages, for the knowledge. Perhaps some day we may return and learn some more.'

'You would be most welcome,' beamed the Historian. 'Let me lead you safely back through the web.'

He escorted them out into the passage and through the gap in the web, closing it after them. They took a last look at it – glowing, glistening and sticky – before heading off to the waterfall. Emerging from behind it they headed back towards the refuge, from where they knew the route to the aberrant hive. They would reach it by mid-morning if they hurried, especially as they were fuelled with Heather's super-honey!

Yarrow also had a fitful night. He was mulling over in his mind what would happen if he had indeed found the Queen bee he was looking for. The description of the trees around the aberrant hive was confusing – it just didn't sound right. Maybe there was more than one aberrant hive with a blue marking? They were barely halfway through this region so it could be a false alarm after all, but if it wasn't, then great things would follow! He began to imagine his strain of Blues in the seven hives around Lower Larch, spreading out to more and more hives until the whole region was theirs. The future was his – no bee could stop him!

Then he paused. What about those bees in the bracken hive? Are they really a threat? Surely they can't do anything about the aberrant hive and its Queen? No. They were just an inconvenient diversion.

Heatrise came and he sent for Kale. After taking on a modest supply of honey, the pair set off for the aberrant hive. Their journey was only one third of that being undertaken by Coppice and friends, so they arrived first.

Yarrow settled at some distance from the hive to begin with. He was trying to recall the 'look' of the surrounding area. It was a long time since he'd last seen his home hive. Trees grow, but not smaller? It didn't look right.

'I think there were tall trees to that side of the hive,' he told Kale,' and smaller ones over there. There's either been a storm of some sort or this isn't my home hive.'

Kale looked at him in astonishment.

'I'll explain in a moment,' said Yarrow, 'if this is the right place. Let's have a closer look.'

They flew over to the entrance. Yarrow noted the blue mark. That hadn't been there in his time, but the entrance – the tube – that brought back memories! Yarrow was actually shaking in mid-air!

Kale asked, 'You recognise it? You recognise the entrance – the blue mark?'

'Not the blue mark, no, but that tube!'

'Could it possibly be a similar hive?'

'Wait – let me fly round the back.'

Yarrow flew round and examined the structure, which housed the hive. He circled it several times.

'I still don't understand what's happened to the trees, but I believe this is the place!'

Yarrow looked triumphant. He then retreated to a suitable branch to decide his plan of action. Now was the time to reveal his aims to Kale, his trustworthy captain.

He began, 'Two cycles before this one, I emerged in this hive, unusually late in the season, I believe. I'd only been flying a few days when the workers expelled all the surplus drones, and that should have been that. However, I was rescued by a pair of bumblebees and taken to their "refuge" as they called it. I didn't stay long – didn't care for it very much, so I headed off on my own to the north-east. I made a stopover – the bumblebees had taught me how to do it – in what we now call Six Hives, but there were only two of them then. After that I flew east and eventually discovered a well-hidden hive called The Glade. It was only a single hive then, but I was successful in mating with the Queen the following cycle, and that's when blue coloured drones like myself started appearing in large numbers. We expanded rapidly that season, deliberately swarming to start two more hives right next to the original one – not what

COPPICE I

usually happens, of course. As a result The Glade became a multi-hive.

One day, as I was exploring some old tunnels below The Glade's combs, I stumbled across an old chamber with markings on its walls. When I returned the next day, the chamber was divided in two and a bee of some sort was in the concealed half. He introduced himself as the "Overlord" and began to tell me all about my future, and that of The Glade.

His plan was to find a Queen for The Glade, one who would produce blue-tinted worker bees – something that hadn't happened before. This Overlord planned an invasion programme, explaining that I would find the Queen I needed in the region I'd come from. I had no idea it was the Queen who ruled in my home hive and I'm still finding that hard to cope with! Anyway, once that Queen is captured, a vast number of worker bees will be flown in from The Glade – something like two hundred thousand! That will reduce The Glade to a single hive for this winter. These workers will take over the breeding programme in the seven hives we've occupied here, plus Six Hives. You, Kale, will be in charge at Six Hives while I remain here. We shall force a mating flight out of season and arrange for some of the resulting eggs to produce Queens for all thirteen hives. From then on, the Overlord assures me, those hives will produce blue coloured workers as well as drones. We shall be strong enough to rule the whole region well before the end of the following seasonal cycle.'

Kale was awestruck, but quick enough to thank Yarrow for his appointment as leader of Six Hives. He then asked what the immediate plan of action was.

'We go and fetch Swarm Force Two and take this aberrant hive today!'

'What about those bees in the hive in the bracken?'

'Forget them. No, on second thoughts, they caused us much delay. Infect their hive with some of those spores you used on that other hive – worked very well, I thought. Let them rot or fly for it! Theirs is one hive we can do without!'

Kale suggested they survey the area before bringing in the swarm force. When they were fully satisfied, they set off back to Lower Larch to round up the blue drones for their most important assault yet.

At that moment, Coppice, Madder and Twenty-three arrived at the aberrant hive.

'Get down!' hissed Madder, spotting a pair of Blues in the vicinity of the hive. The trio concealed themselves and watched as the pair departed in a south-easterly direction.

'That was close,' commented Twenty-three.

'That was bad news!' said Coppice. 'Blue scouts have located the aberrant hive. They'll be reporting to their leaders in due course.'

'Perhaps we should try and stop them,' suggested Madder.

'Too risky. We might need better odds than three against two. Anyway, they've gone now.'

'Scent trail,' Twenty-three reminded him.

'Maybe, but I think we need reinforcements ourselves. We've got to get that Queen out of there somehow, and she won't come quietly, will she?'

'Won't she?' queried Twenty-three. 'What if I go into the hive and try and influence the Council?'

'I hadn't thought of that,' admitted Madder.

'Sounds too easy,' confessed Coppice, 'but it's worth a try. OK, go ahead. We'll fly back to Bracken Bank and see if there's any way we can bring over some of our drones.'

'And when, sorry – *if* – they don't listen to Twenty-three?' asked Madder.

'Then he can wait here for us.'

Twenty-three twitched his antennae and popped over to some flowers to readjust his scent before attempting to re-enter his home hive. When they were sure he was safely in, Coppice and Madder set off.

They were barely halfway to Bracken Bank when they noticed a dark cloud approaching from the east. The pair steered off course to check it out.

'Is that what I think it is?' asked Coppice.

'I think so,' replied Madder. 'I think it's a swarm of Blues.'

It was vast and awful. It threatened everything in its path. Coppice shuddered, then perked up. 'Hang on – if that's the Blues' swarm force, Bracken Bank might be free!'

'Assuming it's not been defeated.'

'That's not like you, Madder.'

'Just looking at all the options. Here's another one; suppose that's only part of their force and the remainder is still at Bracken Bank?'

'Let's find out.'

'How?'

'By flying high above them and estimating their numbers.'

Madder looked at him and had to admit it was a bold idea, and good thinking. They needed to know if they could get reinforcements quickly, and what they might have to cope with at the aberrant hive. Madder agreed and up they zoomed.

High above the swarm force, the pair made their estimate.

'Over fifteen thousand!' shouted Coppice.

'Nearer twenty,' cried Madder. 'That must be most of them, and they'll be at the aberrant hive before very long.'

'So let's get to Bracken Bank smartish!'

Not quite all the Blues were flying with Swarm Force Two. Ragwort and twenty or so Blues had been given the unenviable job of leaving a very nasty present behind for the Bracken Bankers. Kale had delivered a sample of spores inside a small wax pot and ordered Ragwort to 'spill it' inside the hive in the bracken. That meant only one thing to Ragwort – a suicide mission. The only way they could get into that hive was by surrendering and walking in. Even he didn't like doing it but he ordered ten of his Blues into action, keeping the others in reserve in case he needed a second stab at the job. He watched from a safe distance.

The suicide squad took the pot of spores nearer the hive, opened it up, and found small balls of pollen inside. These 'gifts' they held with their middle pair of legs. They then flew slowly towards the hive entrance and hovered outside, heads bowed in a submissive posture. The Bracken Bank guards were puzzled and called for advice. Piper and Fern appeared and observed the Blues for some time.

'Looks like another of their tricks,' said Fern.

'One way to find out,' replied Piper. 'Guards, make a quick attack then return immediately.'

Twenty or so guards shot out and hit the nearest Blues. No reaction – they just took it. One of them was knocked to the ground and didn't get up again.

The guards returned to the hive.

'Odd,' observed Fern. 'They really have given up.'

'This group have, or so it seems. Ask them what they want.'

'Fern hovered just outside the hive and called out, 'What do you want?'

The leading Blue answered, 'We've come to surrender, we're deserters. The swarm force has gone, we've nowhere to go.'

Piper spotted the pollen balls held in the front drone's middle legs and asked him what he was carrying.

'Peace offerings, of rich pollen.'

Fern and Piper discussed what to do for a few moments. This was an odd situation and they decided they wanted to investigate further. They couldn't just let these Blues fly in. Fern spoke, 'All right, we're going to escort you in. Don't move until we've surrounded you.'

The Blues obeyed while the Bracken Bankers flew out to bring them in. They led them just inside the hive where Scruff and Spurge were standing by. It was eerie being so close to Blues and yet not fighting them.

'May we present our gifts?' asked the Blues' spokesbee.

Fern nodded.

All nine Blues moved the pollen balls carefully from their middle legs to the comb beneath their mandibles. Their hosts continued to watch as they solemnly cut into the pollen balls with their mandibles. Suddenly the leader flung his pollen ball as far into the hive as he could, uttering a deathly screech as he did so! Immediately the other Blues followed suit. Chaos broke out as the Bracken Bankers lunged at their 'guests' who turned and tried to smash their way out of the hive. They were all pounced on bar one, who just made the entrance and was about to take off when Spurge caught up with him. It was all over in less than a minute. The de-winged Blues were dumped outside while some of the worker bees examined the pollen balls. They sent for Lavender.

Ragwort waited long enough to see the bodies of his suicide squad thrown out of the hive. Given the amount of time they had spent inside the hive, he felt confident they had succeeded. He indicated to the Blues still with him and they took to the air.

Just as they were leaving, Coppice and Madder made a high drop entry onto

COPPICE I

Bracken Bank. As they approached the entrance the guards flew out to attack them but realised just in time.

'Coppice and Madder are back!' shouted one of the guard bees.

'Great!' exclaimed Piper.

'Quick, over here,' called Fern.

'Guards are jumpy, aren't they?' said Coppice.

'Just had visitors – sort of suicide squad bringing us presents!'

'What?' asked Madder, and Fern told him briefly what had happened. Coppice and Madder didn't like the sound of it, then Lavender arrived on the scene.

'Good to have you back,' was her first comment.

'Have a look at one of these pollen balls, will yer?' said Piper.

'Be careful,' warned Coppice, 'very careful.'

'Where's it come from?'

'A present from some Blues. They were very keen for us to have it.'

Lavender whispered something to Coppice, who then exchanged a few words with Madder before ordering all the bees to stand back from the pollen balls.

'Right,' said Coppice. 'Lavender, appoint three foragers to collect all nine pollen balls, assuming one per Blue, and go and dump them somewhere a long way from here. Better still, bury them!'

'Won't they be attacked out there?' asked Lavender.

'Not any more,' replied Coppice, 'the Blues have gone!'

That brought gasps of amazement and relief from the onlookers and the good news spread rapidly through the hive.

'Something else, Lavender,' continued Coppice. 'You must keep a very close eye on the hive for the next few days. Watch out for any signs of infection of any sort. I reckon those pollen balls were carrying something very nasty.'

'How do you know?' asked Fern, disappointed that he, an intelligence scout, hadn't seen it.'

'We've learned an awful lot just recently but there's no time for that now. Listen carefully, the Blues are after the Queen bee in the aberrant hive I emerged from. We have to stop them taking her and we do have an ally inside the hive. I know the Blues are already on their way there, in fact they should have arrived by now, so we've got to move fast. I want Scruff and Spurge to come with Madder and

I, plus all the fighting drones and workers we can muster. The house bees can guard the hive – I'm sure they won't be bothered. Where are Briar and Teasel? Ah, there you are. Get over to Hollybank and bring all their fighting bees. Fescue and Sorrell have been standing by waiting for the call. Fescue should know the route to the aberrant hive but you can ask Madder before you go.'

While Scruff was talking to Madder, Coppice turned to Piper and Fern. 'We estimated between fifteen and twenty thousand Blues in the swarm force. Do you think you can get any reinforcements from Stonewall? You know where the aberrant hive is, of course?'

'We do,' replied Fern, 'but why that hive, I wonder?'

'Because it's also the original home of the Blue leader, Yarrow.'

'Yer kidding?' asked Piper.

'I'm not. Now let's get cracking. You can think about it when you're flying. Oh, and be careful when you fly over the aberrant hive on your way to Stonewall – it's on your beeline, I believe.'

'We'll check it out from a suitable height,' Fern assured him.

The next few minutes were spent rounding up as many fighting Bracken Bankers as possible. Eventually, about five hundred drones and two thousand workers were buzzing around outside the entrance.

'Looks like our first fighting swarm force,' declared Coppice.

'Yes, but is it a match for the Blues?' asked Madder.

'That depends how we use them.'

'And on the reinforcements arriving in time.'

'Hmm,' muttered Coppice, then he called out, 'Right, let's be away!'

He and Madder made three sweeps around the cluster of bees and then jointly led them upwards and to the north.

Yarrow surrounded the aberrant hive with Swarm Force Two, organising them into four equal groups. Only one would attack at a time while the others waited their turn, although he didn't really expect to have to use them.

Inside the hive, Twenty-three hadn't been idle either. He had called an urgent Council meeting and explained the situation. Of course they didn't believe him – his story was just too preposterous, but he'd expected that, and continued to

COPPICE

advise on defensive methods, 'should they be attacked'.

Yarrow ordered his first wave to attack the tube of the hive, and in they streamed. The guards were taken by surprise and the Blues burst in, quickly filling the tube. Inside the hive, Twenty-three's amazing story was suddenly taken seriously. Knowing they would be late into the defence of the hive, Twenty-three had taken the liberty of gathering his own drone force for the initial skirmish. As the Blues appeared inside the hive itself, the elder bee's drones counter attacked! They went for them with the desperation of a hive in extreme danger and the Blues were taken aback for a short while. Twenty-three screamed at his drones to try and cut off the stream of Blues where the tube met the comb. They rammed and barged for all their worth and succeeded in stemming the tide. At last the hive's worker bees began to join the fray in earnest. They went for the Blues with their stings and the inner entrance area began to clog up with bodies.

'Form a wedge, form a wedge!' yelled Twenty-three. But try as they might, these workers were new to such tactics and needed time to organise themselves properly. Twenty-three, steering clear of the fighting, kept on at them, trying to guide them into a blocking shape of some sort. At least the number of Blues entering the hive was reduced to a trickle, and they could be dealt with.

Outside, Kale had flown to see what had checked the Blues' initial progress. He urged his drones into the tube and tried to increase the pressure on the inner entrance. He was reluctant to call them out while they were still making inroads, however small, so he let them carry on, knowing that every bee who got inside would be taking at least one of the opposition out of action, and he had plenty of drones to spare.

This situation continued for some time – long enough for Coppice and Madder to arrive on the scene with their small swarm force. Scruff and Spurge had scouted ahead and reported back that the hive was already under attack.

'How many Blues?' asked Coppice.

'Thousands,' replied Spurge.

'Right – we'll zoom in and knock them away from the tube if we can. That should give Twenty-three time to form a wedge and block the entrance. OK, Madder?'

'Element of surprise.'

The Bracken Bank bees accelerated into the attack. It was a staggering sight – one swarm flew straight into the other! The initial advantage was with the attackers because they knew what they were trying to do. The Blues had never been attacked like this before and fell into panic. Kale couldn't grasp what was happening at first and by the time he did, several hundred of his drones lay de-winged and the rest were flying anywhere and everywhere.

'Break off!' he yelled. 'Break off the attack! Get away from the hive!'

He tried to get them to withdraw in an orderly fashion but it was more of a mad dash for cover. Yarrow, waiting with one of the other sections of his swarm force, was wondering why blue drones were flying into the trees around him. Shortly Kale arrived, unusually flustered, and explained.

'*What?*' screamed Yarrow. 'What do you mean "you were attacked by a swarm force"? There's only one swarm force around here – and that's us!'

'Not any longer,' gasped Kale. 'They just came out of nowhere, they…'

'No bee comes out of nowhere! They must have come from somewhere!'

'Does it matter right now?'

Yarrow paused, 'What's the situation at the entrance?'

'The newcomers have taken it.'

'Very well then, we'll have to remove them, won't we? How many of them?'

'Erm, difficult to say, it all happened so quickly. Definitely into the hundreds.'

'I should think so – they just chased off four thousand of my drones! So we'll try a fresh group of four thousand. Throw the second wave at them when they're not expecting it, if you take my meaning?'

'I've got it,' said Kale, and he cocked one antenna.

The Bracken Bankers were jubilant at their initial success. The Blues had been driven off in a blind panic and the entrance was retaken. When the remaining drones had been cleared out of the tube, Coppice and Madder went through to find Twenty-three. The elder drone was still near the inner entrance, hoping that the Blues' withdrawal was due to reinforcements from Bracken Bank. When Coppice and Madder appeared, he was delighted.

'What now?' he asked them.

'Get that wedge properly organised, it's not over yet,' said Coppice. 'Where's the Queen?'

'Hidden away in the back of the hive.'

'Well done – give her a strong guard.'

'Any chance of an escape route?' asked Madder.

'Not in an aberrant hive like this,' replied Twenty-three.

'OK, we're fine for the time being anyway. We have the inner entrance, the tube and the area just outside the hive.'

Scruff and Spurge were outside doing some very cautious scouting. The rest of the Bracken Bankers were buzzing around in the close vicinity. Nothing seemed to be happening.

'I can't believe they've given up completely,' said Spurge.

'No, but they've had a bit of a shock, haven't they?' Scruff pointed out.

'True enough – a taste of their own medicine.'

'About time too, I reckon.'

'Hmm, getting rather dull all of a sudden, isn't it?'

'What?'

But it was too late. The subtle change in light was the second wave of Swarm Force Two, dropping from the sky directly onto the hive's new defenders! Now it was their turn to be thrown into confusion. An intense buzzing and zooming ensued as both sides fought for possession of the entrance area. After the initial, painful clash, the Bracken Bankers were at least able to hold their own in the aerobatics. Coppice and Madder emerged from inside the hive to see what had happened. They quickly sent a message back down the tube to Twenty-three before joining the battle. It went on and on. No bee had encountered such a situation before. The bees chased each other with the general idea of two overcoming one before that one could receive assistance. In the process, they were rapidly using up their energy.

The speed of the battle began to slow down. Neither side was winning but Coppice realised they would need honey very soon. However, it was the heavier and hungrier Blues who broke off first. They withdrew in a comparatively orderly fashion this time, having lost only a couple of hundred fighters.

Coppice and Madder immediately ordered a feeding chain. Groups of fifty entered the hive to fill up with honey and then come back outside before the next fifty went in. Twenty-three was greatly encouraged by the action so far, as was the rest of the Council.

Yarrow was upset again.

'They're empty!' explained Kale. 'They need honey!'

'Which is our nearest base hive?' rasped Yarrow.

'Bramble.'

'Right; send them there and have them return as soon as possible. Ragwort can see to that as he's accomplished his little mission successfully,' said Yarrow, emphasising the word 'successfully'.

Kale got the message. 'Shall I take the third wave in?'

'You'll take the third in, then the fourth – as soon as the third begins to tire – understand?'

He did, and he had to admit it was a good move. They would weaken the opposition this way. He zoomed off, collected the third wave, and sent them straight in. He then collected the fourth and stood by. Even though the feeding was only half completed when the attack came, the Bracken Bankers met the challenge bravely and the chasing resumed. Some of them were able to slip into the hive to stock up with honey during the battle, but others weren't so fortunate. As the Blues showed their first signs of slowing down, Kale charged in with the fourth wave. Coppice and Madder saw the change in tactics and were very worried by it.

'We just have to keep going!' yelled Madder.

'Until help arrives,' shouted Coppice. 'Otherwise we'll have to retreat into the hive.'

But help did arrive. Fescue, Sorrell, Briar and Teasel arrived at the head of a force of two thousand bees and saw what was happening. A few seconds later Fescue directed them in, much to the relief of the Bracken Bankers. The Blues maintained their action though, and the fight was still going strong as sunpeak arrived. The weakened first wave of the Blue swarm force re-entered the fray after their feeding trip, eager to make amends for their earlier failure. They inflicted quite heavy losses on the combined defence force before being replaced by the second wave when they returned from feeding. Coppice realised they might soon be forced into the hive. He and Madder began drawing their bees back towards the area close to the hive entrance. Kale spotted this and told

Yarrow, who agreed to send in two waves in at once. The fighting became tougher and more desperate. Yarrow sent in the third wave as soon as they returned from their refill.

'We're losing too many!' shouted Madder above the din.

'Time to begin retreating inside?' asked Coppice.

'Give it a little longer.'

'Hang on, what's that?'

'What's what?'

'Look to the north!'

'Yes, it must be Fern and Piper!'

'Saved again!'

Another two and a half thousand bees flew into battle with Fern and Piper at the head. Again the Blues were taken by surprise, not expecting an attack from the rear. The defenders pushed out from the hive entrance and re-established a defence zone. The Blues retreated and took cover. Yarrow and Kale were forced to reconsider once again. For the very first time in the whole invasion campaign, Yarrow was genuinely worried.

'How many more lots of reinforcements have they got?' asked Kale.

'How did they organise this many?' replied Yarrow. 'How did they know we would be attacking this hive today? Why are they taking so much trouble to defend it? Do they know what we're after?'

That troubled him deeply. Was there some somebee out there who had discovered his target. Impossible! And yet…

Kale remained quiet while Yarrow thought. 'I could do with a visit to the Overlord. What would he say about this? What would he advise?' He made a decision. 'I'll lead the whole storm force myself, at once! We have to finish this quickly!'

Kale seemed pleased with that and offered to join up all four waves.

'Go ahead,' said Yarrow, 'as soon as the fourth wave are back from their feed. This will be my day!'

There was a pause in the confrontation while Kale waited for the missing Blues. The defenders waited patiently but cautiously, until…

'What's that over there?' asked Madder.

'Where?' replied Fern. 'Oh, I see it. Fetch the others, quick!'

Yarrow had brought the whole of Storm Force Two out into the open, but was holding them at some distance from the hive. He then began his own special method of stirring up his forces. He zoomed round and round and up and down. He then made figures of eight in the air, whipping his bees into a state of frenzy.

'I don't like the look of this,' Madder said to Coppice.

'We've seen it before, haven't we?'

'Have we?'

'Remember The Mound hive? They defended boldly but succumbed to an attack led by a bee who stirred his forces up just like this.'

'You're right. So do you think…?

'Yes – that's their leader – that's Yarrow.'

'Watch out, here they come!'

Yarrow's maddened swarm threw themselves at the defenders regardless of personal injury, not caring whether they lived or died. Yarrow himself zoomed around, maintaining the frenzy. The onslaught was too much. The defenders were outnumbered anyway and their previous tactics were not much use against this mass suicide attack. Many more Blues would die this way but there would still be enough left to complete their mission after the defenders were wiped out.

'Any fighting's bad enough but this is plain sinister,' yelled Coppice, as he and Madder ducked and weaved their way back towards the hive entrance. 'We must get as many of our bees as possible inside the hive.'

They tried very hard to retreat in an orderly fashion, but Yarrow kept up his screaming and urging until not a single defender was left in the air around the hive. Some flew off in any convenient direction, many managed to get inside the hive, but hundreds lay dead or dying on the ground. The Blues realised they had won control of the air so Yarrow launched an attack on the hive entrance. In their frenzied state, the Blues worked twice as fast as normal, yanking out defenders from the tube and then the wedge. They also burned up their energy supplies twice as fast, but fresh drones rapidly replaced them. Yarrow kept them at it, with Kale in close attendance.

Inside the hive, Coppice, Madder and Twenty-three were assessing the situation with the intelligence scouts. Briar and Teasel were overseeing the

COPPICE

wedge while Scruff and Spurge went to check the Queen bee's protection.

'We can't hold them off for much longer,' admitted Madder.

'And we can't let them get in either,' responded Coppice.

'Or at least they mustn't take the Queen,' said Twenty-three. 'She's the key, isn't she? If only we could get her away somehow!'

But no bee could see how.

'There has to be some sort of trick we can pull,' reckoned Piper, optimistic as usual.

That did set some of them thinking in a different direction. Coppice, though, was concentrating on Yarrow. What was the answer? There had to be one; there was always hope – as some bee had reminded him recently, probably one of the sages. What had they learned from the Caves of Knowledge that might help them now? He racked his brains and concentrated.

After a little while, pictures began floating through his mind. He allowed them to come and go. He saw the worker bees in his early days at this very hive, dying in their defence against the raiding wasps. Then he saw Madder at Birch Cave when they were in a similar position to the one they were in now. His friend was had been prepared to sacrifice himself to keep the wedge in position while others escaped to Little Birch. The next picture was of himself, as the challenger – as the Historian had described him. He was facing a large blue drone, and realised it must be Yarrow. Now who had suggested that Yarrow was the one to be 'removed'?

'I did,' said Madder.

Coppice looked up, not realising he had spoken out loud, nor that his two best friends had stayed alongside him.

'Any ideas then?' asked Twenty-three.

Coppice pondered a little longer as the idea matured in his mind. He now knew what he had to do, or at least try and do. He turned to Twenty-three, 'Promise me you'll defend the Queen, to the very end if necessary. If the worst comes to the worst, she must not be allowed to fall into Yarrow's possession alive. Do you understand me?'

Twenty-three nodded and flicked a silvery antenna. He already had an inkling of what Coppice was going to do but Madder hadn't seen it yet. Coppice gave

Twenty-three one final, intense look in the eye and turned away. He filled up with honey from a nearby cell.

'Let's go, Madder, we've work to do.'

'What, exactly?'

Coppice remained silent until they reached the inner entrance where the wedge was being badly mauled. Defenders were having to fill the gap at an alarming rate. Coppice found Scruff and Spurge and told them, 'Get as close as you can to the Blues attacking the wedge and shout out that we're going to kill our Queen if they don't call a halt. Got it?'

His friends looked horrified.

'Don't worry, it's not as bad as it sounds. Now do it!'

Off they went and began yelling and shouting. Nothing happened at first but Coppice urged them on. He knew it might take a little time for the message to get back to Yarrow. In fact it reached Kale first, halfway down the tube, and he, knowing its significance, called a halt and sent a messenger to fetch Yarrow.

The Blue leader was most agitated at having to stop his zooming around. He didn't want to lose his own momentum, nor that of his drones, but Kale's message brought him back to reality.

'The Queen, the Queen! They wouldn't dare! Go and ask them what they want, Kale. I'll wait here in case it's a trap of some sort.'

Kale obeyed, flew over to the tube and crawled along to the inner entrance.

'Who speaks?' he called into the hive.

'Coppice from Bracken Bank, Middle Oak, and defender of this hive! Tell Yarrow I want to meet him.'

Kale wondered how the opposition knew his master's name 'Wait here while I tell him.'

Yarrow had a slight sense of foreboding as Kale relayed the message. There really was a connection between the hive in the bracken and the defence here, and even the hive which caused Bugle to come unstuck! This was serious, but surely he could deal with one bee – if he could get at him.

'Tell him I'll meet him,' instructed Yarrow.

Kale went back with the message.

Coppice had pleaded with the intelligence scouts not to interfere. He had also now told Madder what he intended to do, leaving his good friend numb with shock. He addressed Kale; 'You must clear the tube and allow me to meet Yarrow outside the hive.'

Kale looked at Coppice as if to say: 'do you really expect us to concede that ground?' But Coppice insisted, 'Clear the tube or we kill the Queen!'

Kale resumed his shuttle service and delivered the message to his master.

Yarrow paused, then said, 'Fine, if he comes alone!'

Much to Kale's surprise, Coppice agreed. Fern and Piper made an effort to stop him but Madder intervened, 'Let him go, you have to let him go!'

The scouts stared at Madder but challenged no further when they saw the determined look in his eyes. The Blues began withdrawing from the tube, and as they did so the defenders edged forward, with Coppice at their head. Steadily he walked through the tube towards the outer entrance, his eyes adjusting automatically to the light, just as they had done when he first left this very hive. 'I was in trouble then as well,' he reminded himself, his sense of humour not deserting him.

Yarrow, Kale and a few others were hovering in the air a short distance outside the hive. The Blue forces were buzzing around in an ominous cloud behind them.

Coppice eyed up Yarrow. He was indeed a large, powerful drone. He exuded physical strength and he seemed to be producing a distinctive scent. Yet he didn't look entirely confident. Yarrow stared at Coppice. He just looked like an ordinary drone. Could this bee really have caused him so much bother? Not for much longer though. But why was he giving himself up like this?

Coppice spoke, 'I challenge you one to one for the possession of this hive and its Queen.'

Yarrow tried to stifle a laugh but failed miserably. Then he thought again. What did this bee say his name was? Coppice? Coppice! He suddenly remembered that the name meant something. Wasn't it to do with some unusual way of growing trees – an aberrant treatment of trees? It was coming back to him. Those bumblebees at the refuge had tried to explain it to him but he hadn't really taken much notice. The giant creatures would come and hack down young trees, causing them to shoot up again with several small trunks instead of one thick one. When they reached a certain height they were cut back in large numbers. That was what had happened around this hive! That was why he hadn't recognised its location! And had this bee come from this hive as well? Very strange, very strange.

This all led Yarrow to accept that a one to one challenge was the best way to deal with the matter. He had to get rid of this Coppice fellow. He wouldn't be able to rest otherwise, even when he'd taken the hive and its Queen. Now his challenger was giving him a quick way through to victory and total success.

'I accept!' he roared. 'One against one. No bee to interfere.'

With that, Coppice immediately shot up into the air! Yarrow was transfixed for an instant and then shot up after him.

32. ONE ON ONE

A number of Blues couldn't help themselves and flew up after Yarrow and Coppice. Kale sent Ragwort to bring them back. Then he thought about it. Perhaps a simple precaution would be wise, as long as Yarrow didn't know about it.

He called up Fumitory, 'Take your scout quad and follow at a safe distance – and I mean *safe* – don't let Yarrow know you're following!'

'As you wish,' replied a puzzled Fumitory.

He collected Mustard, Stinkweed and Runch and zoomed away in pursuit, knowing that Yarrow's powerful scent would make following at a discreet distance a simple matter for trained scouts.

Up ahead, Coppice had put a distance of about two hundred bee-lengths between himself and Yarrow, assuming correctly that he could outfly him. Yarrow didn't realise that fact and was annoyed that he couldn't close the gap on his challenger and finish him off. He put it down to the energy he had expended in leading his swarm force in its frenzied attack. He was amused, however, to see they were headed in a north-easterly direction. That would take them to the region of Six Hives, should the pursuit last that long, which it surely wouldn't.

Coppice was in fact flying to the refuge first so that he could then take the route he really wanted. It didn't take very long, over the woods, before the large pine with the lightning damage came into view. He deliberately swooped down low over the refuge in an effort to jog Yarrow's memory. The Blue leader recognised the pine tree and vague recollections of the bumblebee's home filtered into his mind. However, his attention was taken by Coppice's sudden change of direction. They were now heading north-west, into a sector of the region that the Blues knew little about.

Fumitory and his scouts followed far enough behind to be out of sight. As they flew past the pine tree on their beeline, the scent disappeared and they slowed up to a hover.

'Quick, begin circling!' ordered Fumitory.

It didn't take the four of them long to pick up the scent again, but the new direction troubled the quad leader for the same reason it had bothered Yarrow.

'Stinkweed and Runch; fly back to Kale and report the route so far. He may want to send reinforcements. We'll mark our route with extra scent.'

If Stinkweed and Runch were disappointed to be sent back, they didn't show it. Fumitory and Mustard shot off, aiming to close the now widened gap as soon as possible, in case there were further changes of direction to cope with.

Back at the aberrant hive, the stand-off continued. Madder said nothing of Coppice's intentions and was encouraged by the fact that Yarrow had not returned. At least Coppice was outflying him. It also meant that the Blues' onslaught was being seriously held up, allowing time for the defenders to take stock of their situation. Thanks to Coppice's demands, they had already regained control of the tube. The Blues kept buzzing around, waiting for Yarrow's triumphant return, until Kale withdrew them to the shelter of the nearest trees. Madder watched him do it, then brought Scruff, Spurge, Briar and Teasel to the end of the tube.

'We'll keep an eye on things from here, Look out especially for the Blue who appears to be left in charge.'

'Will Coppice come back?' asked Scruff.

'I don't know,' replied Madder, 'I really don't know.'

'If he doesn't, do you reckon the Blues will give up?'

'They'd better!' insisted Spurge.

'And if the Blue leader returns?' asked Briar.

'Let's just hope he doesn't, shall we?' replied Madder. 'Let's just hope he doesn't.'

Coppice led Yarrow across the edge of the orchard and over a copse of fir trees set out from the forest. Now the hills beckoned. He actually had to slow

COPPICE

down a little in order to allow Yarrow to keep up. Coppice had deliberately filled up with honey before making his challenge, but Yarrow was flying on a dwindling food supply – after all, he hadn't expected to be making such a long flight. Fumitory and Mustard had closed up sufficiently to just have Yarrow in their sights – at least most of the time. Should he turn round, they might have to dive for cover very smartly, but they reckoned he would be too busy concentrating on his quarry.

It was mid-afternoon when they reached the fork in the stream where the force field or 'warp' began to take effect. As they approached, Coppice allowed the gap between himself and Yarrow to close up. He had to make sure that Yarrow followed him, and not the beeline. Yarrow came to within fifty bee-lengths before Coppice moved off along the left fork of the stream.

Further back, Fumitory and Mustard temporarily lost sight of their master. The pair reached the fork in the stream and automatically veered right, according to their force field navigation. Shortly though, Fumitory slowed to a hover.

'What's happened to his scent?'

'Maybe they turned and we missed it?' suggested Mustard.

'I'm not sure about that. I thought I was on line and we saw him only a short time ago. Look, you circle around here; I'm going to back-track to where we last had visual contact and try again.'

Fumitory did just that but found himself rejoining Mustard.

'This can't be right!' he exclaimed.

'So what do we do about it?'

Fumitory thought before answering, 'I don't like it but I think we'll have to split up.'

Mustard looked at him as if to say, 'no way', but Fumitory could see no other answer to their predicament.

'You follow this stream for a time. If you find nothing, return to where the streams divide. I'm going to look at the other fork. Now be off with you!'

So Fumitory flew over to the left fork and, to his great relief, picked up his master's scent again.

Meanwhile, Coppice was approaching the waterfall. By now he realised his pursuer was tiring considerably. He just began to wonder if he might take him on in combat. It wasn't his initial intention, but a plan was forming in his mind. Could the waterfall provide an ambush site? Maybe it could. He made a spurt for the waterfall, catching Yarrow by surprise. The great blue drone could only lumber along after him, trying to watch where his quarry had gone. It appeared he had flown straight into a waterfall!

Yarrow hovered by the cascading water. It was noisy and he was frustrated. Where had that Coppice got to? He flew slowly around the waterfall. No sign of anybee. By this time Fumitory had come within eyesight and he had to take cover. He watched as Yarrow hovered around the waterfall. There was no sign of the other bee.

At last Yarrow spotted a gap between the falling water and the rock behind it. He was uncertain what to do, but he remembered his calling. He could only go back to his swarm force as victor. In he flew, cautiously. He landed on a bare rock and was immediately thumped hard by something! Coppice had zoomed out of his hiding place and tried to knock Yarrow into the waterfall! He almost succeeded, but the large Blue was too heavy to be moved the required distance. He was stunned for a few moments though. Coppice held his ground. Yarrow turned to face him.

'You! You dare to think..!' and he lunged at Coppice, catching his right foreleg and smashing it against the rock. Coppice shot sideways and began zigzagging through the limited airspace between the waterfall and the rock face. He was furious with himself for not keeping to his original plan. Now Yarrow was very close to him, chasing him through the zigzags, trying to cut off the corners and ram him. Yarrow was very worked up and really angry! He shouted and screamed insults at Coppice.

'Maybe I can use his anger,' thought Coppice as he spun around for the umpteenth time. So he called out, 'What's wrong, mighty leader? Not getting your own way? Well here's another challenge for you. I dare you to follow me through the silver web!'

Yarrow was even more incensed at his opponent's cheek – or was it daring? Coppice turned and twisted so as to enter the tunnel that led to the silver web. Yarrow followed him. As the glistening strands appeared up ahead of them, Coppice allowed Yarrow to get as close as he dared, before accelerating through the last twenty bee-lengths up to the web. Yarrow, pumped up with anger and pride, accelerated after him. Coppice hit the glowing web as hard as he could! Yarrow lost his nerve at the last moment and was losing speed as he crashed into the deadly, sticky threads!

Fumitory observed his master's disappearance into the waterfall. Being a scout, he had some knowledge of waterfalls and guessed what had happened. He flew up and over the water before landing where Yarrow couldn't see him, if and when he left the waterfall. He waited patiently. No bee appeared.

'Time for a closer look,' he said to himself.

Very carefully he hovered down to the gap he'd spotted earlier. He just hoped Yarrow would forgive him if he emerged now. Then again, he was only following Kale's orders – let him take the rap!

Yarrow did not appear. Fumitory edged behind the falling sheet of water. Nothing. He flew around in the space behind the water and found an opening into a tunnel. He paused and listened, but the noise from the waterfall blotted out all other sound. He would have to venture down this spooky tunnel. Slowly he advanced. Next he picked up a faint glow ahead. At first he thought it was the end of the tunnel. Then he heard the noise – a terrible screaming sound. He moved forward with more speed. Now he could see a web, a silvery, glowing, spider's web. And there, near the middle of the web, was a bee, hopelessly caught, struggling and screaming. The bee was a dark shade of blue – it was his master, Yarrow. Fumitory stopped about ten bee-lengths from the disastrous spectacle. Yarrow's screams were beginning to fade, his movements were petering out. He was dying. Fumitory looked all around. Where was the other bee? There was no sign of him whatsoever.

Shattered and depressed, Fumitory retreated from the web without waiting for Yarrow's last breath. He flew back down the tunnel, out from behind the waterfall, and off to the fork in the stream. Mustard was obediently waiting for him there.

'It's all over,' said Fumitory.

'What's all over?'

'Everything. Yarrow's dead, or will be by now.' Mustard was speechless. Fumitory continued, 'He flew into a spider's web. No sign of the bee he was chasing – probably dead as well.'

Still Mustard said nothing.

'We'd better report back to Kale. He'll know what to do.'

Back at the hive it was late afternoon and both sides were getting restless. Both sides wanted to know what had happened – who had won. The Blues would soon have to return to their base hives for heatfall, and the defenders would have to decide whether to stay or return to their home hives. All Kale knew was that Fumitory had sent for back up and he had dispatched three quads of scouts for that purpose. However, they had run into Fumitory and Mustard on their way back with the bad news.

It was Scruff who spotted the minor disturbance and indicated to Madder that the acting Blue leader was on the move, flying around the sweet chestnuts.

'They're preparing to attack!' he warned.

Madder was sad. Did that mean Coppice had failed? But then he realised, 'But if Yarrow's won, they don't need to attack, do they?'

'I think they might be moving away,' suggested Fern.

The defenders watched carefully. Sure enough, the Blues were pulling out – they were actually leaving!

'No, not all of them,' warned Scruff.

A small group of Blues had clustered by a tree opposite the hive entrance. It remained there while the vast majority of Blues departed, heading off back to their base hives with Fumitory and the other scouts leading the way. Kale stayed behind, with Ragwort and about fifty chosen Blues.

Yarrow's captain had been shaken to the core when Fumitory eventually returned and told him what he'd seen. He spent some minutes in silence before ordering the withdrawal. He knew they had failed. The scouts were told to take the swarm force back to the base hives and from there, the following day, they could return to Six Hives. Kale had one more task to perform. He would attempt to take the Queen they had come for, and he would do it after heatfall. That should spoil his opponents' celebrations.

He dreamed he was flying full tilt at a massive spider's web, chased by a monster bee. He hit the web so hard that he burst through it and landed heavily against the rock face on the other side of the web. Then he heard himself screaming. As he came round, he tried to calm himself. It was then that he realised it was not he who was screaming but another honeybee, caught in the spider's web. Then it all came back to him – the pursuit, the waterfall, and the flight into the web. But he had come through to the other side while Yarrow had not!

Coppice eased his battered body over to the web. The screams were dying down as Yarrow's life expired. Coppice just looked at him. All this trouble because of one bee? All the suffering, injury and death. It was too much – monstrous. That was the word which best described Yarrow. Yet now he was a pathetic, dying creature. Coppice turned away and waited for something to happen.

Heatfall came with Madder and the others still at the entrance while the celebrations took place inside the hive. The remaining Blues had tried to hide themselves but speedy Fescue had flown a daring recce to establish the fact that they were still out there.

'Some of us must be on guard throughout the night,' insisted Madder. 'We know what these Blues are capable of. They may yet have a trick or two to play on us.'

'Cheating then, aren't they?' grumbled Spurge, with some justification.

'Scruff agreed, 'Yes, but it was Yarrow and Coppice who made the deal, and...and they're both gone...it seems.'

Madder nodded grimly and explained, 'And it was his decision to risk his life, and if that's what's happened we mustn't let his sacrifice go to waste. Agreed?'

'Agreed!' responded the others.

'Good, so let's get organised!'

Madder had them stock up with honey before settling into a cluster close to the inner entrance. They took it in turns to act as look-out from the outer entrance, changing positions regularly in order not to get too cold.

Kale waited until he was sure the hive guards had left the entrance, not realising he was dealing with such experienced opposition. He gathered his fifty or so Blues, including Ragwort, and started them warming up for the raid. When they were ready, Kale gave the signal and Ragwort shot out towards the hive with the rest in close order behind him. Kale tucked himself in at the rear. Spurge was on watch and he had just enough time to yell a warning down the tube before Ragwort flew right into him! Spurge grabbed hold of his attacker and the pair rolled off the end of the tube onto the ground below. The other Blues shot into the tube and flew along to the inner entrance where the defenders were ready for them. They let them into the hive before pouncing on them, and the scrap began. Fifty Blues, however, were not so much of a match for defenders who were prepared for them. Madder looked out for their leader, without success to begin with. Then he spotted a bee arriving late at the inner entrance. The bee stared at the battle taking place in front of him as if he couldn't quite believe it.

'That must be him,' thought Madder, and he scuttled over to engage him. Kale was late seeing him coming, being too distracted by the trouble his raiding party had flown into. Madder lunged and grabbed hold of Kale, forcing him back into the tube. They rolled over, grappling with each other, gradually moving along the tube to the outer entrance. For an instant Kale broke free and tried to zoom off, but Madder shot after him and thumped him against the wall of the tube. Kale was dazed and Madder attacked, jumping onto Kale's back and hacking at one of his wings. In desperation, Kale twisted free. Madder lunged again. This time he missed and Kale was away. He was just about to escape from the end of the tube when a dark shape came at him from the outside. *Smack!* Spurge thumped into him, sending him sprawling! Madder had time to reassert himself and he was onto Kale's neck, going for the kill. Suddenly Kale stopped struggling. Madder slowly let go and the blue drone slumped to the floor of the tube. Spurge was back on his feet again and he gave Kale a push, sending him into the darkness below, to join Ragwort!

33. EPILOGUE

The day after Yarrow's death and Coppice's disappearance, the Blues were taken back to Six Hives by their scout bees. With Yarrow and Kale gone they had little idea what to do. Many of them felt the need to return home to The Glade, and that's what happened over the next few days. A few stayed behind in Six Hives, but as they weren't replaced, the blue tinted drone soon disappeared from the region altogether.

At Bracken Bank, the spores had done their job and Lavender was terribly upset. When Madder and the others returned, they decided there was only one thing to do. After some manipulation and persuasion, virtually the whole hive swarmed out of the stricken Bracken Bank and headed for the coast. There they found a fallen, hollow tree trunk, which gave them sufficient shelter for the night. The following day they made the crossing, led by Madder, Scruff and Spurge. Briar, Teasel, Lavender, Thyme and Bryony were all in the swarm that flew over to Squill's Island and made their new home at High Oak. It was Madder's intention to return to Little Birch early the following cycle and help them re-establish the Birch Cave hive.

Piper, Fern, Fescue and the newly qualified Sorrell, all stayed on the mainland and took up their duties as intelligence scouts. They saw their region return to near normality by the end of the season. Although many hives were lower in numbers due to Queen replacement, they recovered well during the following season.

Twenty-three, the elder drone, remained in the aberrant hive. He was determined to continue guarding his Queen, and did so until early the following cycle when she was suddenly replaced by a new Queen. Twenty-three guessed it must have been done by aberrant interference because he knew of no Queen rearing inside the hive. What's more, the new Queen had a yellow mark on the top of her thorax. One day, when returning from one of his rare flights to the drone zone, he noticed that the blue marking by the side of the hive entrance had been replaced by a yellow one.

Far to the north, inside the Caves of Knowledge, the Historian had taken Coppice into his chamber after the final encounter with Yarrow. Battered, bruised and exhausted, Coppice had collapsed in a heap onto some cosy bedding and didn't come round until well after the following heatrise.

The Historian gently reminded him of what had happened. When he had fully recalled the previous day's events, Coppice asked the obvious question.

'So can I get back to the others now? They'll be wondering what's happened to me.'

'Don't they know what you intended to do?'

'Well yes, Madder did, and Twenty-three.'

'Then they may understand why you don't appear again.'

'Don't appear? What do you mean?'

'I mean you can't go back.'

'Why on earth not?'

'Because you've flown through the web.'

'Yes, fortunately. I didn't actually expect to come out the other side.'

'Indeed – it takes a most determined bee to fly through. You have to completely overcome your natural reactions to webs in order to accelerate into it. You see, Yarrow hesitated, lost a little speed, and therefore failed to get through. To stay in the web means certain death.'

'Fine, so why can't I go back home?'

'This is now your home.'

'*What?*'

'Look at yourself, Coppice.'

He was about to complain again but did glance back at his abdomen and stopped short. He stared in amazement at the gentle glow coming from his own body. It was the same glow that all the sage bees possessed.

'We've all flown through the web,' explained the Historian. 'You are to join us here, in the Caves of Knowledge.'

COPPICE

Coppice was quite overcome for some time, then he asked, 'But what I am to do here?'

'Ah well, that's a very good question. You may feel you've just accomplished your most important assignment in life...'

'Yes,' agreed Coppice wholeheartedly.

'Whereas in fact that was only the beginning!'

Bugle discovered that the Blues had returned to Six Hives prematurely. When his sources told him Yarrow and Kale were dead, he ventured a visit to the hives. He found very few Blues were left and decided he could safely return to The Glade himself.

On arrival there, two days later, he went directly to Yarrow's chambers, only to find them deserted. He went inside and made his way to his ex-master's personal chamber. He'd always wanted a closer look at the honeypots and the carvings on the walls and...what was this? Bugle detected scratch marks low down, near the floor, where they didn't seem to fit in with the surrounding patterns.

'I wonder,' he said to himself, and he leaned against that part of the wall. It gave way and he was into the secret passage. It was small but its walls seemed to glow somehow. Slowly but surely he followed the passage deeper and deeper into the earth below The Glade.

At last he reached a most unusual chamber, one with a dividing wall across the middle. He could only enter the first part of this chamber. As he stared at the dividing wall, he noticed it was made of surprisingly thin wax. Suddenly he jumped back. There was something on the other side of the wall. Regaining control, Bugle crept up to the partition. Was that the shape of a honeybee on the other side?

He summoned his courage and called out, 'Is anybee there?'

A few seconds later a reply came loud and clear: 'Ah, welcome my chosen one!'